He was about to set Molly down when he paused, stiffening, suddenly alert.

"What is it?" she as

"I thought I heard ____ as if he expected to see ____ d-ows. They both rem ____ he flickering light only ____ ly could hear was the c ____

"Doubtless, it was just my imagination," he said, setting her gently on the bed where she could lean back against the pillows. Then, fetching the pewter goblet, he handed it to her, saying, "Don't drink too fast now."

She sipped, watching him strip off his clothing. That he was in a hurry was plain. When he was naked he turned toward the bed. Molly stared. He was magnificent . . .

PRAISE FOR AMANDA SCOTT

AMANDA SCOTT

The Secret Clan

ABDUCTED HEIRESS

WARNER BOOKS

An AOL Time Warner Company

WARNER BOOKS EDITION

Cover design by Diane Luger
Cover illustration by Franco Accornero
Book design by Giorgetta Bell McRee

Warner Books, Inc.
1271 Avenue of the Americas
New York, NY 10020

Visit our Web site at www.twbookmark.com.

For information on Time Warner Trade Publishing's online publishing program, visit www.ipublish.com.

 An AOL Time Warner Company

Printed in the United States of America

First Printing: November 2001

10 9 8 7 6 5 4 3 2 1

Dedicated to
Maggie and Serendipity,
and to Donal Sean,
with many thanks!

Author's Note ───────────

For readers who enjoy knowing the correct pronunciation of the names and places mentioned in a book, please note the following:

Dunsithe = Dun-sith´-ee
Eilean Donan = Eel´-ee-an Doe´-nan
Dunsgaith = Dun-skaith´
Sleat = Slate
Ceilidh = Kā´-lee

Prologue

Dunsithe Castle, the Scottish Borders, 1527

When they came for her, she was sleeping. Her dreams were untroubled, for she did not yet clearly understand that her father—the big, laughing, teasing man she adored with all her heart—was gone from her life forever.

Powerful Adam, Lord Gordon, having against all odds survived the Flodden bloodbath at fourteen, had died at twenty-eight of a knife wound suffered at the hands of a common reiver—and that after he had granted the villain the mercy of branding rather than death. After his death, Gordon's men had rectified their master's error, but that had made no difference to Gordon, for by then he was beyond caring, and he did not know what a quandary his dying would create. Things might have been different had he left a male heir, but he had not.

"Wake up, lassie." The strange voice was insistent. "Ye mun come wi' us."

Ineffectively, Molly tried to shrug away the big hand that shook her shoulder. She was five years old and sleeping the heavy, deep sleep of an innocent child, so waking was not as easy for her as the man seemed to think it was.

"For Christ's sake, just pick her up, Davy." Another voice, another stranger. "His lordship wants her straight-away, below."

"But she'll need proper clothing," protested the first.

"Whisst! D'ye think the wee lass kens where her clothes be kept? Take her up, man. She's sleepin' like the dead."

Cold air enveloped her when one of them threw back the coverlet, but she was still too sleepy to care, even when he picked her up. He cradled her small body against his broad chest, but hard points jabbed her tender skin through the thin shift she wore as a bed gown, making her squirm to avoid them.

She blinked groggily. It was dark in the room, but where was her nurse? Her father's men did not look after children.

"She'll be cold," the man holding her said. "Mayhap I should take along the blanket, too."

"His lordship will say what the lass needs," the other said gruffly.

She was more awake now and feeling querulous. "Put me down, you," she muttered. "Who are you? You should not touch me."

"Hush, lass," growled the man who carried her. "Ye're tae do as ye're bid."

His curt command silenced her, but it did not ease her annoyance. She was not accustomed to rudeness.

The stranger was carrying her down the torchlit, wheel stairway, into the great hall. It was cold there, too, for although several torches burned in their holders on the arras-draped walls, the hall fire had burned down to embers. She shivered. She should not be here.

"Here be the Maid, m'lord," the man carrying her said.

"Put her down."

That voice was one she recognized. It was her uncle, the Earl of Angus.

More disoriented than ever, because Angus rarely visited them, she watched him, trying to gauge his mood, as the man who held her set her on her bare feet.

Then, seeing her mother in the shadows near the great fireplace, and being a well-trained child, she curtsied hastily and said, "Good evening, Uncle."

Though she stood on a carpet, her feet were cold, and she knew that her mother would condemn her untidy appearance and the fact that she had come downstairs in her bed gown. Nonetheless, her gaze fixed itself on her uncle.

Angus was a handsome, fair-haired man in his late thirties, but his penetrating blue eyes were as cold as the hall, and they stared unwinkingly at her. When he did not respond to her greeting, apprehension stirred within her.

His expression was stern and his voice grim when at last he snapped, "Where the devil are your clothes?"

Swallowing hard past a sudden ache in her throat, and trying to ignore the tears welling in her eyes, she said, "N-no one fetched them to me." She did not dare even glance at her mother.

To her surprise, Lady Gordon said tartly, "Pray, Archie, what did you expect? The child is not yet six years old. Truly, sir, I do not know why you are bent on this dreadful course, for she is far too young to be taken from her home."

Molly tensed and rubbed one cold foot against the other, but she did not protest. Although she was young, she knew better than to complain. Her mother was as unpredictable as Uncle Archie and would not thank her for voicing an opinion.

The earl regarded her mother with disfavor. "You will not set yourself in opposition to me, Eleanor," he said. "You will do what is best for your family, and I will determine what that must be. I have a new husband in mind for you, and although he is willing to take a woman born on the wrong side of the blanket if she is my sister, he is not a man I can allow to control the Maid of Dunsithe or her present heir. I shall control their destiny myself."

"You cannot take Bessie, too," Lady Gordon protested. "She's but a bairn."

"Of course, I will take her. Children die, madam, and if Mary dies, her sister becomes Maid of Dunsithe and inherits all of this."

Had he been anyone else, Molly would have told him quite firmly that she did not like to be called Mary. Her father had always called her Molly.

"You do not care one whit about my daughters," Lady Gordon said resentfully. "You care only about controlling Dunsithe and its wealth, just as you have controlled the King's grace these past years. I am Mary's mother. Surely, I am the one best suited to look after her and to tend to my late husband's property as well."

"Don't be daft," he retorted. "Dunsithe is a Border stronghold and requires a strong man to control it. The King has granted me a writ of wardship and marriage for Mary, so you will do exactly as I bid you, or you will soon find yourself in sad straits indeed."

He paused, watching her, but the child was not surprised when her mother questioned him no further. No one argued with a man when he spoke in that tone.

"That's better," Angus said. "Take the lass and see her warmly dressed. And see to the bairn, too."

"What of their nurse?"

"Keep her here. I'll provide them with nurses I can trust at Tantallon. Now, go, for I've other matters to attend to before I can depart."

Without another word, Lady Gordon snatched up her

daughter, and Molly pressed her lips tightly together to keep from crying out at such rough handling. As she was carried up the twisting stairway, she heard her mother mutter, "Other matters, indeed. He wants only the fortune and control of Dunsithe's heiress."

Upstairs, Lady Gordon shouted for her woman, and when that worthy appeared, said angrily, "We're to dress her to travel, Sarah, so tell their nurse to give you warm clothing for Mary and to dress Elizabeth warmly, too, and to pack more for them to take with them. They go with Angus."

Tears sprang to Molly's eyes at the thought of going away with her grim uncle.

"His lordship be takin' both o' the wee lassies then?"

"Aye, he is," Lady Gordon said, "and I am to marry someone else of his choosing, if you please. Molly is an heiress now, after all, and my esteemed brother does not consider me worthy to look after her. He wants Elizabeth, too, in case Molly should die. By rights, that fortune should be mine to control until Molly is grown, but I am to have naught but what Angus and my soon-to-be husband choose to allow me. Poor Molly will doubtless be married off soon, too."

"Och, but she be gey young for marriage!"

"A girl with a fortune like hers is never too young to marry," Lady Gordon said tartly. "Angus will use her and her fortune to serve his own interest."

"He willna let her go if Dunsithe's treasure goes with her, I'm thinkin'."

"No, but the course of history seldom runs smoothly, Sarah, and young King Jamie does not like my brother. For all that his grace must answer to him now, in time, Jamie will win free, and when he does, Angus will no longer wield the great power he wields now. What if something happens to Molly? What if someone should contest her claim?"

"But who would do such a thing?"

"Oh, think, woman!" Lady Gordon said impatiently. "Such things happen whenever men desire aught that belongs to someone else. It would require only that someone declare her an imposter or suggest some other deceit or conspiracy afoot."

"But ye'll set matters straight if they do, madam. Ye're her mother, after all."

"Aye, but I'll not be surprised if Angus forbids me any contact with her. This abduction—for it is no less than that—does not mean he believes that he is better suited to raise her. He simply does not want me to control Dunsithe and her wealth. Now go and fetch her clothing, or they'll come and take her without it."

The woman hurried away, and the child was left alone with her mother.

"Molly, listen to me," Lady Gordon said. "You are going away with your uncle Archie, and you must be a good girl. Obey him always, for he is very stern."

"But I don't want to go away," Molly said, fighting tears again. "I live *here,* and I don't like Uncle Archie."

"You must go, so you can look after Bessie."

"But why cannot we both stay here with you?"

"Because you can't, that's all."

Her tears spilled over, and hastily she wiped them away. Only babies cried.

The door opened, and both child and mother turned to see the tirewoman enter with Molly's clothing. Sarah looked distraught.

"What is it?" Lady Gordon demanded. "What's amiss?"

"Men came and took the bairn, my lady! They just walked into the nursery and snatched Elizabeth from her cradle."

"Faith, what can he be thinking?"

Sarah had tears in her eyes, and seeing them, Molly began to tremble. Tears trickled down her cheeks again, unheeded now.

Sarah began deftly to dress her as she said sadly to Lady Gordon, "Why would the earl take one as small as wee Bess, my lady?"

"Because if anything should happen to Molly, Bessie will become the Maid of Dunsithe, and he means to maintain control of the Maid's fortune. Indeed," she added thoughtfully, "I would not put it past Angus to create his own heiress if both of the girls should die. If he were to keep them secluded and shift them about from one of his castles to another, who would know the difference? 'Tis likely that as the years pass even I would fail to recognize the true Maid of Dunsithe."

"Surely, that could never happen!"

"We cannot *let* it happen," Lady Gordon said grimly. "I can do nothing about Bess if Angus has already taken her, but I will know Molly, one way or another." Reaching for the ring of keys on her belt, she removed one of the smaller ones and handed it to Sarah. "Stir up the fire and heat this red-hot. I mean to see that no one will ever have cause to doubt the identity of the true Maid of Dunsithe."

"Mistress, ye'll no hurt the wee lassie!"

"Hold your tongue, woman, and do as I bid you. I'll go and hurry Nurse with their clothing, but I'll be right back. Molly," she added sharply, "you stop your weeping if you don't want to feel my hand when I return."

Her tummy clenched, her breathing came too fast, and her hands felt prickly, but dashing an arm across her eyes to wipe her tears away, the child watched silently as the tirewoman stirred up the fire.

Sarah put another log on and blew expertly on the embers to encourage more flames. When the fire was burning lustily, she slipped the little key onto the end of the poker and held it right in the heart of the flames. By the time Lady Gordon returned, the key was red-hot.

"Find me something to hold it with then bare her chest for me," she ordered. "I'll do the rest myself."

Only then did Molly realize her exact intent. Screaming, she tried to free herself from Sarah's grip. Though she was tiny, it took both of them to hold her.

Chapter 1 _____

The Isle of Skye, Scotland, 1539

Outside the little thatched cottage, wind blew and sleet-filled rain pelted down from a lightning-lashed black sky. The rain pattered noisily against the straw thatch, and thunder rolled after each bolt of lightning, but the crofters inside the cottage were used to such sounds. The single, crowded little room beneath the thatch was quiet except for the noise of the storm, the rhythmic whir of a spinning wheel, the crackling and sizzling of the peat fire in the center of the hard-packed dirt floor, and the voice of the long-bearded old man sitting in the place of honor.

"Years ago," he said, "my father did tell me about a woman who were in a great hurry to ha' her wool spun and made into cloth."

Pausing to shoot a twinkling look at the woman seated at the spinning wheel, he drank thirstily from his mug. Then, cradling the mug in his lap between two gnarled, liver-spotted hands, he went on in a more ominous tone. "One nicht," he said, "against advice, she made a wish for someone to help her, and next day six or seven fairy women in long green robes appeared at her house, all chanting magical words that only they could understand. Taking up her wool-cards and spinning wheel, they set to work, and by midday, the cloth were on the loom. When they finished, they asked her for more work, but she had nae more spinning or weaving to do, and she began to wonder how she would get them out o' her house."

Seventeen-year-old Molly Gordon sat on her cloak on the dirt floor near a corner of the room, leaning contentedly against the wall. Arms hugging her knees, she listened to the familiar tale, contented and filled with a rare sense of almost fitting in, belonging, if only for a short time. She knew everyone in the room well, as well as the family that had raised her, and she cared for them deeply.

The fragrance of burning peat wafted through the air, mixed with odors of food cooked earlier over the fire, the damp fur of the dogs curled near their masters, and the wet wool smell of rain-damp clothing. Although everyone in the cottage had heard the tale many times, each listened as intently as if it were the first time.

Everyone had brought food to share, and now that they had finished eating and darkness had begun to fall, the *ceilidh*, or folk gathering, had begun in earnest. While they ate, the conversation had been all gossip, as everyone shared any news gleaned since the last gathering. Then men had heaped the peat higher, and as it flamed and then smoldered, the tales had begun.

Nearly a score of people filled the room, adults and children, most of them sitting close together around the fire, albeit leaving sufficient space between it and themselves for any wee folk who might care to join them and hear the stories. Girls snuggled with family members or friends, and boys perched wherever they found space—three on the solid, square table pushed against one wall and several more in a tangle beneath it.

Near Molly, a man twisted twigs of heather into rope to tie down his thatch while he listened. Another twined quicken root into cords to tether his cows, and yet another plaited bent grass into a basket to hold meal.

At her spinning wheel, their hostess's hands moved deftly through their familiar motions while her eldest daughter carded wool beside her. Another teased the nap on a piece of finished cloth. Other women sewed, knitted, or tended small children. Babies nursed or slept, and on a bench in the corner opposite Molly, an elderly man dozed, his snores occasionally punctuating the fairy tale.

Molly had no task to occupy her hands, no knee to lean against, and no hand to hold. She sat apart from the others, but even so, the evening warmed her heart and contented her restless soul.

The storyteller had reached the point in his story where the housewife complained to her neighbor about the exasperating fairy women.

"'Get ye inside,' the neighbor said to her, 'and tell them to go down to the sea and spin the sand into cloth. That'll keep 'em busy and out o' your house.' And so it did," the storyteller added. "For all we ken, they be there to this verra day."

Chuckles greeted the end of the tale, just as they always did, and before they had died away, another man said matter-of-factly, "Me father and grandfather knew a man wha' were carried by the Host all the way from South Uist to Barra."

"Aye, then, tell us aboot it, man," murmured several members of the audience in a chorus.

After that, the old man told the tale of the *Dracae,* or water fairies, which was one of Molly's favorites. Even the children were silent, eager to hear what happened to the woman seized by the water fairies and taken to their subterranean depths to act as nurse to their brood of fairy children. Then one small lad, who had been struggling to stay awake, fell asleep and toppled over just at the part where the now-escaping captive acquired the ability to see the *Dracae* whenever they intermingled with men. The hoot of laughter from the lad's brothers brought quick shushing noises from their father and several of the other adults. Molly smiled.

As the water fairies' tale reached its happy conclusion, she drew a deep breath of delight. It did not matter how many times one heard the tales. Knowing how each would end only added to one's enjoyment. She could even be grateful for the rain. No one would expect her to walk back to Dunakin Castle until it stopped.

Despite the driving black storm from the Atlantic that raged with unabated fury around the flat-bottomed fishing coble, the little boat's oarsmen moved it with remarkable steadiness from the Kintail mainland toward the looming dense shape of the Isle of Skye. Lightning flashed, revealing the boat's six occupants, one hunched in the bow, one manning the tiller, and the four others manning the long sweeps.

Thunder rolled and rumbled as driving sleet pelted them. The wind carried gusts so fierce and high that the coble's square lugsail was useless and was rolled up and strapped tightly to the beam of the mast.

The next flash of lightning revealed white sea foam billowing like snow around them. Then thunder crashed, and darkness enveloped them again.

In the bow, his oiled woolen mantle gripped tightly

around him and his head turned away from the wind, Sir Finlay Mackenzie, Baron Kintail, enjoyed mixed feelings about the wintry weather. He was cold, and despite his heavy mantle, he was wet. This was not the way he had imagined restoring stability to his life.

Earlier, horses had carried him and the five others to the village called Kyle from Eilean Donan Castle. From Kyle, they had taken the coble into the teeth of the storm. Normally, the trip across the strait would have been quick, for the distance was only half a mile. However, they headed almost due south, so the full fury of the Atlantic storm blasted them from the right, and with the storm thus trying to force them off course, the journey was taking an eternity.

Fin glanced over his shoulder, ignoring the sting of sleet against his face as he searched the darkness ahead. Through the black tempest, a tiny cluster of lights gleamed—their beacon, Dunakin Castle, perched high on its promontory. They were on course despite the storm's attempts to drive them back to Eilean Donan.

He hoped he was doing the right thing. To attempt his mission in such a hazardous way was perhaps foolhardy, especially with so few men in his tail. He was a Mackenzie chieftain, after all, a baron with the power of the pit and the gallows, and therefore a man of considerable authority. Perhaps he might have done better to await a calm day and transport horses to Skye along with a full contingent of men-at-arms to act as a proper chieftain's tail.

However, by the time he could mount such an effort, every man on Skye would know he was coming, and not all were friendly to the Mackenzies of Kintail.

Instead, he had decided that the mission he undertook was best done speedily and without warning, let alone any fanfare. He would stir a hornet's nest, even so, but that did not concern him. In truth, it pleased him that his greatest enemy, Donald of Sleat—the very man who had brought such heavy responsibilities crashing down upon his shoulders—was about to lose one of his most valued assets. The Maid of Dunsithe, greatest heiress in the land, was about to change guardians, and Donald of Sleat—known in the western Highlands and Isles as Donald the Grim—knew nothing yet about the exchange.

The taking of the Maid would stand for little enough in the grand scheme of things, but it was something, and Fin Mackenzie owed Donald the Grim much more. Only months before, in the depths of winter, Donald and others of his clan had murdered Fin's father in cold blood. Vengeance, in any form, was sweet.

It was hard to tell the difference between the seawater dousing him and the driving sleet, but as they drew nearer, the Isle of Skye began to protect them from the worst of the storm. Now, compared to being on the open sea, they were sheltered, and despite the roar of the wind, he could hear the creaking of the rowlocks and the lashing of water against the sides of the boat. In lulls, he could even hear the labored breathing of his oarsmen. Being men who lived by the sea, they all were skilled at rowing, but they were also experienced men-at-arms.

Lightning flashed again, and his gaze met that of Sir Patrick MacRae, his closest companion and best friend. In the Highlands, the MacRaes were called the Mackenzies' "shirt of mail," and Patrick was a true MacRae. Much the same age as his master, he had served Fin since childhood, even accompanying him to St. Andrews University, where they had enjoyed a good many adventures together.

Patrick was grinning, as usual, and Fin automatically smiled back. But when thunder clapped and blackness swallowed them again, his thoughts returned to the Maid of Dunsithe. Specifically, he wondered what he was going to do with her.

His greatest loves were his home and his people. James, fifth of that name and by grace of God High King of Scots, had granted him the right to marry the Maid off wherever she could do him the most good. He could even marry her himself if he chose, but he had no interest yet in marrying anyone.

Fin was more interested in the Maid's fortune, because it could do much to protect his people and add to Eilean Donan's fortifications. There was a problem, though. Men everywhere, from the Borders to the Highlands, agreed that the Maid of Dunsithe was the greatest heiress in all Scotland, which, under normal circumstances, would have meant that one of her earlier guardians—and she had enjoyed several—would have married her off long since. The enticement for each, and the greatest deterrent, was her fortune. It was said that no one had actually ever laid eyes on it, but that tale sounded apocryphal to him. If there was treasure, he would find it, but even so, he was certain that over time men had exaggerated the size of it many times over. Still, whatever it comprised, he would see it, touch it, and take control of it before he did anything else with her.

He could not help but wonder at his fantastic luck. After months of uncertainty and concern over whether he would succeed in filling his powerful father's shoes, he had somehow drawn the King's notice and could now claim a connection to the powerful Earl of Huntly, chief of the Gordons. Huntly ruled the eastern Highlands and was some sort of cousin to the Maid.

Thus, the heiress had grand connections in Edinburgh and elsewhere, but she belonged now to a Highland baron with few influential connections outside the Highlands. Fin was uncomfortably aware that it would take a miracle to hold her if other, more powerful men discovered what James had done and decided to claim her for themselves. He would have to fight to keep her unless those others, including Donald the Grim, also believed that her fortune was mythical.

Unfortunately, the King was fickle in his choice of friends. He loved pitting his nobles against each other, but if there was trouble, Fin believed he could hold his own. Even without the improvements the Maid's fortune could provide, Eilean Donan was a stronghold worthy of the name, and he was a warrior, able to guard what was his. With the Maid to strengthen his position, who knew what blessings might follow?

The oarsmen shipped their oars, and the boat scraped on shingle. Atop the steep bank above them reared the lofty curtain walls and angle towers of Dunakin Castle, stronghold of the Mackinnons of Skye. Below the castle, huddling between the steep bank and the shore, Fin could make out the dense shadows of the fishing hamlet called Kyleakin. It comprised no more than a row of cottages, hovels, and tarred shacks used for smoking fish, but here at last the noise of the storm was muted. All was dark and still, for the village seemed already to be sleeping.

A flutter of eagerness stirred. Mackinnon was unknown to him, but Fin loved a challenge. He did not doubt his ability to take what was his.

A lone dog barked when Fin jumped out on the shingle, then other dogs joined in, but no one stirred from any of the cottages.

His men followed him, and together they dragged the coble high onto the shingle, where it would be safe until they returned. Then, savoring the sweetness of winning a hand without his opponent realizing he was even in the game, Fin set his sights on the towering fortress above and strode forth to claim his prize.

"Wake up, Claud! Drat ye, ye worthless dobby, wake up!"

Shaken rudely from his comfortable doze on the settle by the parlor fire, Brown Claud opened one eye and looked blearily at his tormentor. Recognizing his mother and deducing at once that something had stirred her ever-volatile temper, he said warily, "Did ye want summat, Mam?"

"I want ye tae wake up," snapped Maggie Malloch.

Before he could so much as stir a muscle, two small, plump, but nonetheless amazingly strong hands grasped the front of his tunic and gave a mighty heave. The next thing he knew he was sailing through the air, but his flight was brief. The full length of his body hit the stone floor with a bone-jarring thud, leaving him astonished and winded but certainly awake.

Sitting up awkwardly, he rubbed his aching shoulder and tried to gather his wits. His head swam, but it did not ache. He did not think that it had hit the floor.

His mother stood, arms akimbo, glaring down at him, her plump figure aquiver with anger and some other, less familiar emotion. "The Circle has met," she said grimly. "They ha' decided!"

"What did they say, Mam?" he asked. He had meant to sound casual, but the enormity of his recent actions made it likely that his entire future depended on what the Circle had decided. Thus, his stomach knotted painfully, and even to his own ears, he sounded pitifully anxious.

If his mother detected his anxiety, she ignored it, saying crisply, "Ye ha' only yerself tae blame, Claud, nae one else."

"Am I tae be broken, then, Mam? Will the clan cast me out?"

"I still carry weight enough in the Circle tae ha' my say," she snapped. "For the present, I ha' prevented the worst, but I canna prevent it forever, lad, if ye dinna pull your legs under ye and do your proper, bounden duty."

"But I thought I *were* doing me duty."

"Bah," she snapped. Her head bobbed forward to emphasize her next words. "Ye be bound tae look after the Maid, tae protect her from harm. Instead, ye took on summat well beyond your ability, and grave harm may come of it."

"I meant tae help! So long as she stayed ward tae Donald the Grim, nowt could happen tae do her good. Ye ken that as well as I do!"

She shook her head. "What's come over ye, lad? Ye were always one tae make mischief now and again, but never were ye so feckless afore this. Is it another woman? Ye never think well when there's a woman in it."

He hesitated, but her powers were far greater than his and he could imagine no way to avoid telling her the truth. "Aye," he said softly, "but Catriona's no just any woman, Mam. She's a wee goddess."

"Ah, bah," retorted his mother. She moved nearer, adding grimly, "I thought as much, though. I'll warrant the whole thing were her doing."

"Nay, then, it were not," Claud protested. "It were my doing, Mam, all of it." He did not think it wise to admit that he had wanted to see if he could do the thing, to see if his abilities were great enough to influence even the High King of Scots. He would not let her spoil the amazing success he had achieved, either, certainly not by suggesting that anyone else had had the smallest hand in it.

That Catriona might have put the notion into his head in the first place he would never admit to himself, let alone to his mother.

"Aye, sure, I've nae doubt that ye believe that, laddie,"

Maggie Malloch said with a sigh. Then her voice grew stern again when she said, "But ye've nae business tae be meddling in the King's affairs, let alone causing him tae do what he might verra well no ha' wanted tae do. Ye mustna do such a thing ever again, for I've given my word tae the Circle that ye'll not."

"I'll thank ye, then, for standing by me, Mam."

"Ye're my son, Claud, but I'll no ha' ye shaming our good name."

Her bosom swelled with her lingering anger, and that anger gave her greater size, so that she loomed over him. Hastily, he scrambled to his feet, hoping thereby to ease the fear she stirred in him at such times. "Even them in the Circle canna see the future, Mam," he said, striving to sound brave and hearing only desperation in his voice. Blustering on, he added, "I warrant it'll all work out for the best. Ye'll see. And them in the Circle will, too."

"Ye'd best hope that we do, lad, for the chief himself said that ye're tae ha' but one more chance. If ye overstep again, they mean tae cast ye out, and ye ken fine what will become o' ye then."

Cold terror shot up his spine, making it nearly impossible to speak. He tried, but he could manage no more than a whispered, "Aye, I do."

"Ye're frightened, and so ye should be," she said. "But when ye poke your fingers into a stew o' King Jamie's brewing, ye mustna weep when ye get burnt."

He was silent for a long moment, striving to calm himself so he could make her understand that he had done the right thing. However, when he realized that he could not trust his voice, he moved to pass her, to get away.

"Where be ye going?"

"Out," he muttered.

"Where? Ye'll no be goin' tae that wretched lass the noo."

"Nay, there's a *ceilidh*," he blurted. "I like tae hear the stories."

Pushing past her, he left, feeling her angry gaze upon him like a sharp sword against his back.

Her voice, low-pitched and grim, followed him.

"Remember, Claud—kings, like dragons and clan chiefs, breathe fire when ye poke at them."

Chapter 2

Fires roared at both ends of the great hall at Dunakin Castle, but the reception of six unexpected late visitors was chilly at best. The Laird of Mackinnon sat in his armchair on a slightly raised dais at the end opposite the main entrance, his lady at his right in a chair almost as elaborately carved as his. To his left sat his two burly sons on armless chairs. The chair at her ladyship's right was unoccupied.

When Fin and his men were admitted at half-past ten, shortly before the laird's suppertime, their arrival stirred a buzz of conversation. But the buzz ended abruptly when the laird's porter banged his staff of office on the stone floor, demanding silence before he announced the name of the visiting chieftain.

Then in stentorian tones, he said, "Sir Finlay Mackenzie, Laird o' Kintail, declares that he has business wi' Mackinnon o' Dunakin."

"Welcome t' Dunakin, Kintail," Mackinnon said affably. "We'll be setting aside any business till ye've taken your supper, though. A man should eat well afore he takes up matters of import. Call in your lads and find places at yon tables."

Stepping forward instead, Fin said, "I have brought no others with me, sir. An it please you, my business will not take long."

"Aye, sure, but what will please me most is t' take my supper first, and in peace," Mackinnon said less affably than before. "Sit ye down, Kintail, as I bade ye—ye and your lads—and enjoy your meal whilst I enjoy mine. There be naught ye could say that can be more important than food, lest ye've come t' beg urgent assistance against a common enemy. Will it be battle, then?"

"Nay sir, 'tis naught o' the sort."

"Then sit down, man, sit down. We've salmon and fresh lamb roasted whole on the spit, and I've a hunger on me grand enough to eat it all m'self."

Left with no other choice, Fin and his men sat down and took supper with the laird and his household. But although Mackinnon's servants offered them much food and drink, the six ate sparingly and drank less, speaking civilly when addressed but otherwise remaining silent.

Fin noted that his grizzled host watched him through narrowed eyes and doubtless noted his impatience, but when the servants had set fruit and sweets on the tables, instead of permitting him to state his business, Mackinnon called for one of the Dunakin men to give them a tune on the pipes. When that was done, he called on another to tell them a tale. Then one of her ladyship's women took up a small harp and played a tune while servants bustled about, clearing tables and beginning to dismantle the trestles in the center of the hall. The high table remained as it was.

Fin, sitting on the hard bench and watching the table before him be taken apart, had to exert stern control to suppress his growing frustration. Only the suspicion that Mackinnon hoped he would press again to have his business heard, and would then counsel more patience, kept him silent. Exerting patience of any sort was foreign to his nature.

The hour had advanced considerably before at last the laird made a slight gesture and said, "Step forward, Kintail, and state your business. Ye be Sir Ranald Mackenzie's lad, be ye not, the one they call Wild Fin?"

"I was called so before my father's death," Fin admitted in a commendably calm but carrying voice as he stood up. He saw no reason to add that many who knew him still referred to him by that appellation.

Mackinnon nodded somberly. "'Twas sorry I were t' learn o' his passing."

"It was a sad day," Fin said curtly. Taking the roll of parchment that Patrick MacRae held out to him, he added, "With respect, sir, I have come not to speak of past events but to present this document to you and to collect what is mine."

"What sort o' document would that be?"

"'Tis a writ of wardship and marriage from King James, sir, vacating an earlier writ of the same nature, granted a dozen years ago to Donald of Sleat."

"Indeed?"

"Aye."

"Then it seems t' me that it is t' Sleat that ye should present your document."

"As to that—"

Cutting him off with a gesture, Mackinnon said, "I expect I can guess the ward named in this writ of yours, Kintail, but ye'd best tell me all the same."

"One Mary Gordon, sir, known also as the Maid of Dunsithe."

A surprised murmuring broke out in the hall, but it stilled quickly when Mackinnon glowered at all and sundry and said gruffly, "Doubtless yon writ includes her estates and fortune, as well."

"Aye, it does," Fin said steadily.

Mackinnon grimaced. "I'd like fine t' ken how ye persuaded Jamie t' make ye such a gift, lad. Ha' ye become one o' his favorites o' late? Because if ye have, I'd counsel ye t' take special care. In my experience, any man who trusts Jamie's word takes a fearful chance."

"I have no knowledge of how the King came to transfer the writ to me, sir," Fin said evenly, adding, "A special messenger brought it only yesterday to Eilean Donan. On that, you have *my* word, and you have no experience that can lead you to mistrust me, because when I give my word, I keep it."

At Mackinnon's side, Lady Mackinnon looked troubled. Her hands clutched one another tightly on the table before her.

After a pause, during which Fin could hear angry winds outside hurling themselves against the castle walls, Mackinnon said gruffly, "I still say that ye be presenting your writ t' the wrong man, lad. The Maid be ward t' Donald of Sleat. He be chief o' all the Macdonalds, and they dinna call him Donald the Grim wi'out cause. Forbye, ye must appeal t' him, although I'm thinking that will do ye nae good at all."

"With respect, sir, I'm told you foster the Maid here at Dunakin, and the writ directs that I may collect her from her present dwelling place and take her to Eilean Donan. It explains his grace's wishes quite clearly if you'll only read it."

Mackinnon smiled wryly, saying, "D'ye expect t' collect her mythical fortune, lad? Did our conniving Jamie promise ye riches?"

"As to that, sir, his grace promised me naught, although the writ includes custody of her estate and that which was willed to her by her late father. I come only to collect the Maid. I know little as yet about her fortune."

"Aye, as little, I dinna doubt, as any man in Scotland. Ha' they no told ye, laddie, that cleverer men than ye ha' looked in vain for the lassie's grand fortune? For m'self, I believe 'tis nobbut a golden gleam in Jamie's fertile imagination— aye, and in Angus's afore him."

"I know from the writ that the Maid is kin to Angus, but all it mentions of her personal history is that James granted Donald of Sleat a similar writ of wardship and marriage years ago, which Donald has failed—"

"Och, aye, but then ye must ken that Jamie were nae more than a lad himself when Angus became his stepfather by marrying the sister o' that scalawag Henry of England. Queen Mary soon got shut o' Angus, o' course, but he kept young Jamie under his thumb for two years after that, and it were during that time that Angus forced Jamie t' grant him the Maid's wardship. Her father, Gordon o' Dunsithe, had but just died, ye see, and he were a man o' parts. 'Twas said he were worth more than any o' the King's gentlemen, more even than his cousin the Earl o' Huntly."

"I have heard such tales, of course," Fin admitted. "Still, I thought they were most likely untrue, since no one can claim to have seen any part of her fortune other than the castle and its lands."

Mackinnon shrugged. "They do say there were gold and jewelry, chests full of the stuff, but 'tis true that nae man ha' laid eyes on it since Gordon's death. I, too, doubt that it exists. Still, some do, and nae one who wants the lass cares a whisker about her welfare. Why, I heard that when Angus abducted her—"

"Abducted?"

"Och, aye, did ye no ken that, either? Angus rode t' Dunsithe not a fortnight after Gordon's death and snatched her and her wee sister from their mother's arms. The Maid were nobbut five years old at the time."

"But Angus did not marry her."

"Nay, for he were burdened wi' troubles of his own even then, and the King heaped many more on him when he won free o' Angus's care. The Maid's wee sister had died by then—bairns being ever a fragile lot—and one o' Jamie's first acts as King were t' collect the Maid from the kinswoman into whose care Angus had put her. He didna keep her long, though. He gave her to Donald o' Sleat."

Resting his elbows on the high table, Mackinnon tented his fingers under his chin, frowned a moment in thought, and then went on. "Many men ha' sought her fortune since, including Donald and Jamie himself, but nae one has found it, so ye'd best leave her be, lad. Ye'll never find it, and nor will anyone else."

"That may be so," Fin said, his jaw muscles tightening. "Nevertheless, the Maid is mine now. Will you transfer her custody to me peaceably, or will you not?"

"Well, as t' that, I canna do it straightaway," Mackinnon said glibly. "Forbye, she isna even here at present."

"Where is she?"

"Aye, sure, ye've the right to ask if yon document be what ye claim it be, but I doubt ye'll like the answer. She's away t' the north end o' Skye at Dunvegan."

Lady Mackinnon's eyebrows twitched, and she glanced quickly at her husband as if she would speak. Then, as casually as if the moment had not occurred, she took an apple from a basket on the table before her and began industriously to polish it on her sleeve.

Mackinnon did not look at her. His steady gaze held Fin's.

Fin said evenly, "Perhaps you can send for her, sir."

"Lad, I dinna mind telling ye, ye've put me in a bad place wi' this demand o' yours. There be three chiefs on this island, ye ken—MacLeod o' Dunvegan in the north, Donald o' Sleat t' the south, and m'self here in the middle. I've my good relationship wi' Donald t' consider and that wi' MacLeod, as well. I suggest, therefore, that ye take this demand o' yours t' MacLeod."

"It is devilish late to be leaving for Dunvegan," Fin said, thinking swiftly. That the Maid was at Dunvegan was a blow, for the MacLeods were unfriendly to the Mackenzies as often as not. Moreover, Dunvegan nestled in a distant, easily defended position on a sea loch. "It lies nearly fifty miles north of here, and we cannot go by sea on a night like this."

"Aye, that be fact," Mackinnon agreed, "but I'll gladly lend ye ponies, and the track be plain enough. Ye look t' be stout lads, so I warrant ye'll make the distance easily afore midday tomorrow. Then ye've only t' wait for low tide. Ye can approach the sea gate then wi'out difficulty—if MacLeod welcomes ye, and all."

Kintail gazed steadily at his host for a long moment, then nodded curtly. "I thank you, sir, and accept your offer to mount us. Come, lads. We'll take our leave now, since we've no reason to claim further hospitality here."

Turning on his heel, he walked away, his companions following quickly after him. As he passed through the tall doorway, Fin glanced back and felt his temper stir when he saw Mackinnon exchange a look of profound relief with his lady.

Inside the croft, Molly realized the rain had stopped. Knowing, however, that it might begin again any moment and continue through the night, she got reluctantly to her feet and picked up the cloak upon which she had been sitting.

"Mun ye go the noo, mistress?" the crofter asked, standing at once.

"Aye, Geordie. I do not want to leave all this warmth and good cheer, but it must be nearly midnight by now, and someone is bound to remember that I'm away and come to fetch me if I do not return soon."

"Ye mun let me walk wi' ye," he said, turning to look for his cap and cloak.

"Nay, then," she said, smiling as she laid a restraining hand on his arm. "You need not miss the stories. Wee Hobby has not yet told the one about Joseph and his wondrous coat, and I know that you always enjoy that one."

"Aye, well, 'tis a good one, that," he agreed.

"The path is clear, and I know it well," Molly said, smiling again when she saw others getting to their feet to bid her farewell. "The rain has stopped, and there is no one out and about now. I shall be perfectly safe."

"Ye may be safe enough," one of the other men said, "but the laird will ha' summat t' say if ye walk home all alone."

"If he does, he will say it to me," she said calmly, whisking her dark cloak over her shoulders and putting up the hood. Then, to the entire gathering, she said, "Thank you, all of you, for inviting me to share your *ceilidh*. 'Twas a fine night, storm or no storm."

"Och, lassie, that were hardly a storm, that one," scoffed the one who had worried about what the laird would say. Shaking his head, he added, "Only two or three thunderclaps and a few wee bolts o' lightning afore supper. A storm be when the waves from the sea lash over the mountaintops and swords o' lightning stab at every door and window. Why, I mind, in the autumn o' twenty-three, when—"

"Hush ye now, Lachlan!" cried several of the others. "Wee Hobby's going t' tell us about Joseph's fine-looking jacket!"

As Lachlan muttered apologies, Molly moved to thank her hostess and to speak proper words of farewell to each of the others. By the time she had spoken to them all, the storyteller had begun. Her host hovered over her until she reached the doorway. Then, holding the flap back for her, he bade her good night.

As she stepped into the cold, she heard the storyteller's voice behind her, saying, "Aye, sure, it didna help that Joseph were a wee villain and told his father about all his brothers' bad habits when they were out working wi' the sheep!"

The landscape sloped uphill between the croft and the promontory where Dunakin Castle overlooked the strait, and the track was rugged. To warm herself, Molly walked at a good pace, but she took no chances. She did not want to twist an ankle. Being alone did not bother her. She was accustomed to solitude.

Although the rain had stopped, the night was too dark for good visibility, and the wind still blew in great, noisy gusts. It was a high wind, though, roaring through the tops of trees while barely stirring her cloak. She could hear and smell the seawater to her left, and despite the wind—or maybe because of it—the hoarse cry of an errant seabird drifted to her ears.

Looking around at the eerie, shadowy landscape, she was reminded of some of the stories she had heard. Throughout history, strange things often seemed to have occurred on dark, stormy nights. That thought brought another on its heels, and she looked up at the sky just as the moon peeped through the clouds, spilling silvery moonbeams down to dance on the foamy waves.

"A perfect night for heroic deeds," she murmured to the moon as it showed more of itself, nearly full and lighting the landscape. "In a more interesting world," she added, "one would know of heroic deeds to accomplish and a proper hero to accomplish them—a fine, upstanding man, capable of slaying fiery dragons."

Since the moon made no reply and the wind's song did not alter, she told herself to stop being a ninny and to get on home before someone came in search of her. No one would be angry, of course, but she would feel guilty at having caused any man to leave a warm fire and ride into the night merely to remind her that she should go to bed before morning.

Had Dunakin been her real home, teeming with brothers and sisters to squabble with and her own parents to look after her, perhaps she would not feel so beholden to minions who did her a kindness. But she lived there only because Mackinnon and his lady had been kind enough to take her in when Donald the Grim hadn't wanted her, and although they had continued to be very kind over the years, she felt a distinct obligation not to be more of a burden to them than necessary.

They knew where she had gone, though, and they knew that *ceilidhs* frequently lasted into the small hours. Perhaps no one was looking for her yet.

A cloud sped across the moon, causing the night to darken and then grow lighter again. Ahead of her on the track, six riders appeared.

They seemed to materialize out of thin air, because with the wind blowing toward them from the west, she had not heard their horses' hoofbeats. Nor had she heard voices, if any of the men had spoken. She could not see them clearly enough to recognize them, but there were too many to be searching for her. Rarely was more than one man sent out on such a mission.

A tingling stirred at the base of her spine. Normally, she did not have to concern herself with safety. The three men who ruled Skye knew her. Donald of Sleat, the most fear-some, was her titular guardian. Mackinnon of Dunakin was her foster father, and MacLeod of Dunvegan was friend to the latter if not to the former. None of them would harm her or allow his clansmen to do so.

Likewise, though, she could imagine none of them send-ing a mounted party into the night for any good purpose. Had Mackinnon planned to do so—a remote likelihood at best—she would surely have learned about it before leaving the castle that evening. And had either of the others sent out such a party, she would have heard about it at the *ceilidh*. The most likely explanation, therefore, was that the riders had come from the mainland and were up to no good.

These thoughts sped through her mind in the blink of an eye as she clutched her dark, hooded cloak more tightly around her and stepped off the track to the right, away from the water, toward nearby trees and shrubbery. With any luck, the riders had not yet seen her against the dark, hilly land-scape. Moving as swiftly as she dared and hoping that any movement they detected they would credit to wind through the bushes, she made for cover, finding it quickly amidst shrubbery at the edge of the tree line.

The men rode nearer. Now she could hear the hoofbeats, a steady drumming that made the ground vibrate beneath her. They were not riding swiftly, so it was likely that they did not know the track well. They were strangers then, but they seemed to be riding away from Dunakin rather than to-ward it. Shivering fear shot through her. What if they had at-tacked the castle?

As quickly as the thought struck, however, she dismissed it. All was quiet behind them, and Dunakin was well forti-fied. The three chiefs on Skye protected themselves well, and Mackinnon was the least likely of the three to suffer at-tack.

Donald would attack MacLeod, or MacLeod Donald before either would attack Mackinnon. Men called Mackinnon two-faced, but not as an insult. The tutor she had shared with Mackinnon's sons had told them that Mackinnon was like the two-faced Roman god Janus. Just as Janus looked forward and backward, at beginnings and endings, Mackinnon kept an eye on MacLeod and Donald, and existed on peaceful terms with both.

The riders rode two by two and were too few to be a raiding party.

She wished that the moon would dive behind another cloud; but perversely now, it shone brightly on the riders and the surrounding landscape, revealing that the leaders' horses had strayed from the track. To her horror, she realized that they were riding straight downhill now and would pass within a few feet of her hiding place, but until another cloud hid the moon, she dared not move.

She could hear voices now but could not make out what they were saying, because the wind's song through the trees had grown louder. The leaves around her danced and rustled, and the wind was cold against her cheeks.

They were drawing nearer, too near. Tension filled her. She felt as if she should shut her eyes lest her gaze attract someone else's, but no sooner did she shut them than they popped open again. She had to see.

The two riders in front gazed straight ahead. Whoever was talking, it was not either of them. One rode slightly ahead of the other, and Molly was certain that he was the leader. His profile against the moonlit landscape was well etched, proud. He looked powerful and dangerous, and the way he held himself spoke of great confidence. Broad-shouldered and tall in the saddle, he wore no helmet, and his windblown hair gleamed darkly in the moonlight. His horse was larger than the one beside it, and both animals looked strangely familiar. Did she know them?

Her fascinated gaze shifted back to the leader as a gust of wind greater than the others roared across the hillside making the bush that concealed her seem to part in two. The lead horses were no more than six feet away, the moon was bright, and when the leader's head turned slightly, his gaze collided with hers.

To Fin it seemed as if the girl's face had magically appeared in a whirl of color, forming before his eyes out of the black night. He had been paying little heed to the route his mount chose, caring only about reaching the foot of the promontory before heading back to the beach where they had left the coble, to be sure it was secure where they'd left it.

He reined in at once without taking his eyes from her. Despite the bright silvery moon overhead, he could see only her pale oval face and fear-rounded eyes. The face was enough, though. Full, soft lips, flawless skin, and huge black-fringed eyes. He wanted her to stand up. His imagination created a slender yet curvaceous, naked body to match the lovely face. His loins stirred. It was long since he had enjoyed a beautiful woman.

Raising his free hand as a signal to the others to halt, he said in a deep voice that carried with terrifying clarity to Molly's ears, "Well now, what have we here?"

Leaping to her feet, she turned to run, but the big horse he rode leaped after her, and she knew that he would easily catch her. If she waited until he ran her down, she might be hurt and her dignity certainly would suffer. Therefore, she stopped and turned, straightening her shoulders and meeting his gaze boldly.

His dark eyes gleamed, and the way his lips formed a half smile made him look hungry, even lustful. Responding tension made her dampen her own suddenly dry lips. She clutched her cloak tighter across her breasts, surprised by the tingling in their tips as she did so.

"Why, look at her, Patrick," he said. "She's a little beauty."

Molly heard the other man chuckle, and annoyance stirred beneath her fear.

"Let me pass," she said firmly, taking a step forward.

The man who had spoken drew his horse across her path. "I thought this expedition would prove a complete waste of time," he said, "but that may not be the case, after all. Possibly, you can amuse me, lass."

"I shall do no such thing," Molly said indignantly, trying to ignore her body's quivering response to his blatant hunger. "What manner of man would make such an impertinent suggestion to me?"

He grinned and said, "Why, 'tis myself who speaks to you and no other, so 'tis a fine man, indeed."

His voice was low-pitched, and the sound of it vibrated right into her, but the sensation eased when more chuckles from his men greeted his sally.

He ignored them, saying curiously, "How is it that you speak Scot instead of Gaelic, lass. Hereabouts most folks of your class speak the latter."

"I speak whatever is spoken to me," she retorted. "I have always done so, and I rarely pay attention to what language it is. Moreover, since our laird's lady comes from Edinburgh, many at Dunakin speak both tongues."

The man he had called Patrick said with another chuckle, "She's a saucy one, Fin. I like a wench with spirit."

The one called Fin laughed. "You like anything in skirts, my lad. I'm of a much more discriminating nature, myself, but I believe that she might please me."

"Well, unless you intend to share her, what do you expect the rest of us to do whilst you amuse yourself?" Patrick demanded in a less respectful tone. "And, too, you'll delay us considerably unless you mean to take your pleasure quickly."

"I've no cause for haste," Fin replied. "If what we've seen is aught to judge by, making for Dunvegan now means fifty miles of riding across this island in treacherous moonlight. 'Twould be far wiser to make camp hereabouts, and then I can amuse myself with the lass until morning. What's your name, lassie?"

"I won't tell you, and you will do no such thing," Molly snapped, ruthlessly ignoring the havoc his attitude, looks, and voice were wreaking with her senses. "How dare you even think of trying to take me to your bed!"

"I dare what I like, lassie, and do as I please, so take care how you speak to me unless you want to learn quickly just how much I will dare with you."

Her body's reaction to his threat startled her, for the feeling was unlike any she had ever felt before. Muscles tightened in places where she had not known she had muscles, and jolts of heat flashed through her. At the same time, she wanted to slap him for his impertinence, but she was not a fool, and he was out of reach in any case. In frustration, she nibbled her lower lip as she tried to think how to escape.

"I see that you do have some sense," he said. "Now, I'll ask you again. What is your name?"

She glowered.

"Fin, before you decide to cross the backbone of Skye in broad daylight, perhaps you should consider whether you want to explain our journey to Donald the Grim," Patrick said, making her think for a startling moment that even without knowing her name they knew who she was and had the sense to fear her guardian.

But Fin dismissed the suggestion instantly. "Why should I care a whit about Donald?" he demanded.

"Because," Patrick said, "if you think we can ride for hours across Skye in daylight without his learning of our presence here, you're daft. Moreover, 'tis as likely as not that MacLeod will refuse to admit us when we get there."

"He'll admit us. He respected my father, and when he sees the writ I carry, he'll have no choice unless he wants to anger the King. Donald will not bother us if we camp near Kyleakin, and my bed will be warmer for some company."

He grinned again at Molly. "You've lovely hair, lass. It gleams like molten gold in the moonlight."

Trying to ignore a second surge of heat through her body at the unexpected compliment, she told herself he did not mean it, that her hood had merely slipped and he was just an unmannerly rogue being overly familiar. She was certainly not frightened of him—or the least little bit attracted to him. He was horrid.

"I shall leave you now, sir," she said, striving for a note of dignity and reaching back to pull her hood forward again.

"Nay, lass," he said, bending toward her. "First give me a kiss, and then . . ."

As he spoke, he reached to catch hold of her upraised arm, but his gloved fingers no more than brushed her elbow when his horse suddenly reared. Caught off balance and off guard, he flew from the saddle and crashed to the ground, his head striking it with a sickening thud.

His body lay in a twisted heap, without movement.

The big horse, calm now, turned its head and looked curiously at the still form of its erstwhile rider.

Chapter 3 _____

Molly gaped in dismay at the fallen man as the one called Patrick flung himself from his mount and hurried to kneel beside him.

"Witch! The lass must be a witch!" The words flew from mouth to mouth, whispers at first, then muttering.

Another man followed Patrick but kept his eyes on Molly as he said, "It be true, Sir Patrick. The lass must ha' cast a spell over that horse to make him rear so."

Sir Patrick? Molly stared. If Patrick was a knight, then what was his master?

"Don't be daft, Tam," Sir Patrick muttered as he shook the injured man's shoulder. "Mackinnon's lads warned us this horse had a temper as wicked as our laird's. Just because he thinks he can ride anything that . . . Fin, speak to me!"

No response.

"They did say the beast were unpredictable," Tam said, "but he recognized his match, for the master did say he were meek as a lamb! So there could be no other cause for him rearing like that. The thunder stopped long since, and there were naught else t' fright him but the lass there." He paused, but when no reply was forthcoming, he bent nearer to Sir Patrick, adding, "Be he dead, then?"

Molly shivered. Rogue or not, she did not want the horrid man to die.

"He breathes," Sir Patrick said, "but he's got a lump on his head and he does not stir or open his eyes."

"Don't sit gaping at him then, you cloth-heads," Molly said, speaking sharply in her relief. "You there, you two," she said, indicating two of the muttering riders. "Go into those woods and cut two saplings of a size a bit longer than your idiot master. Have you rope or cording?" she demanded of the nearer of the two.

"Aye, mistress," he replied, responding automatically to the note of authority in her voice.

Sir Patrick looked over his shoulder at her. "What would you have us do with saplings, mistress?"

"You must tie his mantle to them in such a way that you can carry him on it back to Dunakin. He may be badly hurt, but the castle has a healer who can help him. I will ride his horse if you like."

Sir Patrick frowned. "The beast seems temperamental, mistress. I'd not advise you to attempt it."

"Animals do not fear me," Molly said.

"Even so, I'd advise against it," he said. "Our men already believe you to be a witch. You speak Scot when they expected you to speak only Gaelic, and they think you caused their master's fall. If you now manage to ride a horse that could throw a rider of his skill, they will be certain of it."

"I see. Very well, then, but if I follow your advice, will you follow mine?"

"Aye, if you think Mackinnon will take us in. I should perhaps tell you that his welcome earlier was none too warm."

"I will not believe he denied you hospitality, sir, for no

Highlander would do such a discourteous thing," she said, noting with satisfaction that the two men she had sent for saplings were already returning.

"We did not request hospitality," he replied. "Mackinnon gave us supper and lent us these horses, but his manner was not such that my master chose to sleep under his roof. When we are away from home, we prefer to sleep under the stars."

She glanced up. The wind still blew, but there had been no more gusts as fierce as the one that had revealed her hiding place. The clouds were rapidly dispersing, the moon was bright, and a sea of stars glittered overhead.

"Who are you?" she asked quietly, realizing after the words were out that he might demand similar information from her and not certain she wanted to provide it.

However, if he heard her question, he gave no sign, saying only, "I'll help them rig that carrier. It should not take long."

Moments later, the stretcher was ready to receive its occupant. "Lift him carefully," Molly said when all five moved to help. "Dunakin's healer can mend broken bones but only if you do not shift them about too much."

"I felt nothing that appeared to be broken," Sir Patrick said, "but you may be sure that we will take care. Shall I have one of my men escort you to your home whilst we see to our master?"

"I'll go with you," Molly said crisply. "To speak plainly, sir, with your master as their example, I'll feel safer at Dunakin than alone with any of your men."

"As you wish," he said quietly, gathering the reins of the horse his master had ridden. "Back to Dunakin, then, lads. You four carry him for now, and I'll relieve anyone who grows tired, though the distance is short. Would you care to ride one of the other horses, mistress?"

"I'll walk, thank you," Molly said. She did not want to

give them information when they had given her none. Nor did she want to ride, since that would mean accepting Sir Patrick's help in mounting. Doubtless, too, if she rode, he would ride also, and she felt safer with everyone walking. "I'd be happy to lead one of the other horses if you like," she added, watching as they gently straightened the injured man's legs and settled his arms beside him.

Sir Patrick accepted her offer with thanks, his attention focused again on the motionless form of his master.

Molly did not know whether to hope the injured man regained consciousness quickly or remained safely out of his senses, but as she gazed down at him, she realized that her indignation and anger had given way to softer emotions.

Moonlight made him look peaceful and almost boyish, although he was far too large for anyone to mistake him for a child. His features looked less intimidating now, to be sure, but nonetheless attractive. Doubtless, most women would find him handsome and be only too happy to leap at his slightest command, even into his bed. Her feelings were mixed. She could not cheer such an accident befalling anyone, and she could not help thinking that she had somehow spooked the horse into rearing, but she was grateful for whatever had stopped the man from pursuing his intentions toward her.

She wondered what color his eyes were. She had seen only the darkness of their depths and the danger in their expression.

He certainly had made his wishes plain, and she found it disturbing that he had wanted to kiss her and doubtless to fondle her the way she had seen certain men kiss and fondle croft women or female servants in the castle, whether the women were agreeable to such pastimes or not.

His hands were large, she thought, gazing at the nearer

one. One could easily hold her, and if he put the other arm around her . . .

"We're ready to go now, mistress," Sir Patrick said, startling her. He handed her the reins of the horse she was to lead.

Sir Patrick walked, too, leading the two horses that he and his master had ridden. The animals gave them no trouble, and Molly thought it odd that the one had thrown its rider, for she now recognized all six horses as coming from the Dunakin stables. They were spirited beasts but not ill-tempered ones, whatever the men in the stable might have told the strangers.

The little party moved steadily but swiftly, and it seemed no time at all before they were inside the castle walls, where gillies came at once to tend the horses and Molly led the way into the great hall.

Although servants had long since cleared away the supper tables, Mackinnon lingered at the high table. His lady had retired, but it was ever her ladyship's custom to retire to her private chamber after she had supped.

Micheil Love, who had long tutored the laird's sons and Molly, had taken Lady Mackinnon's place, and at the entrance of the little group with their stretcher, both men looked up from the chessboard they had been carefully studying.

A look of annoyance flitted across Mackinnon's face, but he said amiably enough, "What's this, then? Ha' ye come t' grief already, lads?" Then, as his gaze fixed on Molly, his tone altered to one of consternation, "Molly, lass, what are ye doing wi' this lot? Ye should be asleep in your bed."

"Aye, sir, I know, but the storm kept me at the *ceilidh* longer than I'd intended, and then I came upon these men, and their leader was hurt, and . . ."

"Faith, I can see as much," he interjected, "but off ye go

now, and no argle-bargle if ye please. I'll tend t' this business."

"Yes, sir," she said quietly. "But as they have brought the injured man with them, I will go and fetch Gerald the Healer, an it pleases you."

"Aye, aye, that's a good notion. The healer will ken what t' do wi' him."

Worry for the man's fate overcoming her now that her own safety was assured, Molly hurried through an archway at the left of the roaring fire and down a service stairway that twisted through the thick wall to the lowest level, where the healer had his small chamber near the kitchens. Knowing he would have gone to bed hours earlier, she hesitated only long enough to snatch a taper from a receptacle on the wall and light it from a nearby torch. Then, pushing the door open, she said urgently, "Gerald, wake up. The laird needs you at once."

"W-what?" Sitting up on his fur-piled pallet, the healer rubbed sleep from his eyes and looked blearily at her, squinting when his gaze met the candle's light.

"Come quickly," she said. "A man has fallen from his horse and lies senseless in the hall. I fear he may die!"

Bewildered, the healer said, "He fell from his horse in the hall?"

"His horse threw him on the track below the castle," Molly said tensely, seeing no reason to reveal more. "Come now, and do hurry!"

"I'm coming, I'm coming."

She turned away, keeping the taper, and he followed her back upstairs.

Mackinnon met them at the archway opening.

"Molly, ye foolish lass," he scolded, "what be ye thinking? Gerald, go and see if there be aught ye can do for Mackenzie o' Kintail. But ye, lass, get ye gone and dinna come back into the hall tonight. Indeed, I mean t' see ye spirited away from here as soon as may be, t' Dunvegan— Nay," he corrected hastily. "I spoke o' Dunvegan t' them earlier, so that willna do, for 'twould be the first place they'll look for ye, but it will take them a day t' ride there, and in the meantime, I can get ye safely t' Donald o' Sleat. He'll see they dinna take ye away."

"Take me away?" Foreboding swept through her. "But why, sir? I do not want to live with Donald. He may be my guardian, but he is cruel, and Dunakin is more my home now than Dunsgaith could ever be. I want to stay here."

"Cruel he may be," Mackinnon acknowledged, "but when all is said and done, lass, the only thing that matters is that he is your true guardian. I be but fostering ye whilst he tries t' reclaim the Lordship o' the Isles, which, as ye ken, he believes the Crown stole from the Macdonalds years ago."

"Aye, sir," she said, having heard about Donald's many beliefs and schemes over the years, all of which precluded his keeping her with him. "But I do not want to leave Dunakin," she added. "I scarcely know Donald of Sleat, and you have been like a father to me for nearly as long as I can remember."

"Likely, ye'd remain wi' Donald for only a short time," Mackinnon said reassuringly. "But go now, lass, I dinna want anyone realizing who ye be till I get shut o' this lot from Kintail."

"But who are they, exactly? You mentioned Mackenzie of Kintail, but that name is not familiar to me."

"That would be himself in there lying on the floor. He's the Mackenzie chieftain from Eilean Donan Castle, and he carries a writ from the King."

"King James?"

"Aye, and what other king might be making a nuisance o' himself but our own Jamie?"

"As to that, I do not know," Molly said, forcing a smile. "I suppose that, since Henry of England has formed the annoying habit of attacking the Scottish Borders and poking his nose into royal affairs at Stirling, he might decide to extend his impertinence to the Highlands. He certainly has made a nuisance of himself everywhere else for many years, or so they say."

"And who's been talking t' ye about the Borders?" he demanded.

"Why, you have, sir, frequently, and Micheil Love, as well. You said that I should know about what has been happening there in my absence."

"Aye, but your absence, as ye call it, ha' gone on now for nigh onto a dozen years, lassie. I doubt what happens in the Borders these days need trouble ye."

"No, sir."

"Aye, so dinna fratch wi' me more, but go and do as I bid ye, and dinna go t' your own chamber but sleep wi' Doreen or Annie. And if anyone asks ye who ye be, tell them ye be a servant lass here in the castle."

A disturbingly familiar voice said grimly, "We would not believe her."

Molly and Mackinnon turned as one and found themselves face-to-face with Mackenzie of Kintail. He looked even larger than Molly remembered—and more handsome—but the impudent grin was gone.

She had recognized his voice instantly, for it had the same effect on her that it had had before. Even so, she could scarcely believe that the tall, broad-shouldered, dark-haired, and extremely healthy-looking man standing in the archway could be the same one who had lain senseless only a short time before.

Evidently, Mackinnon felt the same, for he said blankly, "So ye're no dead after all, Kintail."

"As you see," Kintail replied. "Your healer was surprised, as well, but I have a hard head." Although he answered Mackinnon, he looked at Molly, and she forced herself to look steadily back.

The flickering light from the taper she still held and from torches in nearby holders made his dark eyes glint menacingly, making her feel as if she gazed into the eyes of Satan himself. She could not look away. His eyes looked brown, she thought, but very dark. That dark gaze held hers and seemed to draw her nearer, although her feet did not move. Her body stirred as if he had touched her.

Stupidly, she said, "You . . . you are standing up."

"You are perceptive, mistress." His voice was honey smooth, but his tone was nonetheless ominous. All sign of the impudent marauder she had met on the hillside was gone. Some undercurrent in his tone kept her silent, although she longed to tell him that both his comment and his manner were insolent.

Mackinnon said abruptly, "If ye're not hurt, Kintail, mayhap we should return t' the others now and let the lass retire t' her chamber. I've a chess match t' win yet, but your lads are welcome t' bed down in the hall, and I warrant we can find a spare chamber for ye and your deputy. He'll be a MacRae, will he not?"

"Aye." Kintail's gaze still locked with Molly's, and she began to feel that to look away now—if she could—would somehow give him a victory. "We thank you for your hospitality, Mackinnon," he added, "but we'll sleep with my men."

"As ye wish. Be they all MacRaes?"

Kintail glanced briefly at him. "Why would you think that?"

"Men do call the MacRaes 'the Mackenzies' shirt o' mail,' do they not?" Mackinnon said. "'Tis only natural t' think MacRaes would make up the greater part o' your tail, lad. D'ye play chess?"

"I do."

"Then if your head's no paining ye, we'll ha' a game, for 'twill be my pleasure t' beat ye," Mackinnon said cheerfully.

Kintail raised his eyebrows. "Do you always win?"

"I do. Does that terrify ye, or will ye play?"

"I'll play," he said, capturing Molly's gaze again. "But before we abandon the lass, I would know her name."

"Dinna tell him, lassie," Mackinnon said urgently.

"As you wish, sir," she said. "He asked me several times earlier, but I did not like his tone, so I did not tell him." She shot Kintail a challenging look, daring him to recall all that he had said to her.

He did not flinch, saying easily, "I thought what any man would think, meeting a lass walking alone at such an hour. If I offended you, mistress, you have only yourself to blame. You ought to have had a companion. In truth, you should keep her more closely guarded, Mackinnon."

"Why should he?" Molly demanded, furious that he would blame her for the incident. "Pray, what business is it of yours if I choose to walk at night?"

"It is very much my business," Kintail replied sternly, "because I believe that you are Mary Gordon, Maid of Dunsithe."

"And what if I am?" She heard Mackinnon gasp but kept her attention firmly fixed on Kintail.

He said evenly, "If you are, I hold a royal writ granting me your wardship."

"But you cannot hold such a writ," she protested, appalled at the thought of this man having any hold over her, realizing at last just what Mackinnon had been trying to explain to her. Desperately, she said, "My guardian is Donald of Sleat."

"No longer, mistress. His grace the King has seen fit to transfer that guardianship to me. Apparently, he learned that Sleat harbors thoughts of reestablishing the Lordship of the Isles."

"I know little about that," Molly said flatly, "nor can I imagine why a matter between Donald and the King should involve me."

"All you need to know is that I speak the truth," he replied with that maddening calm. "Do you deny that you are the Maid of Dunsithe?"

"I'll not deny it, for I am certainly she," Molly said. "But if you seek to control my fortune, sir, you should know that many others have long sought to find it and all have failed. There is land, of course, and Dunsithe Castle in the Borders, although that is doubtless falling to rack by now unless Donald still keeps a garrison there. But although men say that my father was a man of great wealth, as far as I know, no one has laid eyes on anything but the castle and its lands since his death."

"That is my concern now, not yours," he said. "At present, I am interested in collecting what is mine—which is to say, yourself, mistress. You will prepare to depart for Eilean Donan at dawn."

Molly looked from one man to the other, speechless and fighting tears. As she had continually feared, despite being allowed to remain in one household for years, she was again to be uprooted without a moment's thought for her wishes.

"Dinna be daft, lad," Mackinnon said curtly. "The lassie ha' made her home here for ten years and more. Ye canna sweep her away overnight. I warrant it will take a sennight at least, for she'll want t' take farewell of all here who love her. Ye're welcome t' stay wi' us till she's ready, but surely—"

"She may have one day."

"Nay, then, for it lacks but a few hours till dawn, and the lass requires her sleep. Make it four days. There's a good lad. We canna say fairer than that."

"Two."

"Make it three, at least!"

"Faith, Mackinnon, I'll not be taking her to the end of the earth, only to Eilean Donan. It is not as far away as Dunvegan," he added dryly.

"Aye, sure, Dunvegan," Mackinnon replied with a twinkle. "Well, I did think I'd sent the lass there, ye ken, but 'tis true, I ha' a dreadful memory."

Gathering her scattered wits, Molly said, "Do you not think that someone should ask me if I *want* to go with him? Even if I did—and I don't—I could not possibly prepare to leave Dunakin so quickly."

"You have nothing to say about it," Kintail said. "As it is Tuesday morning already, I'll give you until noon Thursday to pack."

"We dinna dine until one," Mackinnon said. "Ye'll no want t' go afore ye eat, for ye'll need your strength, lad. 'Tis a wonder and all that ye can keep your feet after such a clout as ye must ha' taken, falling off your horse. And how ye come t' do such a fool thing, I dinna ken. My man's a wizard training horses, and I ha' never had trouble wi' the one that gave ye a toss, but mayhap ye—"

"There is naught amiss with me or the horse," Kintail said, shooting a look at Molly. "Indeed, sir, so mild was his temper before that moment that my men still suspect witchcraft."

"That is not what your men said about his temper," Molly said. "They said it was as wicked as your own—although," she amended hastily, "they did say, too, that he was as meek as a lamb with you. It *was* odd, sir," she said to Mackinnon.

"Naught occurred to spook him, I promise you. He reared for no reason."

"Well, there be little accounting for beasts," Mackinnon said amiably. Turning to Kintail, he added in the same tone, "We're agreed, then. Ye'll remain until after dinner on Thursday—or mayhap till Friday morning. Ye'll no want t' be sleeping on that stone floor in the hall all that time, either, for ye'll need your sleep, and in a bed befitting your station. My people will look after ye nicely. Now then, Molly, ye run along t' bed. We'll speak more o' this business anon."

"Aye, lass," Kintail said. "You and I will also speak more anon."

Ignoring the little shiver that shot up her spine at his stern tone, Molly curtsied to Mackinnon but spared only a nod for Kintail. She was pleased when he frowned. Let him learn that she was no woman to bend her knee to a man merely because he thought he wielded power over her.

"Come along, lad," she heard Mackinnon say heartily as she strode briskly away from them. "Unless ye be lying and your head aches like the devil—as it should—I'll teach ye how t' play chess properly."

Chapter 4 ————————

Fin accompanied his host willingly enough, but it was as well that no one asked him just then what he thought of his new ward. From the moment of receiving the King's writ, he had thought only of what the transfer would mean to Donald of Sleat and perhaps to Eilean Donan. He had scarcely given a moment's thought to what it might mean to him. Had anyone asked what he had expected her to look like, he would have had no answer. Indeed, he would not have thought such a detail important, but he certainly had not expected her to look as she did—deliciously, intoxicatingly beautiful.

He had never seen anyone like her. He doubted that most men ever had, and it occurred to him then that James could not possibly know how beautiful she was, or he would have seduced her himself before offering her to anyone else. Such was his grace's reputation, after all, and if her fortune was half what they claimed, her purity would not matter a whit. Doubtless, James thought of her still as a child, no more than a pawn in his favorite game of pitting noble against noble.

Fin realized that he, too, had thought of this new ward as a child, but she was no such thing. Even dressed as she was and bedraggled after hiding in the shrubbery, she was exquisite. Her pale red-gold hair was soft and silky-looking, encouraging a man's touch. He could easily imagine burying his face in her long, thick curls. Her complexion was pale, translucently so, with a stubborn little chin, a tip-tilted nose, and undeniably kissable lips. And her eyes were extraordinary—large, with black-rimmed gray pupils, or so they had seemed in the dim torchlight of the corridor. Black lashes—long, curly ones—fringed them and made her look vulnerable, until she opened her saucy mouth.

She had a truly elegant figure, slender, graceful, and enticingly curvaceous. Indeed, he could complain of nothing in her appearance, and if the truth were told, he looked forward to seeing her again. But her behavior and manner of speech would have to change if they were to get along. That much was certain.

Following Mackinnon to the high table, he wondered what the man had been thinking to let her grow up speaking so impertinently to him or to anyone else. As Fin watched him finish his game, an image flashed before his mind's eye of the lass naked and spread out like a feast before him, her mouth bound shut. He chuckled at the thought. Doubtless, she would unman anyone foolish enough to try gagging her.

When Mackinnon's opponent relinquished his place at the chessboard, Fin took it with alacrity, certain that he could beat the older man. But although they played several games, no matter what he did, no matter how clever his strategy seemed, luck eluded him. When Mackinnon said kindly, as he offered him more of the heady *brogac* that the islanders drank, that Fin's losses were probably due to the clout on his head, Fin wanted to believe him, but his head did not even ache.

That seemed strange, too, because since he had hit the

ground hard enough to render himself unconscious, his head ought to hurt like the devil.

One benefit came from the busy night, however—or the *brogac*—for although he rarely slept well in strange surroundings, he slept soundly in the bedchamber allotted to him until a sharp rapping at the door awakened him.

"Enter," he growled, shifting his pillows and sitting up against them.

"You're in a pleasant humor," Patrick MacRae said with a teasing grin. "I came to see if you mean to sleep the day away. 'Tis nigh onto eleven."

"Faith, it cannot be so late!"

"Aye, but it is. I'd have come sooner, but Mackinnon told me you wanted to sleep late. He passed that information to Tam, as well."

"The devil he did! After this, my lad, unless you or Tam hear such an order from me, you will pay it no heed."

"Aye, well, normally I would not have believed him," Patrick said with a wise look, "but you stayed up till nearly dawn, after all, letting the old man beat you at chess and drinking his *brogac*, so I thought he might be right to let you sleep."

"Where is the lass? Is she still abed, as well?"

"Nay, the old man said she went hunting shortly after dawn."

"Hunting!"

"Aye, I thought it strange, myself, but I did take the precaution of sending a pair of the lads to keep an eye on her so she'd not winkle her way off the isle whilst you slept. They have not returned, so doubtless they managed to follow my orders."

"Good man," Fin said.

"Aye, unless Mackinnon is more devious than we think," Patrick said thoughtfully. "He could have murdered our lads and hidden the lass somewhere. This is his ground, after all."

"Men say Mackinnon is a man of his word," Fin said, "but I do not trust the lass. Unless I miss my guess, she'll leap at the first opportunity to escape me."

"How odd that she did not take to you at once," Patrick said, grinning again.

"You mind your manners, my lad," Fin growled, "or even you will soon find it difficult to laugh. I may allow you frequent liberties, but—"

"I'll hold my peace," Patrick said, sobering hastily. "There is still food set out in the hall," he added. "Shall I send a lad up with a platter of it?"

"I'll go down," Fin said. "Tell someone to saddle a horse for me. I mean to follow that hunt as soon as I've broken my fast."

An hour later, Fin rode out of the castle with Sir Patrick at his side, and it did not take them long to find the hunters. To his astonishment, the Maid rode ahead of the men, and she rode like a young goddess.

Her mount was of the highest quality, a fine bay gelding with four black stockings and a white blaze on its face. Its black mane was strung with tiny silver bells that tinkled musically as it paced along with its long black tail arched high. Her plushly padded saddle was inlaid with ivory and gilt. Her silver-tipped stirrups, her elegant gray velvet dress, and her plumed black hat—all augmented her beauty and the magnificence of her appearance. The fair huntress held her reins gracefully in her left hand and her bow in her right. A quiver of arrows hung from her belt. Her thick, reddish blond curls hung in a loose cloud down her back.

The sight reminded him of his Viking ancestors, any one of whom would have been delighted to capture such a treasure and carry her back to his home, to plunder at will until she squirmed with delight beneath him. The thought stirred tension in his loins.

Three huge gray deerhounds followed her closely, their heads held high, nostrils twitching eagerly as they sought to catch scent of her prey on the wind. Still staring at the alluring huntress, Fin found himself wondering next how much it all had cost. Becoming to her as it was, he hoped she did not expect him to clothe or mount her so finely at Eilean Donan—not unless he discovered that her fortune was as large as everyone claimed it was and it somehow came into his hands.

He had expected her to be riding with the hunters but not actually to be hunting, herself. He wondered again what Mackinnon was thinking, to let her ride with a company of men in such a fashion. He would certainly protect her better than that. Had the man no common sense at all?

It would not have shocked him to see her—with a proper lady companion or two, of course—hunting larks with a merlin whilst the men escorting them hunted with larger hawks or falcons. But the lass carried a longbow, and that, to his mind, was an absurdity. The longbow was a man's weapon, not a woman's, and meant for warriors, not willow-slender lasses, who could spend their time more wisely learning how to please a man. Surely, she could not even draw that bow properly. She was too small and lacked the necessary muscle. Nonetheless, she rode astride, she rode well, and she carried the bow as if she knew what to do with it.

Even as the last thought danced through his mind, the

hunters flushed a flock of gray-brown wood pigeons and she swiftly raised her bow, dropping her reins to her horse's neck and letting an arrow fly in almost the same short span of time that it took him to notice what was happening. The arrow flew true, and the bird fell.

Fin glanced at Patrick to see that gentleman's mouth hanging open.

Patrick looked at him. "You saw that?"

"Aye," Fin said. "She might not be as skilled as you are, but if I'm not mistaken, that shot was as fine as any other archer might make."

"I've never seen the like," Patrick said. "She handles that bow as well as any man I've ever trained."

Molly saw Kintail watching her, but she carefully avoided looking at him, because she did not want him to detect her curiosity and mistake it for anything else. Better that he think she had more important matters on her mind. Nevertheless, she was delighted that he was watching when she shot the wood pigeon. Men thought them difficult prey for an archer, because of their fast, steep, erratic flight. When the arrow struck true, it was all she could do not to throw him a smile of triumph, and when he and Sir Patrick rode away, she told herself the disappointment she felt was merely because he could not see her repeat the shot.

Back at Dunakin an hour later, she handed her bow and quiver to a gilly and nodded to another to help her dismount. Before the lad could do so, however, a muscular arm pushed him aside and Kintail stepped up beside her horse.

"Pray, sir," she said, raising her chin, "stand aside and let me dismount. I have much to do, and Lady Mackinnon is doubtless awaiting my return."

"I don't doubt that you have much to do," he said evenly. "What I do not understand is why you were careering about the countryside all morning instead of attending to your preparations for our departure."

"Because it is a magnificent day," she said airily, avoiding his intense, disturbing gaze. "The storm washed everything fresh, and I wanted to hunt."

"Do you always do as you want, mistress?"

"Always," she replied.

"You will find life at Eilean Donan rather different, I'm afraid," he said as he clasped her firmly around the waist and lifted her from the saddle.

To her surprise, he did not set her down at once but held her with her feet dangling. The position was undignified, and she felt her temper stir. His expression challenged her to protest, and she had a feeling that he was spoiling for a fight. When she did not respond at once, his eyes narrowed and he frowned.

She was sharply aware of him physically. In her present position, she looked him eye to eye. His hands at her waist were warm and strong. His body was large—huge compared to hers—and she realized that until he chose to set her down, she was powerless to make him do so. That helpless feeling was unlike any she had experienced since early childhood. Her nerves tingled and her breathing quickened.

She swallowed, hoping she could control her voice long enough to insist that he set her down, without revealing the disturbing effect he had on her.

Before she could speak, he said, "Eilean Donan is an islet, mistress, much smaller than the Isle of Skye. If one had such power, one could pick up our islet and Loch Duich—the entrance to which it guards—and put them both down anywhere on Skye without disturbing much of this island's present landscape."

"Have you a point to make, sir, before dinnertime?" she asked.

"I do," he replied, his strength apparently unstressed by her weight. He was still gazing steadily at her, and briefly meeting that gaze, she saw that his eyes were not dark brown, as she had thought the night before, but a deep blue so dark as to look nearly black. In an area where many men revealed the coloring of Viking forbears, his was unusual.

"The point," he said, giving her a shake as if to be certain that he held her attention, "is that once we reach Eilean Donan, you will go nowhere without my permission. It is clear to me that Mackinnon has allowed you far more liberty than simple good sense would dictate. That will change."

"You take your new authority much too seriously, sir," she said, hoping that she sounded as determined as she did. "I am quite capable of looking after myself, and I would ask you to put me down now. You have shown off your splendid strength to everyone in the stable yard. I warrant that they are much impressed by it, but in truth, such a display is unseemly."

He looked around and his rueful expression revealed that he had forgotten their surroundings. To her relief, he set her gently on her feet. When he shifted his hands to her shoulders, holding her, relief turned to apprehension.

She realized then that the top of her head did not even reach his shoulder. Thus, he seemed larger than ever when he put a finger under her chin and raised it, making her look at him again as he said quietly, "Hear me well, mistress. You no longer answer to Mackinnon but to me, and you would be wise to remember that. Not only am I not a man you can safely cross, but I am now your legal guardian, and by the King's authority I hold the right to marry you myself or to arrange a marriage between you and any other man I choose. Do not stir my temper."

A mixture of fear and something less easily identified shot through her, but she repressed the feeling, licked dry lips, and said with careful calm, "Am I to have naught to say to such plans, sir? I tell you now that I will not willingly marry you. Nor will I marry any man simply because you say that I must. I tell you also—nay, warn you—that if you believe Donald of Sleat will ignore this . . . this usurpation of his authority, he will soon make you see your error."

His eyes gleamed. "I hope that Sleat comes to Eilean Donan to debate the matter with me, lass, for he will meet a warm reception. If he dares to set foot anywhere in Kintail, my men and I will be ready for him."

He seemed suddenly like a different man. Although he had scarcely been gentle before, by comparison to the violence she sensed now just below the surface, his previous demeanor had been lamblike.

Abandoning her airs, she said quietly, "Why do you hate him so?"

"He killed my father."

"Men kill other men frequently," she said, struggling to conceal the instant sympathy she felt. To that same end, she added hastily, "For years now, ever since the Crown took unto itself the Lordship of the Isles, the Macdonalds have had to fight to keep what they hold. Other clans, clans the King chooses to set against them, have taken their land by trickery. Indeed, I believe the Mackenzies . . ."

"Aye, we had Lewis from them."

"Well, if your father—"

"You know not of such matters," he snapped. "Hold your tongue."

Fearing that he might become violent if she pressed him too hard, Molly fell silent, although she burned to inform him that she knew a great deal about the history of the Isles. But if Donald was responsible for the death of Kintail's father, she was sure Kintail would not willingly discuss that with her. Objectivity in such a discussion would be difficult for him if not impossible.

He waited, as if to be certain that she would not compound her impertinence, and then said quietly, "My father was leading men to Kinlochewe, to help fight off an attack there, when men told him a boat was foundering on the north shore of the loch. When he and his men ran to assist the boatmen, the Macdonalds ambushed them. Sleat is a scoundrel without honor, and he wants to rule the Isles as his ancestors did. Indeed, he would be King of Scots if he could."

She could think of nothing to say. She did not like Donald the Grim. The only thing that had made his guardianship acceptable to her was his continued absence, for the few times she had met him he had both irritated and frightened her with his fierce looks and abrupt manners.

"Go inside now," Kintail said curtly. "You will want to change your dress for dinner, and it cannot be long now before we dine."

"That is true," she said, wishing she could think of something to say that would bring a smile to his face. Glancing at the bright, cloudless sky to find the sun directly overhead, she said only, "Someone will be ringing the bell shortly."

"Go then," he said again. "And, lass . . ."

She had turned away—gratefully—but at these words, she glanced back over her shoulder at him. "Aye, sir?"

"Wear a blue dress. I would see how well blue becomes you."

All desire to cheer him vanished.

"Arrogant knave," she muttered under her breath as she turned away again. Despite the undeniable attractiveness of his person and the irritatingly seductive quality of his voice, his forcefulness annoyed her. She immediately began a mental survey of her wardrobe, trying to decide which of her dresses would declare most loudly to him that she refused to obey his absurd, arbitrary commands.

Fin drew a deep, steadying breath as he watched her walk away, her round little backside twitching in such a way that he wanted to run after her and either paddle her or make love to her until she agreed to submit to his will or he surrendered to hers. The unexpected rider to his thought made him want to smile, but he did not, fearing she might look back and see it and think she had already vanquished him.

For the past fifteen hours or so, he had felt disoriented. Doubtless much of that was due to the swiftness with which he had acted after receiving the King's messenger, and then his fall from the horse, but for that fall and for much of the rest he had no hesitation in blaming Mistress Gordon. The exasperating fact was that the lass did not know her place. She behaved more like a spoiled princess than the foster daughter of a Highland chieftain.

He had not behaved well either, though, and admitted as much to himself as he walked toward the keep's postern door, where a narrow service stairway led to the chamber allotted to him. It irked him that the lass could throw his own behavior in his face if he found cause—as he was sure he would—to take her to task again. He had never known anyone so impertinent, or so tauntingly fascinating.

She was different from any woman he had ever met. Border-bred, she was smaller and more slightly built than the Highland women he knew, who tended to be built along the larger, more robust lines of their Norse ancestors.

Clearly, serving as Mistress Gordon's guardian was not going to be as easy as he had thought, and just as it now seemed absurd that he had not once thought about what she might look like, that he had not thought about how she might act was an equally foolish oversight. If he had, of course, he would have assumed that she would simply obey him. Now he feared that she would not.

He sighed. She would learn, one way or another. He would not allow a mere lass whose head barely reached his armpit to make trouble at Eilean Donan. She would have chores to tend just like everyone else, and she would do as she was bid or she would answer to him. How difficult could it be?

Trying hard to ignore the lingering itch of doubt in his mind and an equally disturbing sensation much lower down, he reached his chamber and, finding Patrick within, demanded that gentleman's aid in finding a suitable change of clothing.

Molly reached her bedchamber still contemplating how best to show Kintail that domineering males did not impress her. Irritated by the constant echoing in her mind of his command that she wear blue, she pushed open the door hard enough to send it banging against the wall. Then she stopped at the threshold, stunned at the sight of one of the largest wildcats she had ever beheld, curled up on her bed.

Golden eyes gleaming wickedly, the beast growled at her.

"Mercy," she murmured, too stunned even to be afraid. When the first prickling of fear stirred, she decided that she could jump back and slam the door before it could attack, but even as that thought flitted through her mind, she noticed something even odder than the presence of a wildcat in her bedchamber. At first, it was as if a swirl of mist formed in front of the cat. Then, slowly, a solid-looking outline took shape.

The hair stood up on the back of her neck as, before her eyes, where no one had been before, a little woman appeared. Molly shut her eyes and opened them again, but the woman was still there. About two-thirds the size of the wildcat, she was leaning comfortably against its furry side, her legs stretched out before her, primly crossed at the ankles. In her right hand, she held an odd-looking implement like a stick with a small white bowl at one end from which a narrow stream of whitish gray smoke wafted upward.

"Good day to ye," the little woman said. "Did ye enjoy your hunt?"

"I did, thank you," Molly said, responding automatically to the woman's matter-of-fact tone. Then, still finding it hard to believe that the woman and cat had simply appeared out of thin air, she said warily, "Who are you?"

"Why, I be Maggie Malloch, that's who."

"I am afraid that name means naught to me," Molly said.

"Aye, sure, and I expected as much," Maggie Malloch said, "but we've nae time tae discuss me name now. It takes a deal of effort for me tae remain visible, ye see. I must speak quickly, so if ye'll be so kind as no tae interrupt me—"

"Remain visible!"

"Whisst now, I told ye, ye mustna interrupt," Maggie said impatiently. "I declare, mortals be as rude as any o' the wee people, for all that many in both worlds would say different."

"Wee people!" Molly's voice went up on the words in a

thready shriek, although she had begun to suspect as much when Maggie's figure formed out of the swirling mist.

"Whisst now, whisst," Maggie said sternly. "Ye'll do nae good by settin' up a screech, for if anyone else comes in, I'll ha' tae be taking me leave o' ye straightaway. Would ye mind shuttin' that door now—and quietly, mind."

Fascination replaced the lingering remnants of Molly's fear and disbelief. She had heard tales of the wee people all her life, but never had she actually seen one before—or two, if one counted the cat, as she hoped one could. "But you cannot be a fairy," she protested. "Fairies are much smaller than you are."

"How small? Like this, d'ye think?" Maggie shrank until she was smaller than the wildcat's paw. The beast looked much more menacing now.

"I-I'd prefer larger, if you don't mind," Molly said, eyeing the cat warily.

"Aye, well, that's what I thought," Maggie said, returning to her previous size. "Now, shut the door if ye'd like me tae stay and chat."

Molly pointed to the wildcat. "What about him?"

"Dinna fash yourself. He'll be doin' ye nae harm." Maggie snuggled deeper into the wildcat's thick fur.

To Molly's astonishment, the beast began to purr.

"There, now, ye see," Maggie said. "But we canna be wastin' time. What d'ye think o' yon Finlay Mackenzie o' Kintail?"

The question caught Molly as she moved at last to shut the door. Using more force than necessary, she said bluntly as she turned, "He is hateful and arrogant."

"Aye, well, I were afraid ye wouldna like him, though he seems tae be handsome enough."

"I suppose," Molly said, "if one likes dark-haired men with eyes that seem to look right through one. I do not."

" 'Tis a pity then, but once our Claud had stuck his finger in the pie, there were little I could do. He's in lust again, Claud is, and bein' in such a state turns his brain tae porridge. Nobbut he's no so strong in that area most days, come what may. I fear our Claud didna come out o' the womb wi' all his bits in such fine order as I did m'self, ye see, even though he had the good fortune tae ha' me for his mam."

Thoroughly bewildered, Molly stepped nearer and said, "Whatever are you talking about, and who is Claud?"

"If ye'd but listen, I told ye, he's me son, though it isna summat I care tae brag about most days. Aye, sure, and ye can believe me when I say that!"

"But who are you? Or, more to the point, *what* are you?"

"Aye, now that would ha' been a better way tae put your question in the first place, instead o' taking it for granted that I were one o' them feckless Highland fairies," Maggie Malloch said, nodding. Making a gesture with the white implement in her hand, she said, "Ha' ye no heard tell o' the household spirits, then?"

"I don't think so, although I have heard many stories about the wee people," Molly said, "about fairies that steal babes from their cradles, and about the evil Host that flies at night, seeking stray souls to collect."

"We'll no speak o' the Host, if ye please. As for fairies stealing bairns, them would be Highland fairies or the Irish lot, and I've nae truck wi' such. Foolish creatures they be, always spouting o' kings and queens and the like, and making mischief—stealing grown folks away, too, and then returning them twenty years later tae everyone's consternation. I dinna hold wi' such fractious goings-on."

"Are you a Highlander of another sort, then?"

"Nay, lass, I be nae more a Highlander than ye be yourself. Me and Claud, we traveled wi' ye from the first, when your uncle took ye away tae Tantallon, and later we followed ye tae Dunsgaith when that misbegotten fool that's presently ruling Scotland sent ye here tae Skye. And we ha' been wi' ye at Dunakin since Donald sent ye here." She put the stick end of the white implement in her mouth, sucked on it, and then blew out another stream of smoke.

Watching this process in fascination, and feeling that she somehow owed the little woman an apology, Molly said, "I am sorry if I caused you to leave your home, but you can scarcely blame me when I did not even know you existed."

"Pish, tush, I dinna blame ye at all. 'Twas a dreadful night, that."

"It was, indeed," Molly agreed, involuntarily putting a hand on her left breast as a sudden, unexpected memory swept over her of the pain she had endured.

The little woman nodded, watching her. "I ken fine that ye sometimes still ha' nightmares about it, for all that we try tae divert them tae others wha' deserve more tae suffer them," she said quietly. "But in time, an all goes well, that scar will fade, mayhap even disappear, just as memories fade and disappear."

Again, Molly had the feeling that Maggie Malloch could read her mind, but she did not like thinking about that night and was grateful when curiosity pushed the uncomfortable memories aside. "You divert my nightmares to others?"

"Aye, well, it be me bounden duty tae look after the Maid o' Dunsithe—mine and Claud's, as well—and we ha' done it right cheerfully, although it required little effort whilst ye lived here at Dunakin. Nae more than aiding ye in learning tae speak the Gaelic and helping wi' your lessons—and keeping the laird happy by seeing that he always wins at chess."

"Is that how he does it?"

"Aye," Maggie said with a long sigh.

"Forgive me for saying so, but you do not appear to be very cheerful now."

"Nay, then, but ye can lay me dour face at Claud's door. I'll grant ye that, like him, I had begun tae fear that Donald the Grim didna mean tae to his duty by ye and see ye suitably wedded. That man be as wicked as a man can be, and nae mistake, but I'd no ha' taken such a rash step as what Claud did, and he shouldna ha' done it, either—on anyone's account. I canna doubt it ha' vexed ye, too, since 'tis sure ye'll feel some alarm at leaving the only home ye've known for years."

Despite years of practice at shielding herself and others from her deeper emotions, Molly had felt more than a twinge of alarm about leaving Dunakin, especially at having to leave with Kintail. She said with careful calm, "I would remind you that, altogether, men have uprooted me three times before now—from Dunsithe to Tantallon, then to Dunsgaith, and from Dunsgaith here to Dunakin. Most young women know they must leave home when they marry, of course, but the sudden way this happened does put me forcibly in mind of the night my uncle snatched my sister and me away from Dunsithe."

"Ye were both too young tae take from your mother," Maggie said with a grimace. "And Angus were nae man tae look after bairns. 'Twas a pity and all, though, that the wee one were so delicate and failed as quick as she did."

Not wanting to dwell on thoughts of wee Bessie's death, which even so many years later had the power to devastate her, Molly said, "But what did Claud do, exactly, that was so rash and annoyed you so?"

"Why, 'twere my Claud who caused that feckless King James tae transfer your writ o' wardship from Donald tae Kintail. Claud said he thought such an act would move things along and soon see ye married. Tae that same end, it were Claud who revealed ye tae Kintail last night when he and his men were riding past."

"May God have mercy," Molly exclaimed. "Why would he do such a thing?"

She spoke to air, however, for Maggie Malloch had vanished and the wildcat had vanished with her. Even the spiral of smoke had disappeared.

Chapter 5

Molly stood gaping at the now vacant bed for several moments and then rubbed her eyes. But the hallucination—for it surely must have been one—failed to reappear. Indeed, no sign whatsoever remained to show that a large furry wildcat and a plump, middle-aged woman two-thirds its size had been resting there only moments before. The coverlet was not even indented.

"Will ye be wantin' hot water, mistress?"

The maidservant's voice, sounding from the doorway behind her, startled her into remembering why she had come into her bedchamber in the first place. So intently were her senses fixed upon the bed that she had not heard the door open.

"Aye, Doreen," she said, struggling to sound normal. "Just have someone fill the ewer, so that I can wash what shows. Then, help me change into another dress for dinner—the embroidered yellow wool, I think."

The maidservant nodded and hastened to do her bidding. She had no sooner left the chamber, however, than Lady Mackinnon bustled in. Plump and comfortable-looking, she did not attempt to hide her relief at seeing Molly.

"Thank heaven you're back, my love," she exclaimed. "I knew that ye'd gone out, but I did not think ye meant to stay away the entire morning!"

"I apologize, madam, if you have been awaiting my return with impatience," Molly said with a fond smile. "It was such a fine day, you see."

Lady Mackinnon threw up her hands. "Say nae more! I see exactly how it was. 'Tis ever the same thing when ye fling yourself onto the back of a horse."

"Come now, madam," Molly said, moving to kiss the older woman's soft cheek. "I do not believe that I still fling myself onto horses. You have taught me to behave more properly than that. Once, perhaps, when I was small, but—"

Lady Mackinnon chuckled. "I expect I should allow myself credit when it is due me," she said. "I have indeed had some influence over ye, I believe."

"Much influence, madam, and I am grateful for it. You taught me how to go on in many ways. I—I shall miss you." The little hitch in her voice surprised her, and she strove to regain her customary control.

"I would ha' done the same for a daughter o' my own, love, had I been blessed wi' one," her ladyship said. "Ye filled that void, and thus 'twas my duty, for heaven kens Donald o' Sleat wouldna ha' bothered to teach ye deportment."

"Nor, I warrant, would he have taught me my letters and numbers."

"Now, to be truthful, that canna be laid to my account, for I scarcely ken them myself," Lady Mackinnon said. "Ye did that yourself, for when Mackinnon hired Micheil Love to tutor our three lads and ye insisted on bearing them company during their lessons, there were naught anyone could do to gainsay ye."

"I was barely seven years old when I came to you, madam. Surely, you will not say that I held sway over your entire household."

Lady Mackinnon's pale blue eyes twinkled. "I willna say that," she replied, "but in the face of the dreadful temper tantrums ye threw when anyone denied ye, it did seem wiser to let ye ha' your way about the lessons. Many Highland families of rank educate their daughters, after all."

"Is such education not so common in the Borders, then?"

"As to that, I dinna ken, but when Mackinnon told Donald of Sleat that ye shared our lads' lessons, Donald didna object."

"He will object to the present situation, though, will he not?"

"Och, aye," Lady Mackinnon said, her brow knitting in worry. "That man—nae one kens what to expect from him any day, but it be rarely anything good. One only prays that— What do *ye* want, lass?" she interjected in a sharper tone when Doreen appeared in the open doorway, carrying a ewer of hot water in one hand and Molly's yellow dress draped over her free arm.

The maidservant stopped abruptly at the threshold.

"She is to help me change my dress for dinner, madam," Molly said with a reassuring smile for Doreen.

Lady Mackinnon said briskly, "Come ye in, then, come ye in! But fetch out another dress for your mistress. She willna want to wear such a fine one to dine in today. And be quick about it, lest all the food be gone afore we get to the table."

Doreen moved swiftly to set the ewer by the basin, but Molly said nothing immediately to contradict her ladyship. She knew Lady Mackinnon exaggerated the need for haste, but it was true that their midday meal was a hastier affair than supper would be. At midday everyone left chores to eat, and everyone knew that dalliance was not allowed. Supper, however, was more leisurely, accompanied by conversation and music from the pipers' gallery. Afterward, people tended to linger in the hall, and a number of the men slept there each night on the floor.

Diverting her train of thought to a mental list of what remained to do before she could depart for Eilean Donan, she moved toward the basin to wash her hands and face, and saw that Doreen still held the yellow dress. The maidservant was looking uncertainly from her to Lady Mackinnon.

Lady Mackinnon said, "Quickly, lass, fetch a more suitable gown."

"That one will do," Molly said. "I told her to fetch it."

"But ye willna want to wear anything so splendid, my dear, and I ken fine that your ordinary clothing hasna yet been packed into the kists ye'll take wi' ye."

"Aye, madam, but I have good reason for choosing this gown."

"I canna imagine what it could be," Lady Mackinnon said, her tone inviting confidence. When none was forthcoming, she frowned and then suddenly smiled. "I see how it is," she said. "Indeed, I do! The man is handsome, to be sure, but oh, my love, I do hope he willna disappoint ye. To my mind, he is rather brash, rather . . . Well, no to put too fine a point on it, he is an arrogant laddie and of such great size as to be intimidating. Of course, Highland chiefs—nobbut what Kintail is only a chieftain like Mackinnon, but with a family as powerful as the Mackenzies, it is much the same thing. For all that he is young, he—" She broke off with a comical look. "Faith, but what was I about to say afore I carried on about Kintail?"

Well aware of where her ladyship's thoughts had been taking her but in no mood to encourage her, Molly said gently, "I chose this gown, madam, because Kintail ordered me to wear blue. He told me in a most authoritarian way that my life will be different from now on, and although I do not doubt the truth of that, he will not choose what I shall wear—not now or ever."

"Nay, then, of course he canna treat ye so," Lady Mackinnon agreed. Frowning, she went on in her scattered way, "That is to say, I expect he can, for men do, ye ken—some men, at all events. But he has nae cause for tyranny, and if he were a heartless man, I dinna believe his grace the King would ha' consigned ye to his care and protection."

Molly did not know his grace the King, but she did not believe that he had given any thought to her well-being. Had he done so, he would not have given her in ward at the tender age of five to her uncle Angus or at the age of six to any man with "the Grim" appended to his name. Had James had the least care for her, he would have allowed her to grow up in her own home with her own mother and her beloved little sister; and had that been the case, Bessie would still be alive.

She did not point out any of this to her ladyship, however. Not only was it an uncomfortable subject to discuss with anyone, but being fully occupied with taking off her hunting dress and donning the gaily embroidered yellow wool, Molly was content to listen while the others listed tasks that awaited their attention after the meal. Her imagination insisted on presenting one image after another of the powerful Kintail, usually frowning, but she banished each one as it appeared. It was enough that he would control her future. She would not allow him to occupy her mind. Her ladyship offered a stream of orders and advice, but despite her own straying thoughts and these well-intended interruptions, Molly was soon ready.

Leaving Doreen to tidy up the room before she joined the other servants to eat her meal, the two ladies went together to the great hall, where they found men and maids surging in through the main entrance and hurrying to take places at several trestle tables set at right angles to the laird's table.

Clatter and noisy conversation accompanied this invasion, and the conversation continued unabated while the two ladies wended their way to the high table. Two of Lady Mackinnon's three sons—one a year younger than Molly, the other several years older—stood at their places. The other places were still empty.

Try as she did to appear calm and disinterested in Kintail's absence, she could not help glancing around, wondering if he would dare comment publicly on her choice of attire. A flutter of apprehension and the little she had already experienced of the man told her that he might.

When he entered a few moments later with Mackinnon and Mackinnon's eldest son, Rory, the embroidered collar on the loose smock Kintail wore belted over his russet hose and rawhide boots told Molly the smock was one of Rory's. Despite its excellent cut, it was too short and fitted too tightly across his big shoulders, making his arms and legs look like those of a boy who had outgrown his clothes. There was nothing boylike about the rest of him, though. He looked formidable, and she knew in a flash that he had seen her, noted the yellow gown and thus her defiance of his request—nay, his command—and that he was displeased.

The flutter of apprehension turned into a shiver that shot up her spine, but that served only to stiffen it. She raised her chin and gave him back look for look.

Mackinnon spoke to him, and when Kintail turned to respond, Molly felt a rush of gratitude to her foster father for diverting that stern look from her. Her gratitude was short-lived, however.

"See ye, Molly lass," Mackinnon said bluffly, "d'ye take her ladyship's chair this once and I'll shift mine wi' Kintail's, so ye and he can sit together. He tells me he's hardly had a moment t' tell ye aught o' his Eilean Donan, and I dinna doubt but that ye'll be yearning t' hear all about it."

She could think of no polite way to refuse, but it did not matter, for as soon as those below them in the hall saw that their laird was present, a silence fell and what little opportunity she might have had was gone.

Obediently, she stood behind the chair Mackinnon indicated, trying to ignore mounting tension as Kintail moved to stand beside her. She knew he was watching every move she made, because she could feel his gaze, and his displeasure.

Mackinnon said a few words to serve as grace-before-meat, and the meal officially began with a rumble and scrape of people taking their seats on the long benches at the trestle tables.

Kintail held Molly's chair for her, deftly sliding it in as she sat down.

Good manners demanded that she thank him, but over-conscious of his daunting presence and determined that he would not know how strongly he affected her, she could not bring herself to do so.

Servers moved among them, plunking down platters of meat and trays of bread trenchers on the tables.

As Molly waited for the laird's carver to serve her meat, her tension increased. She wished she could turn and engage Lady Mackinnon in conversation, but her ladyship was issuing orders to a gilly setting side dishes on the table. Bereft of aid from that source, Molly signed to another lad to pour her some ale.

"Art color blind, mistress?"

His voice sounded like she imagined the growl of a tiger might sound.

"I believe not, sir," she replied, avoiding his gaze easily when the gilly reached between them to pick up her goblet.

"I believe you must be," he said when the gilly stepped

back. "That dress is yellow. I cannot deny that it becomes you—better than such a bright color would become most women, in fact—but it is not blue."

Flattered despite her determination to let nothing he said affect her more than his looming presence already had, she said, "I chose not to wear blue."

"I see." He was silent while the gilly set down her goblet again and departed, and for a long moment after that. Indeed, he waited almost long enough to make her look at him. Then he said, "Very well, I will allow the lapse this time, because I can see that you chose well, and because perhaps you did not understand that I meant for you to obey me. You may wear blue to supper tonight instead."

"I am not accustomed to letting anyone dictate what I shall wear," Molly said, glowering at her trencher and wishing that his sternness did not incite such a turmoil inside her.

"I am rapidly coming to believe that you are not accustomed to anyone telling you anything," he retorted. "Such license is not appropriate for a young, unmarried female. You must learn to look to others to guide you."

"Why?" She did look at him then, astonished.

He stared back steadily. "Because you cannot otherwise know how to go on. Females don't. They lack the education and experience necessary to make wise decisions on their own."

Indignant now, she said, "I warrant my education must be the match of most men's educations."

"Is it?" He smiled patronizingly. "What university did you attend?"

"You know very well that females do not attend universities, and I think that it is a great misfortune that they do not. Nonetheless, when I took my lessons with Rory Mackinnon and his brothers, I frequently knew the correct answers to our tutor's questions when they did not."

"You had a tutor?" He was clearly surprised.

"Aye, I shared Micheil Love with the lads, of course, but he often said that I was his best pupil and that it was a shame I could not study Greek and Latin. He believed that I would excel at those subjects, too."

"Why did you not study them, then?"

"Because Rory and the others did not want to do so, and the laird would not pay Micheil to tutor me alone. I could share only what they were willing to learn."

"I see." His brow furrowed, and she expected him to make another acid comment about what females could and could not do, but to her surprise, he did not. Instead, he smiled wryly and said, "I'll admit that you are not what I expected, mistress. Are you perhaps apt with numbers then, as well?"

"Aye," she said, seeing nothing to gain with false modesty. She added frankly, "I can do sums and subtractions, at all events, and I can multiply and divide if the numbers are not too great. I do not know more than that, though, for the same reason that I did not learn Greek."

"That is enough," he said thoughtfully. "You might prove more useful at Eilean Donan than I had reason to suspect."

"Indeed?" She would not give him the satisfaction of asking what he meant, although she was dying to know.

He did not tell her, either. He smiled enigmatically, and then, just when she thought he would at last turn his attention to his meal, he added, "First, of course, you must learn obedience. I look forward to seeing that blue dress this evening."

Molly sighed. Clearly, it would take time to show Kintail that he could not so easily master her. The foolish man seemed to think that he had only to speak and everyone would obey.

Mackinnon diverted Fin's attention just then to suggest that they enjoy another game of chess later, but although Fin agreed, he did not allow his host to divert him long. He was more interested in taking the opportunity to study his ward.

Her magnificent hair no longer tumbled in a cloud of curls down her back. She had tamed it, confined it in a coil at the nape of her slender neck, where escaping tendrils trailed enticingly. Others escaped her coif, softly caressing her rosy cheeks.

She seemed unnaturally interested in her food, peering at the juicy slices of rare beef on her trencher as if she were oblivious of the noise and chatter in the hall, and blind and deaf to his presence, as well. She selected a narrow slice, picking it up daintily and raising it to her lips. When her little pink tongue darted out to lick running juice from the meat, his loins tensed sharply.

He had picked up a leg of roasted chicken, but it remained hovering, forgotten, halfway between his trencher and his mouth, while he watched her.

She seemed to be lost in thought, for surely no one could keep her attention so solidly fixed on a bit of food. Still oblivious of his attention, she sucked on one end of the meat, drawing out the juices, savoring the taste.

His throat tightened. When she bit off the end she had been sucking and set the rest down on the trencher to reach for her goblet, he stifled a gasp of protest.

She sipped the ale, and he watched her swallow. When she set down the goblet, he continued to watch her lips, waiting for her to lick them. She did, and he realized with a jolt of desire that he would have liked to lick them for her.

Just then, she turned, looked him straight in the eye, and

said, "Do you mean to eat that chicken, or will you wave it about all night?"

Realizing that she had been aware of his gaze all along, and feeling flames in his cheeks that he had not felt since the earliest days of his puberty, he said curtly, "Impertinence is not becoming in a young woman, mistress. You must learn to curb your tongue."

A sweet smile touched her lips. "If we are to speak of manners, sir, you should know that here at Dunakin we consider it rude for a man to stare at a woman whilst she is eating."

"I was not—"

"You were."

"Nevertheless, it is not for you to criticize my conduct."

"Someone should," she retorted. "If you mean to act the guardian one moment and revert to your previous role as seducer the next, I can promise you that we will not get on well at all."

Without waiting for him to reply, she returned her attention to her food.

It was just as well, for he could think of nothing to say. Remembering the way he had behaved at their first meeting, he winced inwardly, knowing that he had given her good cause to condemn his manners. It was just as he had feared, though. Guardianship presented pitfalls that he had not anticipated. He certainly had not expected to feel such a physical attraction to his ward.

Since he could not act on that attraction, he would have to get over it, for seducing her would gain him nothing unless he could lay hands on her fortune. He would do far better to use her to form an alliance with another powerful clan.

He saw her breasts heave and realized that she was repressing emotions of her own—anger with him, no doubt. The soft curve of her bosom made his fingers itch to touch her. He looked away. She was right to rebuke him, but he could control himself. Duty demanded it, and since duty also demanded that he teach her obedience, he would have to do so without allowing his baser instincts to interfere.

Turning back to her, he said quietly but nonetheless firmly, "We will get on better, mistress, if you do not defy me. I promise, you are safe from me, except insofar as you flout my authority."

When she pressed her lovely lips tightly together but did not speak, he decided that he had made his point. He could handle this guardianship business as well as he handled everything else. It was just a matter of practice.

Elsewhere, shafts of sunlight filtered through a dense green canopy into a trackless woodland glade. They gave Brown Claud the impression as he approached the pool in the center of the glade that a few daring rays had escaped the firmament and slipped through the maze of greenery to play on the moss-covered ground and sparkle on the calm green water.

A stream fed that glassy pool, and if one stayed perfectly still and no breeze rustled the leaves, one could hear the water bubble gently as it flowed.

"Catriona, wake up, do!" Claud cried to the slender little lady who was the glade's only other occupant.

Had he given the matter any thought, he might have hesitated to wake her, for she looked so beautiful, sleeping there on a bed of the soft moss, her clinging, gauzy green gown blending nicely with the rest of the greenery. The sight made his heart thud in his chest and stirred another part of his body to life, as well.

Flaxen hair curled softly from beneath her bell-shaped green cap, framing her lovely face. Her rosy lips pressed together at the sound of his voice, and her exquisitely arched eyebrows knitted in a frown before her eyes opened. They, too, were green, the soft green of the moss from which she had made her bed.

"Claud, why do ye disturb my slumber?" she demanded petulantly. She yawned, exerting herself only to the extent of raising one slender, pink-nailed hand to cover her rosy lips. When he hesitated, looking stricken, she held out her arms in invitation and added in a more sultry tone, "My naughty laddie."

"Oh, my heart, forgive me," he said, hurrying forward to kneel beside her and clasp her hands in his.

"I will, for ye ha' captured the Maid of Dunsithe for Mackenzie of Kintail," she said, slipping her hands from his and settling onto her back, arching sensuously as she put one hand behind her head to fluff the moss into a soft pillow.

"Aye, I did," Claud said, unsurprised that she knew what he'd done and more interested in watching the rise and fall of her soft, firm breasts beneath their flimsy covering. Before coming to the Highlands, he had not known anyone like her.

"I am pleased with ye, Claud."

"Are ye, Catriona?" He bent nearer until his face was but a few inches from hers. "Art really pleased wi' me?"

She smiled. "Would ye like to kiss me, Claud?"

"Aye, I would," he said gruffly. "I'd kiss every inch o' ye an ye'd let me."

"I think I would enjoy that," she murmured, her voice low and sultry. "You may begin with my breasts if you like."

With alacrity, he bent to kiss the swell of the nearest one, his hands slipping under the slender straps of her green gown to slide it off her shoulders and down.

He had just taken one firm nipple into his mouth when she said lazily, "But what is the so-important news that brought you here today?"

Tensing, his tongue still touching that splendid nipple, Claud tried to think and could not seem to do so. Without releasing the object of his attentions, he looked up, willing her to wait a few minutes.

"Tell me your news, dearling," she said softly. "Ye'll remember well enough where to begin again after ye do."

Reluctantly, for he did not want to spoil the moment with unhappy tidings, he raised his head, noting with approval that she made no move to cover herself.

Clearing his throat, he muttered, "Me mam did say that the Circle ha' met."

"Is such a meeting momentous?" Her look was intense, her interest and curiosity plain. At least he was not boring her.

"Aye, it is. Mam said I did a bad thing, mucking about in royal affairs."

"But ye were that clever, Claud, and ye did it for me. I knew your Maid's wardship would serve Kintail well, and I must look after him, just as ye look after her. Still, I never thought ye could make the King give her to him, and ye did!"

"Aye," Claud said. His conversation with his mother had killed his delight in that cleverness, but it swept back now. "It wasna easy," he said. "We canna sway emotions, ye ken, only events, and them only when naught else interferes."

"But nothing else did, and ye did succeed."

"Aye, but me mam be furious wi' me now, and the Circle likewise."

"Tell me more about the Circle."

"I ha' tellt ye afore, and forbye, ye should ken their

power, Catriona, for it be as fierce here in your part of our world as it be in mine."

"Aye, but they trouble me little, so tell me again," she urged.

As always, he was wax in her hands.

"The Circle be our governing body, like the King's Privy Council in the mortal world, for ours be similar tae theirs, wi' chiefs and chieftains and the like. Them wi' the most power form the Circle and decide who can be in and who mun be out. If they cast me out, the Host will take me and force me tae fly wi' them through endless night till I expiate me sins. I'm gey afeard o' the Host, Catriona."

"Ye did only what I asked, Claud. It will be well."

"But what if—?"

"Hush," she said, laying two smooth fingertips against his lips. "My poor laddie, do ye recall what ye were doing a few minutes back when I interrupted ye?"

"Aye, I do," he said, his body stirring to life again.

She touched him then, and although her touch was delicate, its effect was powerful. All thought of his troubles vanished.

Chapter 6

At Dunakin, Molly spent the rest of the afternoon and early evening with Lady Mackinnon, sorting and packing clothing and other items that she would take with her. Her ladyship talked less than usual and seemed lost in thought.

"Perhaps you should rest, madam," Molly said. "You seem overtired."

"I'm well enough," her ladyship said with a sigh. "It is just settling into my mind that I'm going to miss ye sorely. I dinna ken how I'll get on without ye."

Touched by this admission, Molly hugged her, saying, "I am grateful for all you have done, madam—and the laird, too. You and he have been as much a mother and father to me as anyone could be, under the circumstances."

"Ye must ha' missed your own parents, though."

"I scarcely knew them," Molly said, speaking what was only plain truth. "My father seemed to enjoy my company, but my mother paid no heed to me, leaving my care and that of my sister to nursemaids. My strongest memory of her is the day we parted, when she burned me with that red-hot key."

"And a wicked thing it was to do," declared Lady Mackinnon with feeling. "Ye still bear that dreadful mark, as I ken, and I canna think what possessed the woman to do such a thing to her own bairn."

"She said it was to mark me so that she would always know me as her true daughter," Molly said. "But I agree that it was cruel. Many people knew me then, and many know me now, so how did she think I could become unknown?"

"We canna ken what were in her mind," Lady Mackinnon said fairly. "But ye be a grand heiress, Molly lass, and powerful men would control ye."

Molly smiled as she said, "You do not want my fortune."

Lady Mackinnon sighed. "In truth, we ha' nae hope o' possessing it. I canna deny I'd be pleased could our Rory or one o' the other lads wed ye and gain the lot. But we knew that Donald wouldna agree to it, and no more would the King. We expected Donald to wed ye to his own whelp, but he be a canny man, and without he laid hands on your fortune first, he couldna like the notion. 'Tis gey strange the way the treasure disappeared."

Molly shrugged, and Doreen entered then, so the topic of conversation, of necessity, reverted to the task at hand. Nevertheless, Molly's thoughts soon returned to her position and what lay ahead.

The Gordon treasure seemed mythical, for she had never seen it and had no notion what it comprised. Her memories of the castle where she had spent the first years of her life were dim. She remembered walking with her father, holding his hand as they climbed a golden hillside and stood at the top, looking back at Dunsithe. She remembered riding her pony, albeit not the first time, because she had ridden as long as she could remember. And she remembered her nurse and Bessie's, but other adults were unidentifiable figures in the whirl of servants and others who had lived with them or visited.

All those memories included lots of color, but they were more dreamlike than real. She could not remember a single room, even her own bedchamber. She had had a room of her own, though, for she had stronger memories of visiting Bessie in the nursery and being allowed to sit and hold her, and of looking down at the sleeping, rosy-cheeked baby in her cradle when Bessie was new.

She did not linger on such memories, however, particularly ones of Bessie.

She had lived at Dunakin for more than half her life. It seemed unfair that she had to leave whether she wanted to go or not, but life was like that for women, and so it would ever be.

She had learned over time that men who ordered her destiny paid little heed to her once they controlled her. Keeping her or winning and controlling her had always been more important to them than knowing her. Clearly, Kintail was like the others and expected to keep and control her easily. She had learned to find her way, though, first at Tantallon, then at Dunsgaith—although she had stayed but a short time—and then at Dunakin. She would do the same at Eilean Donan, whatever its domineering master might think to the contrary.

That natural skill she had discovered at six for getting her own way she had honed to a fine art in the years since then. Kintail would learn that she was no pawn to push around as he pleased.

She would be on her own, for she could expect little if any support from Mackinnon or his lady. Being on her own was nothing new, though, for despite what she had told Lady Mackinnon, she did not think of them as parents, nor had they ever really encouraged her to do so. They had been kind to her always, but they had never let her forget that her true guardian was Donald the Grim. Nor had their sons let her forget that she was Border-bred, not a Highlander, or that they considered Highlanders somehow superior.

Since she could outwit the lads in the schoolroom and outshoot them with bow and arrow, and since they had not otherwise been unkind to her, she had easily shrugged off their teasing. But she felt little kinship to any of them. For years, she had kept her own counsel and gone her own way, her previous experience having warned her that to form close relationships was unwise, lest she be ripped away again. Now that it was happening, she could congratulate herself on her good sense.

A niggling notion stirred that Kintail might not keep the same emotional distance from her that Mackinnon and his family had. Nor could she persuade herself that even in time he might become as casual a guardian.

That thought stirred again the odd feelings that seemed to ripple through her whenever she thought about him. Even now, she felt a constant awareness of his presence in the castle. What would it be like when he confined her within the walls of his own home? Heat surged through her at the mental image, and she hastily turned her attention to her packing, engaging her two companions in desultory conversation and ruthlessly reining in any wandering thought after that until increasingly gusty sighs from her chief companion drew her attention and she realized that most of the afternoon had passed.

"You are tired, madam," she said then. "I know you must be yearning for your usual nap, and we have all of tomorrow to finish this. In any event, I want to have a wash before I dress for supper. I feel musty and frazzled."

"I dinna mind saying I'll be glad of an hour's rest," Lady Mackinnon admitted. Pushing a stray lock of gray hair from her cheek, she looked around the chamber with a frown. "I'd no idea we'd find so much to do."

"I have lived here for years," Molly reminded her, "and you have been more generous than you should in giving me things to take with me."

"Well, one canna imagine what ye might need in your new home, and we dinna want ye to go without such as we might provide for your comfort. Doubtless, though, the number of sumpter baskets and kists will astonish Kintail."

"Let him be astonished," Molly said with a smile. "I want to astonish him."

"Aye, I saw how ye taunted him with that yellow gown of yours at noon, but dinna underestimate the man," Lady Mackinnon said, returning the smile. "Ye've spent most of your life amongst them who want only your happiness. Ye may not find that at Eilean Donan."

"Then I shall write to King James and command him to return me to you," Molly said with a saucy grin.

"Aye, and I wish ye could do that," Lady Mackinnon said with sudden dampness glistening on her eyelashes.

Seeing those tears, Molly experienced a sense of loss and wondered if they indicated that her foster mother might have welcomed a closer relationship had Molly but let her know she wanted one. Deciding that to ponder such a possibility would lead only to more grief, she said, "You are very kind-hearted, madam. I pray only that Kintail may prove to be half as kind to me."

"I, too," Lady Mackinnon said, wiping her tears away. "Doreen," she added more briskly, turning to the maidservant, who was folding clothing from a pile on the bed, "I'll leave ye now, but do ye see to finishing Mistress Molly's mending straightaway. We canna ha' our lass taking shabby garments to Eilean Donan."

"Aye, my lady, I'll see to it," Doreen said complacently.

"Never mind the mending, Doreen," Molly said as soon as the door had shut behind her ladyship. "Order me a bath, and then fetch the red velvet gown I wore at Christmas, the one with the sable trimming round the wrists and hem."

"Mistress, ye'll never wear that to supper," Doreen protested. "It be far too grand, that gown! Recall that the laird did say that, by the sumpter laws, that sable should be worn only on truly festive occasions."

Dismissing the warning with a careless gesture, Molly said, "I am feeling festive. That devil Kintail ordered me to wear blue to the midday meal, and when I wore yellow instead, he declared that he was permitting it only because he feared I had not known that he meant his request as a command. I am to wear blue to supper now, if you please."

"Then mayhap the blue silk with the embroidered trim, mistress. That gown becomes ye well, I think."

"Aye, it does, but Kintail will not see it. I shall begin as I mean to go on, Doreen. That man will not call the tune for my dancing. The red, if you please. Shake it out well and brush it. I must look my best, for I want him to see that he has more than a meek little miss to deal with."

She washed everything that showed, and when Doreen helped her don the elegant, fur-trimmed crimson gown, Molly shook out the skirts with a chuckle. Seeing the maid-servant's disapproving look, she said, "Fear not. He cannot murder me, and he must learn straightaway that I am no ewe for his shearing. He may do as he pleases with my fortune if he can find and hold on to it."

"Ha' ye truly got a grand fortune, mistress? What would it be, and all?"

"Heaven knows," Molly said with feeling. "Her ladyship says I do, that men have searched every stick and stone at Dunsithe, trying to find it. She said Donald keeps men-at-arms there to guard it, lest someone else find what he has not. At least that may change now that Kintail has thrust himself upon us. He claims to have little interest in my fortune, but he would be an odd sort of man if that were true."

"Aye," Doreen said quietly. "Men be ever a greedy lot."

Realizing from the tone of her voice that Doreen was not speaking now about Kintail or Donald, and being in no mood to indulge the girl's personal troubles, Molly said, "I shall wear my silver pomander. Fetch it, please."

"Aye, mistress." Doreen hastened to do her bidding, and while she did, Molly dabbed onto her wrists and into the hollow of her throat some of the lily-scented French perfume that Mackinnon had given her for Christmas. Had anyone asked why she bothered, she would have said that she liked its scent. That it would compete with the scent of cloves from her pomander did not trouble her in the least.

Her thoughts darted ahead to the hall and the man who awaited her there. Although she looked forward to proving that she could manage him, she suffered a few misgivings when she tried to imagine how he would react to her dress. Having sensed more than once the passionate nature beneath his stern demeanor, she knew he was a man who would not ignore defiance. Still, she could not imagine him bellowing at her before all and sundry in the hall, and surely he would not harm her.

Doreen adjusted the pomander on its chain for a second time, and suddenly annoyed by her fussing, Molly dismissed her, saying, "I would be alone for a few moments. I've little time left, after all, before I must leave Dunakin. You may return to finish whatever you must here after you eat your supper."

"Aye, mistress." Without another word, Doreen left the room.

Drawing a deep breath, Molly moved to the single arched window embrasure. Lifting her skirt to put a knee on the padded bench under the window, she leaned forward to look outside, hoping to clear her mind of all thoughts of Kintail, at least for a moment or two.

To the west, in the darkening peach-colored sky, gray mist swirled like a living thing over and around the stark, jagged peaks of the Cuillin, drifting lower as the sky darkened into night. The mist was the sole lingering sign of the previous day's rain. If the weather cleared, nothing would prevent Kintail from taking her away on Thursday.

" 'Tis no use grievin' afore ye've summat tae grieve over, though ye're bound tae miss this place and all within its walls."

The voice startled her but not nearly as much as did the appearance on the flat cushion beside her of the plump little woman, leaning back against the arching stone wall of the embrasure. This time she appeared to be no larger than a bairn's doll, but once again, she held the odd stick with its white bowl at one end, and gray-white smoke issued forth in a thin stream. Molly was close enough to note its pleasant fragrance.

"Why do you haunt me?" she demanded, struggling to recall the woman's name. "I hoped you were naught but a dream or hallucination!"

"Maggie Malloch be nae dream," the little woman said, as if she had read her mind. "The last time we spoke, if ye'll recall it, I were just beginning tae sort out what from what when ye so rudely interrupted me."

"Interrupted you?"

"Aye, for ye called upon spirits that be none o' my world or your ain. Forbye, if ye wish tae hear all I mean tae tell ye, ye mustna do that again."

"I'll try not to," Molly promised, wondering what spirits she had called up before. That she had somehow conjured up this little woman was bad enough. Surely, there were no odder creatures about. "What is that object in your hand?"

"'Tis called a pipe," Maggie said, taking another puff. "'Tis a fine thing, too, though it comes from a faraway land. Folks often smoke them there, but ye willna see any hereabouts for a few odd years yet. D'ye recall all I told ye afore—about me and my world?"

"You told me that you are a household spirit from the Borders, that you followed me here to the Highlands out of some sort of duty, and that your son, Claud, is responsible for my having to leave Dunakin. I fail to comprehend how he can be, however, since I am leaving by royal command."

"Aye, well, it happened as it did because ye made a wish whilst ye were leaving yon *ceilidh* last night," Maggie said.

"A wish! What wish? And how could anything I did after the *ceilidh* have aught to do with King James's having transferred my wardship to Kintail? Surely that happened sometime before."

"I do be getting ahead o' myself," Maggie said, nodding. "I canna blame ye for what James did, because that grievous mischief occurred on account o' Claud fallin' in lust again. I do recall tellin' ye that bit, though," she added. "Forsooth, and though it grieves me tae say it about me own son, he's no got wit enough tae ha' dreamed up such a trick on his own."

"He falls into lust?"

"Aye, and 'tis a wicked thing, lust is. 'Tis my belief Claud were goaded into mischief by one who would put Dunsithe's treasure into Mackenzie hands. Men do things for lust, ye ken, that they wouldna do for any other cause, and most times, they regret what they ha' done once it be too late tae do aught about it."

"And is it too late now?"

"Aye, sure, for didna the King command, and hasna Kintail acted? When yon villain, Donald the Grim, learns what ha' come tae pass, will he no send the armies that killed Kintail's da months ago tae reclaim his so-valuable ward?"

Molly frowned, saying, "But if your Claud had the power to make the King act, why can he not simply turn things back the way they were?"

"Because that isna in his power. What they ha' done be done, both in your world and in ours, and we must all make the most of it. That be what I meant when I told ye about Claud hearing ye make your wee wish."

"But—"

"Dinna interrupt," Maggie said sharply. "I told ye afore, I ha' only a short time tae make m'self visible tae ye. If ye had the gift o' second sight, I wouldna ha' tae exert m'self, but ye dinna have it, so I must. When Claud stirred the King tae act, he displeased the Circle—them wha' govern our clan. They take a dim view o' mucking about in royal affairs, ye see, and many in it spoke against him. I persuaded them tae give Claud another chance, but the reckless lad took a pet when I told him he must let his wicked lass be—the strumpet wi' which he's in lust—and he stormed off tae the *ceilidh*, your *ceilidh*. When ye left the cottage afterward, my Claud heard ye wish ye could know a proper hero tae accomplish heroic deeds—a man capable o' slaying dragons, ye said."

Vaguely recalling that she had muttered some such foolishness, Molly said, "I was air dreaming. Do you mean to tell me that Claud thought he could grant my wish by casting me into Kintail's path?"

"Aye, summat o' the sort," Maggie said, grimacing. "I grant ye, it makes no sense tae anyone wi' a brain that isna fashioned o' porridge, but doubtless my Claud thought he could make up for the first error if ye could just see Kintail as that hero ye wished for. I kent m'self it were hopeless, so I intervened afore—"

"You?"

"Aye," Maggie said with a twinkle. "I feared Claud might get up tae mischief, in the state he were in, so I kept me eye out. When Kintail mistook ye for a serving maid and reached for ye, I stirred his horse tae give him a toss."

"And then you mended him afterward," Molly said, beginning to believe in Maggie Malloch despite her more sensible self's insisting such things could not be.

"Aye, I did, and I dinna mind tellin' ye, it were a good thing for Claud that I ha' such powers," Maggie said. "Many in my world can take a dust mote from a man's eye or even stop blood flowing at a distance, but few can do as much as me. 'Tis Claud's greatest folly that he seeks tae emulate me wi'out the power tae do so."

"Then can you not just make Kintail not want me anymore?" Molly asked.

"Nay, for we canna affect any man's emotions. I can stir a single puffy white cloud into a dark and dangerous storm, but for all that I *can* do, I canna make a man care about summat that he doesna care about, or take away his greed or anger or even me own Claud's lust. Would that I could do that!"

"I see," Molly said with a sigh. "I don't suppose then that you can make Kintail happy to see me in this dress rather than in the blue one he ordered."

"Nay," Maggie said, twinkling again, "I admit, though, that Claud may be right about one thing. It would be gey helpful an ye could see your way clear tae falling in love wi' the wretched man."

Unable to help herself, Molly laughed. "Merciful heaven," she exclaimed, "you cannot honestly think that there is the slightest—"

But again, she spoke to air, for Maggie Malloch had vanished, and just then the castle bell began to ring, summoning the household to supper.

When Fin saw the Maid enter the hall dressed in sable-trimmed scarlet, he stifled an oath. Heaven knew how many people at Dunakin knew that he had ordered her to wear blue, but from his place at the high table, he saw nearly every head turn her way and he could not blame any of them for staring.

She wore no coif tonight and her beautiful hair, worn in a thick plait over one shoulder, glinted brightly in the flickering light. She looked magnificent, but if he intended to maintain control of his household at Eilean Donan, he would have to make his position clear now.

Beside him, Patrick cleared his throat, and when Fin glanced at him, the appreciative twinkle in his friend's eyes told him that Patrick, at least, knew exactly what she was doing. His jaw tightened at the thought, but he could not deny that the scarlet gown became her even better than the yellow one had at noon.

She moved slowly, and he could have sworn she avoided his eye. So at least she had sense. She was also damned attractive. Her movements were sensual, displaying a willowy grace that kept every masculine eye riveted to her body.

Able to think of only one thing that might teach her that he controlled her destiny, he waited until she reached the high table. Then he turned to Mackinnon and said in a clear, carrying voice, "I have changed my mind, sir. We will depart at dawn tomorrow for Eilean Donan."

She looked at him then, and her magnificent eyes flashed with anger.

Fin felt his body stir. He wanted to shake her, but he knew he dared not lay his hands upon her, for if he did, lust would vanquish any sense of duty he felt toward the lass and every ounce of common sense as well. He would carry her from the hall and teach her—

Mackinnon's voice shattered his reverie. "But she will not have finished her packing! Surely, one more day—"

"Anything that she has not packed by morning you can send after her," Fin snapped, looking sternly at his ward.

She gazed back, sparks still flashing from her eyes, and said, "If this display of pique is merely an attempt to show me that you will not brook defiance even in such trivial matters as allowing me to choose what I shall wear, you waste your time. And if 'tis a show of arms, sir, you abuse your power."

"There is nothing trivial in my decision."

"I disagree."

He held her angry gaze as he said to Mackinnon, "I must hold a baron's court in less than a sennight, sir. Therefore, as much as I'd like to let you keep her longer, the truth is that I have much to do and would be wiser to depart at once."

She continued to glower at him, but he knew she understood that he would not change his mind. Although the alteration in plans clearly infuriated her, she did not debate his decision further. Once again, he gave her credit for good sense.

Believing that he had won an important point, Fin turned his attention to his host when that gentleman diffidently suggested that moving Molly and all her things might require another boat or two. When she sustained her silence through the rest of the meal, he began to wonder what she was up to, but he told himself she was just learning to behave better. He realized that he missed the sound of her voice, but he managed to suppress the wish that she would speak again, if only to rail at his domineering ways.

Nevertheless, and despite reassuring himself that he was only doing what was necessary, when she bade Mackinnon good night after supper and spared only a nod for Fin on her way out of the hall, the evening suddenly seemed dull beyond bearing. It grew worse, for his host beat him soundly at chess, twice.

At Stirling Castle, the court of James the Fifth, High King of Scots, was also sitting down to its supper. The King, however, was otherwise occupied, entertaining himself in the way that he had most favored from about the age of thirteen, when his otherwise objectionable guardian, the Earl of Angus, had introduced him to the wonders of the female form. Since then, James had relished sexual encounters of every description.

Despite now being twenty-seven years old and a bridegroom of less than a year, he had not altered his predatory habits.

To his present companion, he said, "Faith, but you are a bonnie lass, Nell! I vow, I have never seen bubs as firm and smooth as yours, nor ones so perky." He stroked her breasts gently for some moments and then bent to savor them at length.

His grace showed every sign of being deeply enamored, and Eleanor Douglas Gordon, now Lady Percy, sighed as much in relief as in feigned passion.

She had taken a great risk in coming to Stirling, for she could not doubt that Henry Tudor would learn of her visit. The King of England had spies everywhere. And when Henry learned of it, her brother Archie, Earl of Angus, would hear of it soon afterward. If she feared Henry the

Eighth—and any sensible person who had contact with him did fear him—she feared her brother far more.

Everyone knew that James of Scotland was fond of the fair sex. However, as a result of his unabated fury with Angus, no one who bore the name Douglas was safe, least of all Angus's sisters—legitimate or otherwise. That their father had never married Nell's mother had posed no obstacle when Angus arranged her first marriage to Lord Gordon or her second to an elderly knight in the powerful English Percy family, now thankfully deceased. Her birth would pose no obstacle to James, either, if he should decide—as he had two months before in the case of her half sister Janet Douglas—to try Nell for witchcraft and burn her at the stake.

Still, the success of her present mission was vital. She had ridden all the way from Northumberland, reaching Edinburgh the previous day. Upon learning that the court had moved, she had followed it to Stirling after a short night's rest, and by the time the sun had risen that morning, she and the three other members of her party were close enough to see the thrusting skyline of Stirling's massive fortress, perched like a sleeping lion atop its rocky plateau.

Clattering up the steep streets of the town, the party of four had drawn little attention from townsfolk who had enjoyed a royal procession only days before. Nell was glad they ignored her, certain she must look a fright.

She had not visited Stirling for years—not since Angus had ruled the King's household—but everything looked much the same. Hammers banging and a clatter of wooden planks suggested changes in the making, but the only notable difference she saw was that, unlike the days when Angus ruled, the portcullis was up and the drawbridge down.

The double gates were shut, of course, but it took no

more than her name being shouted to open them, and in moments the horses' hooves thudded across the timber drawbridge. The castle forecourt was as she remembered it, but renovations were indeed occurring, and workmen hurried to and fro.

Inside, however, all was in order, albeit bustling. She excused the two men-at-arms who accompanied her so that they could see to the horses and baggage and then to themselves. Then she and her woman followed a servant who showed them to a private apartment, where Nell spent the morning preparing to greet the King.

When she made her way to the great hall shortly before one, the castle seemed to be overflowing with fashionable people, but she paid little heed to any of them. She had come to see James.

At thirty-four, Nell was still a remarkably beautiful woman, but she had known she could leave nothing to chance. James had a judicious eye for feminine beauty, and although she was seven years his senior, she did not think she would disappoint him. She rarely looked her age, and it would not bother him in any event, for his only interest in a woman's years was his desire to discover how much experience and imagination she had managed to acquire. Nell possessed both, and thus far, as she had hoped, his grace had been as wax in her soft, smooth hands.

She realized as soon as she clapped eyes on him that she had forgotten how handsome James was, how tall and well built—and how charming of manner. She had not seen him since his stripling years, though, and a redheaded, blue-eyed stripling's promise was not always kept as the man acquired height and bulk. James's looks had fulfilled their promise and more.

Aware that he recognized her name when his herald announced it, and that he knew exactly who she was, she held her breath until, with relief, she saw his interest stir when she curtsied deeply before him. She bent her head to make the obeisance look as yielding as possible. Then, daringly, she looked up from beneath fluttering, dark lashes and was well satisfied to see his gaze fixed on the softly thrusting swell of her breasts above the low-cut neckline of her blue velvet bodice.

Drawing a deep breath to increase the impact, she hid her satisfaction at hearing his gasp. Since she had ordered the gown cut daringly low on purpose, so that her magnificent breasts would look to him as if they threatened at any moment to pop free of the gown, she knew in that moment that she had judged her man well.

Smiling appreciatively, the King offered first his hand to assist her to rise and then his arm, but to her disappointment, he relinquished her soon afterward to one of his nobles. That gentleman squired her to table, where she did her best to look as if she were pleased with the arrangement. She even managed to deal patiently with the inane comments of a particularly annoying, elaborately coiffed and garbed woman who presented herself and her two homely daughters to Nell in an unbecomingly forward way. Nell did not bother to remember their names.

The hall was crowded, and people lingered into the late afternoon. The King lingered with them, although his advisors frequently sought him out, since rumors were flying about trouble in the western Highlands, where Donald Grumach apparently was stirring clans to support his bid to reclaim the Lordship of the Isles.

Nell listened carefully to all she could overhear, dismayed to learn that they already suspected so much about Donald's activities but hoping to turn any new knowledge to good account. Whatever Angus or Henry might think, she had been right to come to Stirling before blundering alone into the treacherous Highlands.

She had nearly given up hope of speaking to James again before supper, if then, when suddenly he appeared before her and gallantly offered his arm.

As she smiled and placed a hand upon it, he bent to murmur in her ear, "I trust you will not mind if we seek privacy, madam. We have much to discuss."

"Your wish, sire, as ever, is my command," she replied demurely.

James chuckled. "I shall test that, I promise you."

Guiding her to a private chamber, he had bolted the door and, turning, had said only, "We understand each other, I hope."

"Aye, your grace. I am yours to command."

Without further ado, he bared her breasts and ordered her to help him undress. Entirely willing, Nell obeyed that command and others, and now as they lay together in bed, James continued to savor her breasts for some minutes before moving atop her and taking her with gusto. When he was spent, he lay still for so long that she began to fear that he had fallen asleep.

His weight was uncomfortable, but when she tried to shift him, he murmured, "Don't wriggle, lass. Tell me instead how it is that I do not recall having granted you permission to return to Scotland."

"I did not know that I required permission, sire," Nell murmured, hoping that he could not hear her heart thudding. "I was but coming home, after all."

"Then why come here to Stirling?"

"To beg your forgiveness if I require it and to beg a boon if I do not," she replied, struggling to sound calm, and to keep her increasing tension at bay.

James lifted his head to look at her.

"A boon, madam?" Mockingly, he quirked an eyebrow, adding, "I trust you do not ask this boon on your irksome brother's behalf."

"He would not thank me if I did," Nell answered honestly. "Nor do I think you such a fool, sire, as to bid Angus back to Scotland, if that is the boon you fear he would seek. In truth, I have no more reason to trust him than you do. He has used me abominably." And that, she thought, certainly *was* the truth.

James slid off her, lying on his side next to her, his intense gaze searching hers. "What would you have of me then?"

The moment had come. Her lips were dry, but she dared not wet them lest he deduce the extent of her nervousness and draw unwelcome albeit possibly accurate conclusions. Thinking swiftly, she said, "I hope to be of some use to you, sire, and perchance to serve my own end as well."

"How might you be of use to me," he asked, "other than as we've just seen?"

"Donald the Grim," Nell blurted. "I . . . I am told that you fear he may be causing strife, may even be seeking to reclaim a certain Highland title."

"True." He frowned. "I hoped to keep him friendly. Instead, the traitor has turned against me. Do you fancy yourself a spy in his household, madam?"

"Mayhap you forget, sire, but Donald holds my daughter in ward."

James was silent for a long moment, and then he said quietly, "Have you no other children, madam?"

Bitterly, Nell said, "I bore Gordon two daughters, sire, but the younger died soon after Angus took them from me. I had no children with Percy, for he was elderly when we married. Molly is all I have left." Having no wish to speak more of her past, she added earnestly, "I am told, sire, that she is yet unmarried. It is my fondest hope that Donald might grant me permission to visit her."

"Do you know what became of her fortune, Nell?"

"Nay, sire," she replied evenly, careful to look him directly in the eye. "I never knew where Gordon kept his wealth. After his death, I discovered that he had hidden the jewels I wore. Other things disappeared, even the castle's furnishings."

James looked long at her before he said, "I find it hard to trust the word of any Douglas. Is it not likely Angus took it all himself?"

"I certainly never saw any sign of that," she said, glad she could speak honestly. "Pray, sire, grant me leave to seek my daughter."

"I suspect more in your yearning than simple mother's love," James said shrewdly. "I will grant this much, madam, that I shall think on the matter. However, I should first mention one wee problem with your plan."

She did not speak, refusing to let him make her beg for the information. Not only did she possess the Douglas blood but also her share of the Douglas pride.

A glint in his eyes told her that he understood, and gentleness touched his voice when he said, "Your daughter is no longer ward to Donald of Sleat."

"Where is she, then?"

"In good time, madam, in good time."

Nell forced a smile. If she let him know how important his decision was to her, he would only tantalize her more. As it was, she hoped that she could continue to interest him long enough to get what she wanted. She had more freedom as Percy's widow than she had ever known before, and she did not intend to lose a jot of it. But continued freedom required continued independence, and independence was no easily won commodity for any woman.

Chapter 7

Before daylight, Fin and his men arose, broke their fast, and then went down to load Mistress Gordon's remaining baggage into the boats. The sky was black and starless, and the air was damp with a heavy mist that swirled eerily around the torches they carried down to the shore to light their work.

Most of her things were already stowed in two of the galleys that Mackinnon was lending them—Highland galleys, nothing like their great Venetian namesakes but more like Viking longboats of old. Narrow of beam and high of prow, they could be rowed or sailed, which made them useful for inter-island travel.

He had not slept well, and as a result his temper was short. Not only had the Maid retired early, leaving him to Mackinnon's mercies at the chessboard, but the older man had taken it upon himself to offer advice.

"She's a good, kindhearted lass," he said.

"Perhaps," Fin replied, seeing nothing to gain by arguing.

"If she doesna seem easy wi' ye, 'tis doubtless because she fears leaving wi' ye. She doesna ken ye, lad. Ye'd do well t' treat her gently for a time."

"I am scarcely an ogre, sir, but women have a duty to obey those who wield authority over them," Fin said bluntly. "For her own safety she must learn, and she will learn more easily if she does not continue to defy me."

Thinking of that exchange now as he watched the men preparing the boats, he believed he was right to remain firm. His mother had died when he was small, but experience with other women had shown him that they would take as much liberty as a man allowed them and more, and if a man could not control his household, he could not expect to control much beyond it.

With responsibilities and duties as vast as his were over the lands of Kintail, he could not risk rebellion from one small, clearly overindulged female. Still, it had not been thoughts of her overindulged childhood that had rendered his night a sleepless one. Thoughts of her slender, curvaceous body had done that, images of how she might look naked and what it would feel like to wrap his hands in her silky-looking hair or to stroke her smooth skin. Despite his determination to keep his mind on other things, no matter what else he forced himself to think about, only moments had passed before his imagination turned again to her.

He sighed, again having to force his thoughts back to the moment at hand.

Mackinnon oarsmen and a third Mackinnon boat carrying armed men would accompany Fin's party to Eilean Donan as protection in case Donald the Grim should already have learned that his guardianship of the Maid had ended. No one doubted that in such an event he would take speedy action. Fin's hope was that he would see his charge safely inside the walls of Eilean Donan before that happened—if she had not already taken flight.

That fear had alternated with the other thoughts of her that had teased him through the long night and since rising.

Her anger the previous night had been plain to see, and he doubted that it had eased in the meantime. She had made it clear that she would not submit easily to his authority—or, indeed, to any man's.

It occurred to him again then, uncomfortably, that his duties as her new guardian included finding her a suitable husband, preferably one whose connection would prove advantageous to himself. Before he could think of arranging such a match, however, he had to teach her to mind him and thus to mind the husband who would wield authority over her. Anyone could see that she was not prepared for marriage. Since she had not learned to submit to any man, she would doubtless lift that stubborn little chin of hers to Jamie himself, should his grace ever venture past the gateway to the Highlands and demand that the Maid of Dunsithe kneel to him.

That mental vision tickled Fin's sense of humor, but he quickly reminded himself that the reality was no laughing matter. The plainest fact of life was that women, by far the weaker sex, were dependent upon men to protect them. In return, they owed their protectors quick and absolute obedience.

Simple duty demanded that he teach the lass her proper place. Mackinnon certainly had not done so. He had spoiled her, in fact, and had done the Maid no favor thereby. Jamie's reaction to her sauciness, should he ever experience it, would not be pleasant. Indeed, the King was not the only one who should concern Mistress Gordon, since he was not the only man who could do what he pleased to punish insolence. Any laird who possessed a barony held the power of the pit and the gallows, as Fin did himself, and could speedily put an end to insolence—to life, for that matter. The thought of her incredible beauty wasted in such a harsh manner banished the last lingering gleam of humor from his mind. The image that he had stirred to life made him feel sick, and he resolved that before he had finished with the lass, she would be as meek as a nun's hen.

He was a man born to duty, after all. He had not shirked the responsibilities thrust upon him when his father died, nor would he shirk his responsibility toward the Maid of Dunsithe, no matter what effect she had on his libido.

The sky had lightened considerably by the time he and Patrick returned to Dunakin, leaving the others to guard the boats and cargo. Members of Mackinnon's household were still seated at the long tables, eating, and Fin's gaze swept the huge chamber, seeking the shapely form of Mistress Gordon.

When he did not see her, his jaw tightened, and his fears increased, for if Mackinnon had helped the minx run away, he could do little to retaliate. In the present political climate, with a soon-to-be-outraged Donald the Grim on the loose with armies and fleet, to attack anyone on Skye would be sheer folly.

He saw her then, standing beside Mackinnon, one dainty hand resting on his forearm while she chatted with some of their people. Fin relaxed, the strong relief he felt warning him that he had been more worried than he had realized.

Beside him, Patrick murmured with a chuckle, "I'll wager you're damned relieved to see that lass. As besotted over her as Mackinnon is, I feared he might find a way to winkle her into hiding."

" 'Tis as well that he did nothing of the sort," Fin retorted.

"Aye, it is," Patrick agreed, still with a touch of that annoying humor. "We'd never have found her, you know, for the mountains here are devilish treacherous and keep their secrets well."

Fin shrugged. With Mistress Gordon standing before

them, he had no need to waste any thoughts on Skye's mountains.

She turned then and looked at them, and when he saw her chin tilt up defiantly, he fought a sudden, unexpected urge to smile.

Molly had noted the entrance of Kintail and his deputy at once. But she had taken care not to react visibly. Obliquely, through narrowed eyes, she had watched their approach, and as others made way for them, she realized that both mainlanders were much larger than most men. Seen singly or even as a pair, the difference in the two was not particularly noteworthy. But surrounded by so many others, the contrast became remarkable. Most Highlanders were taller than she was, and most men seemed to tower over her. Kintail certainly did, but she had credited his intimidating manner as much as his size for creating that sensation.

Perhaps, she thought idly, his horse had thrown him simply because he was too heavy for the poor beast to carry. Then she remembered Maggie Malloch and sighed, uncertain whether to hope that the woman was only a figment of her overactive imagination or to hope instead that somehow Maggie wielded sufficient power to help defend her against Kintail.

Upon waking and before Doreen had come to help her dress, she had tried to invoke Maggie Malloch's presence, hoping to persuade her to work whatever magic she could to put off the journey to Eilean Donan, but her attempts had failed. If Maggie had heard, she had not deigned to respond.

Molly had eaten only a few morsels of bread to break her fast, and when Mackinnon had urged her to eat more, she told him she was not hungry. Her insides were muddled enough, without taxing them to digest food.

When she saw Kintail's dark gaze sweep the chamber, she knew he was looking for her, and although she quickly returned her attention to the tenants who had approached to bid her farewell, and had done her best to listen to them, her skin prickled at the thought that he might be watching her. Curiosity soon overcame resolution, and she turned, unable to avoid looking to see if he had found her yet.

Her gaze collided with his, firing unfamiliar sensations through her body. Reacting automatically, she straightened her shoulders and raised her chin.

His dark eyes narrowed, although she saw his lips twitch and then press together tightly. But he continued to look at her, his dark gaze like a gimlet, until she wished he would look away. She could not seem to do so, and he was making her blush. Not only did her face feel hot but also her entire body. It was as if the very temperature in the hall had risen to an unnatural degree.

Mackinnon's touch on her arm made her jump.

When she turned, wide-eyed, to face him, he said gently, "It appears, lassie, that Kintail be ready for ye."

"I . . . I wish that you and her ladyship were coming with us," Molly said impulsively. The unexpected wish spilled out without thought.

Mackinnon looked both rueful and uncomfortable. "I, too," he said, "but Kintail ha' deemed it otherwise. He thinks it be better an ye go alone."

"Well, at least I shall not be completely alone," she said, forcing a smile. "Doreen will go with me."

The smile vanished with his next words.

"Doreen canna go either, lass," he said, avoiding her gaze. "Kintail said Eilean Donan isna large enough to accommodate more servants, but he ha' promised ye'll no be lonely."

"He will not try to marry me off to someone straight-away, will he?" That possibility distressed her more than she had thought it might, for she had long known the time would come when her guardian would arrange a marriage for her, one likely to be advantageous to himself if not to her. The thought that Kintail, rather than Donald the Grim, was the guardian who would make that choice was somehow even more upsetting.

"He'll no fling ye into marriage," Mackinnon said, clearly more comfortable with this topic. "He isna interested in marrying yet himself, and he said he'd think a bit on his choices, but in the meantime he says ye'll ha' companions aplenty."

"He said 'companions'?"

"Aye."

For a moment she wondered if Kintail meant to make a servant of her to remedy the lack of space to house more of them. The thought almost stirred a smile, for she knew that she lacked the household skills necessary for such a posi-tion.

He was upon them before she could consider the matter longer. His manner was easy, though, revealing none of the tension that she had discerned in him when he entered the hall.

He said quietly, "Art ready to leave, mistress?"

"Aye, if I must," she replied. "Is it true that you refuse to allow my personal maidservant to accompany me?"

"I was told that she intends to wed in a month's time," he said, his manner still calm, even reasonable. "Taking her with us if she will only have to return soon and is likely to pine for her man in the meantime seemed pointless."

"She is loyal to me," Molly said stubbornly.

"Aye, that would be the real reason that I will not take her," he said with a teasing smile.

She gasped, as much at her body's reaction to that smile as to the idea that he could be taunting her about such a thing. To cover her confusion, she said more sharply than she had intended, "You dare to admit that?"

His smile disappeared, but he said only, "If you want her to accompany you, mistress, I will not forbid it, but she will have to share your bedchamber, and it is quite small. I doubt she will make good company for you if she is unhappy, but if her unhappiness does not trouble you . . ."

When he paused, letting her fill in the rest of the sentence for herself, she wanted to slap him for making her seem uncaring. That Doreen might not want to accompany her to Eilean Donan had not occurred to her, but memories washed over her again of her departure from Dunsithe—the terror and misery she had felt at being ripped by veritable strangers from the only home she had ever known. She remembered now that she had scarcely spoken a word for weeks after that terrible night. Neither pride nor compassion would let her subject Doreen to such an ordeal.

"Perhaps someone else can accompany me," she suggested, turning to Mackinnon. "I know that her ladyship would say it is unsuitable for me to travel amidst all these men without at least one other female to bear me company."

Kintail said quietly, "Since you travel with your lawful guardian, lass, it is perfectly suitable. I'll let no harm befall you. My men would not cause you grief in any event, and certainly not whilst I am at your side."

She did not look at him, unable to say aloud that she was beginning to fear that his being at her side might prove to be the most dangerous thing that threatened her. Instead, she watched Mackinnon, but that gentleman looked doubtful, and she realized then that few women at Dunakin would be willing to move to Eilean Donan. All were loyal to the laird and would obey if he ordered them to go, but it occurred to her that although she had lived among them for years, she was not a Mackinnon and had little claim on the members of that clan.

"An ye wish it, lassie," Mackinnon said gently, "I'll ask about and see who else may be willing."

"No," Molly said, gathering her dignity. "I hope that you and her ladyship will visit me, though. I shall be glad to see you both."

"Aye, we'll do that, and right soon," Mackinnon replied, shooting a look at Kintail that dared him to refuse them permission.

He did not. "You will be welcome," he said. "And 'tis not far, after all, only eight or ten miles by boat—two hours with a good westerly breeze."

Nodding agreement, Mackinnon signed to a nearby gilly, who held Molly's cloak over one arm. The lad handed it to him, and facing her, Mackinnon draped it over her shoulders and tenderly fastened the clasp under her chin.

One of his fingertips gently stroked the line of her jaw, and tears glistened in his eyes. "We'll miss ye, lass, and that be plain fact," he said.

"Aye," she said, astonished to see him display his emotion before such an audience. She found herself unable to say more and glad that Lady Mackinnon had declared it too difficult to bid farewell to her.

Had her ladyship been present, too, and perhaps dissolved in tears, Molly would not have been able to keep her composure. As it was, she felt a strange mixture of relief and gratitude when Kintail offered his arm in a clear indication that it was time to depart. Indeed, the casually domineering gesture gave her the impetus she needed to collect her wits.

Ignoring the outstretched arm, she gently touched Mackinnon's and said, "Do you not mean to accompany me down to the boats, sir?"

"Aye, of course I do," he said, taking her hand in his and leading her from the hall, leaving Kintail no option but to follow.

Responding warmly to members of the household who had lingered to bid her farewell, Molly took care to avoid turning her head far enough to see the two men following in their wake. She was nearly certain that she had heard Sir Patrick MacRae chuckle, and if he had, she did not doubt that a cloud of bad temper had engulfed Kintail. The thought added a touch of delight to her smile.

Outside, mist still hung heavy in the air, concealing the sharp peaks of the Cuillin from view and revealing the hilly mainland opposite Skye as only a dense, eerie, dark shadow.

The mist muffled the sound of their footsteps on the track, and other ordinary island sounds. Only the lapping of the water against the shore seemed normal. No one shouted, although folks from the hamlet stepped out of their cottages to bid her farewell. Every face was familiar, every man, woman, and child a dear friend. She would miss them all.

To her surprise and gratitude, Doreen stood near a Mackinnon boat, waiting for her. Since Molly had expected the maidservant to accompany her—had not imagined earlier that it could be otherwise—they had not yet said their goodbyes.

Stepping away from Mackinnon, she held out both hands, saying, "How glad I am to see you, Doreen! I expected you to come with me, you see, but I own, I never thought to ask. I just assumed that you would."

"Aye, and so I would, mistress," Doreen said firmly, casting a speaking look at a stalwart, grim-faced young man-at-arms standing nearby. "Thomas did say that 'twere the master's decision that I canna go—because ye'll no ha' need o' me at Eilean Donan, he said—but it be in me mind that these menfolk ha' decided it all betwixt them. And so I came to tell ye that I'll go if ye want me—unless the master himself forbids it," she added with a quick, wary glance at Mackinnon.

Molly, too, looked at him. "Well, sir?"

Mackinnon, however, looked at Kintail.

That gentleman hesitated, and Molly sighed, certain that she knew what his answer would be.

Wanting to make plain her gratitude for Doreen's bravery in standing up to them all, she said to her, "It is kind of you to offer to do this, Doreen. Indeed, I wish that you *could* go, but I am afraid that you must stay here."

Abruptly Kintail said, "I have heard it said, lass, that you want to marry."

Molly looked at him in surprise. Had he really meant that he would let Doreen accompany her had it not been for the maid's marriage plans?

Doreen bobbed a curtsy. "It be true that I did agree to marry Thomas MacMorran, sir," she said. "But I ha' told him that my duty lies wi' my mistress. I ha' served her since we were bairns together. So if Mistress Molly wants me and if the laird will permit it—and . . . and ye," she added belatedly, "why, then, Thomas will just ha' to wait until the mistress requires me service nae longer."

Kintail exchanged a glance with Sir Patrick MacRae and then looked speculatively at the young man-at-arms standing in grim silence near Doreen. "Would you be Thomas MacMorran?"

"Aye, my lord."

"What say you about this?"

MacMorran's annoyance with his intended was plain in the black look he cast her. "We be promised, sir, and the laird ha' agreed to our wedding."

If the black look fazed Doreen, she gave no sign. Fixing her intense gaze on Kintail, she made her determination clear to everyone.

Molly waited for Kintail to dash their hopes, but to her astonishment, he turned to Mackinnon and said, "Have you dire need of MacMorran?"

Mackinnon's bushy eyebrows shot upward, but he said only, "I ha' need o' every man who serves me. Why d'ye ask such a thing?"

"Because I could manage to accommodate another woman if she were to come with an experienced man-at-arms. What say you to losing them both, sir?"

Mackinnon smiled at Molly. "I say aye, then, but only if the lad himself be willing. MacMorran's a skilled swordsman, and I would gladly keep him here."

Every eye turned toward Thomas MacMorran, causing that stout fellow to turn fiery red and look at the ground. Then swiftly, searchingly, he looked at his beloved. And in reply to his clear, unspoken question, she nodded.

"What say you, MacMorran?" Kintail asked. "Will you swear fealty to me and serve me as loyally as you have served Mackinnon?"

MacMorran straightened, looked him in the eye, and said calmly, "Aye, sir, I'll swear—if the wicked lass will agree to behave herself an I do."

The light that shone from Doreen's eyes told Molly just how much that young woman had offered her. Tears welled into her eyes, and finding it hard to swallow, she was thankful that everyone else watched Doreen, waiting for her to speak. Then her peripheral vision caught movement that drew her attention to Kintail, and warmth rushed to her cheeks when she saw that he was watching her rather than Doreen.

Determined not to let him see how much he had discomposed her, she looked directly at him and said sincerely, "Thank you, sir. I am grateful."

Curtly, he said, "I do not want your gratitude, mistress, but if it will help you to recall this moment the next time it crosses your mind to defy me, mayhap the memory will encourage you to obey me instead."

Since it had made her feel agreeably noble to express gratitude to him when she had really wanted nothing more than to spit in his eye, the imperious response infuriated her. Knowing, however, that no good purpose would be served by revealing her anger, she continued to return look for look and held her peace. Indeed, she could think of no adequate response to his nonsensical suggestion. Only a fool would promise always to obey another person's commands.

Mackinnon, either assuming that things now were settled to everyone's satisfaction or recognizing that no good could come of further delay, said heartily, "I feel a breeze stirring, lad. The oarsmen must be glad o' that, because a stout breeze means ye'll be putting up your sails afore the morning's done."

Sir Patrick MacRae put a finger in his mouth to wet it and held it up, saying cheerfully, "Quite right, sir. I reckon we'll be home before Eilean Donan's bell rings for the noonday meal. That is, we will if we get onto the water soon," he added with a quizzical look at his master.

Molly turned from Kintail to link arms with Doreen. "I am delighted that you are going with me," she said. "I felt sad just thinking about being alone in a new place, but now perhaps it will not be so bad."

"Aye, mistress," Doreen said.

Molly heard a note of doubt in the other's voice and saw that she was looking from MacMorran to Kintail. The former had turned to help launch the two boats that held most of the baggage, but the latter was still watching Molly.

"Come along then," she said, forcing a light laugh as she moved toward Kintail's coble at the water's edge, her arm still linked with Doreen's. "Let us choose our seats at once, or I warrant these horrid men will make us row. But stay," she exclaimed. "What about your clothing and such?"

The maidservant grinned. "Dinna fash yourself, mistress. I didna doubt that I'd be going, so I brought what I need wi' me, and it be already stowed in one o' them galleys. Howsomever, I doubt that Thomas has any clothes but them what he stands in. We'll just see how the braw laddie copes wi' that wee predicament!"

Finding Doreen's good humor contagious, Molly stepped ahead of her into Kintail's boat. Two of the oarsmen and Sir Patrick, who would man the tiller, were already in place, and so with the prow still resting on the shingle, out of the water, it was necessary to make her way carefully toward the narrow central thwart that supported the mast, but her heart felt lighter than it had for days.

That feeling lasted only until Kintail and the other two oarsmen joined them. The latter got in first. Then Kintail took his place in the bow of the coble. All three men faced Molly and Doreen, but only Kintail dared to fix his stern gaze on Molly.

She had not thought about where he would sit, but if she had, she would have expected him to sit as she was, facing the direction they would travel. She saw then that his long legs would not fit comfortably in the small space in front of the bow seat. He would therefore face her for the duration of their journey, and since the stout breeze that Mackinnon had promised had yet to materialize, heaven alone knew how long that would be.

Chapter 8

The slowly stiffening breeze did not help them much until they had passed the easternmost point of the Isle of Skye, but Molly had not been off the island since her arrival and scarcely noticed the lack. She had never been in a boat on such a misty day before, and she was fascinated to see what was generally familiar territory from this eerie, new perspective.

Kintail's boat was much smaller than the Mackinnon galleys, but they were heavily laden, making the speed of all four boats nearly equal. They moved steadily along, but because of the poor visibility, they stayed just far enough from the Skye shoreline to avoid dangerous rocks until the mist began to clear.

Molly enjoyed being on the water, and when the oarsmen shipped their sweeps and two of them moved with care to put up the square lugsail at last, she watched to see how they did it. Men in the other boats were doing the same thing in much the same fashion, and the process looked easy enough, making her wonder if she could learn to do it by herself or with Doreen's help. Doubtless Kintail would refuse to teach them, just as Mackinnon had refused to teach her to swim when she had asked him to do so years ago. She had found her own teacher then, and if she decided to learn to sail, she would find a way to do that, too.

Expecting the breeze to carry them along briskly now, she was surprised when the men in all four boats began rowing again as soon as the sails were set.

As if he read her mind, Kintail said, "The wind is not strong enough yet to do aught but ease the job of the oarsmen. Still, it should soon clear away this mist."

Tempted to ignore him, she found that curiosity made that impossible. Raising her voice to make it heard over the still flapping sail and the knocking of the oars against their rowlocks, she said with a gesture, "That point of land yonder is still part of Skye, is it not?"

"Aye," he replied, glancing in the direction she indicated. "The island extends farther to the east than you can see from here. That point is where Kylerhea joins the loch. It's the strait leading south from Loch Alsh, where we are, through the Sound of Sleat to the Atlantic Ocean. When we reach the far side of the strait's mouth, we'll be almost halfway to Eilean Donan."

"Mistress Molly said that your Eilean Donan sits on an island," Doreen said.

He smiled. "'Tis more islet than island, and it sits in the mouth of Loch Duich, near the mouth of Loch Long. If you can imagine all the water ahead of us as a forked stick with Loch Alsh as the end one might hold, we are sailing toward the stick's fork. A boat cannot sail into Loch Duich or Loch Long without being seen from Eilean Donan's ramparts."

"Are there horses at Eilean Donan?" Molly asked casually.

The shrewd look he shot her spoke volumes, but he said, "We keep several inside the wall but most of our stock stays on the mainland. When the tide is at its ebb one can ride across the channel that separates us from the mainland and Dornie village, but we usually row a boat to shore and take horses from there." Turning to Doreen, he added, "A number of my men-at-arms and their families live in Dornie."

"Thomas and I ha' no need of a cottage yet, sir," Doreen said. "An ye dinna forbid it, I'll bide wi' my mistress whilst she has need o' me."

He nodded and Molly gazed in astonishment at Doreen, never having suspected that the maidservant possessed such temerity.

No one spoke again for some time, during which the only sounds were the thumping of oars, the occasional fluttering of their still fitful sail, the waves lapping against the sides of the boat, and the stertorous breathing of the oarsmen. Molly found the lack of conversation peaceful, however, and was glad that it lasted until they were well past the wide opening into the strait called Kylerhea.

The breeze stiffened then, and the lingering mist cleared rapidly to reveal an azure sky with a few puffy white clouds skimming along. A lone, streaky-brown curlew soared lazily above the boat, commenting occasionally with its musical, bubbling trill as it sought a suitable landing place on the nearby shore. When it found what it sought, a squabble of black-and-white, orange-billed oystercatchers in its path took wing, their shrill cries shattering the peace.

Seeing them, Molly smiled, remembering, as she often did when she saw oystercatchers, the day in her childhood when one had first caught her eye as it industriously jerked a fat lugworm from a freshly turned garden. Demanding to know what sort of bird it was, and hearing its name, she had been astonished to learn that oystercatchers did not always eat oysters. To find one eating a worm still struck her as odd and tickled her sense of humor.

Fin wondered what had brought the soft, secret little smile to the Maid's face and marveled at how so small a change of expression could transform her from the chilly, stiff-featured lass he usually saw. The smile disappeared as quickly as it had come, however. Had he not been watching, he would have missed it.

She was staring into the distance now, and he wondered if she felt lonely. One could not wonder at it if she did. As Mackinnon had pointed out, anyone leaving one home for an unknown one was bound to feel unsettled. Doubtless he had felt so himself the day he left Eilean Donan for university at St. Andrews.

Recalling that day, however, he knew that he had not felt lonely at all, because he and Patrick both had looked forward to university life as a huge adventure. If they had missed familiar things after they reached the bustling university town, any small ache was overshadowed by all the new and fascinating experiences they had shared. Perhaps he misjudged the Maid and she, too, looked forward to some sort of adventure. He could not imagine that she would find much at Eilean Donan, but neither could he doubt that she would come to love the place as he did. Of course, he told himself firmly, before long, she would be off to a new home somewhere, married to someone who could do him some good.

He shifted on the hard seat, trying to get comfortable. They had been out for little more than an hour, and he had endured much longer journeys, but the coble was not intended for more than short jaunts, certainly not for a man of his length. Even sitting in the bow, behind the oarsmen, he could not stretch out his legs.

Glancing at the other boats, and seeing that their sails were not full, he knew that the men in them were probably cursing the coble's slower pace. They probably knew, too, that he could have left it for someone else to return to Kyle, but he had not wanted Mackinnon to deliver him and his new charge to Eilean Donan.

He began fidgeting again. This was a snail's pace, and he had already tarried too long away from home. He had work to do, his baron's court to prepare.

How could women sit still for so long, he wondered.

The Maid's eyes were closed. Had she fallen asleep? She looked childlike, vulnerable, her beauty tender now, alluring. She had better take care, he thought, lest she tumble into the water. Not that there was much fear of that, for she was small and Doreen or one of the oarsmen would grab her if she began to topple. Besides, if he warned her to take care, would she not simply ignore him? Or, as likely as not, she'd fling herself into the water just to defy him and create trouble.

Molly was savoring the sounds and scent of the sea and the caress of the breeze on her cheeks. Curlews and gulls overhead called to one another, and she heard a seal barking in the distance. The breeze was warm, and it smelled wonderfully fresh and clean, with a salty tang.

"Yonder lies Glas Eilean," Kintail said abruptly a half hour later with easily detectable relief.

Molly kept her eyes shut, not yet ready to relinquish her peaceful reveries.

" 'Tis just a wee bit o' land barely showing itself in the water," Doreen said.

"Aye," Kintail agreed, "but Eilean Donan lies not far beyond it."

Molly slitted her eyes open to see that he had twisted around to look ahead and was gazing toward a small, nearly flat islet in the water ahead. She opened her eyes completely then and began to keep watch. As he had promised, the castle soon came into view.

After the steep, towering hills that faced Dunakin across the strait and the impressive sharp-pointed Cuillin of Skye, her first impression of Eilean Donan was that it sat low on a bit of land of singular flatness. The setting was picturesque, though, for Highland hills and mountains jutted up around it on three sides, framing the castle magnificently, and snow-capped peaks in the distance looked even higher than the Cuillin. Still, the small, rocky islet was unimpressive, not much larger than the base of the castle.

The pinkish brown stone castle was more impressive. At its northwestern corner, a square tower—undoubtedly part of the keep—anchored a high curtain wall dotted with arrow loops. From Molly's vantage point, the tower appeared to be five stories tall. The main portion of the keep was a story lower but also possessed its share of loops. Crenellated battlements punctuated with bartizans encircled the structure at a level even with the top floor of the keep, indicating a walkway there.

For some time their oarsmen had been rowing intermittently, leaving more work to the ever-stronger wind, but they took up the sweeps again when the four boats began wending their way around to the south and east shores of the islet.

The castle's architecture became more intriguing as more of it came into view. Its entrance appeared on the east side, which Molly saw also had room enough on the shore to land the four boats. Others were beached or anchored nearby—

two galleys the size of Mackinnon's and a smaller, twelve-oared birlinn.

Men hurried to help them land, and Kintail greeted his people heartily.

She noted how eager they were to welcome him home. They welcomed Sir Patrick MacRae, too, and soon both Kintail and Sir Patrick were laughing and chatting with their men as they pitched in to unload the boats.

Left to climb out of the coble by herself, with only Doreen to help, Molly watched the others with increasing annoyance. The newcomers shot her curious glances and eyed Doreen, too, but no one seemed in any hurry to welcome her to Eilean Donan. Thus, she stood where she was with Doreen at her side, waiting, uncertain for the first time in years about how to act or what to do next.

Although many of the men milling around the boats were men she knew from Dunakin, she could not be certain that they would obey her commands as willingly here as they had there—not when they knew that she was now Kintail's ward. Her courage, normally strong, wilted considerably.

"You lot, down there! What be ye at, then?"

Looking up, Molly beheld a plump, redheaded woman standing at the top of the rocky slope, halfway between the boats and the castle entrance. She was perhaps ten years older than Molly. The wind, assailing her from both sides as it swept around the castle walls behind her, tangled her long hair wildly around her face, but she ignored it, standing with her hands on her hips, glaring down at the men.

They all looked toward her. Then, bewildered, they looked at each other.

Kintail shouted, "What manner of welcome is that to your master, Mauri MacRae? Is our dinner awaiting us?"

"Aye, it is," she shouted back. "Thanks to one o' the lads seeing your boats and recognizing from your banner that 'twere yourself. And plenty o' food there be, too. But what are ye about, amusing yourselves—the whole lot o' ye—whilst them ladies ye brought wi' ye stand like posts? 'Tis like heathens ye're behaving, every last one o' ye. Ye should be ashamed, offering them such poor welcome!"

Molly hid a smile, thinking that perhaps she would like at least one person at Eilean Donan. She looked at Kintail to see how he would respond.

He was still gazing at the woman above them, and he was frowning.

She remembered then that they called him Wild Fin, and a hope flitted through her mind that he would not react too harshly to the woman's scolding.

He did not. Instead, he shifted his fierce gaze to Molly.

"Why do you stand there?" he demanded. "Everything in these boats must go up to the castle, and Mackinnon's men are here merely to protect us until we unload and they can leave. Both of you should be helping."

Doreen stepped forward before he stopped speaking, but hearing his last statement, she paused and glanced back at her mistress, clearly shocked.

Utterly astonished, Molly stared at him. "Help?" she demanded. "Is it as I suspected, then, Kintail? Do you mean to turn me into a common servant?"

"Don't talk nonsense," he snapped. "Do you not see that I am carrying things, myself? Do you think that I consider myself a servant here?"

"But it is the business of servants—"

He cut her off, saying sharply, "Unfortunately, we do not always have time to observe such formality, exposed as we are to attack when we are outside the wall. 'Tis best you understand as much from the outset, so come and help carry these things up unless you want to debate the matter further with me here."

Appalled by such ill grace when, by rights, he should be guiding her up the rugged slope and welcoming her properly to his home, Molly felt sorely tempted to refuse. A tiny voice in the back of her mind suggested, however, that a man so lost to the proprieties as Kintail was might react unhappily to such defiance.

Unwilling to test him before such a large, unknown audience, she resorted to chilly dignity instead. Making her way carefully to the nearest of three laden boats, she accepted a small bundle from Thomas MacMorran and turned to walk up to the castle. As she did, she saw Kintail turn abruptly toward a grinning Sir Patrick MacRae at the far end of the line of boats, as if the other man had spoken to him.

Sir Patrick stood with his feet apart, his thumbs hooked over his belt, and his back to the inflowing tide where it swept through the channel between islet and mainland. Still grinning, he spoke again to Kintail, and Molly heard chuckles from the men nearest them.

The chuckles ceased when Kintail's fist flashed out and caught Sir Patrick solidly on one shoulder, knocking him off balance. Shouting curses, arms waving wildly, he fell backward with a great splash, into the current and under.

The other men burst into howls of laughter, but quick as thought, Kintail bent and snatched up a rope, flinging one end of it to Sir Patrick and hauling him back to shore, where he extended a hand to help him to his feet.

As Patrick bent over, hands on his knees, dripping, gasping, and coughing, Kintail clapped him on one wet shoulder with a blow that nearly sent him back into the water, and said in a tone clear enough for them all to hear, "Is that insolence of yours dampened yet, or does it require another ducking?"

For a moment, Sir Patrick's eyes flashed dangerously, but

meeting Kintail's cool, intense gaze, he shrugged and a wry, rueful smile touched his lips.

"Pax," he said. "I'll mind my tongue."

"See that you do," Kintail said.

No one was laughing now, and when Kintail's gaze flicked toward Molly, she looked away quickly and began to hurry toward the castle, followed by Doreen, who carried a bundle much larger than her own.

When they reached the top of the slope, the redheaded woman reached to take Molly's bundle, saying with a wide, gap-toothed grin, "Welcome, Mistress Gordon. I be Mauri MacRae." Tucking Molly's bundle under her arm as she made an awkward curtsy, she added lightly, "Will ye come inside now?"

"I will, indeed," Molly said. Although she was certain that Kintail expected her to carry more than one small bundle, she followed Mauri MacRae and did not look back. Prickling between her shoulder blades warned her he was watching, doubtless with disapproval, and with every step, she expected to hear him shout.

He did not, however, and when she and her two companions reached the tall arched portcullis entrance to the castle, she dared at last to glance back.

Led by the still dripping Sir Patrick, a line of men bearing goods from the boats snaked its way up the short slope. The Mackinnon men-at-arms were helping the others carry her belongings.

Beside her, Doreen chuckled and said, "I gave my Thomas a look, mistress, and I'll warrant he had no trouble comprehending it. If those Dunakin men mean to dine here, they can be earning their bread, and that's all I'll say about it."

Mauri MacRae put back her head and laughed. "Come

along, ye two," she said, still chuckling. "I'll show ye where ye're to sleep."

"You are very kind, Mistress MacRae," Molly said gratefully as they followed her across a courtyard lined with shedlike outbuildings.

"Aye, sure, I am that," the woman said cheerfully. "But ye'd best be calling me Mauri, the way everyone else does, Mistress Gordon. There be so many MacRaes hereabouts that we'll none of us ken who ye're wanting, else."

"I am Molly to my friends," Molly said impulsively, "and this is Doreen."

"Ye're both welcome," Mauri said, leading the way up a wooden stairway that led into the second level of the keep. "We can always use extra hands, Doreen."

"I serve Mistress Molly," Doreen said with a smile. "But whenever she has nae need o' me, I'll be glad enough to oblige ye."

Passing a stout iron yett, or gate, they followed their guide through a short archway, and entered what was clearly the great hall of the castle. Clan banners fluttered from poles set at an angle high on the walls, just as they had at Dunakin. Mauri did not pause but crossed the hall and stepped through another archway, where a twisting stone stairway took them up two flights to a landing. A pair of doors faced each other there. Mauri paused and turned to face Molly and Doreen.

"I'm thinking that I should tell ye I heard what the laird shouted at ye below, mistress, and whilst I dinna hold wi' ladies dirtying their hands without there be a need for it, I'd be fashed wi' m'self did I no warn ye that ye'll find little to do here if ye dinna help wi' the chores. The laird will be holding a baron court now he's home, and we ha' much to do to prepare for it."

Molly knew about such courts, because Mackinnon held

them, too, but she had never had anything to do with their preparations. "Are there no maidservants to attend to such things?" she asked.

"Faith, mistress, although we've a garrison of men here, besides yourself and your Doreen, ye'll find few other women most days." She held up fingers as she added, "Altogether, there's me, my husband, Malcolm, my uncle Ian Dubh, who's away now but who acts as constable of Eilean Donan when he's here, and our wee bairn Morag, though she's nobbut four months old. Then there's my cousin, Tam Matheson, who looks after the master's clothing and such. We ha' two daily women, too—wives o' garrison men—who come in to help me most days, and more o' the same to help when the master holds a justice court. We'll ha' a few visitors then, too. As to the rest here, there be only the master, our Patrick, and lads who look after Patrick, Ian Dubh, and my Malcolm."

"Sir Patrick MacRae cannot be your son!"

"Nay," Mauri said, laughing again. "He is my husband's elder brother and the laird's closest friend besides." Sobering, she added, "Patrick and Malcolm's father, Sir Gilchrist MacRae, were ambushed wi' the laird's father on the way to Kinlochewe. Likely, ye'll meet Patrick's mother and sister when the laird holds his court. They dwell at Ardintoul, a point that juts into Loch Alsh just beyond Glas Eilean. The south shore o' Loch Alsh be part o' Kintail, too, ye ken."

"I've heard men call the MacRaes 'the Mackenzies' shirt of mail,'" Molly said. "Is that true? Do they always protect the Mackenzies?"

"Aye, it be ever the MacRaes' duty, that. But we'd best hurry," she added, moving to open the door on the right of the landing as a thudding of booted feet echoed below on the stairway. "Those men be coming up straightaway wi' your things, mistress, and this be your bedchamber. We'll pitch out a pallet in the wee chamber across the way for your Doreen to sleep on, so ye'll no ha' to share this room."

The room was not large and seemed smaller when the men arrived with Molly's things. When they put their burdens down and retreated down the stairs, Molly was dismayed to see how much she had brought. It had not seemed so much at Dunakin, or piled in the boats, but here in this small chamber, she had trouble believing all her things would fit.

"I hope you brought enough to make yourself comfortable," Kintail said sardonically from the doorway as his critical gaze swept the crowded room.

"We'll help her see to everything, laird," Mauri told him confidently.

"Not now, you won't," he retorted. "Mackinnon's men want their dinner, because they want to be off, since they'll be sailing against wind and tide, going back. You run on down now and see to them, and take Doreen with you. I want a private word with Mistress Gordon."

The stern note in his voice sent a shiver up Molly's spine, and she was not surprised when Doreen and Mauri departed without a word of protest. She would have liked to go with them.

When he shut the door behind them, she stiffened warily, remembering what he had done a short time earlier to his "closest friend" with but small provocation.

He said, "I spoke sharply to you on the shore, mistress. I said naught that was not true, but I ought to have conducted myself with better grace."

Astonished, she said, "Then I need not act as a servant here?"

"You put more meaning into my words than I intended," he said ruefully. "You are no servant, but neither are you a guest. Eilean Donan is your home now until I find you a suitable husband, and since we are not overburdened with people to do the chores, I'll expect you to do your share."

"My home," she repeated, unable to suppress a sigh at the thought that this place was no more a real home than Dunakin had been. And at least Dunakin's master was predictable. That thought brought another on its heels. "Do you frequently knock people who displease you into the water, sir?"

"Patrick was impertinent," he replied.

Since he had called her the same, and more than once, the blunt statement was not reassuring. She would have liked to ask just what it was that Sir Patrick had said, but as she tried to find the words, Kintail said with a smile that softened his expression considerably, "Tidy yourself now and come downstairs to eat."

Without another word, he left the room and shut the door behind him.

Molly stared at the door, uncertain about what had just happened, until a voice behind her said tartly, "Dinna stand like a stock, lass. He is what he is, Mackenzie o' Kintail, and there be nowt ye can do tae change the man."

With a surge of delight, she turned and exclaimed, "Maggie, you're here!"

"Aye, and where else would I be?" Maggie Malloch demanded.

"But— Oh, there you are," Molly said when she located the little woman atop the tallest pile of stuff. "Faith, but you're smaller now, no bigger than my fist!"

"Aye, well, it takes less energy for me tae stay visible tae ye at this size," Maggie explained, grimly surveying the cluttered chamber from her perch. Gesturing with her pipe, she added tartly, "I tell ye, this isna the sort o' place tae which I ha' grown accustomed. Does the wretched man expect a fine lass like yourself tae live in this drab wee hole?"

"I expect I shall find it adequate once we've managed to put all these things away," Molly said. "I don't suppose you have the power to make the room larger, do you?" she added wistfully.

"Nay," the tiny woman replied. "That I canna do. However, I can help ye find places for your things when the time comes, and I can help ye tidy yourself now. Ye'd best stir your stumps, too, else that Kintail be like tae return in a temper and carry ye downstairs over his shoulder."

The thought of Kintail picking her up and carrying her being more than she wanted to consider right then, Molly turned her attention to her appearance.

Fin's mood had improved, but the reality of his position had struck him hard, nearly as hard as he had struck Patrick. He had reacted swiftly to Patrick's teasing, all the more so, he was sure, because what his friend had suggested was no more than what his own unruly imagination had suggested. He could not strike back at his thoughts, but Patrick was not so elusive.

On the other hand, Patrick would not repeat his mistake, but his imagination was not so trustworthy. If his mind continued to fill itself with tantalizing images of Mistress Gordon's body—usually unclothed—he would have to keep his distance from her. He owed her protection, and if that included protection from his baser instincts, so be it.

Chapter 9

Mackinnon's men-at-arms departed shortly after their meal, and for the next few days, Molly saw little of Kintail or his men, for they were out and about passing word of the justice court he would hold in the great hall at the beginning of the week. The castle buzzed with activity, as its inmates prepared for the event.

Bearing Mauri and Doreen company in the kitchen while they and a few women from Dornie village prepared supper the evening before the great day, Molly said, "I look forward to seeing what such a court is like. Mackinnon held them at Dunakin, of course, but he never allowed me to be present."

"Nor will the laird allow it," Mauri said gently. "'Tis men's business, mostly, these courts, unless some poor woman be accused o' witchcraft, and Malcolm and Patrick ha' both assured me there'll be none o' that tomorrow. The laird may ha' to condemn someone to die, though, and ye'd no want to watch them drown a man or hang one, would ye?"

"I would not," Molly replied firmly, "but I doubt that he will hang anyone on the spot, and if I am going to make my home here until he finds me a husband, I should know who is friend and who is felon, should I not?"

"Aye, sure," Mauri agreed, "but ye'll mostly bide wi' us females, and we can tell ye everything there be to ken about other folks."

"But I want to see what happens tomorrow," Molly insisted stubbornly.

"Then ye must ask the laird, but I doubt he'll agree to it."

Molly doubted it, too, but if she had learned anything about Kintail, it was that he was unpredictable. He had surprised her the day of her arrival when he had come as close as any man ever had to apologizing to her. Until then, she had thought of him only—or nearly so—as stern, humorless, and domineering.

He was handsome enough, to be sure, and there was that odd tendency for her body to react when he smiled or when she met his gaze unexpectedly, but usually she thought of him as fearsomely large and irritatingly grim. His presence certainly filled any room he entered and drew every eye. And although his behavior since her first day at Eilean Donan had given her no cause to believe he had changed his ways, his apology then and the boyish smile that had followed provided a glimmer of hope that she could persuade him to let her watch the court proceedings.

Her reaction to his smile and the twinkle that usually accompanied it had altered her first impression enough to make her spend much of the little time she had spent in his company since, covertly watching him. She did not expect to see that smile when she asked permission to view his court in progress, but it was not her nature to wish for something without making a strong push to achieve it.

She certainly was no help to the women in the kitchen. Although she was accustomed to relaying Lady Mackinnon's wishes and commands to servants at Dunakin, and to doing a number of other things capably that most women did not do at all, she had never had to attend to menial tasks like cooking and cleaning.

Savoring the delicious odors of roasting meats and bubbling stew that wafted around them, she watched with near envy as Mauri deftly shoved a heavy pan into the oven in the fireplace wall, to keep warm, then whisked around Doreen—who was stirring a pot on the hob with a long spoon—to turn the birds on the spit. All the while, Mauri issued a stream of orders to the helpers scurrying around her.

When she turned away from the fire at last and briskly crossed the room to supervise two women at a table laden with platters, baskets, and already-prepared side dishes, Molly said with a sigh, "I am useless to you."

From her place at the fire, Doreen looked over her shoulder and brushed a wisp of hair back under her cap with her free hand as she said, "Ye can stir this stew if ye like, mistress, but it be gey hot over here."

"Nay, then," Mauri said, beginning to count bread trenchers from a large basket as she put them into a smaller one. "She'll muss her gown an she does that."

"I can count those trenchers for you," Molly suggested.

"I've done them," Mauri said, shouting for someone called Ian to come take the trenchers into the hall. She turned back with a smile and said, "Truly, mistress, there be nae need for ye to dirty your hands here. Much of this be for tomorrow, but there be little enough left to do that even Malcolm's mam and sister, who arrived an hour ago, be taking their ease. Ye should do the same."

"But if I help you now, I'll know better what I can do tomorrow when you will have so many more to feed and will need everyone's help."

"Aye," Mauri agreed. "We'll ha' as many as a hundred or more to dine. But, even then I'll ha' these women from the village to help, and in truth, mistress," she added gently, "we'll all be so busy that ye'd be more hindrance than help. I'll gladly teach ye all I can in time, for I believe a woman should ken as much as her servants do about running a household, but I canna do it this evening or tomorrow when I've me hands full just showing Doreen her duties. Mayhap the laird be in the hall now. Ye should go and ask him if he'll let ye attend his court."

Feeling sadly inadequate for the first time in her memory, Molly went away without argument.

Kintail was not in the hall. A few men-at-arms were there, but not many, for before meals, they tended to congregate in the garrison hall below. One man stirred up the fire, while another dumped a stack of peat into a basket nearby. Two others were casting dice at one of several trestle tables where most members of the household would sit.

"Be there aught we can do for ye, mistress?" the one stirring the fire asked.

"The laird," Molly said, "do you know where I might find him?"

"Aye, he's above," the man said, gesturing with a thumb toward the ceiling. "Third level, door on the left."

Thanking him, she hurried to the stairs and up them, knowing that the bell would sound for supper at any moment and preferring to ask Kintail about watching the court proceedings without having to do so in front of the entire household. As she stepped through the archway onto the third landing, she heard a shout of masculine laughter from behind the arched oak door on the left.

Believing that Kintail and Sir Patrick must be inside together, she grimaced at the thought of trying to persuade the former while the latter stood by and grinned mockingly at them or, worse, added his masculine—and doubtless disapproving—opinion to the conversation.

She had learned that Sir Patrick was seldom serious. Moreover, he flirted with her outrageously. At first, she had wondered if he had notions of trying to persuade Kintail to allow him to marry her, but she had quickly seen that Sir Patrick flirted with anyone in skirts, even with his temperamental sister-in-law.

The day after Molly's arrival, Mauri had responded to his passing pat on her backside by throwing a wet rag at him, catching him full in the face with it. But the gesture had barely fazed Patrick. With a shout of delighted laughter, he had deftly caught the towel and flung it back at her, his aim as true as hers had been.

These memories flashed through Molly's mind in a blink as she rapped firmly on the door.

"Enter." There was lingering laughter in Kintail's voice, and as she pushed the door, he added with a chuckle, "Just look at the wee fish I've caught, Patrick."

The shriek and the splash that accompanied his words stopped Molly in her tracks, but it was too late. She stared in shock at the scene she had interrupted.

His hair full of suds, Kintail sat in a large tub in what clearly was his bedchamber, with a fully clothed, very wet young female sprawled atop him.

The room was not much larger than Molly's. A high, curtained bed took up the space along the far wall, and with the washstand flanking a window embrasure at her left, and chests and a wardrobe occupying the wall to her right, little room remained for the tub. It sat in front of the doorway a few feet from her, with puddles surrounding it and the large water pail beside it.

Both occupants of the tub stared back at her in dismay,

for although her entrance had caught the female with her back to the door, she had twisted about to look over a shoulder. She appeared to be at least two years younger than Molly, and at first glance seemed apprehensive, even frightened. But when she saw Molly, that apprehension turned to visible, albeit deeply blushing relief.

"Who are you?" she asked faintly.

At the same time, Kintail snapped, "What the devil are you doing here? I thought you were Patrick, or I'd never have told you to come in."

Collecting her dignity with an effort, Molly said quietly, "I know that, sir, and I beg your pardon. It never occurred to me that he was sending me to your bedchamber, and not having a clear notion yet of which rooms are where, I—"

"*Patrick* sent you here? By heaven, I'll throttle him! Stay where you are, lass," he added sharply, jerking the girl back as she tried to get out of the tub.

"I have not seen Sir Patrick," Molly said, taking a step back, wanting only to leave and never see either of them again. She was shocked, embarrassed, and rapidly growing angry.

"Then who—?" He broke off, adding hastily, "Mind your hand, Bab, unless you want more of a ducking than you already got."

Molly's temper flared then, but the girl chortled, giving him a slap on one bare shoulder as she said, "You mind *your* hands, Fin, or by heaven—"

She broke off with a shriek and Kintail roared when Molly snatched up the water bucket by the tub and upended its contents over the pair of them.

Without a word, she turned on her heel and stormed out of the room. Had anyone asked her how she dared do such a thing, she could not have answered sensibly. She was more than a little shocked at herself, and equally fearful of how Kintail would retaliate.

The drenched pair in the tub remained silent for a long moment after the door shut behind Mistress Gordon before Fin gripped his companion firmly around her slim waist and lifted her off him.

"Take care when I set you down, Bab," he said. "The floor will be slippery."

"Don't lean over so far!" Barbara MacRae exclaimed, her feet dangling above the stone floor. "You'll have the whole tub over!"

Setting her down, he said, "If I do have the tub over, I won't wait for your brother to take a switch to you for this little prank. I'll do it myself. I may do it, anyway."

Busy pulling her clinging, wet skirts away from her legs to wring them out, she paid no heed to his threat. "Who was that, Fin? Is that the Maid of Dunsithe? Does she frequently enter your bedchamber?"

"I *will* take a switch to you," he said grimly, putting both hands on the sides of the oblong tub and shifting his weight to get up.

"Don't get out!" she shrieked, backing away so quickly that she slipped in a puddle and nearly fell. Grabbing a bedpost to steady herself, she eyed him warily, but when he settled down into the tub again, she said, "What am I going to wear? At least she rinsed the soap from your hair, but I cannot return to my mother looking like this, let alone go down to supper!"

"You should have thought about that before you decided to sneak in here and help with my bath," he said unsympathetically. "Ask Mauri to lend you something, or ask the Maid. She brought enough clothing with her to outfit Dornie village, as well as any guests we might entertain for the next year or two."

"I am certainly not going to ask Mauri," Barbara said. "She'll only scold." Coaxingly, she added, "You won't really tell Patrick, will you? He may be the best of brothers, and he never cares when his behavior shocks people, but he frequently displays uncomfortable notions of propriety where I am concerned."

"Out," he said, pointing toward the door. "There's the bell for supper, and neither of us can go below until we've put on dry clothing."

"But—"

He started to get up, whereupon she shut her mouth and fled.

"The Maid's room is below this one on the right," he bellow after her, "but first find someone to tell Tam Matheson I want him!"

Knowing that she had heard him but not certain she would obey, he got out of the tub and picked his way barefoot across the puddle-drenched floor to the washstand to get a towel. As he dried himself and sought clothing to wear, he recalled the look on the Maid's face when he had demanded to know what she was doing there, and his ready sense of humor stirred. He subdued it easily, however.

She could not have known she was entering his bedchamber, that much was clear. But why had she come? Her very presence teased him—nay, distracted him at every turn—and that, too, was something she could not know. Even in her fury, she was distractingly beautiful. Not a day passed without moments when he wanted to shake her, spank her, or kiss every lovely inch of her. Undeniably, James had done him a favor, but he was not certain that he would ever feel properly grateful.

Molly, too, had heard the supper bell, but instead of continuing down to the hall, she darted into her bedchamber on the floor below Kintail's. Shutting the door behind her, she leaned against it, breathing hard.

Squeezing her eyes shut, she tried to regain control. What was wrong with her? It certainly was not the first time she had seen a man's bare chest and shoulders, and thanks to the girl sprawled atop Kintail, that was all she had seen. Even if she had seen more, she supposed it would not have meant the end of the world. In even the finest houses—or so Lady Mackinnon had told her—it was not unusual for a daughter of the house to assist with a gentleman's bath. But gentlemen, in general, did not bathe often, and no one at Dunakin had ever asked her to perform such a personal service.

Still, she doubted that Kintail's bareness alone had disturbed her so much.

Drawing a deep breath, she considered the matter but could think of no excuse for her odd behavior other than that finding herself in his bedchamber, confronted by such a scene, had disordered her senses. As her breathing settled into a more normal rhythm, it occurred to her that perhaps her mischievous household spirits had had something to do with what had occurred.

Narrowing her eyes, she searched the chamber—tidier now than it had been, for miraculously and just as Maggie Malloch had promised, she and Doreen had found places to put everything.

"Maggie? Maggie, are you here? I need you."

Was that a swirling of the air yonder on the cushion below the window?

A loud rap-rap on the door behind her startled her half out of her skin. Holding her breath, certain that a furious Kintail stood on the other side, she was still wondering at her unnatural, trembling cowardice when a voice that definitely was not his begged her to open the door.

"Mistress Gordon, it is Barbara MacRae. If you are in there, please be so kind as to let me in—and quickly, I pray you!"

Suspecting that her visitor was the girl who had been with Kintail, Molly did not want to open the door, but when she saw the latch move, she snatched it open, saying icily, "Go away. I have naught to say to such a brazen female."

But her annoyance quickly eased, for the girl on the landing, dripping water on the stones, looked utterly wretched. Dusky curls had escaped her headdress and hung in limp, damp strands to her shoulders, and her gown was soaked through.

"Please, mistress, have pity," she said urgently. "The supper bell has rung already, and I cannot go down looking like this. Oh, haste! Someone is coming up the stairs. If 'tis Patrick—!"

The next moment she had whisked herself inside and shut the door behind her. Standing with her back against it, in much the same way that Molly had stood only moments before, she said, "Pray, Mistress Gordon, we are of size, and Fin told me that you have dresses to spare. Can you not find it in your heart—?"

"Fin?" Molly had moved only because otherwise Barbara MacRae, in her haste, would have run into her.

"Aye, Fin Mackenzie—Kintail."

Her temper stirred again. "Do you always address him so informally?"

"We have known each other since childhood, mistress. I am Patrick MacRae's sister. When our father died with the previous laird, my mother insisted on moving back to our home across the loch, so I went with her. But I grew up here in the castle just as Patrick did, earning my keep by helping Mauri with her chores."

"You speak very well for a servant," Molly said.

Barbara's blue eyes twinkled, giving her a mischievous look similar to her brother's. She said, "Although we MacRaes are sworn to serve the Mackenzies, mistress, we are not servants. Nor are we tenants, although it must seem to many that we are. My family owns land across the loch in Kintail. My brother went to university with Fin, and I was fortunate enough to learn to speak as they do."

"Did you share their lessons?" Molly asked, sensing a kindred spirit.

"Alas, no, my father would not permit it. They did teach me to read enough to understand recipes and such, and to write some, but that is all. Oh, bless you!" This last was because Molly had turned to open a chest and extract a clean shift, skirt, and bodice from it.

"Whatever were you doing in the tub with him?" Molly asked as she handed Barbara a towel and began to help her remove her wet clothing.

"It certainly was not by choice," Barbara replied with a laugh, adding while she did her best to dry herself, "I met Tam Matheson coming up the stairs with that bucket of water you poured over us. I took it from him and went into the chamber, meaning to surprise Fin, because he did not know that my mother and I had arrived to help Mauri and the others prepare for the court."

"Do you customarily just walk into his bedchamber?"

Barbara blushed. "I did when we were children, but I suppose I should not do it anymore. In any event, Fin was bent over in the tub when I went in, soaping his hair. He assumed I was Tam and told me to pour water over his head. I was beside him by then, and since he had his eyes shut, I put the bucket down far enough away so that he couldn't reach it himself and told him that I thought it would be better if I waited until he washed his mouth with soap for all the names he had called me when we were children. He came the laird over me then and ordered me to give him the bucket and get out, but I'm afraid I taunted him as I did years ago, saying I'd do it in my own good time. I forgot how long his arms are," she added ruefully.

"He grabbed you and pulled you into the tub," Molly said.

"Aye, just as you knocked at the door and dismayed us both. He said you were likely Patrick, since if Tam had given me that bucket, he'd know better than to show his face again anytime soon. I was terrified then, because I knew that Patrick would not like my being there at all, let alone with Fin in that tub."

Molly flung the skirt over Barbara's head. The young woman's skin was still damp, but there was no time to do much more about drying her.

"Could you also please lend me a fresh cap to cover my wet hair?" Barbara asked when Molly had hastily laced up the bodice and shaken out the skirt.

Molly did so, and if the result was not what either of them might have hoped, at least Barbara was presentable.

She sighed as Molly opened the door. "Patrick is going to be most annoyed."

"Well, I do think you should have realized that before you went into Kintail's chamber," Molly said with a smile. "Still, perhaps he will not notice."

"Patrick? You don't know him yet if you think that, mistress. Patrick takes more careful note of clothing than anyone else I know. Certainly more than Fin. I heard about Fin pushing him into the loch the day they brought you here. They say the only thing about it that dismayed Patrick was that he was wearing a pair of brand-new boots. He gave them to Tam, saying they were no longer fit to wear."

"Did he, indeed?"

"Aye. Fin might not notice a woman's gown, but I'd wager my finest silk bodice that Patrick will see in a twinkling that this dress is not mine."

Her guess proved right, but the result was not as bad as she had feared, for her brother only laughed when he saw her and hurried to give her a hug.

"You should have told me that you had arrived, Bab," he said, stepping back and cocking his head critically. "That dress doesn't suit you, and you've kept us waiting a devilish long time for our supper, but Fin told me what happened."

Both Molly and Barbara turned as one to look at Kintail, who was lounging at the table as though he had been waiting some time for them to arrive. The teasing look he sent Molly made her wish she had another pail of water.

"Aye," he said, grinning at Barbara, "and I confessed that it was my fault for splashing so much water about before you brought the rinse water in for me, and how you might have split your head on one of the stones when you slipped, had I not caught you. Still, I'm sorry I tumbled you into the tub, lass."

Had Molly not already heard Barbara's explanation, she might have believed him, so glibly did he offer his version. As it was, she regarded him speculatively, wondering if he always lied so easily.

He met her gaze with a bland look and suggested that they eat at once, so that his men could set up more benches for the next day's court. Afterward, however, when she and Barbara got up from the table, he got up, too, saying, "One moment, mistress, if you please."

Barbara paused beside her, and Molly was grateful, for she was certain she did not want to hear what Kintail had to say to her.

However, he dismissed the girl with a gesture, and when she hesitated, he said, "Don't tempt me, Bab. You have already compelled me to lie to Patrick—"

"Compelled you!" she exclaimed indignantly, but as she did, she shot a wary glance at her brother, still seated at the table.

"Aye," Kintail insisted, "and if you do not want me to tell him the truth straightaway, you had best run along. I want to speak privately to Mistress Gordon."

Grimacing expressively, Barbara stalked off, and Molly, still not wanting to hear what Kintail would say, said hastily, "You won't really betray her to her brother, will you, sir? It seems to me that you were far more at fault than she."

"Aye, I was," he admitted, "although if you hadn't knocked when you did, I'd have soon sent her about her business. You startled us both just as I'd grabbed her, though, and the result was that she slipped and I tumbled her into the tub. Had it been Patrick, as I'd thought, I'd have told him at once what had happened and he would have seen the humor. He might have scolded her for entering my chamber uninvited, but that would have been the end of it. I did not know how he would react to hearing the tale secondhand, however, especially considering your part in it, and I did not want him to take her to task over supper."

"So you lied to him," Molly said with a challenging look.

"I did," Kintail said, glancing ruefully toward Sir Patrick, "and I will have to own up to it soon, before we leave the hall."

"So you will tell him what happened," Molly said, feeling sorry for Barbara.

"I will, but I will also have the chance then to explain the whole business. Must I explain it to you, mistress? I ken well how it looked."

"You need explain nothing," Molly said. "Barbara told me how it was. She ought not to have gone into your chamber, though, any more than I should have."

"You did not know that it was my bedchamber, however. How came you there? If one of my men was playing tricks . . ."

"No," she said swiftly. "I believe his part in it was unintentional, and perhaps you will say that I ought to have known your chamber, but I did not."

"Why were you seeking me?"

"To ask if I might observe your court tomorrow," she replied.

"Surely you will have too much to do, with so many chores to attend on such a busy day."

"Mauri says I would be more hindrance than help to her," Molly muttered unhappily. "I was not raised to cook or clean, you see, so she has to show me."

He was silent for a moment, but although she expected him to lecture her about a woman's need to learn such skills, he said instead, "You told me at Dunakin that you do know how to do sums and such."

"Aye, I do."

"Then, perhaps I can arrange for you to do something that you'll enjoy more than cooking or cleaning. Patrick's father attended to the castle accounts, and since his death, Patrick and I have had to attend to them, but we have talked about training someone else. Do you think you could do them if we showed you how?"

"Aye, I could. You would really let me?"

"I would," he said. Then he rather spoiled her delight by adding, "We will have to check what you do, of course, but if you learn quickly and do not make too many mistakes, you could save us both a great deal of time."

"I'd like to do that," she said, "but will I not do a better job if I come to understand more about castle affairs?"

His eyes twinkled responsively. "I can see that you are determined to observe my court, lass, and since I have taken sufficient of your measure to know that you will find a way even if I forbid you—"

"I would," she said. "Mauri tells me there are laird's peeks aplenty, overlooking the hall. I have seen the one on the stairs, myself, so I could—"

"Would you so willingly accept your punishment for disobeying me?"

She hesitated, then cocked her head to one side and said, "Is it so horrid, then, what you do to the people who seek justice in your court?"

Grimacing, he glanced over his shoulder as though he suspected that even then someone might be watching. Then he said, "Justice is not always pleasant to witness, lass, but you may watch if you want. I warrant Bab has watched more than once if it occurred to her to, because I did and so did Patrick, before my father invited either of us to be present. She can sit with you if Mauri has no need of her."

He bade her good night then and turned away, but as she walked up the stairs to her bedchamber, she realized that once again, he had astonished her, and the thought warmed her. Perhaps life as his ward would not be so bad after all.

"That went well, I think," Catriona said as she nibbled Claud's ear. The pair of them sat in a stone niche near the stairway and had easily overheard the conversation between Kintail and Mistress Gordon.

"I dinna think they like each other much," Claud said.

"She poured water over him, did she not, when she found him with that Bab person?" Catriona snuggled closer. "That was clever of you, Claud, to think of sending your Maid in to find them together."

"But I didna do any such thing," Claud protested, trying to think—a process he found difficult even when Catriona was not putting her tongue in his ear. "I—I be more concerned about what I'll do when he chooses a husband for her."

"He must not give her to another," Catriona murmured, resting one slender hand on his thigh. "Her husband will get her treasure."

"But we canna stop that," Claud said reasonably. "In their world, a husband be entitled tae claim his wife's fortune."

"Then we must think, Claud dear." She slid her hand between his legs.

He gasped. "Och, Catriona, I canna think when ye do that!"

"Then we will do this first and think later."

Claud groaned, but he said nothing more about thinking.

Chapter 10 _____

Men and women began to arrive for Kintail's court early the next morning. They rowed across the water in small boats and larger ones, and several even poled across from Dornie village on a log raft. The hall was crowded and noisy.

Sir Patrick, looking like a lord in an elegant blue velvet doublet and black hose, informed Molly and Barbara when they arrived that Kintail had left orders to seat them near the rear.

Molly had hoped to sit as close to the proceedings as possible, but when she protested, Patrick said flatly, "I'm to put you out if you make a fuss, mistress. As for you, Bab," he added, turning to his sister, "you and I are going to have a serious talk before the day is done."

Neither protested any further. When they had taken the places he indicated and he had walked away, Barbara said, "I wonder what I have done now."

Realizing that she had gone straight to her bedchamber after speaking with Kintail the previous night and had not seen the younger girl again, Molly said, "I believe he knows now what really happened in Kintail's bedchamber."

"But how could he? Fin did not tell him yestereve. We know he did not."

Molly explained, adding, "Will your brother truly be angry, Barbara? Surely, he trusts Kintail not to have taken liberties with you."

The worried look disappeared when Barbara chuckled. "I would certainly call it a liberty to topple me into the bath with him."

"He told me that my knocking startled him, and at all events, you know what sort of liberties I meant," Molly said.

"Aye, but I doubt that Patrick would fully trust Fin near anyone wearing a skirt. The pair of them often got up to mischief together before our fathers were killed, and since nearly any woman in Kintail would gladly submit to either one of them, who knows what Patrick is thinking?"

Shocked, Molly said, "You cannot mean that Kintail would—"

"Oh, no," Barbara said, controlling her merriment with visible difficulty. "He would not, and hopefully, now that Patrick has had time to think about it, he will realize that Fin would never harm me, so I *am* glad that Fin did not tell him straightaway. Patrick's temper is like his, you see. They both flame up easily, and when either one is blazing away, it is best to leave at once—if one can do so."

"They had better not blaze at me, either of them," Molly said coolly.

Barbara looked at her in wonder. "Are you not afraid of a man's anger, then? They can be very fierce."

Molly shrugged, ignoring the chill that shot up her spine at the thought of Kintail being fierce. They had no more time to talk, however, for Sir Patrick had moved to the front of the hall. When he raised a hand, the assembly hushed. Feet shuffled, but the few lingering whispers were quickly silenced.

Sir Patrick said only, "The laird," and everyone arose as Kintail strode in and sat in the lone armchair on the dais where the high table generally sat.

Molly stared. She had thought that Sir Patrick looked splendid, but Kintail put him in the shade. Both men were dressed in the French fashion common to west Highland gentry on formal occasions, but Kintail wore red-and-black striped netherstocks. His upper stocks were slashed and banded with red satin, his elegant red doublet patterned to match. His black velvet cap sported the two eagle feathers proclaiming his rank as a Mackenzie chieftain. His attire was much more formal than anything else she had seen him wear, and she thought he looked magnificent.

Acting as baron's bailie, Sir Patrick demanded order and called the first case, a claim of simple assault filed by a Mackenzie against a Matheson.

Kintail listened to both sides, decided in favor of the Mackenzie, and ordered the Matheson to pay a fine of two merks and to keep the peace in the future.

"If you fail to obey me in that, Will Matheson," he added with a fierce look, "I'll think of a harsher penalty to remind you."

"Aye, laird, I'll mind ye," the young man said, nodding emphatically.

Molly had expected more interesting crimes, like murder or mayhem, and she wondered if Kintail always found in favor of the Mackenzies. She learned as the morning progressed that he did not, but the claims seemed petty, and she did not know the people involved, so she soon grew bored. She saw that Barbara shared her feelings, but she dared not suggest they leave. She had worked too hard to gain entry and feared that if she left, he would say that he had warned her what to expect and would forbid her attendance on future such occasions.

When his gaze met hers, she saw his lips twitch and detected a twinkle in his eyes. Did he know what she was thinking? She found herself watching him rather than heeding the cases presented to him, until one of two men standing before him said pleadingly, "Please laird, it were the fairies what did it."

Her interest piqued, as good-natured chuckles rippled through the hall.

Kintail, not amused, said curtly, "Explain yourself, Ranald MacVinish."

The second man protested, saying urgently, "Laird, it were Ranald himself that shot my cow, for I saw him do it, and I only had but the one."

"I know that," Kintail said. "Let him speak."

"But fairies, laird? Nae doubt he's lost his mind, but fairies, indeed!"

Spreading his hands, Ranald MacVinish said, "Aye, sure, but 'tis true, Ian MacMurchie." Turning back to Kintail, he said pleadingly, "I were walking home late at night after hauling a foundered sheep from a ditch when I heard a rush of air like some'un had flushed a hundred birds. 'Twere the Host passing by, laird, and they swept me right up off me feet."

A mixture of gasps and chuckles greeted this tale, but Molly listened avidly now to every word.

"Aye, there's a tale," his accuser said scornfully. "'Tis like I said afore, Ranald. Yon fairies must ha' dropped ye on your head."

More laughter rippled through the audience.

"Aye, ye laugh now," Ranald MacVinish said, clearing his throat nervously.

Even from the rear of the hall, Molly could see that he had gone pale and that sweat beaded on his forehead.

He went on grimly, "I trow ye'll alter your thinking, man,

when I tell ye your daughter Anna were milking that cow when we passed overhead. The Host ordered me to shoot her, but when they put me down, I shot the cow instead, for it be well known that so long as an animal be killed, the command o' the Host be fulfilled. Ye should be glad 'twas your cow and no your daughter, ye sniveling ingrate."

His accuser was silent, and Molly thought he looked taken aback.

Kintail said harshly, "You do admit to shooting the cow, do you not, Ranald?"

"Aye, laird, but it happened the way I said."

"You will pay Ian MacMurchie for his cow. Have you the means to do so?"

The man's face fell, but he did not argue further, saying only, "I ha' but the four sheep, seven bit chickens, and a dog, laird."

"I canna milk one o' your wretched sheep, Ranald," Ian MacMurchie said.

"It is a fair price, however," Kintail said. "I will take one of your sheep, Ranald, and I will give Ian MacMurchie a milk cow. Is it time to eat yet, Patrick?"

"Aye, laird, they've been waiting to bring in the food this quarter hour past."

Nodding, Kintail announced that the court would resume after dinner. When he stood, everyone else in the hall stood as well, and when he left, the men set up trestles at right angles to the dais, where they replaced the high table. In a short time, Mauri MacRae's numerous helpers were setting out food.

Everyone sat down together at the long tables, sinners and sinned against, and as far as Molly could tell, no one seemed to mind in the least.

Seated between Barbara and Kintail, she surveyed the assembled company, trying to think of a graceful way to excuse herself from the afternoon proceedings, when a clamor at the entrance heralded new arrivals.

At least three men-at-arms accompanied them, and heads craned to be sure the newcomers were friend and not foe.

A Mackenzie man near the entrance took it upon himself to act as Kintail's porter, announcing in stentorian tones, " 'Tis Mackinnon o' Dunakin, laird."

"Enter and welcome, sir," Kintail said, standing to welcome the older man.

Mackinnon strode forward, leaving his men at the entrance.

Molly smiled at her foster father, but although he smiled back, she detected lines of worry etched into his grizzled face. His lady apparently was not with him.

Conversation faded into silence as the diners watched him, and she knew that she was not the only one to read warning in his grim expression.

"Will you dine, sir?" Kintail said, reaching to shake Mackinnon's hand.

"Nay, lad," the older man replied, bending to kiss Molly's cheek. "You're looking well, lass. This place seems to agree wi' ye."

"Thank you, sir," Molly said, but his attention had shifted back to Kintail.

In a gruff undertone, Mackinnon said, "We must talk, lad, and straightaway."

Kintail nodded and turned to Sir Patrick. "You can begin the afternoon session. Get Tam Matheson to act as your bailie. I've a notion this business with Mackinnon will take more than a few minutes."

Mackinnon nodded. "That it will, lad. We ha' some serious planning t' do."

"Come with me, then," Kintail said.

Sensing that what they would discuss concerned her, Molly said, "What is it, sir? What has happened?"

Mackinnon turned toward her as if to speak, but Kintail said curtly, "If you require to know, mistress, be sure that we will inform you in good time. You are not to attend the afternoon session, however. When I want you, I will send for you."

Her temper stirred, but knowing that it would be foolhardy to defy him in front of so many people, she held her peace.

A tall, lanky young man, whom she assumed to be the same Tam Matheson who had acquired Sir Patrick's wet boots and who had given the bucket of water to Barbara, announced that the session would begin as soon as the trestles were dismantled. Men got up at once to deal with that task.

Barbara said, "If we are not to attend the session, then I had better see what chores my mother and Mauri have kept waiting for me. Will you come with me?"

"No, thank you," Molly said. It had occurred to her that with all the men occupied in the hall and the women busy elsewhere, the opportunity was excellent for a walk outside. She had had scant time to examine the islet since her arrival.

Not wanting to take the chance that one of the men-at-arms at the entrance might take it upon himself to forbid her going outside, she went instead to a postern door at the foot of the northwest tower that she had discovered upon taking a wrong turning the second day of her stay. In moments, she stepped out into the sunlight.

"What is it, sir?" Fin asked as he shut the door to the little office into which he had shown his guest.

Tersely, Mackinnon said, "Donald kens where the Maid is, and he means t' stir trouble wi' ye."

"I expected as much," Fin said, but the information hit harder than he had imagined it would. He was not ready to relinquish the Maid to Donald of Sleat.

Gesturing toward the single chair in the chamber, he took a stool for himself and leaned against the stone wall between his worktable and the olivewood stand that held his iron-bound desk box. "She will be safe enough here. Eilean Donan is impregnable to attack without cannon. The last I heard, Sleat had none."

"True," Mackinnon admitted, "but the man be gey dangerous all the same, lad. He ha' decided t' take the Maid back, and he says he'll do what he must t' get her. He ha' gathered an army, ye ken, and his galleys be many and swift."

"You have talked with him," Fin said.

"Aye, and the sour-natured devil threatened me," Mackinnon said, grimacing. "Says he meant t' offer our Molly t' Huntly in exchange for Huntly's promise no to interfere in his attempt t' reclaim the Lordship of the Isles. Now, Donald says, he has naught t' offer Huntly and Huntly will side wi' the King."

"Aye, he will, as I will," Fin said.

"Donald believes his cause is just," Mackinnon said. "And 'tis true that they carried off the last Lord o' the Isles when he were but a bairn. I dinna hold wi' abducting children," he added with a speaking look.

Fin raised his eyebrows. "You would compare the Crown's annexation of the Lordship of the Isles to Angus's abduction of the Maid of Dunsithe?"

"Aye, and why not? Just as the Crown gave Macdonald land to its cronies ha' Jamie passed our Molly about like a prize at an apple-bobbing."

Controlling his annoyance with effort, Fin said, "If you have come seeking my support for Donald of Sleat, you have come in vain, sir. I would remind you that the man killed my father and many of our people."

"Whisst, lad, 'tis Molly I care about. I want only t' remind ye what Donald believes and mayhap t' offer ye another lesson in the fine art o' chess."

"I do not doubt that Sleat has persuaded himself of his rights," Fin said, "but he will find it hard to rally other clans in the name of a defunct title."

"The Macdonalds number in the thousands, lad. Moreover, he's threatened t' move against MacLeod and me if we dinna help him reclaim the Maid, and he's as good as promised to attack Eilean Donan and all of Kintail to get her. Only if ye can reduce the value o' the prize that draws him might ye prevent true disaster."

"I'll do what I must to protect Eilean Donan and my tenantry," Fin said. "The castle cannot support the entire population of Kintail through a determined siege, so Sleat will wreak havoc if we cannot stop him."

"Aye, I ken that fine," Mackinnon said. "We canna raise an army t' match his in a twinkling, but ye're bound t' discourage him if ye wed Molly straightaway."

Fin inhaled deeply, not trusting himself to speak. To tell Mackinnon that if he suggested marriage to Molly, she was more likely to murder him than to submit willingly did not seem to be the most sensible course. Nor did he think it wise to admit to Mackinnon or to anyone else that the thought of wedding and bedding Molly tempted him more than he would have believed possible a sennight before.

Mackinnon's eyes twinkled. "I ken how it is, lad. Dinna think I do not. I ha' lived wi' the lass for nigh onto a dozen years, ye ken, and I took her measure long since. Still, ye can manage her, and ye've the royal writ t' support ye."

"My marrying her would make no difference to Sleat," Fin said more curtly than he had intended. In a more reasonable tone, he added, "He would simply declare the marriage null and do as he pleases with her. I'm told he expected to marry her to that whelp of his, although she'd have eaten the brat alive."

"Aye, she would that," Mackinnon said with a fond smile. "But I'd as lief keep her out o' Donald's clutches, and ye be forgetting Huntly. Recall that 'tis Donald's hope t' use the lass as a bargaining piece."

"Huntly is a clan chief," Fin reminded him. "He also can declare any marriage null and void and then marry her where he chooses."

"Aye, that would be true most places in the Highlands, but ye forget that Huntly be a devout Papist. Ye ha' a priest o' your own in Kintail, d'ye not?"

"I do," Fin said, seeing where the older man's thoughts had taken him. "You think that if I were to marry her in a proper, priestly ceremony, Huntly would support the marriage and refuse Sleat's offer."

"Aye, and dinna forget that presently, at least, Huntly supports Jamie."

Fin said, "Then he won't want to go against Jamie's writ. There is no need for me to marry her."

"Ye make it sound like a penance, lad. D'ye ken how much land the lass will bring ye? Even an ye never find her treasure, Dunsithe alone be worth a marriage."

"But I'd have to secure it, which is no easy task at such a distance," Fin pointed out. "In any event, it is too soon to think of marrying her, and 'tis my belief that she'd be unwilling. So, if Huntly is likely to refuse Sleat's offer—"

"Sakes, I didna say he would refuse it, only that he would refuse to undo a Papist marriage t' seize the lass and her fortune. The point o' marrying her, I'd remind ye, is t' make it less desirable for Donald t' snatch her from ye. He's smart enough t' see that Huntly would be loath t' anger both the Pope and the King."

"Almost do you persuade me, sir."

"Think carefully on it," Mackinnon advised. "Donald will want t' gather his forces afore he attacks such a stronghold, so ye've some time, but no verra much."

"She won't like this," Fin said, wondering how much he would like it himself. He was undeniably attracted to the lass. She had only to enter a room for his body to respond to her. Even now, the thought of taking her to his bed argued more strongly in favor of exercising his right to marry her than anything Mackinnon had suggested, persuasive though that gentleman's arguments were.

Still, he had done little to tame the lass, so heaven alone knew to what lengths she would go to prevent the marriage or, if he were successful in hailing her before his priest, what she would do to retaliate.

Molly had found a comfortable seat on a rocky outcropping conveniently shaped like a chair, where she settled to enjoy her solitude. The only thing that would have pleased her more would have been riding her horse at Dunakin, or anywhere—galloping full out with her hair loose and streaming behind her.

As it was, the wind blew softly from the west, and the air held a fresh salty tang, a pleasant change from the crowded hall with its odor of too many unwashed bodies. Gulls and curlews soared and darted overhead, their cries contrasting likewise to the buzz of human conversation she had left inside. Solitude was heady stuff if one chose it rather than having it thrust upon one.

Thanks to the wind, the day was clear, and away to the west she could see the shadowy, humped shape of Skye. Her thoughts rambled idly, and although they lingered frequently on Kintail, they turned to Mackinnon more than once, and to the reason for his unexpected visit.

That Lady Mackinnon had not come with him made it clear from the outset that his visit was not social. It did not take much imagination to decide that its most likely cause was that Donald the Grim knew that she had left Dunakin and where she was now.

She wondered if Mackinnon himself had informed Donald and knew that for him to have done so would not be against his nature. One reason he had been able to maintain the uneasy peace with MacLeod and Donald was his honesty, a trait that both of his fellow leaders admired in him even if neither saw fit to adopt it.

"What the devil are you doing out here?"

Sighing, realizing that she had lost track of time and had been just staring at the water and listening to the birds and the wind, and to the waves lapping against the shore, she turned reluctantly to face Kintail.

"It is peaceful out here," she said.

He loomed over her, and she realized that the sounds that had fascinated her had deadened any noise behind her. She had not heard the postern door open or shut, nor had she heard his footsteps approaching over the rocks.

Although he looked angry, he did not speak at once but drew a deep breath instead, as though to curb his temper. That frightened her more than a fit of pique, for it warned her that he thought what he was about to tell her would upset her.

"Is it her ladyship?" she demanded, scrambling hastily to

her feet. "Has something happened to her? Don't stand gaping at me, Kintail! Tell me!"

"Peace, lass, it is nothing like that."

"Then why do you hesitate to speak?"

"Because I am tempted to shout at you," he retorted, his voice louder than before. "Do you not realize how dangerous it is for you out here?"

"I'm not going to be swept into the sea by a few waves spitting against the shore," she said. "The water is calm today."

"A sensible person does not heed only the sea at Eilean Donan," he said, still controlling his temper with visible effort. "Do you not see how near we are to the shore yonder? A skilled archer with a longbow—"

"He would have to be skilled," she said, eyeing the distance, "and his bow would have to be stout."

"Patrick could do it," he said bluntly. "He has done it. More to the purpose, however, I have done it, and I am not as skilled with a bow as Patrick is."

"Aye, perhaps," she said, nodding, knowing that in truth a man of moderate skill could accomplish such a feat. "Still, I doubt that you'd do much damage to a target—if, indeed, you actually hit one. The wind being what it is presently—"

"Enough," Kintail growled, glancing around. "I did not come out here to debate archery with you. I told you that you are not to leave the castle without my permission. I doubt that you can have forgotten that order so quickly."

"Nay, I did not forget," she said, eyeing him warily, "but you told me only that I could not leave Eilean Donan without permission. That is the islet, is it not?"

She could almost hear his teeth grind. Standing as he was on a small rise, he towered over her, and she knew that he was strong enough to pick her up with one hand if he chose to do so. It was perhaps as well that he did not know she could swim. By the look of him, he might have been tempted to fling her into the water, as he had Patrick, and it was still icy cold at this time of year.

When he did not speak and seemed still to be struggling with his temper, she attempted a diversionary tactic. "How did you chance to find me?"

"Chance had nothing to do with it," he retorted. "I do not leave the castle unguarded, lass, least of all when so many are gathered here. Watchmen stand above on the battlements, and one sent a lad to tell me when you came out here. Had I not been closeted with Mackinnon, I'd have come for you sooner."

"Why did he come? Has Donald learned that you brought me here?"

"Aye, and Mackinnon says the scoundrel's in a foul temper over it. Apparently, Sleat hoped to use you to barter with your cousin."

"My cousin? What cousin?"

"Huntly."

"He can scarcely know who I am," Molly said, wrinkling her nose. "My father was indeed his cousin, but I doubt Huntly's ever clapped eyes on me."

"Nonetheless, Sleat believes that if he can present you to him, Huntly will agree not to take up arms to fight his claim to the Lordship of the Isles. To that end, Mackinnon thinks Sleat means to attack Kintail."

"But he could not take Eilean Donan!"

He eyed her speculatively for a moment and then said, "You need not worry, mistress. Most men believe that a single man, woman, or child could defend this castle. You are quite safe here."

"I doubt that I'd feel safe with only one other to defend me, but you'd never leave Eilean Donan to be defended so," she said, certain that she already knew him that well, at least.

He sighed. "Believe me, lass, there are moments when I might cheerfully *say* that I'd leave you to look after yourself, but you're right about Eilean Donan. If I truly had control of that fortune of yours, the first thing I'd do is build a defensive hornwork here, and then I'd do similar things elsewhere to defend Kintail."

"So you are just like all the others and care only about my fortune," she said, surprised by the strength of her disappointment. "I should have known, for that is all anyone has ever cared about."

"That would not matter now, even if it were true," he retorted. "What I care about now is your safety and that of my people. And, as to that—"

"I'm going inside if only to stop you from barking at me any more," she said.

"But—"

"Men's words are nonsense, mostly. 'Tis their actions that speak the truth."

It hurt more to hear him speak so casually about acquiring her fortune than it had to hear him speak lightly about leaving her to defend herself. Then, she had known he was goading her, but accustomed though she was to her fortune being the primary reason men paid her heed, she did not want Fin Mackenzie to be like the others, and certainly not to say as much to her face. He stood too close to her, in any event. Her skin tingled. She needed distance.

When she turned toward the castle, he stopped her. "Wait," he said. His warmth burned through her clothing where his hand grasped her shoulder.

She stopped and let him turn her to face him, but she avoided his gaze even when his warm fingers cupped her chin, gently tilting her face up.

"Molly, look at me."

His tone was persuasive, compelling, and every nerve in her body shouted at her to do whatever he asked. But she kept her eyes downcast, resisting, certain that he expected submission and would take full advantage of it if she relented. Moreover, to give in so easily would render her vulnerable in other ways. If she let herself care, if she set even tentative roots at Eilean Donan, then leaving would be that much harder to bear when he found it expedient to give her to another man.

When his lips touched hers, shock swept through her like a firestorm. The hand on her shoulder slipped down to her waist, and the one holding her chin moved to caress her right arm, his thumb brushing against the side of her breast. She stiffened at the desire his touch aroused in her, and her eyes flew open.

With a teasing smile and a swift glance around as if he expected someone to see him and object, he murmured close to her lips, "I have wanted to kiss you since the night I first saw you."

Fighting the feelings he stirred in her, she pulled back, saying tartly, "So you still regret that you did not take me to your bed that night. Well, you will never do so, sir. Good day to you!" Turning sharply, she wanted to rub her burning lips, but she would not give him the satisfaction of knowing that he had affected her so.

"Nay, lass, wait!" He caught her arm again. "I should not have— Pray, do not go in yet. There is something else I must tell you . . . that is, something that I should discuss with you," he amended hastily. Glancing around again, he added, "I keep feeling as if someone were watching us. Perhaps we should go in."

"What can you possibly want to discuss with me?"

A shout from the slope drew their attention to Mackinnon's hurried approach. As Molly waved to him, she heard Kintail swear under his breath.

"Did ye tell her yet?" Mackinnon said as he hurried down to them. "What did she say?"

"Tell me what?" Molly demanded, turning to Kintail.

To her surprise, his face reddened and for the first time since they had met, he seemed reluctant to look her in the eye.

Mackinnon caught her in a fierce hug, saying heartily, "Well, lass, is it t' be your wedding or his funeral that I'll be helping ye t' organize?"

Shooting Kintail a gimlet look, she said grimly, "What is he talking about?"

"This is not how I meant to bring up the subject," he said ruefully.

"Ye didna tell her yet?" Mackinnon clapped a hand to his head. "I'd never ha' taken ye for a coward, Kintail, and that be plain fact." Grinning at Molly, he said, "The man's decided that he must marry ye t' protect ye from Donald, lass. And a fine notion it is, too. I say that the quicker ye're wed, the better!"

"Not unless he'd enjoy a corpse for a bride," Molly snapped, adding as she moved toward the castle, "because I'd be dead first!"

Mackinnon stepped out of her way, but Kintail did not.

"Wait, lass," he muttered, reaching for her.

Dashing his hand aside, she swept past him, head high, practically daring him to lay a hand on her again, only to feel disappointed when he did not. Telling herself that she had just hoped he would give her an excuse to slap him, she continued miserably to the postern door and inside.

"Now, that did *not* go well," Catriona said, watching Molly's stormy departure through narrowed eyes. She and Claud sat side by side on a bit of rock near Molly's natural chair.

"Dinna be vexed, lass," he said. "I told ye they dinna fancy each other."

"What matters what they think of each other?" she replied lazily. "My laird requires your lady's fortune, and she requires only firm management. Think, Claud! Can you not *make* her care more for him?"

"Ye ken fine that I canna do any such thing," Claud said. "Nae more can ye, unless ye o' the Highlands ha' more power than we do. And sakes, lass, I be in enough trouble already, wi'out doing what I've nae business doing."

She pouted. "I just want what is best for my laird, Claud."

"Aye sure, lassie, I ken fine what ye want."

"Moreover, my clever one, if they should marry, both of us will have done our duty, for you will have provided your Maid with a husband and I will have provided my laird with a proper fortune. Even the nay-sayers in the Circle will see then that making the King give her to Kintail was an excellent notion."

"Aye, perhaps," Claud said. But recalling the Maid's anger, he wondered if anyone wielded enough power to change her opinion of Kintail.

He soon forgot about her, however, when Catriona diverted his thoughts in her own special way.

Nell Percy was bored and growing frustrated, fearing that all her careful planning might come to naught.

The company in the hall at Stirling was lively and loud

that evening, and since Nell hoped to draw James's attention again, she was exerting unnatural patience. That patience was weakening rapidly, however, due to the annoyingly talkative matron she had met her first night at Stirling.

Surreptitiously watching the woman's two homely, silent daughters while attempting to listen to the mother, it occurred to her that the girls' silence was due to nothing more than knowing they could not get a word in if they tried.

With bright enthusiasm, their aggravating mother said, "It is such a pleasure at last to be able to converse at length with you, Lady Percy."

"So you have said, madam," Nell replied, but the woman was still talking and barely acknowledged Nell's words with a gesture as she babbled on.

"Your so charming brother Angus—so dreadful your being separated from him, madam, although I must own that I do not comprehend what all the fuss was about or why he has stayed in England all these years. In sooth, I believe his grace the King is jealous of the Douglas power."

She tittered behind one hand as she added, "I know I should not say so in such a place as this—the King's own palace, and myself but a royal guest—but then, no man ever expects us poor females to understand these things, and I am not a Douglas by birth, thank heaven! One can only wonder at your nerve, madam, coming here so soon after your poor half sister's unfortunate demise at the stake. My husband, who claims a slight connection, said he is persuaded that Janet Douglas had no acquaintance with the powers of darkness or with poison and that her husbands both died quite natural deaths. Her misfortune, Sir Hector said, was merely that she was a Douglas who had chanced to displease the King."

"You say your husband is a Douglas, madam?"

"Well, not to say a Douglas, exactly," the woman replied,

apparently deciding that this query was worth heeding. "Sir Hector could claim cousins with your uncle of Kilspindie if he chose, but thankfully, under present circumstances, the connection is slight—through his mother, you see. Our Elspeth is more closely connected of course," she added with a sly look, "but no one heeds a maidservant's antecedents even in these days of unrest. I should not rattle on, though, when doubtless the less you hear about Elspeth, the happier you will be. She was not as fortunate as you, or course, her mother being of common stock, whilst yours was well born. Although," she added thoughtfully, "in view of your half sister's dire misfortune, perhaps you do not view the circumstance of your birth as unhappy. At all events, I am persuaded that Elspeth is happier with us than she would be if her father had taken her with him to serve in his English household."

Nell's attention had wandered, but this statement reclaimed it, and noting the birdlike look of expectation on her companion's plump face, she decided that the woman had intended to pique her interest.

Gently, she said, "You need not mince words, madam. Do you suggest that a maidservant of yours is Angus's natural child?"

"I suggest nothing, madam. I speak plain fact. Our little scullery maid is your own niece, left with Sir Hector and me when your brother fled to England. Angus promised to send money for us to pay for her wages when she was old enough to earn wages, and he did—but, sadly, only for a short time. Since then, we have borne the cost, but perhaps my meeting you here is a sign of heavenly intervention. Perhaps you might see your way to . . ." She paused, showing delicacy for the first time since Nell had met her.

Nell's patience, however, was spent. She let the pause lengthen until the other woman fidgeted and looked as if she might speak again, perhaps to rephrase her suggestion in less spiteful terms.

Without giving her a chance to do so, Nell said in a chilly voice, "I am sorry to disappoint you, madam, but Angus's sexual accidents are not my concern. If you want something from him, you must tell him yourself. Doubtless one of your people is brave enough to risk carrying your message to England where he can easily learn Angus's whereabouts. Whether Angus will deign to respond, I cannot say."

"Pray, Lady Percy—"

But Nell cut her off, saying frostily, "Forgive me, but I see his grace the King beckoning to me."

James was doing no such thing, but when she strode toward him, he looked up and smiled. Taking the smile for an invitation, she approached, albeit slowing her angry pace to one of greater decorum.

"Good evening, sire," she said, curtsying low.

"Faith, but you are just what I need this evening, madam," he said with a grin. "These men have been boring me witless with tales of Donald the Grim—his damnable great army and his more damnable fleet of galleys. I want pleasuring instead, see you, and what with the Queen being at Linlithgow and sundry others of my wom—" He broke off, chuckling, and looked around as if to be sure that any courtiers who had heard him were joining in his mirth.

They were, and Nell discovered that she was still capable of blushing. To divert him, she said, "Is Donald of Sleat behaving badly, sire?"

"Aye, he is," James said, his tone turning gruff. "The traitor has threatened to raise the entire Highland west against me."

One of the courtiers hovering at James's side said condescendingly, " 'Tis said that Sleat can command as many as fifteen thousand broadswords and over a hundred galleys.

He may soon be marching south with his fleet escorting him."

"You are too solemn," the King said grumpily to the man. "Mackenzie of Kintail and others who remain loyal will halt this Sleat."

He shot an enigmatic look at Nell, but she was at a loss to interpret it, for besides looking annoyed, he looked rueful. Unable to imagine an appropriate way to respond, she remained silent, hoping the men would continue to discuss Donald. Even if he were no longer Molly's guardian, she had to learn where he was now and where she might find him later.

The other men seemed happy to discuss Donald's forthcoming rising, but James, looking more and more uncomfortable, suddenly stood, silencing them all.

"Come, madam, I have had a surfeit of politics for one day. Surely you can think of something better calculated to amuse your king."

"Willingly, sire," she said, resting her hand on the forearm he offered her and allowing him to lead her from the hall.

He took her to his private chamber, and conversation lapsed for some time while he enjoyed his fill of her. Not until he lay back against the pillows, sated, did he say, "There is something you should know about your daughter."

"You told me she is no longer ward to Donald the Grim. Where is she, sire?"

"Aye, that's the rub, and I fear you will be wroth with me. You will perhaps recall my mentioning Mackenzie of Kintail earlier."

"Aye, sire, I remember. One of your loyal Highlanders."

"Kintail is the Maid's new guardian. If Sleat passes through Kintail on his way south, as we expect, she sits directly in his path. You can be sure he wants her back or, at the least, that he wants to punish Kintail for taking her from him."

"But was it not you who warded her to Kintail?" Nell asked, turning this new information over in her mind in an attempt to see how it could aid her.

"I did. My intent was to bolster Kintail's loyalty by giving him control of an excellent Border estate and of the lass's fortune if he can find it."

"I'll wager you also desired to punish Donald," Nell said dryly. "My daughter is still a pawn to be pushed about at will by whoever controls her."

James shrugged. "She and others of her ilk have always served so, madam, as you know from your own experience. Increasing one's power requires position, wealth, and above all, connections to others of like and greater power."

He was telling Nell nothing she did not know. "I would see my daughter, sire," she said. "Mayhap, if you permit, I can be of use to you."

"How so?"

"With Donald's army running rampant in the western Highlands, you might benefit from a safe means of communicating with this Mackenzie. I could take him a message from you and see my daughter, as well. Who would dare harm a lady of rank traveling with an armed escort?"

"Royal messengers do risk interception," James admitted. "Indeed, I sent word to Mackenzie a fortnight ago, when I first learned of Sleat's increased activity. I've received no message in return."

Nell's eavesdropping had told her as much. She waited.

"I will consider your offer," James said at last. "But, madam, do not think to fool your king. I have not forgotten that you are Angus's sister or that you entered Scotland from England without first seeking my permission to do so. Also, it has been suggested that Henry of England may be sup-

porting this madness of Sleat's. If I find you have more reason for your journey than a mother's natural wish to see her
daughter, you will rue the day that you came to Stirling."

A shiver shot up Nell's spine, but she looked him in the
eye and smiled as she said, "I assure you, sire, I am only a
mother in search of her long-lost child."

Chapter 11 —————————————

When Molly left Kintail and Mackinnon so abruptly on the shore, she had expected Kintail to follow her inside or to send a gilly with a command to present herself to him for further discussion, but he did neither. Instead, he returned to take command of his baron's court, and for the next few days she saw little of him. Since Barbara, her mother, and Mackinnon departed along with the many who had attended the court, and since Maggie Malloch had not put in another appearance, she had no one except Doreen or Mauri with whom to discuss his irritating behavior.

Throughout her childhood, she had confided in Doreen, but the habit had waned even before leaving Dunakin. To discuss Kintail with her at all seemed wrong, let alone to reveal that he had kissed her. Nor was she tempted to speak about anything so personal with Mauri, whom she scarcely knew.

Oddly, the temptation was greater to confide in Sir Patrick—if only a little—when he introduced her to Eilean Donan's account books the day after Kintail's court. However, although Patrick behaved in his usual charming, cheerful way, she recalled his behavior that first night when

Kintail had wanted to bed her, and she knew she could not speak frankly to him, either. His demeanor was unexceptionable as he explained how the accounts were organized and showed her how to enter MacVinish's sheep and the cow sent to Ian MacMurchie, but she was glad he did not seem disposed to chat. Soon she was engulfed in household details, but by the lesson's end, she knew nothing more of any consequence about Kintail.

She did learn that he and Sir Patrick spent most mornings hunting or hawking and most afternoons dealing with tenants' problems and attending to other duties of landownership. She also learned from Mauri that Kintail had sent out running gillies to see what they could learn about Donald the Grim's movements, but what those gillies reported to him on their return, she knew not.

Thus, when Sir Patrick came to her in Mauri's solar the fourth day after Mackinnon's visit to tell her that Kintail wanted to see her, Molly felt both eager to confront him and wary of what he might say or do to her.

"Where is he?" she asked Patrick, setting aside the needlework with which she had been pretending to occupy herself while she waited for Mauri to join her.

"Below, in the hall," he said.

That did not sound as if Kintail intended to pick a quarrel, she decided, for surely he would have chosen a more private place. Nevertheless, she felt increasing tension when she entered the hall and saw him standing near the fireplace, talking with one of his men. The banners overhead stirred in the ever-present draft, but the fire, for once, was small. The days were growing warmer.

Kintail's stern gaze met hers. He dismissed the man with him but did not move, waiting for her to approach him, regarding her speculatively, as if he were judging her mood. He did not look as if he intended to kiss her again.

Thinking about that kiss sent a surge of heat through her. She had to exert herself to sound dignified as she said, "You sent for me?"

"Did you doubt Patrick's word when he told you I had?"

Ignoring what was obvious provocation, she said, "I hope you do not mean to press me again to marry you, for I have not changed my mind."

He smiled and shook his head. "I won't beg you, lass, now or ever. If I decide that we'll marry, then marry we will. I am lord here, in all things. I even beat Mackinnon at chess the night he stayed here," he added with satisfaction.

"I'm surprised to hear that," she admitted. "I have never known him to lose, but even so, you are not lord of the world, sir. You may have the power of pit and gallows in Kintail, but I believe that even here you do not rule the Kirk. Micheil Love told me long ago that in Scotland a woman has the right to refuse marriage if the proposed union does not suit her."

Kintail shrugged. "Scotland has many laws, lass, but Edinburgh and Stirling are far from Eilean Donan. To whom will you make your complaint?"

"The priest—"

"—is my priest," he interjected. "He depends upon me and my people of Kintail for his food and shelter, and therefore, he will not deny me what I want. His wife and children would suffer."

"He should not have a wife, let alone children," she snapped. "Priests are suppose to be celibate."

"You see," he said, as though she had proven his point for him. "As I told you, we are far from Edinburgh and Stirling, farther yet from Rome and the Pope. Now, do you want to know why I sent for you or not?"

"Only if you do not mean to take more liberties and if we need not discuss marriage again."

"Would such a marriage be so distasteful to you?"

To her surprise, she detected a wistful note in his voice as he asked the question, and she could not make herself reply with a flat negative. Instead, she said, "I have scarcely seen you for days. Why did you send for me now?"

"Did you miss me?" His eyes twinkled. "You should be glad I gave my temper time to cool before sending for you. Had I followed my inclination when you left Mackinnon and me the other day, I'd have made you regret your rudeness."

She could think of nothing to say. Remembering her disappointment when he let her go so easily, she felt flames in her cheeks, but she did not understand herself or her feelings where Kintail was concerned, and she could not read him at all. The twinkle in his eyes said he was not angry with her, but the reminder that she had given him cause to be made it hard to feel confident or to know how to deal with him. After a long moment, she forced herself to meet his gaze.

"Why did you send for me?"

"I thought you might be missing your horses," he said gently.

Delight instantly replaced bewilderment. "You will let me ride?"

"I will take you riding," he amended. "You are not to go out alone, mistress. Not now, not ever. If you do, you will not sit a horse again for three full months. Do you understand me?"

Striving to conceal her annoyance at what sounded like intentional provocation, she said, "I am accustomed to having an escort, sir."

"Perhaps, on occasion," he said. "But it strikes me that you also are far too accustomed to going your own road without consulting anyone. That must stop. On Skye, where everyone knew you, things were different from the way they are here, particularly with Sleat on the loose."

"Where is he, then? I collect that he is not presently in Kintail."

To her relief, he did not press his point but accepted the new subject. "I'm told he is still sailing amongst the Isles, gathering men," he said, "but soon he'll move south, and the easiest route for his army lies through Kintail and Glen Shiel. This may be our only chance for some time to ride safely. Will you come?"

Delight at the thought of riding overcame any momentary annoyance with him. Nodding, she followed him down to the inlet where his boats lay. Fluffy clouds floated in a sunny blue sky, and a soft, light breeze blew from the northwest.

Commanding her to get into the stern of a small rowboat beached on the shingle, Kintail pushed off, jumping into the craft as it slid into the water and deftly taking up the oars.

Surprised that he had not commanded one of his men to do the rowing, she watched him, noting that he managed easily and with skill.

"I can sail, too," he said. "I am no carpet knight."

She smiled, seeing no reason to tell him that she had never taken him for one. Instead, she watched to see what she could learn from him and to enjoy the play of his muscles as he rowed. When their eyes chanced to meet, she blinked and forced herself to concentrate on studying his technique with the oars. She could row a little, too, but one was wise to seek always to improve one's skills.

The journey to the Dornie shore was brief, and in what seemed to be no time at all, they walked to the place where Kintail kept his horses. To Molly's astonishment, the horse that the gilly led out for her was her own bay gelding from

Dunakin. Happily, she stroked the soft, white blaze on the horse's face.

"Mackinnon thought you might be happy to see this fellow," Kintail said, patting the bay on the neck and holding out a lump of sugar for it on his palm.

"Mackinnon brought him over?"

"Aye?"

"Four days ago!"

"Aye." He said nothing more, watching her.

"Why did you not tell me?"

"The opportunity did not arise," he said glibly, but she knew it was more than that. He had meant to punish her.

"Are we going to ride?" she asked, to break the sudden tension.

"Aye."

Without further ado, he gripped her firmly round the waist and lifted her to the saddle.

As she arranged her skirts, she said, "I am glad to see him, sir. Thank you."

"You need not thank me," he said, adding with a straight look, "I am pleased to find that you are capable of gratitude, however."

She bit her lip, knowing that she deserved the censure but disliking it nonetheless. He moved without further comment to the big gray he would ride.

When he had mounted, she noted that four of his men had mounted horses, too. Since they were armed, and since Kintail did not seem the sort of man who would insist upon always having his proper chieftain's tail in attendance, she concluded that he had not exaggerated their danger, even now.

Once they rode out of the yard, however, she forgot everything except the agreeable caress of the breeze on her face and the familiar smells and sounds of riding in the open air. She was content to let Kintail take the lead and set the pace, happy to be doing what she loved. A niggling little voice at the back of her mind suggested that she was also happy to be riding with Kintail, but she ignored it, and when the same niggling voice suggested that marriage to him might provide many such pleasant moments, she ignored that, too.

He led the way through Dornie village, pausing every few feet to speak to a villager and to introduce her, and Molly's impatience soon stirred. She wanted to ride. They left the village at last, and she was glad when he let the horses stretch their legs. However, it was not long before he drew rein again in a cottage yard.

Before she could protest at yet more delay, the cottager emerged with a pair of barking dogs and a wobbly toddler, so she found herself smiling instead, acknowledging Kintail's introduction and the cottager's polite welcome. Soon the man's wife and other children joined them to receive their share of attention.

After this scene had repeated itself several times, Molly rebelled, saying, "Do you mean to introduce the whole of Kintail to me in one day, sir?"

"If necessary," he said. "Mauri packed a dinner for us if we get hungry."

"But why should it be necessary? Surely I need not meet everyone at once."

"I thought you should meet the people who will find themselves in Sleat's path when he comes to collect you," he said, giving her a direct look.

She glared at him, trying to repress the gory picture his words flashed before her mind's eye. "That sounds as if you *want* me to marry you, Kintail, and I *know* that cannot be the case."

"I have a duty to protect you," he retorted. "Moreover, I

have a duty to marry suitably and produce an heir, for the sake of my tenants, and Mackinnon makes a persuasive argument for *our* marriage when he says that Sleat will likely lose interest when he learns that he cannot control you or your fortune."

"Persuasive only because it points out that *you* will then control my fortune," she snapped back, anger making her speak louder than she had intended.

He glanced over his shoulder, then signed to his men riding behind them to fall back a little. When he turned back to her, the look on his face sent a thrill of fear through her and reminded her that she was with Wild Fin.

"Now, you listen to me," he said grimly. "You may cut up at me all you like in private, but you will keep your voice down when others are about, or I promise, you will not like the consequences."

"Nor will I like them if you force me to marry you," she said, trying to sound undaunted but fearing that she sounded only peevish and regretting it if she did.

He took a deep breath. Then, more evenly, he said, "Whilst you remain unwed, your fortune is a prize Sleat can use to bargain, but to do so he must hold you. I'd think you'd want to do all you can to avoid being used that way."

"But you want the same thing he wants," she retorted stubbornly.

"That's not so."

"It is," she insisted. "It was Donald's duty to protect me before it became yours. How do you know he does not believe he will be rescuing me from you?"

His eyes crinkled at the corners, and she saw his lips twitch. He did not share whatever it was that amused him, but she welcomed the near smile.

To her surprise, he said, "What do *you* want?"

She stared at him in astonishment, for no one had ever

asked her that before. Opening her mouth to speak the first words that came to her mind, she shut it again.

"Tell me," he urged, his voice unusually gentle. "I shan't eat you simply for answering a question that I asked, even if I don't like the answer."

"I did not think that you would," she replied. "I'm just afraid that you will not understand."

"Try me."

"Very well," she said, adding bluntly, "I want a home."

He shrugged. "That you will have, regardless of the choice you make. You have a home at Eilean Donan for as long as you like, and another with Mackinnon at Dunakin, should circumstances ever require it. And, whoever you wed—"

"Home is not merely where one keeps one's clothing," she said, cutting in before he could continue his useless argument. "I thought Dunsithe was my home when I was small, but in the space of a few midnight minutes, that changed. I do not remember Tantallon, where my uncle kept me for several months after his men snatched me from my bed and carried me away. Nor do I recall much about my time at Dunsgaith before Donald passed me to Mackinnon. The plain fact is that I have not had a home since my father died."

"Mackinnon gave you a home for nearly a dozen years."

"But I always knew my stay was temporary, just as I know that Eilean Donan is temporary until you or the King decide I can be more useful elsewhere. Don't you see?" she pleaded, willing him to understand. Seeing no sign that he did, she added with a sigh, "At least you asked, sir. No one else has done that."

"I'll go further yet, mistress. If you want me to send you to Donald, you need only say so. Similarly, if you prefer to marry someone else, I will try to arrange that, if you can persuade me that he will protect you as well as I can."

"There *is* no one else!" she snapped, instantly if inexplicably infuriated by what even she recognized as an eminently reasonable suggestion. She did not want him to be reasonable.

"Then there is no impediment," he replied on a note of satisfaction. "You need simply choose between returning to Sleat or marrying me, and only one of those choices provides what you desire. Eilean Donan will remain your home."

He made it sound like a matter of practicality, as if nothing else mattered. Perhaps if he were more interested in her than in her fortune, she would feel differently. She pushed that disturbing thought away, however, for such thoughts were a waste of energy. If anything other than her fortune came into it, it was that controlling her when Donald wanted her gave him some sort of satisfaction.

That he could be so casual, so smug and self-satisfied, made her want to hit him with her riding whip, but his men were watching, and she did not want to give them more grist for rumor. Moreover, she knew she could not trust Kintail to react to such a gesture in a gentlemanly fashion, even before such an audience. Thus balked, she did not deign to reply at all.

Fin did not press her, knowing she did not want to return to Sleat's guardianship. When she did not answer, he was content to ride in silence, indulging himself again in the thought that had nearly made him chuckle earlier, of Sleat rescuing her from him. Had someone told him a week before that he would now be considering marriage of any sort, let alone marriage to the unpredictable Maid of Dunsithe, he would have thought he was the one needing rescue, and the thought that he could possibly need rescuing from any female struck him as funny. Not so funny, however, that he would share the thought with Patrick.

In childhood, his favorite tales had been those about his Viking forebears, men who sailed the wild northern seas in search of booty, adventure, and women. Sitting by the hall fire on cold winter nights, he had listened to his father's men tell the same tales over and over again. But although he had easily imagined himself such a warrior, carrying off willing ladies by the score, he had never understood the Vikings' apparent lust for taking the unwilling ones. If in those days, childish pride had made it impossible to imagine any lady unwilling to go with him, his present situation made it plain that such women did exist. Why, then, did he apparently welcome the challenge to make her change her mind?

The errant thought of rescuing Mistress Gordon from Sleat had stirred the old fancies, but the reality spun all such images into absurdity. Despite himself and despite her continued defiance, he knew that he was increasingly attracted to the lass and had grown to like her. Nonetheless, his duty to her remained clear.

She could not protect herself against the likes of Sleat, and unless he could manage somehow to make her understand that she must not defy him, he could not protect her either. Perhaps he had made a small start by letting her know that she might have ridden earlier had she behaved, but he could not be sure she understood that. He could not tell what she was thinking—not now, not ever.

The more he considered his choices, the more he believed that Mackinnon was right. The only sure way to protect her was by marrying her, but that would work only if

Sleat reacted as Mackinnon had predicted, and Sleat was an unknown quantity, never predictable.

Fin had spoken with Dougal Maclennan, the priest of Kintail, and Dougal had declared, as expected, that faced with a royal writ of marriage, he had no objection to performing the ceremony, with or without the bride's consent. Fin remained reluctant, however. The notion of marrying Molly was daily becoming more appealing, but although he had every legal right to command her, he had a strong notion that if he did his life thereafter would be a living hell.

Deciding that it would be best to speak plainly now, he ended the long silence, saying, "I hope you will think carefully on this matter of marriage, mistress, before rejecting it. I have no wish to force you into a union for which you have no taste, but neither will I shirk my duty to protect you."

"You don't care about protecting me," she muttered. "You'd not think twice about that if you could control my fortune without controlling me."

"I won't deny that I could use it," he replied honestly. "But as I'm no more likely to lay hands on it than anyone else, it need not concern either of us now."

"You will have my land, in any case," she reminded him.

"Aye, and a sore trial that is, whether I control it as guardian or husband, since it lies hundreds of miles from here and is unlikely to move," he retorted.

Again, she fell silent, and again he let the silence lengthen before he said quietly, "All I ask, Molly, is that you do not dismiss the notion of marriage out of hand but consider carefully the most likely ramifications if you refuse."

She nodded, and he had to be satisfied with that. By late afternoon, when they returned to Eilean Donan, the clouds had darkened and Fin feared that the gathering storm might prove to be an omen. They had exchanged no more conversation about marriage, so although he had enjoyed the out-ing more than he had expected to, he could not flatter himself that his arguments had been persuasive.

Molly did think about what he had said, but his introduction to his people made a stronger argument than his words had. At the baron's court, seeing the sundry persons gathered in the great hall had given her but a small sense of their personalities—save for the man who claimed the fairies made him shoot his neighbor's cow. But seeing Kintail's people as she had today, standing in their own yards, surrounded by their wives, their children, and their aged parents, had cast them all in a more personal light. The thought that her presence in their midst could endanger them disturbed her deeply.

Alone after supper in her darkening bedchamber, she told herself that marrying Kintail could make no difference to his people's safety. Although her presence might endanger them, it was not all that did.

"Donald is determined to reclaim the Lordship of the Isles, and Kintail will do all he can to stop him," she muttered to the ambient air. "That's the danger."

"Aye, it is," replied the now familiar voice. "But 'tis gey possible that Kintail's people will fight harder tae defend his lady than they would if they were only tryin' tae stop Donald from claiming some ancient title for himself."

Startled, Molly looked around the chamber. "Maggie, where are you?"

"Here, in the corner. If ye'd light a candle and stir them embers into a decent fire, ye might see me. Night be fallin', and it be brewin' up tae storm outside."

In no mood to cater to the little woman's brusque temperament, Molly said, "The embers' glow provides light enough for my mood at present. Can you not make yourself visible in the dark?"

"I can, but the effort be greater, and I canna stay visible as long."

Molly could see her dimly. Stepping nearer, she said, "What should I do?"

"I canna tell ye that," Maggie said. "Ye must decide for yourself, ye and Kintail, betwixt the pair o' ye."

"He does not want to hear what I say," Molly said with a sigh. "He always thinks he knows what is best."

"Then make him heed ye," Maggie said, rather spoiling the effect of her decree by adding, "if ye can."

Puffing on her pipe, she sent up a cloud of smoke, then kept on puffing gently while Molly tried to think how she could force Kintail to do anything.

"It still seems odd to see smoke billowing from your mouth," she said at last, "especially when I can barely see *you*."

"Aye, but I like it. Now then, did ye speak aloud before only tae hear yourself speak, or did ye ha' summat ye wished o' me?"

"Can you grant wishes?"

"I expect I could if I saw good reason and if ye wished for summat that lies within me powers tae grant ye."

"Then tell me where I can find my fortune," Molly said.

"I canna do that," Maggie said, smiling ruefully. "I can tell ye, though, that when the right time comes, ye'll find it."

"When will be the right time?"

"Ye'll ken that when ye should."

"The treasure lies at Dunsithe, does it not?"

"Perhaps."

"But Dunsithe lies far from here. Will Kintail have any part in finding it?"

"He might," Maggie said. "He has the gift if he would acknowledge it, and meantime, he has the power tae keep ye safe."

"What gift does he have?"

"I told ye afore—second sight—if his grand education hasna spoilt him."

Frustrated, feeling as if her head had begun to spin but curious to learn as much as she could about Kintail, she said, "What has his education to do with it?"

"Only that men who leave the land tae live in cities and towns, even for a short time, be apt tae take pride in being free from what they call superstition and tae smile pityingly at them who believe in fairies and their ilk."

"Kintail does not believe in fairies," Molly said, remembering his court.

"Aye, men like him develop an unnatural insulation from nature," Maggie said with a sniff. "A laird wi' a grand education can make himself believe that he hasna seen what he has seen. Peasants, no being informed that they should ken better, believe what they do see."

"But I am educated," Molly reminded her. "Perhaps not so educated as Kintail but more so than most women."

"Aye, but one doesna ha' tae be *un*educated tae see the good people," Maggie said. "One need only admit that one sees what one sees."

"Then I must have the sight, too, for I can see you."

"Nay, lass," Maggie said, shaking her head. "Had ye the gift, ye could see me wi'out me having tae expend so much effort. And ye could see the others, too, when they're about. Kintail, now, he could an he would, but he will not."

"By heaven, I swear I do not understand you. How could that be?"

But evidently, Maggie's energy had expired, for she had vanished.

Molly stared at the empty space in the shadows, then walked over and waved her hand around in the dark corner. Only air remained where a moment before Maggie Malloch had sat smoking her pipe.

Outside, a rumble of thunder announced the onset of the storm that had threatened all afternoon, and soon winds howled and rain lashed the castle walls. Molly quickly closed the shutters on the bedchamber window, stirred up the fire, and lit several candles. Then she sat down in front of the cheerful fire to think.

Her thoughts were disordered and remained so until Doreen came to help her prepare for bed, because no sooner would she tell herself that all anyone cared about was her fortune than an image of Kintail would present itself, smiling, eyes twinkling, and she would remember the warmth she felt when he smiled at her. Then she would imagine him grim and unsmiling, and wonder what had possessed her to forget, even for a minute, how implacable he could be.

Nor did her thoughts order themselves after Doreen had gone away and she lay sleepless in bed. She tried to imagine how she could prevent Kintail from forcing her to marry him if he resorted to force, but she found herself, instead, imagining what marriage to such a man might be like. Those thoughts stirred feelings in places she had not previously suspected she could *have* feelings.

When she tried to remind herself that she did not like him, her imagination presented a picture of him on horseback beside her, gently asking what she wanted.

Remembering then that he had allowed her to help keep the castle accounts, she tried to imagine herself as his partner, helping him rule Kintail and Dunsithe. Unfortunately, the mental image of him that leaped to mind then was that of a large, determined, domineering man, unwilling to accept any opinion of hers without question, let alone to accept her as a consort ruling his domain. Trying to imagine him otherwise staggered her imagination.

Maggie Malloch had been no help. Her suggestion, that Molly simply make him heed her wishes, seemed absurd when she could not even make him understand how much she valued the freedom she had had at Dunakin. At Eilean Donan, she had practically none, and although he had not tried to turn her into a drudge as she had first feared, she still had little opportunity to do the things she most enjoyed.

She missed her solitary rides on Skye, where people knew her, and wherever she went, willing hands would help if she ran into trouble, and where trouble rarely involved more than a broken rein or a strained fetlock.

She had been at Eilean Donan only a short time, but already she knew that if things did not change, the confinement would drive her mad, married to him or not. Therefore, she had to make him see that she would not submit to thoughtless, arbitrary orders. His commands had to be reasonable, and he should discuss them with her, not simply issue them and expect her to obey.

She realized, however, that to make him understand all that, she first had to show him that he could not make her obey if she did not choose to do so.

Fine, she thought, an excellent start, but how could she show him any such thing? He was rarely around during the day to see what she did or did not do, and she would not let Mauri or Doreen suffer for her defiance. Moreover, as long as she remained tamely at Eilean Donan, she could do nothing but what he allowed.

Kintail must see that she was pitting herself against him alone. He must see that if he did marry her, he would be marrying a woman with thoughts, opinions, and capabilities of her own. The people at Dunakin had understood that.

Surely Kintail would come to do so, too. He might be block-headed, but he was not stupid.

So, she would have to leave Eilean Donan, at least for a short time, and preferably before Donald and his armies arrived, for she had no wish to run into them. She was not a fool, so she would attempt no more than what she had done at Dunakin. She would simply ride out by herself and . . .

That would not do. She tried to tell herself it would not do because Kintail's people were unlikely to let her row across the channel and take her horse from the stable without his permission, but she knew the truth was that she knew he would make good his threat if she did, and forbid her to ride for three months. That he might do more than that, she did not want to consider. She would not ride.

The first thing, then, was to get off the islet. She could row one of the small boats, perhaps even manage to sail one of the fishing cobles. The storm would not last forever, but would Kintail's men permit her to take any boat?

Not if they saw her, she decided, but what if she arose before dawn and slipped down to the beach? Could she launch a rowboat quietly enough to get away without any watcher on the battlements seeing her?

The idea appealed to her. Most likely, they did not watch their own beach as carefully as they watched the water and the shorelines. They would be watching for attackers from the mainland or Loch Alsh. If she drifted whichever way the current flowed for a short distance before she used the oars, perhaps she could succeed.

But where would she go?

The notion stirred that she could somehow get to Dunsithe to search for her fortune, but she rejected it. Her intent was not to do something foolhardy, and a trip alone of over a hundred miles would be nothing less.

She had to do something ordinary, something that she

would have done at Dunakin without any soul-searching—without thought, in fact—like hunting.

"He knows I like to hunt," she muttered to the surrounding silence. "He and Sir Patrick hunt every day, yet he has not once asked me to join them."

Like any other castle, Eilean Donan required constant replenishing of its food stocks, and that was something with which she could help. Smiling, sure now of her plan, she turned over and went to sleep.

To Nell's vast relief, after nearly a sennight had passed, James not only agreed at last to let her carry a message to Kintail and depart straightaway but also gave her a warrant commanding hospitality along the way. Most households would give shelter to any passing traveler, but she knew that a woman with a small escort would receive more agreeable treatment at the King's command than on her own.

The distance being more than a hundred and fifty miles, much of it through the roadless Highlands, the journey would take three days at least, and that only because Nell and her women were Border-bred and thus excellent horsewomen.

James had suggested that she might prefer to travel to Dunbarton and take ship from there but agreed that, with Donald the Grim gathering a fleet, she might run into trouble before she reached Eilean Donan. That a royal navy was being hastily assembled to deal with Donald's fleet would not make her journey safer, since she could count on neither side to accept her bona fides.

Ordering her woman to pack their things, she sent word to her men-at-arms that she would depart within the hour and would require a guide who knew the Highlands and could get them to Kintail safely and by the fastest route. She was taking a last look around her bedchamber to be sure she left nothing behind when a sharp rap sounded at the door.

Her woman opened it to find a girl in a blue gown and white cap. The latter concealed her hair, making her large, dark-fringed gray eyes seem enormous.

"Beg pardon, m'lady," the girl said, "but my mistress, hearing that you mean to leave the castle, asked me to bring you this message." When Nell had taken it, he girl bobbed a curtsy and hurried away.

"How odd," Nell murmured, breaking the wax seal. She understood little more when she read the following:

> *Dear Madam:*
> *Your haste precludes a more formal farewell, but I did think you would appreciate a glance at the bearer to reassure yourself that she is well cared for. With Respect, Discretion, and in Haste, I am, as ever, your affectionate —Lady F*

"Be aught amiss, my lady?"

"Nothing, Jane. I believe this message comes from an extremely encroaching woman, who insists on believing that I retain interest in my brother's affairs. I do not, of course, but I could not tell her so if I wanted to, for I do not recall the wretched creature's name and her absurd discretion has prompted her to sign only her initial."

"Shall I attempt to identify her, my lady? Perhaps one of—"

"No, Jane, I want to put as much distance between ourselves and Stirling as we can before dark. Art ready?"

Being reassured on this point, Nell led the way to the courtyard, where she found her escort and their guide. The latter caused her some annoyance, for it seemed that James had also recognized her need for such a person and had provided a wiry little man of his own. The guide would be useful as far as Kintail, but to fulfill her mission, she would have to get rid of him soon after their arrival.

"We'll make for Loch Lomond first, my lady," he said politely, "and thence up the Great Glen to Glen Garry and west to Kintail. Portions o' the route be rugged, but your people assure me that you and your woman be intrepid horsewomen. I pray that be so."

"It is," Nell said curtly. "Let us depart at once."

He assisted her to her saddle, and within minutes, the little group was crossing the timber bridge, leaving Stirling Castle behind them.

Chapter 12 _____

Molly's preparations took much of the day, for not only did she require food but clothing, too. Too many people would recognize her in her customary garb, thanks to Kintail's introductions, and those who did not would want to know why a well-dressed young woman was strolling alone in the woods or practicing her bowmanship in some clearing or other.

Even an ordinarily dressed young woman might draw unwanted attention, so masculine clothing was preferable, but she could not imagine herself daring to appear in one of the raggedy, kilted garments that so many of the common men and boys wore. Over the course of the day, however, she managed to acquire a knee-length saffron tunic and a pair of ragged braies, to which she added leg bandings and rawhide shoes. The shoes were too big, but by extending the bandings to cover her ankles and feet, she could make them fit.

Completing her wardrobe with a flat blue cap and a woolen mantle of the indigo and dark green pattern the Highlanders called tartan and that nearly every male in the area seemed to wear, she tucked everything into a wooden chest in her bedchamber, ready to wear when the opportunity arose.

It rained all day, making her fret that the bad weather might continue indefinitely. Kintail need only receive word that Donald the Grim had landed in Kintail, and he would hail the priest straight to Eilean Donan and order the feckless man to marry him to her on the spot. It was imperative that she prove to him before then that he could not act the tyrant over her.

Waking before dawn the next morning, she looked outside and saw stars twinkling in the still black sky. The rain had stopped. Dressing as hastily as she could in the unfamiliar tunic, braies, and leggings, she fastened her quiver of arrows around her waist, kilted the tunic over the belt, tucked her hair into the cap, and wrapped the tartan mantle around her. Taking up her bow, she slipped downstairs to the double-barred postern door at the base of the northwest tower.

She could manage the bars alone, and she could be reasonably sure that no guard stood just outside it. In any event, the door was the only way to leave the castle without being seen.

Not only did men-at-arms sleep in the great hall, through which she would have to pass to reach the castle entrance, but the entrance was guarded by the tall, heavily timbered portcullis and a second, interior timber gate that was nearly as solid. Both would be shut, and no one in Kintail's service would open them for her.

Each of the bars scraped when she lifted it, being too heavy for her to manage with deftness. The door creaked, too, but although each sound stopped her breath in her throat, no one demanded to know her business.

Outside, she breathed more easily. Waves slapped hard against the shore, and the wind blew hard enough to interfere with any man's hearing. There was no moon to shine upon her, so the dark mantle would conceal her as long as she stayed near the wall as she made her way around to the eastern shore.

Although the distance to the boats was not great, it seemed to take forever, but she reached the nearest rowboat at last, without seeing or hearing anyone.

Just then, a clank from above stopped her in her tracks. Voices drifted on the wind from the battlements, but soon they faded, and she knew that the time had come to move again if she could just make herself do so. Silently feeling her way, she laid her longbow in the boat and then slowly, carefully, eased the small craft into the water, hoping that the scraping sound of the boat over loose pebbles would not carry above the louder sounds of wind and slapping waves.

Attempting to imitate the movement Kintail had made, launching their boat two days before, she grabbed the gunwales on either side of the little craft's bow, then pushed and leaped, swinging one leg over and in, then gasping and holding on for dear life when the other foot plunged into the icy water. The boat tilted and an oar slipped, thudding dully against its gunwale.

Although she expected to hear an alarm, none sounded, and the boat was moving, drifting toward the Dornie shore. She was still too close to the castle, and there were steep cliffs on that side of the loch and fewer places to beach. The opposite shore was heavily wooded, more welcoming. Using an oar, as silently as she could, she guided the little craft out into the tidal current. When she decided that she was far enough away that no sound she made could reach the castle, she began to row in earnest, and twenty minutes later, she beached on the opposite shore.

Dragging the boat high enough so that the rising tide

would be unlikely to carry it away, and tying its painter to a tree root to make doubly sure, she took her bow and moved uphill into the trees until she came to a flat rock where she could sit and wait for dawn. She had no idea what time it was.

Resting her arms on her knees and her head on her arms, she dozed with her bow across her lap, waking to the sound of a crane's whoop to find that the sun had risen. Beyond the tree line, in the distance across the loch, she could see Eilean Donan gleaming like bronze in the pale yellow sunlight. She could discern no unusual activity, but she realized that she should have taken Doreen into her confidence, so that the maidservant would not raise the alarm when she entered Molly's bedchamber and found her gone.

Men searching the shoreline would soon find the rowboat and would recognize that it belonged to the castle, so she hastened to put distance between it and herself. Hiking up the steep hillside until she came to a grassy clearing, she turned to get her bearings again. The three lochs lay before her. She could even see Skye in the misty distance. She would not get lost.

Movement drew her attention to the far shore—horses and mounted men, perhaps a half dozen. Had someone raised the alarm while she dozed? No, she decided, they were too bunched up to be searching and too small a group to be raiders or—worse—a vanguard of Donald the Grim's invaders.

Knowing that the riders could not see her, she watched until they reached the head of the loch and crossed the burn. When they turned toward her, she slipped into the shrubbery again. Keeping an eye on them would be easy. She would find a place where she could practice her bowmanship and when she was quite ready, she would return to the castle.

"'Tis a fine day for sport," Patrick MacRae said cheerfully. "We must hope that Donald Grumach does not spoil it by attacking Kintail today."

"Aye," Fin said, but his attention was fixed on the moody young goshawk he carried on his gloved left fist. Although hooded and jessed, the bird still tended to bate at unexpected noises and had been ruffling its wings ominously for the past several minutes. Fortunately, Fin's mount was seasoned and would not bolt if the bird began thrashing around and fighting its tethers, but it would be as well if the young she-devil behaved. It could injure itself or break a primary feather if it got too excited. Looping his reins around his wrist, he stroked the bird's underbelly gently to calm it.

Patrick's hawk was smaller and more even-tempered. He seemed to pay it no heed, choosing to engage in merry conversation instead, but Fin knew his careless attitude was deceptive. Patrick was as skilled with a hawk as with a longbow, sword, or gun. Both he and Fin had learned the art of hawking from the old laird's chief falconer, for Sir Ranald Mackenzie had believed that both his son and their future constable should be as skilled at such arts as their hirelings were.

"Is Smoke giving you trouble, laird?" Tam Matheson asked. He, too, had learned from the chief falconer, for that worthy was his father. Having helped train birds for Fin and Patrick, Tam tended to blame himself for the birds' few faults.

Patrick grinned. "Everyone is giving the laird trouble these days, Tam—his birds, his women, his—"

"Mind your tongue," Fin said, repressing the picture of

Molly that leaped to his mind's eye. "If you recall, I'm still capable of schooling your manners."

"Aye, master," Patrick said with a chuckle, adding, "How do those boots of mine fit you, Tam?"

"Excellent well, as ye see," Tam said, raising a foot to show him.

Fin said nothing, trying to keep his thoughts on the goshawk and off Molly.

Patrick shot him a measuring look, then said more soberly, "Uphill yonder is that long, heathery meadow we like. Shall we try them there? It'll give that vixen of yours room to stretch her wings, and we'll be able to keep a better eye on her if she takes to the trees."

"The laird's Smoke be belled, Patrick," Tam said indignantly.

"Aye, Tam, but if she catches sight of a grouse and the grouse dives into the trees, we'll want to see which way they go, in the event that Smoke loses him and keeps going. Bell or no bell, she'll be hard to follow through woodland, and she is still young."

Tam shrugged, and Fin smiled, knowing that Tam was thinking—and rightly—that he'd be the one to hunt for the goshawk if they lost sight of it. Patrick wasn't one to waste his time with tedious tasks if he could avoid them, and the goshawk would respond to Tam's whistle as quickly as it would to Fin's.

When they drew rein in the meadow, Patrick shot Fin a challenging look. "I'll wager that my Kit takes his prey at first flush and that Smoke will fail."

"How much?"

"Ten merks."

"Done," Fin said, pulling the glove off his free hand with his teeth and tucking it into his jerkin so that he could loosen the braces that closed the goshawk's red-plumed Dutch hood. "Smoke can outfly anything. Easy, lass," he murmured to the tense, quivering bird. Starting at every sound and too-quick movement, the goshawk pulsated like a plucked bowstring. He could feel the low vibrations humming through his gloved fist and fingers.

The goshawk seemed to glower at all it surveyed, but Fin knew it was merely seeking and would soon spy its prey. Its tension stemmed from hunger and anticipation, not from nerves.

He could hear distant twittering in the woods, but nearer at hand, the denizens of the meadow apparently had the good sense to lie low and keep still.

On the far side, a coppery grouse broke cover, clacking wildly, the rapid flapping of its wings making a noisy whirr as it hurled itself skyward.

Fin released Smoke's jesses, and in the same instant the goshawk's great wings unfurled and her powerful thighs thrust her into the air. Her wings' strong, slow beat belied her startling speed from the fist. Already nearing the target, her wings flattened into a glide, tips pointed, edges trailing.

The grouse, belatedly recognizing its danger, shrieked and tried madly to take evasive action.

A split second before the goshawk struck, a long yellow shaft streaked through the air ahead of it, and the grouse plunged to the ground, still flapping wildly in its death throes, its shrieking stilled.

"What the devil?" Fin exclaimed.

"Some fool shot an arrow from the woods!" Patrick shouted.

"Yonder," cried Tam, pointing.

Following the gesture, Fin saw a saffron-colored flash through the trees. Tossing the goshawk's hood to Tam, he wheeled his horse, saying, "Fetch Smoke, Tam. I'm going to have words with that villain. He nearly killed my hawk!"

Urging the gray into the woods, he watched for movement that would again reveal his quarry's direction, and immediately glimpsed another flash of saffron, a figure darting swiftly through the trees.

Digging his heels into the gray's flanks, he felt its muscles tense as it leaped forward. Highland-bred, the horse took the rugged woodland terrain in stride, and just ahead, the darting runner was flagging. Flat ground lay between them, and Fin leaned over the horse's neck, urging it to a greater speed.

Riding alongside the running figure, he reached down, grabbed a fistful of saffron-colored fabric, and hauled the struggling villain—bow, quiver, and all—facedown over his saddlebow, losing one of the fellow's shoes in the process. Holding him there with one hand while he reined in the gray with the other, and deducing from the size of the figure he held that it was only a lad, Fin gave the backside so temptingly presented a couple of angry, hard smacks.

The shrieks he evoked were decidedly unmasculine in nature, and his captive began to struggle more wildly than before. The blue cap fell off, and a massive cloud of curly red-gold hair tumbled free. Seeing those familiar silken tresses, Fin clenched his jaw in a flash of raw fury and smacked again, even harder.

"Stop that, you villain!" she screamed.

He smacked again. "If you don't want more, be silent and keep still," he ordered grimly. "You nearly killed my hawk! What the devil were you thinking? Where did you get those dreadful clothes, and what in the name of all that's holy are you doing outside the castle walls?"

Molly gritted her teeth. No one had laid a hand on her at Dunakin, and it had not occurred to her that anyone might ever dare do so again. Her backside felt like it was on fire, and although she could remember her mother and nurse spanking her when she was small, she did not remember that it had hurt so much.

She had no acceptable answers for Kintail's questions, either, reasonable though they were. She had not expected the hawk to fly so fast to its target, but she did not think that telling him so would help much.

She had been watching the men from the woods, and having heard Kintail boast that his bird could outfly anything, she had decided to deprive it of its prey, showing him that an arrow could certainly fly faster. The thought that the fiendish bolt might have harmed as much as a feather of the magnificent hawk both sickened and appalled her, so she could not blame Kintail for his fury. She was glad, though, that he had stopped smacking her, and she did not want him to do so again.

"Well?" The grim note in his voice was not encouraging.

She drew a ragged breath to steady her nerves, and as if the gray sensed her unease, it sidled, then steadied again at a slight movement of its master.

She said with careful calm, "May I get down?"

"That depends."

"On what?"

"On what you say to me beforehand."

"What if I have nothing to say?"

"Then you must think of something." His hand came to rest on her backside. The powerful fingers twitched ominously.

She swallowed. What did he want her to say? Would he settle for a simple apology, or did he want more? Surely, he did not expect her to agree to marry him just to keep him from smacking her.

The fingers twitched again, then the hand lifted.

"I'm sorry!" she said hastily. "If you want me to say more than that, you'll have to tell me what I am to say. I . . . I don't know what you want!"

Two strong hands gripped her waist, and he lifted her to sit sideways before him. Since her backside still ached, the position was less than comfortable, but she did not think that complaining or reminding him that she wanted to get down would do her any good. Besides, she had lost one of her shoes.

When the horse sidled again, she felt his thighs tense as he steadied it.

Gazing blindly into the distance, she waited for him to speak, but before he did, approaching riders diverted his attention, and she heard him mutter a curse.

The riders were Sir Patrick and another man she did not recognize.

Patrick shouted, "Ho, Fin, what have you caught?" As usual, laughter tinged his voice, but Molly felt no appreciation just then for his sense of humor.

"Where are the others?" Kintail asked.

"Yonder," Patrick said, gesturing toward the meadow. "Smoke took to a tree after the grouse fell. She perched there and glowered down at it for a time, as if she wondered why it was flapping around like a beheaded chicken. But when the flapping ceased and nothing else of a disturbing nature occurred, she flew down intending to feast. She responded to Tam's whistle as prettily as you please, however, so I told the others to wait there and came to see what you'd caught." He bowed gallantly from the waist. "Mistress, 'tis a pleasure, as always, to see you."

Molly glowered at him.

Directing his attention to the second man, Kintail said sternly, "Talk of this incident goes no further. Do you understand me?"

"Aye, laird. I'll say naught."

"Good. You and the others go on ahead. Patrick, you ride with me."

The second man turned back the way they had come, and Molly was relieved to see him go, but if she hoped that Sir Patrick's presence would spare her from Kintail's anger, Kintail quickly disabused her of that hope.

As the two men turned their mounts toward home, he said in the same stern tone he had used earlier, "Now, mistress, I want an explanation, and it had better be a good one if you do not want more of what I gave you before."

Shooting a glance at Patrick to see if he realized from these words what Kintail had done, she saw that he was looking straight ahead, his normally expressive countenance now wooden. She would find no ally in him.

Deciding that since nothing she could say would appease Kintail she might as well say what she was thinking, she said tartly (but without looking at him), "Do you frequently beat females, sir? Because if you do, I must tell you that I do not approve. Nor do I think such violence is necessary. As large as you are, you probably frighten most people witless simply by bellowing at them."

Heavy silence greeted this observation.

Then Kintail said abruptly, "Did you intend to shoot the hawk?"

"Don't be daft," she snapped. "I never miss my aim."

Patrick, surprised, said, "Never?"

She hesitated, knowing that neither man would believe her if she spoke the truth. "Rarely," she said, prevaricating.

"Well, it was a fine shot, and I am an excellent judge of such matters. Who taught you to shoot?"

"Never mind that," Kintail said sharply. "You keep silent, Patrick. She doesn't need encouragement. You had no business even to be there, mistress."

But Molly had had enough. "Sir Patrick," she said firmly, "would you please ride on ahead of us? I would speak privately with your laird."

Patrick shot her a look of astonishment, then glanced at Kintail.

"Go," he said, gesturing.

Without another word, but likewise without disguising his relief, Patrick gave spur to his horse and disappeared into the woodland ahead.

Fearing that Kintail might begin scolding again, she said swiftly, "I was wrong to shoot. I had no idea that your hawk could cross the meadow so quickly, and I'd heard you say that nothing could outfly it. That challenged me, I'm afraid, to show you that an arrow could take the grouse before your hawk could."

He did not reply at once, and in the interval, she felt unnaturally aware of his nearness and size. His body felt too warm against hers, his muscles too hard. She could feel him breathing, could feel his heart beating. He was too large for comfort.

At last, quietly, he said, "You were not running away."

"Only from you, just now," she muttered.

"You had reason for that."

"Aye." Her backside still ached.

"How did you come here?"

She remembered the rowboat, having forgotten it until that moment. "I slipped out through the tower door and took one of the boats."

"You left that door unbarred?"

She nodded, not looking at him.

"For that alone, you deserved beating," he growled.

To divert him from that painful thought, she blurted the first thing that came to mind: "Do you still intend to marry me?"

"I'll not force you into a marriage you do not want."

Strangely, considering how hard she had fought the notion, his response disappointed her.

"But you still believe it is the right thing to do," she persisted, "even though you despise me. Mackinnon told me that you had no wish to marry at all."

Seeing his lips twitch into a near smile, she breathed more easily.

He said, "First of all, I do not despise you. As for marriage, whilst 'tis true that I resisted my father's efforts to marry me to one suitable female after another, I thought I had years ahead of me before I need worry about an heir. I learned differently when he was killed. Life can end abruptly, lass, and I care deeply about my people. I take my duties seriously, to them and to the castle. Were I to fall suddenly as my father did, I would leave them bereft of more than their laird."

"So you want me just to get heirs." The thought brought an ache to her throat strong enough to make her forget her earlier pains.

"Also to get your fortune," he said dryly. "Do not forget that."

She knew he was teasing her, but truth underscored the teasing. Because her fortune and her woman's ability to produce children would be useful to him, he wanted to keep her even if it meant marrying her.

His hand moved slightly where it touched her hip, and yearning shot through her, frightening her with its strength. He had more power over her than he knew, but if she submitted, she was in danger of losing her soul to him. And if he should decide, as others had, that she would prove more useful elsewhere . . . But that thought did not bear completing.

She could not speak, and he said no more for a time. They reached a hard-packed trail along the shore, and he turned the gray toward the head of the loch.

"The boat," she muttered.

"I'll send someone to fetch it later," he said.

The silence between them continued until they had crossed the plank bridge over the tumbling burn at the head of the loch. The thudding of the horse's hooves on the planks above the rush of water beneath them seemed very loud. On the far side, when even the water sounds had faded behind them, the silence seemed heavier than before. There was less foliage, and halfway between them and the castle, Molly could see the other riders on the track above the cliffs.

"I am not generally defiant by nature," she said then, looking at him.

"Indeed," he said, his mocking disbelief plain.

"In sooth, sir, I am not accustomed to having orders hurled at me," she said. "I am accustomed to discussing things, to knowing that others heed my opinions. You treat me as if I were a halfwit. If we *were* to marry, I would not like that."

He looked into her eyes, his gaze searching hers.

Her body seemed more alive than usual, unnaturally aware of every movement of his horse, even more aware of Kintail, his woodland scent, his steady breathing, his dark gaze and stern countenance. When he dampened his lips with his tongue, it was as if he touched his lips to hers. The moment lengthened.

Then he said gently, "If I hurl orders, lass, I do so because you challenge my authority at every turn. Is that not what you did today?"

"You make me feel like a prisoner," she said. "I went out

with my bow, because I often did so on Skye and because I enjoy the solitude of the hunt. I understand about the danger, though—particularly now," she added hastily, seeing his quick frown. "But I took care. I was not raised as most girls are, you know."

His lips pressed hard together, and at first, she thought she had angered him again, but then she saw that he was struggling to suppress laughter.

"I said nothing humorous," she said indignantly.

"You certainly spoke the truth," he said, chuckling.

He sobered then, saying, "Forgive me if I mistake the matter, but it appears to me that you have begun to think favorably on a possible marriage between us. Given your earlier distaste . . ." He let the words hang in the air.

She nibbled her lower lip, trying to think how to explain her tumbled feelings when she did not understand them herself.

"It was not distaste, exactly," she said at last. "I know that I must marry someday. Indeed, Lady Mackinnon often said it was a miracle Donald had not forced me into an advantageous marriage. I am in my eighteenth year, after all, and many women marry much earlier, particularly heiresses."

"Then your dislike is merely for me," he said evenly.

"For the circumstance and . . . and for your treatment of me," she said. "If you were more—"

"More like Mackinnon?"

"Aye, perhaps," she said, wrinkling her brow, unable to imagine herself married to the hearty but carefully neutral Mackinnon or to anyone like him.

"Lass, I am not like Mackinnon, nor will I ever be. I am my own man. I can protect you, which is something that you should consider, and I can provide for you even without your fortune—albeit not so well as with it, I'll admit. It is, in any event, my duty to find you a suitable husband, and in this present circumstance, I can think of no one better suited than myself to protect you from Sleat, certainly no one to whom I can arrange your marriage in the little time we have."

Frustrated, as averse to his thinking that she would marry him for protection as she was to his wanting her only for her fortune and womb, she nonetheless found it impossible to declare again that she did not want to marry him. But neither could she confess outright that she did.

"I—I do not want to go back to Donald," she said at last.

"I should warn you," he said, his eyes narrowing in a way that belied his gentle tone, "that if you hope a pretense of submission will spare you from punishment for your defiance today—for it was no more, say what you may—you will find that you have misjudged me."

Heat flooded her cheeks, and she said angrily, "I would not do that!"

"Then I apologize for mistrusting you. I will send for Dougal Maclennan, the priest, straightaway. Shall I send for Mackinnon and his lady, as well?"

Wondering if she had lost her mind, she nodded. Then recalling his earlier words, she said, "What will you do to me—for this . . . for what I did today?"

"I told you what I would do," he said. "You must learn to trust my word, lass. You will not ride for three months."

"But that was only if I took my horse out! I didn't!"

"I did not say that. I said that you were not to go out alone, ever."

"But we were talking about riding!"

"You may have been talking about riding. I was perfectly plain. Also, you will not take your bow out again until I grant you leave to do so."

"I do not think I want to marry you, after all."

"If you refuse to keep your word because I am keeping

mine, so be it," he said. "But you should know that it will make no difference to your punishment. I am still your guardian, and you will not ride again until I say you may."

Her dignity had already suffered much, but now she felt small. "I do keep my word," she muttered. "And if I must marry, I'd as lief marry a man who lives near Dunakin and . . . and one who keeps *his* word. But need we not call the banns?"

"We have no time for that," he said. "The priest will make all tidy." When she did not speak, he added gently, "Shall I send for him then, and for Mackinnon?"

She hesitated, her mind a whirl of conflicting images, not least of which was an unnerving image of herself in bed with Kintail. Reminding herself of Donald and how much worse it could be, she said quietly, "Aye, send for them."

"The day after tomorrow then, if Mackinnon and his lady can get here. I'll send Patrick to fetch them as soon as we reach Eilean Donan."

"Very well," she said, certain that she would come to regret her decision. A woman's lot in life left her few choices, though, and at least she could feel that she had had some say in this one, however small.

Chapter 13

Fin saw that Molly was uncertain about the decision she had made, and he knew better than to press her further about her reasons. He wanted to say something to reassure her, but he had no idea what that might be. It would not do to express the feelings coursing through him now that he had persuaded her to marry him, even if he could have expressed them clearly.

Holding her as he was, he could not think about anything clearly, because his body wanted to do his thinking for him. His loins stirred with every motion she made, and when he began to suspect she would not continue to fight their marriage, his head had filled with images he was sure even a Highland priest would condemn.

He had wanted her from that first night, but if he were to tell her that, it would only reinforce the image she had of him from that night. From his viewpoint, a marriage between them was imminently suitable. His father certainly would have approved of it, and not only because of the lass's fortune, assuming he ever found it. That he was attracted to—nay, lusted after—her was an added advantage.

As they continued toward Eilean Donan, he found himself watching her, letting his gaze dwell on the soft pink cheek turned slightly toward him, and on the rosy fullness of her lips. He had wanted to kiss her again since the day on the shore, before Mackinnon had joined them, but kissing was not enough now. His imagination was busy feeding him lustier notions. However, if he acted on any one of them, she would instantly change her mind again, and if she did, he did not know if he had the strength of character to allow it. He would do better to set things in train for the wedding as soon as they returned to the castle.

Because Molly had lost her shoe, he had to carry her inside, and holding her tempted him nearly beyond what he could endure. He noted with humor that while his people were astonished to see her dressed like a peasant lad, they were even more astonished when he announced that he intended to marry her straightaway.

Patrick, after a speechless moment, gathered his wits and shouted, "To the laird! 'Tis a fine thing he does for Eilean Donan."

The others cheered, and conscious of Molly's tense body in his arms, Fin said, "I'm glad to have your approval, friend. Send a running gilly to tell Dougal Maclennan I want him to perform the ceremony here two days from now. Then get something to eat, for I'm sending you to tell Mackinnon. Take an armed escort, in case you meet Sleat, but bring Mackinnon and his lady back for the wedding."

Grinning, Patrick executed an elaborate bow and said, "At once, laird. And has your lady any commands for me?"

Molly shook her head, saying nothing, and from her heightened color, Fin knew she was wishing herself elsewhere. To Patrick, he said, "If she thinks of any, I'll let you know before you leave. Now get about your business. Someone tell Mauri the news, and then the rest of you take your orders from her."

With that, he carried Molly to the stairs and up to her bedchamber, conscious all the way of the way her body felt in his arms. Inside her room, he set her on her feet but did not release her. Hands on her shoulders, he forced himself to say evenly, "Art sure, lass?"

"Would you let me change my mind?" she asked, looking into his eyes.

"I don't know," he replied honestly, holding her gaze. Her eyes were so beautiful. The thought of looking into them every day for the rest of his life gave him a sense of rightness. He doubted that he had the strength to let her go.

"You wouldn't," she said, her lips curving into an enigmatic little smile.

The smile did it. He bent and kissed her, meaning only to kiss her lightly, as if to tell her—what? Before he could bring his thoughts to bear on the question, her lips twitched responsively against his, and he was lost. Pulling her close, he moved his hand over her back and sides, possessively, delighting in the idea that he would soon know every inch of her. That thought stirred others, and as his tongue explored the soft interior of her mouth, one hand moved to untie the strings at the neck of the saffron shirt. The hand slipped inside the opening, stroking the soft skin beneath.

Molly gasped and stiffened, pulling away.

"It's all right, lass," he murmured.

"No, it isn't; not yet," she said, breathing rapidly, as if she had been running.

Her cheeks were flushed, her lovely eyes bright. His body ached for her. But he would gain nothing by infuriating her and much, perhaps, with forbearance.

"I'm a patient man," he said, putting the thought to words.

"No, you are not," she said, stepping back.

He grinned at her. "I'm willing to practice, though. I've offered you a bargain, lass. You'll soon have the home you've yearned for."

"You aren't offering me your home," she said with a sigh. "It is as Sir Patrick said, and you are doing it for your beloved castle. Moreover, on the slightest whim, you could order me to live somewhere else, could you not?"

"Aye, well, here's a better bargain then," he said, undaunted. "Tell me before the wedding that you've changed your mind, and perhaps I'll let you out of our agreement. In the meantime, put on a proper dress. Looking like that, in lad's clothing, you make me feel like a lustful sodomite."

He left, chuckling.

Molly stood where he left her, shaken and wondering what demon had made her agree to marry him. She could hardly tell herself that she had taught him to value her opinions or understand her need for freedom. If she had accomplished anything, it was the exact opposite. What could she have been thinking?

Would he really let her change her mind? And if he did . . .

Her thoughts turned instantly to his handsome face and strong arms, to the twinkle in his eyes when he smiled, to the way that smile lit up his features and warmed her to her toes. Then she thought of what he had done when he had hauled her up across his saddle, and she remembered his stern frown and harsh words.

Then she remembered his kisses and the passionate way he had caressed her.

The more tangled her thoughts became, the more she expected to find herself talking to Maggie Malloch, but the little woman did not appear even when she called her name. Evidently, fairies or household spirits, or whatever they chose to call themselves, appeared only when they wished to do so.

Downstairs, Fin discovered he had to deal with Mauri.

"Such a hasty wedding doesna be seemly," she said, arms akimbo.

"To find Donald the Grim on our doorstep demanding Molly's return at sword's point would not be seemly either," he retorted. "Just do your best, Mauri. None of our guests will expect a grand occasion."

"What guests?" she demanded. "Who will ken aught about it?"

"We'll send running gillies to spread the word," he said. "People will come. Perhaps not many from any distance, but we'll not find ourselves alone."

"Aye, well, we'll see," she said darkly, "but 'tis nae the way for a Mackenzie chieftain tae wed, and if that lass be willin', I've seen nae sign of it afore now."

"She's willing enough," he said, hoping he was right. He was rapidly growing accustomed to the notion of having her as his wife, but she was perfectly capable of changing her mind at the last minute and refusing to take her vows.

As he turned from Mauri and gave his orders to the running gillies, he had an odd sense of someone moving just at the edge of his peripheral vision, but when he turned his head, no one was there.

Doreen came to help Molly change her clothing, clicking her tongue and scolding as only a servant who had known one from childhood could do. Molly, however, had long since learned how to deal with Doreen.

"What has become of Thomas MacMorran?" she asked casually when the maidservant paused to take a breath. "I have not seen much of him lately."

"Well, ye might ha' done had ye looked," Doreen said sharply. "Not only does he sleep wi' the others in the hall at night but he were here in the castle all day yesterday, making a nuisance o' himself."

"How so?"

"The man wants to live in one o' the wee cottages the laird gives them what ha' families to provide for," Doreen said. "It makes no matter to Thomas MacMorran that other folks ha' their duty, as well. Only Thomas MacMorran's needs matter to Thomas MacMorran. Forbye, here today he's gone off to Skye wi' Sir Patrick MacRae and wi'out so much as askin' a body did she ha' any messages for her folks there. So much for Thomas MacMorran's notions o' love."

Molly began to feel sympathy for Doreen.

"Men," she said with feeling.

"Aye," Doreen said in fervent agreement. "A sorry lot, most of 'em." Then, however, she spoiled this moment of harmony by adding, "Except for the Laird o' Kintail, o' course. A grand man, that one, and lucky ye be to marry him."

Repressing an urge to growl, Molly said, "Kintail is just a man like any other, who thinks he rules the earth." Even as the words spilled forth, she knew they were not true. No one could look at Kintail and see just a man like any other.

Doreen stared at her. "Faith, mistress, if all men were like that one, there'd be nae room left on the earth for the women."

The image of an earth covered with men as large as Kintail, wearing swords and mail, and standing shoulder to shoulder, struck Molly's sense of the ridiculous so hard that she laughed aloud. "Very well," she said when she could talk, "Kintail is larger than most but no less stubborn or sure of himself. What is it about men that makes them think they know more about any subject than a woman can know?"

Doreen grimaced, clearly agreeing, but after a few moments of silence as she helped Molly into a fresh bodice and skirt, she said, "I warrant he'll do well by ye, mistress. I own, though, I were flat astonished to learn ye mean to marry him."

Molly sighed. "Do you think I'm being foolish, Doreen? I own, I don't even know what stirred me to say that I *would* marry him."

"Ye'll ha' a home at last that's truly your own," Doreen said gently.

There was that, Molly thought. Although she had contradicted Kintail when he'd said the same thing, Eilean Donan would be her home unless he decreed that she live elsewhere, and that seemed unlikely. Indeed, perhaps the chance to gain a proper home at last was what had persuaded her. She would belong. That thought comforted her more than any other that had passed through her mind that day.

From the day that her uncle had so abruptly removed her from Dunsithe, she had felt displaced. Even at Dunakin, where everyone was kind to her, she had felt apart from the others, different, but the thought of calling Eilean Donan home had distinct appeal.

"I do want a real home," she said wistfully to Doreen.

The maidservant smiled. "Aye, sure, I ken that fine, mistress. Every woman wants a home of her own and a man and bairns to look after. 'Tis natural, that."

"Perhaps," Molly said. She found the thought of bairns—hers and Kintail's—rather startling. A son of her own—doubtless one just like his father—was a daunting but nonetheless intriguing prospect.

Kintail would kiss her again. Indeed, he would do much more than that. She was not sure exactly what the "much more" entailed, but married people did often sleep in the same bed. Thinking of his kisses made her lips burn, and thinking about sharing his bed and creating bairns stirred other parts of her body to burning as well.

These thoughts and others like them tumbled in a continuous but unhelpful stream through her mind as that evening and the following day passed. Aside from the long hours of the night when she lay abed without sleeping, trying not to think about the wedding night ahead, she seemed to be surrounded by people attending to one task after another, talking and making plans. They consulted her from time to time, but whatever she added to the proceedings, she would never recall afterward.

She saw Kintail occasionally in passing, but although he smiled at her, he seemed to elude conversation, and she was just as glad, for she knew not what she would say to him, and she did not want to stir coals with the wedding so near.

During the afternoon before the wedding, she was dimly aware of Mauri and Doreen sorting through her clothing in search of just the right gown for her to wear for the ceremony, but she did not care which they chose. She tried on one after another as they bade her, obediently turning this way and that.

If anyone noticed her distraction, they attributed it to pre-wedding nerves and said nothing. As for herself, she could seem to think of nothing other than that she would soon be

Kintail's bride and, more than ever, subject to his authority. Her uncertainty grew, but at the same time, she felt as if the wedding had taken on a momentum of its own so great that nothing could stop it. The priest would obey Kintail's orders, and so would everyone else, including herself.

That thought nearly shook her out of the spell under which she seemed to have fallen, but then Mauri told her that it was time to go down to supper, and she rose obediently to go with her, feeling a sudden desire to see Kintail and be warmed again by his reassuring smile.

She entered the great hall, expecting to see the same scene that had greeted her eyes every evening at that time, but the reality was so different that she stopped at the threshold and stared. The hall teemed with people, and new arrivals crowded the main entrance. The din of conversation was such that she wondered how she had missed hearing it on the way downstairs. Indeed, she wondered if more hours had passed than she knew, and it was time for the wedding.

She looked for Kintail and saw him a short distance away, speaking to Tam Matheson. Other men turned to greet newcomers just then, and when she saw muscles clench in Kintail's jaw, she followed his gaze.

First, she saw Sir Patrick, looking unnaturally grim. Behind him, she saw the familiar figures of Mackinnon and his lady, and her spirits rose. Eager to greet them, she followed Kintail as he moved toward them, but she stopped when she saw the glowering face behind Mackinnon. It was a memorable face, for all that she had seen it only three or four times in her life.

Mauri bumped into Molly. Hastily apologizing, she said, "Who is that? He has two eagle feathers in his cap, like Mackinnon or the laird, but I dinna ken . . ."

"That is Donald the Grim," Molly said, her uncertain mood evaporating as apprehension took its place.

Fin strode toward the newcomers, barely concealing his outrage at Sleat's audacity. He did not require Patrick's warning glance to remind him of the need to remain calm, however, so he centered his attention on Mackinnon and his lady, rapidly estimating the number of men-at-arms with them.

"Welcome, sir," he said to Mackinnon. "And you, my lady, are even more welcome. Mistress Gordon will be delighted to see you, I know. She stands yonder," he added, gesturing toward the doorway where he had caught sight of Molly moments before, only to see that she had disappeared.

"I'm here," she said quietly from behind him. She looked wary and as if she were not certain that she wanted to show herself.

Lady Mackinnon bustled past him to hug her, saying brightly, "My love, how well ye look! I vow, the change o' residence has done ye good."

"That remains to be seen," someone growled behind Fin.

The curt tone, cutting off Molly's reply, told him who had spoken. He turned back and said just as curtly, "To what do we owe your visit, Sleat?"

Donald Grumach "the Grim" of the Isles, Chief of Sleat and Uisdean, was a tall, broad-shouldered, fair-haired man with light blue eyes. He had the proud look of his forebears, the sons of Somerled, King of the Isles, and arrogance underscored his words as he snapped, "Ye'll kindly refer to me as Donald, or Macdonald, as I've assumed my rightful, heritable title as Lord o' the Isles."

Hastily, Mackinnon said, "There were naught else to do but bring him along, Kintail, for he were wi' me when Sir Patrick brought me your good news."

"I do not agree that it *is* good news," Sleat said gruffly.

With a heartiness belied by the measuring look in his eyes, Mackinnon said, "Now, Donald, ye canna do anything about this, for ye've only a half score o' lads in your tail. Moreover, ye promised no t' make trouble an we let ye come wi' us. Sakes, lad," he added in an audible aside to Fin, "there were naught else t' be done wi' the man!"

"He slaughtered my father and Patrick's," Fin said, striving to control his temper. "He has no business to set foot inside the walls of Eilean Donan."

"Their deaths were unfortunate, but they fell in battle," Sleat said. "'Tis the chance a man takes when he raises his sword against an enemy, but 'tis a worthy death. As to my purpose here, I claim hospitality to attend my ward's marriage."

"He comes in peace," Mackinnon interjected swiftly, clearly recognizing that Fin would see little glory in battle deaths that had resulted from base trickery.

Sleat added smoothly, "I trust ye'll no forbid my attendance at the Maid's wedding, or refuse such hospitality as I have every right to claim."

"And I trust that you do not mean to make trouble, Sleat," Fin replied, putting emphasis on the name but seeing nothing to gain by pointing out to the villain that Molly was no longer his ward.

"Mayhap your hearing failed you," Sleat said gently. "I'm no longer merely Sleat but Macdonald, Lord of the Isles."

"Elsewhere, perhaps, but not here," Fin said, giving him a straight look. "Last I heard, Jamie was still Lord of the Isles."

Sleat grimaced but did not press the point. Shifting his attention to Molly, he said abruptly, "Ha' ye lost your mind, lass?"

"I do not believe so," she said, surprising Fin with her apparent calm.

Sleat snapped, "For all that Jamie had the bad manners to do me a mischief, ye need not compound it by marrying this fellow. Ye can do better! Say only that ye want no part of this, and I'll look after ye myself. I'll take ye to your cousin Huntly, for even Kintail, with all his wild ways, won't dare go against him." Shooting a glance at Fin, he added, "I have heard no man call ye a fool, Kintail, for aught else I might have heard."

Refusing the bait, Fin said, "We are about to take supper, Mackinnon. Perhaps you and your lady, and these others, would like to refresh yourselves."

"Aye, we would," Mackinnon agreed, his relief plain. "And later we'll ha' a game o' chess, lad. Ye'll no beat me a second time, I promise ye."

"One moment," Sleat said gruffly. "I'll hear from the lass's own lips that this marriage meets wi' her favor. We still ha' laws in Scotland, even in the Highlands, and I'll no see her forced into any union against her will. What say ye, lass?"

Fin forced himself to keep silent, resisting the impulse to beat Sleat to his knees and order him dragged out and hanged for the deaths of Ranald Mackenzie and Gilchrist MacRae. Highlanders did have certain rules that they lived by, and one was that a man did not order the death of another who sought hospitality in his house. Still, the temptation was heady, especially when every eye in the hall shifted to Molly, and everyone waited to hear her answer.

As Molly returned Donald the Grim's challenging look, her dilemma suddenly resolved itself, making her choice clear.

She could remain with Kintail, who promised to protect her and whose word seemed trustworthy, or she could declare that she had no wish for the marriage and trust Donald to keep his word to her. Just hearing a declaration of the rule of law from the man who was exerting himself to raise the west Highlands against his king made her wonder why everyone in the hall had not laughed him to scorn. Deciding which man to trust was easy.

"Well, lass?" Donald said. He had thrust back his cloak to hook his thumbs over his belt, and he looked supremely confident of her reply.

"I am content, sir," she replied quietly but nonetheless firmly.

"Ye *want* to marry this fellow?"

"I will marry him," she said, raising her chin. Just so that no one could mistake her decision for anything else, she added firmly, "I shall then be done with being a hostage that my guardians may pledge whenever they want to achieve political gain. I'll have a husband instead, and a proper home."

Continued silence greeted her words, but it was now silence fraught with tension, and it lingered, as did the angry glint in Donald's eyes. Then he jerked a nod and said curtly to Kintail, "Your people will look after mine, I expect."

"They will," Kintail replied with a gesture commanding Tam to see to it.

Molly turned to Lady Mackinnon. "May I take you to your room, madam?"

Lady Mackinnon accepted the offer with visible relief.

As they left the hall, Molly allowed her ladyship's familiar chatter to divert her mind from what Donald might be planning.

Having sent Sleat and his body servant off with Tam, who would show them to a bedchamber, Fin turned back to Mackinnon, saying, "Now then, sir, what the devil is that scoundrel *really* doing here?"

Mackinnon shook his head ruefully. "Truly, lad, there were naught else t' be done wi' him. He came t' me, demanding I throw me lot in wi' his. I want naught t' do with any of it, o' course, but I dinna want Donald banging on me door wi' a cannonball if he ever figures out how t' mount cannon on his galleys."

"We must all be grateful that he has none yet."

"Aye, well, but wi' Donald, one can always expect the worst. At all events, Sir Patrick arrived in the midst of our conversation, and at first, I were glad o' the interruption and invited him t' take a flagon of *brogac* with us, believing he knew Donald. He didna, though, and explained his mission t' me straightaway."

Ruefully, Patrick said, "I'd never seen Sleat before. I thought he must be a friend of yours, sir."

"Whilst I," Mackinnon said, "believed ye must ken him all *too* well."

"Neither of us was present when he organized the attack against my father's party," Fin explained. "We were rousing nearby villagers, so they could prepare to take in survivors of the supposed shipwreck."

"Aye, well, when Donald heard about your wedding, he invited himself t' join us," Mackinnon explained. "He had only the small tail of men wi' him—doubtless t' lend an appearance o' peaceful intent—and Sir Patrick had the wit t' say we should depart at once."

"Is this possibly some sort of ruse on Sleat's part?" Fin asked. "Might his army even now be approaching, hoping to catch us all in one place?"

"Sir Patrick thought o' that, as well," Mackinnon said. "I took Donald at his word—foolishly, ye'll say—but Patrick didna do any such thing."

"I gave orders for our people to keep watch over the Kyle and to send word to us here at so much as a hint of anything unusual," Patrick said.

"Good," Fin said, adding to Mackinnon, "You will be wanting to refresh yourself before we sup, sir. One of my lads will show you to your chamber." When the older man had departed, he said to Patrick, "What think you of this? Sleat must have something in mind other than merely attending my wedding."

Patrick shrugged, but Fin detected a gleam of humor in his eyes as he said, "I hardly think he will mount an attack whilst he rests within our walls himself. Even so, I've arranged for enough of our men to sleep here tonight to keep his lads out of mischief, and I've sent word to those ashore to keep watch there. I told our lot to toss Sleat and his men in the dungeon if anyone reports an unusual number of boats entering the loch, or any other such devilry."

"Good man," Fin said, clapping him on the shoulder.

Patrick grinned. "They came in Mackinnon's boats, don't forget. They should return the same way, but we'll keep a sharp eye out after the wedding."

Deciding that things were well in hand and that Eilean Donan and her people would be safer with Sleat under their eye than elsewhere, making mischief, Fin relaxed, saying lightly, "I'll leave that duty to you, old friend, at least until my wedding night is over."

Patrick laughed. "Fair enough," he said. "If I am any judge of such matters, and I am, you will need to keep your wits about you if you are not to lose your manhood before you've made good use of it. However, you may see to your bride in relative peace, because I'll keep all safe elsewhere."

Fin nodded, smiling as erotic images of the wedding night that lay ahead of him flooded his imagination. It was just as well that he could trust Patrick, for once he was in bed with Molly, he doubted that there would be room in his mind for thoughts of anything, or anyone, else.

Chapter 14 _____

With rare exceptions, thoughts of the wedding night that lay ahead of her had plagued Molly and teased her from the moment she had agreed to marry Kintail, and they did so right up to the morning of her wedding. When she tried to imagine what would happen, she remembered his kisses and caresses, even thoughts of which stirred the fiery feelings they had stirred at the time, but beyond that, her imagination failed her. On Skye, she had heard newly wedded young women giggling to their friends and being teased by them, but she could recall nothing specific that anyone had said in her presence to describe what actually happened.

From the time she awakened to Doreen's rap on the morning of the wedding, tense anticipation filled her mind. Since she had come to terms with what she was doing and why she was doing it, she wondered why she seemed unable to attend efficiently to the simple routines of dressing and breaking her fast. She dropped things and seemed unable to speak the sensible sentences that formed in her brain. Instead words got mixed or the sense turned to nonsense when thoughts of Kintail pushed in to distract her. She would have liked to confide her confusion to Doreen, but she doubted that the maidservant, being still unwed herself, would understand her feelings any more than she did.

Mauri entered while Doreen was brushing Molly's hair after her bath. As she went to the wardrobe to take out the dress they had selected, she said without preamble, "Molly, d'ye ken aught o' the bedding ceremony?"

Flushing deeply, and feeling as if her thoughts had been invaded, Molly shook her head. "I know that married people frequently share a bed, that they kiss and ... and so forth, but no one ever told me that any ceremony is involved."

"It be just as I thought, then," Mauri said, gesturing for her to stand so she could slip the gold-embroidered, pale blue skirt over her head. " 'Tis only the first night, and maidens dinna take part, so I thought ye might no ha' heard of it," she went on as she dealt with the lacing. "I'd heard naught o' such, myself, afore I wed, so it came as a shock to me to learn that the men who attended my wedding would undress me for my wedding night."

Molly stared as that same shock swept over her. "The men!"

"Aye," Mauri said, nodding to Doreen to hand her the matching embroidered bodice. "Everyone accompanies the wedding couple to their bedchamber, and wi' much merriment the men undress the bride and the women undress the groom, and then they deposit them naked on the marriage bed."

"Everyone?"

"Aye. They ... they dinna depart, neither, till they be satisfied that the marriage ha' been consummated in good order."

"That sounds horrid," Molly exclaimed, albeit with only a vague notion of what Mauri meant by the last. "I ... I won't do it!"

"Ye'll ha' no choice," Mauri said, pulling the bodice

laces tight. "Everyone does it, although most brides dinna like it. I canna speak for the grooms. Malcolm said he wished it needna be, but he seemed to enjoy it all the same." She sighed, adding, "I should tell ye, too, that Malcolm and Ian Dubh ha' returned. They'd ha' been gey disappointed to miss your wedding. But come now, it be almost time!"

Molly nodded, but as she let Mauri twitch the skirt and long, full-bottomed sleeves into place, she was not thinking about Malcolm or Ian Dubh. She had to speak to Kintail, for surely he could stop the dreadful bedding ceremony if he chose. Had he not proclaimed himself lord of all? She understood that she had a duty—or would have a duty as his wife—to share his bed if he demanded it, but this was different. She had to be certain that he understood she wanted no part of it.

"I found these pretty blue and silver ribbons to weave round your kirtle and into your garland," Mauri said. "They look new. Ye must never ha' worn them."

They did look new, but Molly had never seen them before, so either Lady Mackinnon had slipped them in among the things she had brought to Eilean Donan, or they were a gift from Maggie Malloch. Since she did not recall seeing them when she and Doreen unpacked, she decided they had come from Maggie, but she did not dwell on the thought. She was still trying to think how she might speak to Kintail.

"There," Mauri said when she had finished arranging the ribbons. "Now, turn about and let us ha' a look at ye."

Molly obeyed, realizing that she had no time now to seek out Kintail. The wedding was to take place in but a few minutes, at noon, a time chosen so that all who expected to attend would have time to get there. Perhaps, though, she mused, some delay might result from the fact that everyone had to be ferried to Eilean Donan from the mainland if from nothing else.

However, when she suggested as much while Mauri adjusted the bridal garland on her head, Mauri assured her that Patrick, Malcolm, and Ian Dubh had everything in hand. And if the crowd that awaited her entrance in the great hall minutes later was anything to go by, their arrangements had gone all too smoothly.

When Fin saw Molly step into the doorway, his breath caught in his throat. He had always thought her beautiful, but now, at this moment, her beauty was almost ethereal. Her magnificent red-gold curls fell in a cloud to her hips, and the simple, well-fitting, sky-blue and gold gown looked like something an angel might wear. Her cheeks were flushed, her eyes bright. Her hands were clasped at her waist over her silver-gilt kirtle, from which dangled a silver mirror and her pomander.

Mackinnon moved to stand beside her, ready to escort her to the dais where Fin, Patrick, and Dougal Maclennan stood beside the makeshift altar. Sleat stood nearby, for even as forceful as he was, he had not had the temerity to suggest that he, and not her foster father, should stand up with her.

Mauri preceded them as Molly's sole attendant, and the scent of rosemary wafted through the air. Not only had village women strewn the herb among the rushes on the floor but they had provided each person with sprigs of it—dried, since the season was yet too early for fresh rosemary. Even the men wore bits of the herb tucked into their shirtfronts or caps, or elsewhere on their persons.

As Mackinnon led Molly forward, her skirt clung to her softly rounded hips and swirled around her dainty feet. Fin could not take his eyes off her, and when she looked at him and smiled shyly, he felt as if his body would betray his lust for her right there in front of everyone.

Molly looked straight at Kintail as she approached the dais and its makeshift altar, thinking that he looked particularly splendid for the occasion. He wore a gold-and-green-embroidered black velvet doublet over a kilted basc made from the black and green tartan favored in the area, and black trunk hose. His sleeves were puffed and slashed with dark green satin, his square-toed black shoes embroidered with matching green silk. The sword at his side and the two eagle feathers gracing his flat black velvet cap reminded everyone of his power and rank.

Molly moved to stand beside him, and Mackinnon stepped back. As always, she was struck by her instant reaction to Kintail's nearness. Vitality radiated from him, making her feel certain that she would recognize his presence though he approached her through the blackest of nights without making a sound. Nonetheless, when he took her hand in his, she started and looked up at him. His eyes were twinkling, and his expression warmed her. It was as if everyone else in the hall faded away, leaving them so completely alone that she might have spoken to him then about her worries, had the priest not spoken first and broken the spell.

Much of the ceremony was in Latin, but for certain key portions, Dougal Maclennan spoke the Gaelic. As Molly repeated the words he commanded her to speak, and heard Kintail speak his bits, it seemed to her that her share included a great number of awkward promises to obey and submit, including one to be always meek and obedient in bed and at board. Was that the sort of marriage it would be, one of convenience for him and total submission for her?

Kintail's share certainly contained no such words. He promised only to take her as his wedded wife, for fair and foul, rich and poor, in sickness and health, until death parted them, and that only "if the holy Kirk so ordains."

The twinkle in his eyes remained throughout, as though he knew exactly what she was thinking.

Slipping an intricately engraved gold ring on her finger, he announced that now, with the ring, he was wedded to her. Then he promised to worship her with his body and to honor her with his worldly chattel, but although he sounded perfectly sincere and even touched her arm in an intimate, reassuring way, she heard naught of obedience, submission, or even ordinary consideration for her wishes.

It occurred to her that God did not have a wife, so what could he possibly know of women's wishes or needs? Startled by the sacrilegious thought, she shot a wary glance at the priest.

He had lapsed into Latin again, however, and was paying her no heed. Slight warm pressure on the hand Kintail held drew her gaze to him.

He was smiling again, but the smile was different and the gleam in his eyes as they looked into hers sent warmth flooding through her—and something else, too, nerves stirring again in those places she had never expected to feel such things.

Moments later, the priest presented them to the assembly as man and wife, and a great cheering broke out, only to be drowned out by the triumphant skirling of pipes from the back of the hall.

Gillies and maidservants hastened to turn the altar back into the laird's high table, after which the bride and groom, their primary guests, and upper members of the household took places there. Servants bore in platters and baskets of food, and the bridal supper began with a toast from Constable Ian Dubh to the couple. One from Kintail to the company followed, and many more followed thereafter.

Merriment and feasting continued through the afternoon, while the bride and groom sat chatting with Mackinnon, his lady, Patrick and his kinsmen, and—because of his rank—Donald the Grim. All the while, a steady stream of well-wishers approached to welcome the bride and congratulate their laird.

Molly was so occupied with friends and guests that not until Kintail took her hand and stood up did thought of the bedding ceremony flash into her mind again.

She realized then that she had not yet spoken privately with him, and thus had not revealed her strong aversion to the horrid ceremony. Now, looking at him, her nerves suddenly reeling, she could think of no proper way to express her feelings. His friends and tenants surrounded them, and Mackinnon stood within earshot. So did Donald the Grim, looking exactly as one might expect.

Kintail made a slight gesture toward Sir Patrick, and that gentleman jumped onto a bench and raised both hands, shouting for quiet.

When the general uproar faded to a rumble, he said, "The laird bids you all stay and make merry as long as you like. There is plenty still to eat and to drink, and we will have dancing, as well, since no reformers were invited here today."

Hearty laughter greeted this sally, but one wag bellowed, "We still ha' the bedding to see to, laird!"

Kintail waved in the direction of the bellow, and Molly slipped behind him, grateful for once that he was so large. No one would see her blushes or, for that matter, detect her rising fear.

Kintail said in an even voice but one that carried easily, "I will bed my own bride, lads. Tradition is all very well, but you are here at my invitation, and anyone who seeks to create a nuisance on my wedding night will quickly learn that he should not take my hospitality—or my amiable nature—for granted."

Sir Patrick gestured to someone at the rear of the hall, and when a lone piper began to play a reel, Kintail grabbed Molly's arm and urged her through the doorway to the spiral stairs.

"Make haste, lass," he said. "Patrick can hold them for a few moments, but most of them are already ape-drunk, and if you give them encouragement by so much as flashing an ankle, they'll be upon us."

"We ha' done it, Catriona," Claud said with satisfaction as, from the laird's peek, he watched Molly and the laird hurry from the hall, then past them and on up the spiral stairs. "The Circle canna say now I were wrong tae put them together, no when Kintail and my lady be married and all. Art pleased wi' me, lass?" he asked, moving to put his arm around Catriona, who had watched the proceedings with him. Now, he thought, perhaps he could spend more time alone with her.

As his hand brushed her shoulder, however, he realized that she was getting to her feet. "Come on, Claud," she said. "I want to see what happens above."

"But, Catriona—!"

He spoke to air. She was already flitting up the stairway.

Chapter 15

Nervous and unusually aware of Kintail behind her as she hurried up the stairs, Molly gripped her skirts in one hand and the stiff oiled-rope banister in the other. Even so, her steps were uncertain and she felt dizzy and out of breath.

Over her shoulder, she said, "I . . . I wanted to tell you that I didn't think I could go through with that dreadful bedding ceremony." When she nearly tripped on the step before the landing, she added, "Faith, but the wine must have been unusually potent. It seems to have gone straight to my—"

Her last sentence ended in a shriek as, without a word, he scooped her up from behind and carried her to his bedchamber, managing the door latch easily despite his burden, and nudging the door open with a foot. The mixed emotions that had been building all day overwhelmed her, and she did not say another word.

A warm, orange-and-yellow glow greeted them from the cozy fire crackling in the fireplace and from candles burning in sconces on two walls. The window curtains were closed, but those on the bed were not. The oblong tub sat where it had the day she had surprised Kintail with Patrick's sister, Bab, and in that first instant she assumed its presence meant that Kintail had bathed before the wedding and someone had forgotten to empty the tub. She was thus surprised to see steam rising from the water. More steam rose from a kettle hanging on the swey over the fire.

She had only a moment to take it all in before Kintail set her down and stood gazing at her. For a moment, she thought he might be experiencing the same sense of disorientation that she felt, but she dismissed that thought the moment it formed. He was too large, too vital, too decisive, and much too sure of himself to be concerned at such a moment about what might happen next.

She looked searchingly into his eyes. A reflection of the firelight danced there, making them gleam, but firelight was not responsible for the hunger she saw, a hunger that made her body hum with nervous anticipation.

He reached out and touched the left side of her face, slowly stroking her cheek and then the line of her jaw with one finger.

His hand was warm, the fingertip slightly rough against her skin.

Gently, he said, "Have you any notion of how beautiful you are?"

The world righted itself, and she said with an unexpected chuckle, "Now, how am I supposed to answer that? If I say 'yes,' you will think me conceited. If I say 'no,' you will think me insipid."

"Never insipid, lass," he said, his voice low and vibrant. "Many other things, perhaps, but not that."

His hand slid around to grasp the back of her neck.

She smiled shyly, watching his expression for a hint as to what he would do next, and when he just smiled, she said, "Should I know what to do now, sir?"

"Do you know what men and women do when they bed, lass?"

"Aye, somewhat," she said, feeling fire in her cheeks. "It is like . . . like horses and such, is it not?"

He chuckled. "I promise you, I'll try to behave in a more civilized fashion than any stallion at rut."

A rap at the door startled them both, but Kintail smiled reassuringly at her and said, "Enter."

Mauri breezed in, carrying a pewter goblet. "Good," she said, looking around the room with a critical expression. "I see they ha' prepared the tub for ye, mistress." Casting a pointed look at Kintail, she added, "Laird, they forgot the cold-water pail. Would ye shout at someone, or better still, go yourself to fetch it? If ye shout, you'll likely ha' that lot below up here demanding a proper bedding."

Kintail shook his head, still smiling. He said only, "What is in the goblet?"

"Just a wee posset o' warm wine and milk," Mauri said, eyeing him warily now. "I . . . I thought that a bath and a warm drink would help the mistress relax after such a . . . a long day. I can help her undress whilst ye're below."

"Leave the goblet," he said, "but take yourself off. I'll help with her bath."

"But the water still be too hot!"

"Then we'll think of some way to pass the time whilst it cools," he said. Shooting an oblique, teasing look at Molly, he added, "I don't think I dare trust my bride yet with a bucket of cold water in my bedchamber."

Molly knew she was still blushing, and Mauri hesitated, looking from her to Kintail. When he frowned, Mauri yielded.

"Very well, then," she said, shooting a sympathetic look at Molly.

When the door had shut behind her, Molly drew a deep breath and let it out slowly. "She is just trying to be kind, sir."

"She's being a damned nuisance," he retorted. "Art nervous, lass?"

"Aye," she said honestly. "You do fill a room."

"I expect I do," he said, grinning. Then, he turned his head sharply.

"What is it?" she asked.

"My mind playing tricks," he said. "I thought I saw movement toward that window, but there is no one here but us, so let's get your clothes off and get you into that tub. I've never played maidservant before, but I believe I can learn."

Feeling uncharacteristically bashful, Molly wanted to tell him she had bathed before the wedding and that she would prefer to have Doreen or Mauri help her if he expected her to bathe again before bed (although surely, one would have heard of such a strange custom if it existed). But she knew where her duty lay, and she still felt the weight of the priest's numerous exhortations regarding wifely obedience. Moreover, Kintail seemed different in this mood, less intimidating.

When he turned her around to remove her garland and kirtle and loosen her lacing, she remained as he placed her, but her heart pounded so hard and fast that she wondered why they could not both hear it. Her bodice laces were quickly loosened, and the ties of her skirt yielded similarly to his deft fingers. In moments, the lovely pale blue gown lay in a heap on the floor, decked by myriad blue and silver ribbons and Molly's garland, and she stood in only her shift. He pulled her back against him, his hands gently cupping her breasts from behind. She felt his warmth through the thin material of her shift.

"So soft," he murmured, nuzzling her neck until she felt his lips caress her, sending fire through her body. His right hand tensed on her breast.

She had trouble finding her voice. "Is . . . is something wrong?"

He chuckled, and his breath ticked the back of her neck, firing tremors of heat to her midsection and lower. "Touching you makes me tingle," he said.

"M-me, too," she said.

He held her against him, stroking one bare arm lightly, then more firmly, before his fingers moved toward her breasts again.

"What of your clothing?" she asked hoarsely."Does only the bride take off her clothes?"

He chuckled again, put both hands firmly on her shoulders, and turned her to face him. "Do you want to take a bath or not?"

"Not," she said. "I bathed before the wedding. Mauri knew that, too," she added. "She cannot have been thinking only that I might be nervous. She must have worried that I might be afraid."

"Are you afraid?" he demanded. "Tell me truly now, lass."

She considered the question seriously for a long moment, then said, "I don't think so. I am a little nervous, perhaps, but all brides must be nervous."

"Then suppose I put you in bed with Mauri's posset to sip whilst I get out of my clothing. You can play maidservant to me another night."

Without waiting for a reply, he picked her up again, shift and all, and although the bed was but a few steps away, he carried her there.

"But this is excellent," Catriona said, settling her slender but enticingly curvaceous body comfortably against the cushion in the window embrasure. "We can watch everything from here."

"I dinna think we should be here," Claud protested, unable to take his eyes off her despite his concerns. "It isna proper."

"I do not care," she said, patting the place beside her invitingly. "I want to see, and after all, if Kintail had not forbidden all others to come, his bedding would have had a much larger audience."

"Aye, but he did forbid it," Claud reminded her.

"You may leave if you think you are intruding. Of course, if you do, I probably shall not speak to you for days," she added, stroking his upper thigh.

"Catriona," Claud groaned.

"Hush," she said. "Watch now. Why is he just standing there by the bed, holding her? Does the great daffy not know what to do next?"

Kintail had reached the bed and was about to set Molly down when he paused, stiffening, suddenly alert.

"What is it?" she asked.

"I thought I heard voices," he said, looking around as if he expected to see someone step forth from the shadows.

They both remained silent for a time, but in the flickering light, only the shadows moved, and all Molly could hear was the crackling of the fire.

"Mayhap Mauri is returning," she said.

"She would not dare."

"Then your friends. Mightn't they dare?"

"Doubtless it was just my imagination," he said, setting her gently on the bed where she could lean back against the pillows. Then, fetching the pewter goblet, he handed it to her, saying, "Don't drink that too fast now."

She sipped, watching him strip off his clothing, aware that he, too, was accustomed to having a servant help him, but his movements were deft and sure. That he was in a hurry was plain. He cast off the last article of clothing and turned toward the bed.

Molly stared.

"Oh, good, very good, indeed," Catriona said, sitting up straighter and removing her hand from Claud's thigh.

Hearing such a strong note of approval in her tone, Claud wandered if she were wishing that she could bed the huge man rather than himself.

"He's all right, I guess," he said with a glance, "for a mortal."

"All *right*?" She did not so much as flick her intense gaze away from Kintail. "The man is magnificent!"

Fin stopped in midstride, certain that this time he *had* heard voices, a female and a male. They seemed to float on the air from nowhere in particular, but glancing at his bride, he could see no sign that she had heard them.

She was staring at him, round-eyed, and he could not blame her for that. Even if she had seen a naked man before, she probably had never seen one in his present state of lust, a state, admittedly, that had slackened at the sound of the voices but was improving again rapidly with each second that he feasted his eyes on her enticing beauty.

With one candle alight on a nearby chest and the fire's diminishing glow to guide him, he moved to the bed, took the goblet from her, and set it on the chest beside the candle. Then, pulling back the coverlet, he resisted the temptation just to stand and gaze at her and slid gently in beside her, gathering her into his arms.

"I am going to take off your shift," he murmured a few moments later, reaching for it. "I want to kiss you all over."

"All over?" she sounded half intrigued, half fearful, as she wriggled helpfully, shifting her weight to make it easier for him to take off the thin garment.

"Aye," he said, casting it aside without a thought as to where it might fall. "Mind you, lass, my body is telling me to take you swiftly and be done with it, but I'd like you to know some pleasure, too."

"Pleasure?" She seemed surprised.

"Aye, like this," he said, beginning to caress her body from tip to toe with his lips and hands. As he moved upward again, intending to savor her full, soft breasts with his lips, he had to fight a renewed urge to take her swiftly. Her skin was so soft, so smooth, and the scent she used filled the air around them with its enticing aroma, filling his mind with delightful images of what lay ahead.

The soft glow of firelight made her body look golden, the tips of her breasts so inviting that he moved to take the right one between his lips. As he did, he cupped the breast in his hand, letting his fingertips stroke it gently as he focused his attention on the soft, berrylike nipple. Involved as he was, it took a moment to realize that his stroking fingertips had encountered something unusual.

Curious, he shifted his position so that light from the candle fell on her breast, and he saw then what his body's shadow had hidden from him before. The oddly shaped mark was not as long as his little finger, but it was dark red, rippled, and slightly raised, a rough blemish on her otherwise perfect skin.

Gently, he touched it with one finger, stroking it lightly as he said, "This is an odd sort of a birthmark. I swear it makes my fingers tingle when I touch it."

"It is not a birthmark," she said. "The night Angus took me from Dunsithe, my mother marked me with a red-hot key."

"Faith, what sort of mother would brand her own child?"

"She said that she did it so that people would always know me as the true Maid of Dunsithe," she said with a grimace. Then, more cheerfully, she added, "Maggie says it will fade away to nothing in time, that such marks do."

"Who is Maggie?"

After a momentary silence, she said, "Just someone who looked after me. Different people have done so, you know, for I was not yet six when they took me from my mother. Even before, I spent more time with my nurse than with her."

"I think it is as well that I do not know your mother," he said.

"I do not know her either," she said. "I never saw her after I left Dunsithe."

"Do you have any other memories of Dunsithe?" he asked. He had never thought to ask if she knew anything that might lead to finding her fortune. He wondered if anyone had ever asked her. Someone, sometime, must have said something, given her some clue to help her find it when the time came to do so.

"Why does he waste time talking?" Catriona demanded.

"Hush," Claud said. "Listen."

Remembering Kintail's interest in her fortune and wondering how she had let herself forget why he had married her, Molly said bluntly, "Is it so important to talk now about Dunsithe?"

His attention had wandered, but he looked directly at her when she spoke and seemed to give himself a shake. His gaze held hers for a long moment before he said quietly, "It was but a topic of conversation, lass, nothing more. Let me see now. Where was I?"

His eyes twinkled then, teasing her, and she cast her worries aside.

"I think I'll leave that to you to remember—if you can."

"Oh, I certainly can," he said, chuckling and reaching for her again.

Feeling Molly relax, Fin breathed a sigh of relief. The tension in her eyes had told him what she was thinking as clearly as if she had put it into words. He had been a fool to mention Dunsithe. He could not think what had come over him to do so at such a time as this, because her thoughts, like his, had naturally gone straight to her fortune.

Speaking of her mother had turned his thoughts to Dunsithe, of course, but the fortune was important only insofar as what he could achieve with it at Eilean Donan, and that was not anything he intended to discuss with her tonight.

He had heard the voices again, too. Only briefly, to be sure, but again just hearing them had been enough to divert his body's interest from Molly. Still, when it happened before, it had not taken long to renew that interest, so he settled beside her again, saying lightly, "I think I was just about here when I stopped."

Bending to her breast again, he stroked it gently, then took the nipple between his lips, sucking gently for a moment before he released it. Hearing her gasp, he looked into her face again and said with a smile, "Have I got it right?"

"Oh, yes! Should I not do something, too, to give you pleasure?"

"Not tonight," he said, returning to his task. "Tonight, this gives me pleasure. Later, I will teach you other ways." With his lips on her breast again, he focused on her reactions, using everything he knew to stir her passions until he had her gasping and writhing. At last, knowing the time was right, he eased himself over her.

"Now, it comes," Catriona exclaimed with satisfaction. "Now, we shall see what he is truly made of, this mortal."

"Catriona, hush!" Claud wailed.

"Stop telling me to hush!" She leaned forward, resting her elbows on her tucked-up knees with her chin in her hands. Turning her head, she added, "Having small regard for human antics, I have not heeded the laird's lusting before now, but I see that I should have. If he can keep this up, he has great potential."

Claud sighed as she riveted her attention to the bed.

Hearing the voices again, and as clearly this time as if they were only a few feet away, Fin stopped what he was doing to look around the bedchamber. The dying fire cast flickering, dark shadows on the walls, but they were all that stirred. He could see nothing out of the ordinary, and certainly there was no hiding place large enough to contain a spy.

With a gasp of frustration, Molly said hoarsely, "Why did you stop?"

"Did you not hear them?" Fin felt himself wilting.

"Who?"

Realizing that she had no idea what had disturbed him, and fearing that she might begin to think him demented, he tried to regain his previous ardor, but no matter what he did, or how hard he tried to forget the voices, he continued to hear them. They were too faint to make out exact words, but the fact that he could hear them was enough. He could not concentrate, and his body refused to do its part.

"Is something amiss?" Molly asked. "Is it something that I did?"

"Just look at him, Claud," Catriona said disgustedly, falling back against the cushion again and stretching out her legs. "He is inept, after all. Mortals simply are no good at this sort of thing."

"We disturbed him," Claud protested, feeling guilty.

"A good lover," Catriona said sternly, "is aware of nothing and no one but his woman. His gaze devours her. It feasts upon her beauty until he can think of nothing but possessing her, conquering her. His whole body should ache for hers."

Involuntarily, as if he had needed no more than the suggestion, Claud felt himself begin to harden and throb, even to ache. "Perhaps mortals dinna feel things as strongly as we do," he muttered.

"Then they should strive to do so," she said. "But in truth, Claud, any man can stir a woman to feel things if he will but concentrate. Mortal men simply do not consider women as they should." She sighed. "I could teach this one, if he would just notice me."

"He did hear us just then," Claud pointed out.

"He heard only our voices, not the words," Catriona said as her fingers teased him. "Since he refuses to see what is before his eyes, we need not heed him."

Claud groaned. "Catriona, stop. Whether they see or dinna see, I feel as if they do. Canna we no leave them tae theirselves, for I canna concentrate, much as I want tae gi'e ye me full attention."

"Then you shall, dearling, for I've something important I want to ask you."

"Anything! Only come away first!"

"Oh, very well," she said.

Delirious with gratitude for her understanding, and in a rush to leave, he scarcely noticed when she turned back and made a slight gesture toward the couple on the bed before following.

"What did I do?" Molly asked urgently.

"Nothing, lass," he replied, but his voice lacked its usual strength.

She was certain something was amiss, for he had been moving atop her and had just stopped. Before then, he had been as eager to continue as she was.

"Then why did you stop?" she asked.

He hesitated for a moment, then settled down beside her again. "I think I just want to hold you for a while first," he said.

Having no objection to that, she let him gather her into his arms. He kissed her gently on the lips, and although she hoped for a moment that he would stir her passions as he had before, she felt nothing but deep contentment. With her head resting in the curve of his shoulder, she snuggled close to him. It seemed odd to be in bed with a man, odd but nice. She felt safe, for one thing, and she felt . . . but even as the thought began to form, she slept.

When Molly awoke, the curtains were open and the morning sun flooded the bedchamber with its bright yellow rays. She was alone in the bed, but Doreen stood at the washstand, folding a towel.

"Good morning," Molly said, rubbing sleep from her eyes.

Looking over her shoulder, Doreen said, "I'm sorry to wake ye, mistress, but I didna think ye'd want to sleep the day away."

"No," Molly said, sitting up and plumping pillows behind her. Realizing that she was still naked, she tucked the coverlet up over her breasts. "What is the hour?"

"Nearly ten," Doreen said. "Ye must ha' been awake long into the night, to sleep so long."

Unable to remember much about the previous night other

than the wondrous feelings Kintail had awakened in her, Molly did not reply. It seemed as if they had scarcely begun when he said he heard voices, but she remembered little after that other than a sense of contentment and pleasure.

"I must have been very tired," she said. "I did not hear Kintail get up."

"He were up and out afore dawn," Doreen said, picking up a skirt that lay ready with the rest of what Molly would wear that day atop one of the chests. "He and Sir Patrick and Sir Patrick's uncle Ian Dubh ha' already escorted the last o' the guests to their boats."

"All of our guests have gone?" Molly sat up straight in dismay.

"Aye," Doreen said calmly, shaking out the skirt.

"But I should have been there to bid them farewell, especially Mackinnon and her ladyship!"

"Nay, mistress, they didna expect it. Ye forget it be the custom for a bride to remain secluded for at least four days after her wedding."

"Is the groom not supposed to remain with her?"

Doreen shrugged. "That be up to the groom, I expect. The laird did say he wanted to make certain Donald the Grim were well away from Eilean Donan."

"Did Donald not return with Mackinnon, then?"

"Nay, I think not. He had men and horses waiting near the village, my Thomas said. Donald told the master he did have business up north somewhere."

"Wicked business, most likely," Molly said.

"Aye, but he did no mischief here in the castle, thanks to our men keeping watch. Moreover, Ian Dubh and Mauri's Malcolm will follow them for a time, my Thomas said. They be taking that Tam o' the master's, too, and Thomas says Tam were a running gilly afore the laird took him for his personal servant and Tam can still run like the wind for hours. The way be rugged, but they'll send him back if they need more men. Will ye dress first, or shall I fetch ye your breakfast here?"

"Fetch some food, please, but then I'll dress. You may fetch me a fresh shift before you go." She adjusted the coverlet, adding, "Surely, no one expects me to stay in this room for four days. I'll not do it."

Doreen did not reply, and when she had gone, Molly slipped the clean shift on over her head but decided not to get up until the maidservant returned. Again, she tried to recall what had happened the previous night, but although she remembered pleasurable feelings, her brain remained otherwise uncooperative.

"A bride shouldna be alone the day after her wedding," Maggie Malloch's familiar voice declared with strong disapproval.

"Good morning," Molly said as the little woman took form at the end of the bed, leaning comfortably against a bedpost with her neatly booted feet stretched out before her and her pipe in hand, its smoke curling gently upward.

"And a good morrow tae yourself," Maggie replied. "Did ye send him away, then, the laird?"

"Do you not know where he is?"

Maggie shrugged. "'Tis nae business o' mine what he does wi' his time."

"But you just *asked* where he was," Molly reminded her.

"Aye, but that were because I ha' found ye alone, and a bride shouldna be alone the morning after her wedding day."

"Well, he was gone when I awoke. Doreen said he arose before dawn to make sure Donald the Grim got up to no mischief and had departed as planned."

"Aye, that one's a menace, and no mistake." Gesturing airily with her pipe, Maggie added, "Did ye enjoy your wedding night then, and all?"

"Do you not know about that, either?" Molly knew she was blushing.

"Whisst now, lassie, it were your night and no an event tae which others should be party, for all that the custom in these parts remains sadly unmannerly."

"Well, the wedding guests did not follow us up here, but nonetheless Kintail said that he could hear voices, so perhaps someone was watching."

"Voices, eh?" Maggie sat up a little straighter. "What sort o' voices would these ha' been, then?"

"I did not hear them," Molly said. "Kintail said he thought he heard someone—three times he said so, in fact—and after the third, the only thing I remember is snuggling down beside him and waking up this morning."

Maggie frowned. "Be that so, in troth?"

"Aye, but there was no one about, and there is nowhere for anyone to hide."

"None that ye could see, at all events," Maggie amended. "Mayhap it isna such a bad thing that the laird could hear them, for it shows that he's summat improved in his ways. Nonetheless, I must look into this business straightaway."

"But how could anyone—?"

The sound of a step outside the door interrupted her, and as she shot a glance in that direction, the door opened to admit Doreen with her breakfast tray.

When Molly looked back, Maggie was gone.

Chapter 16

"Claud! Ye pernicious dunghill-strumpet's fool, where be ye hiding?"

Maggie's fury reverberated through their little abode, making the very walls vibrate, and in the little parlor, Claud trembled at the sound.

He leaped to his feet, but before he could take a step, the parlor door flew back on its hinges and Maggie swept into the room, saying angrily, "What the plague ha' ye been at now, ye witless trull-bender?"

Backing away from her anger, Claud sputtered, "N-nothing, Mam!"

"I suppose ye and that Highland giglet were never in the laird's bedchamber, rattling like a pair o' fractious magpies and preventing the poor man from seeing tae his business!"

"Catriona be nae giglet!"

"A black plague on Catriona—and on ye as well," Maggie snapped. "By my troth, I should hand the pair o' ye tae the Circle and let them ha' their way wi' ye."

Claud gasped. "Nay, Mam, ye wouldna do such a thing!"

"Mayhap, I will, or—an ye heed me—mayhap I willna

tell them yet," Maggie said, her voice suddenly low and almost gentle.

The new tone terrified Claud even more. "What then? What *will* ye do?"

In answer, her hands flashed up, palms out, and Claud suddenly found himself flung backward, hard, against the wall. He slumped to the floor, winded but otherwise unhurt, realizing only when he looked up that her hands still were raised.

She was muttering.

"What be ye saying, Mam?" His voice sounded weak and unnaturally high, more like some ancient crone's than his own.

The muttering continued for another few horrible seconds, but then she lowered her hands and said in that terrifyingly calm voice, "I ha' but two questions tae ask ye, Claud, and ye'd best answer them straight, because what I ha' done will make ye gey sorry an ye dinna speak the truth."

"What will ye ken, then?"

"Who put the laird and our lady tae sleep last night?"

"It must ha' been Catriona," he admitted, too afraid of her to prevaricate.

"Why did that bed-swerver put them tae sleep?"

"I . . . I dinna ken why." The moment the words were out, his body began oddly to twitch and tingle. "What did ye do tae me, Mam?" he shrieked.

"Naught that will harm ye so long as ye speak the truth tae me, Claud. Think now. Why did the wicked trull put them tae sleep?"

"She wanted tae watch, but she said the laird were inept, and she let me take her away, but I dinna ken for sure that . . ." He fell silent, remembering what had happened next. He was not analytical by nature, but neither was he stupid, and the tingling in his body was growing warmer—not pleasantly so, either. "I—I think she went wi' me only because . . ."

"What?" Maggie said, her tone calm now, as if she knew that he could not refuse to answer.

Nor could he. "She asked me where Dunsithe's treasure lies hidden," he said, looking at the floor, his voice no more than a whisper.

"And what did you tell the malevolent slut?"

"That it were your spell cast over it, Mam, that I ken naught o' its ways."

"Then what did she say?"

It occurred to Claud that his mother had exceeded her two questions, but he did not have the courage to point that out, although he would have preferred not to answer this one. Nevertheless, the words spilled from his lips, and he seemed unable to stop them. "She said I must ask ye tae tell me its secret."

He did not dare look at her, and the silence that followed made him tremble again. An odd little voice in his head chose that moment to list all the things he had done to sink himself into this mess, and his fright blossomed into dread.

"Ye mustna see her again, Claud," Maggie said quietly. "Forbye, lad, but ye ken now that her sole interest lies in how easily she can manipulate ye and make ye act for her and for her laird. She covets Dunsithe's treasure for him, and she hopes ye can help her acquire it. Ye canna help, though, and that ye'd best believe, lad. Even I couldna help her find Dunsithe's treasure."

"Truly, Mam?" That she could not sort out her own spell was hard to believe.

"Truly," she said. "The spell I cast that night will dissipate only when them what deserve the treasure discover the means tae retrieve it."

"But the treasure still lies at Dunsithe, does it not?"

"Aye, but that be nae concern o' yours or yon feckless Catriona. What powers ye possess were no intended tae serve such a witless broomstick as that one. Heed me now, lad, for I'll tell ye what I ha' done."

Claud braced himself.

"What time ye spend now in her company will only weaken your powers. Moreover, each time ye use them, ye'll feel their use in a way tae make ye value them more. D'ye accept this punishment, Claud?"

Bitterly, he said, "Do I ha' a choice?"

"Aye, lad, ye do. An ye refuse my punishment, I must take the matter up wi' the Circle, for ye ha' meddled wi' your lady tae serve yourself instead o' her—and that for nae reason but pleasuring. Your duty be tae the Maid o' Dunsithe above all else. So now, Claud, will it be my punishment or the Circle's? Ye must choose."

He sighed. Just as he had thought, the choice was no choice at all.

Nell and her party reached Glen Shiel, and by late afternoon, they were riding along a narrow track with the river to their left and high, steep peaks rising on either side of them. They had ridden hard from Stirling, stopping only to request hospitality for each of the two nights, and then continuing on each day at dawn.

"How much farther?" she asked their guide.

"If memory serves me," he began, as he had every time she had asked such a question, "it will take us about an hour to reach Loch Duich and half an hour more to reach Eilean

Donan. At least we are blessed with fine weather," he added. "It may rain later, though. I feel mist in the air."

Nell could feel the mist on her face, but it was a lovely, soft day, and she would soon accomplish at least one of her goals. What to do about the others, she did not know. First, she would have to rid herself of Jamie's too-observant guide.

They slowed to rest the horses, and when the steep embankment on the north side of the River Shiel suddenly became a sheer cliff to the water's edge, they paused at a convenient ford to water the horses before crossing to the south bank.

Nell strove to conceal her impatience. She glanced at Jane, her tirewoman, and saw that she looked tired. No wonder, Nell thought. They had ridden long and hard. The men who had ridden with them to Stirling had shown no surprise at their stamina, and even the guide Jamie had provided had soon taken their measure. The first night, surprised at learning that Nell expected to be on the road again at dawn, he had dared suggest she rest longer. The second night he just nodded obediently in response to her commands.

"Not much farther now," he said a half hour later.

Hearing Jane's sigh of relief, Nell smiled at her and said, "If Kintail proves hospitable, perchance we'll linger a few days with him and have a good rest."

"We cross this river again near the mouth of Loch Duich," the guide said. "The land there is particularly boggy, so we must take special care."

Nell was accustomed to bogs. The Scottish west march was rife with them, and for that matter, Douglas land in all three Scottish marches contained bogs. She had learned their secrets. The one ahead did not concern her.

When they came to it, it proved to be woodland with soft, mushy ground but none that she considered treacherous.

They rode through the first part of it without incident and crossed a plank bridge over the river. To her left lay the waters of Loch Duich, and the sight filled her with eager anticipation. Molly was near.

Nell smiled, although tears stung her eyes, and just then, without warning, men dropped from trees and burst from the shrubbery, surrounding them.

The attackers had no horses, and most were bare-legged, wearing only long saffron-colored fabric kilted round their waists with belts, from which hung scabbards for dirks or swords. The scabbards were empty, though, for the weapons were in the men's hands. Errant shafts of sunlight sparkled on cold steel.

The riders had scarcely seen man or beast since entering Glen Shiel, and the men of her escort, overwhelmed, were no match for the assailants. The guide reached for his sword but fell with the weapon halfway out of its scabbard. The two men-at-arms fell, too, leaving the women to fend for themselves.

One attacker grabbed Nell's reins and spoke to her, but he spoke the heathenish Highland Gaelic, and she could not understand him.

"Does no one amongst you speak plain, broad Scot?" she demanded, dashing an impatient sleeve across her still damp eyes.

"If ye mean the tongue spoken by the villainous English, lass, I speak it well enow," one of the men said. "Who be ye and what possessions ha' ye got that we might find useful— after your pretty selves, o' course." He leered at her.

"I am Lady Percy," Nell said, retaining her dignity with effort. "I come on the King of Scot's business and bear his warrant, granting me safe conduct."

"Och, does yon wee bletherer, Jamie, think he rules the Highlands, then?"

"You know that he does rule them," Nell said, striving to keep her increasing fear from revealing itself in her voice. "He is High King of *all* Scots."

"I ha' heard that," the man said, still grinning. "All the same, I ha' never laid eyes on the man, so I'll wait till I do to decide will I follow him or no."

"Even if you do not recognize James's power, surely you recognize the Laird of Kintail," Nell said, remembering how near Eilean Donan was and assuming these must be Kintail's men. "I am bound for Eilean Donan, because my daughter abides there. She is Mary Gordon, Maid of Dunsithe, and she is Kintail's ward."

The man's eyebrows shot upward. "Aye, so? Then I've a notion my master will want to speak wi' ye, lass, straightaway."

"I warrant he will," Nell said gratefully. "Will you kindly ask your men to look after mine, since you are responsible for their present condition?"

He glanced at the fallen and shrugged. "I canna do other than bury them," he said. "They be dead, and I canna seek help fra' the local priest just now, ye see."

She wondered what he could have done to alienate the priest but decided it would be undiplomatic to ask. So, with a reassuring nod to Jane, she prepared to follow her new escort, striving to quiet her fears by telling herself that, horrid as it all was, at least she need worry no longer about how to rid herself of Jamie's guide.

The man with whom she had spoken, clearly the ruffian leader, took her reins from her, insisting that she let one of his men lead her horse. Another led Jane's, but to Nell's surprise, they did not continue along the shoreline of Loch Duich. They turned north up a side glen, away from the loch where their guide had said that Eilean Donan sat on an island, so the castle was not their destination. But when she demanded to know where they were going, no one deigned to reply.

Making their way through twisting, steep-sided glens, they came in less than an hour to a tent encampment in the midst of dense woodland. The leader ran ahead and disappeared inside the largest tent. Minutes later, he emerged with another man, tall and fair-haired, who strode ahead of him to confront Nell.

"Lady Percy," he said, eyeing her shrewdly, "I understand ye've expressed a wish to see your daughter."

"I have," she replied firmly. "If you are Mackenzie of Kintail, I must tell you, sir, that I do not approve of the way you welcome people to your land."

"Ah, but you are mistaken, my lady. Your daughter does reside with Kintail. Indeed, she has married him, but I am not he. I am Donald, Lord of the Isles."

"Are you?" Nell said. Quelling her shock at learning of Molly's marriage, she forced a smile. "H-how delightful, sir. I must tell you, this meeting solves a problem for me. I bring messages from Henry of England and my brother, the Earl of Angus, so you can imagine how confounded I was to learn that expressing a desire to see my daughter no longer provided a suitable excuse to visit you."

"I can certainly arrange for you to see your daughter, madam," he said, returning her smile, "but I hope you bring me more from England than messages."

The castle was quiet except for hushing noises the servants made as they tended to their work. Having grown bored with her own company, Molly searched for Mauri and

Doreen and found them in the kitchen, supervising the daily women.

"What would ye, m'lady?" Mauri asked.

Molly started at hearing her new title on Mauri's lips. Although guests had undoubtedly used it when paying their respects after the wedding, Doreen had not, and she had not yet grown accustomed to it. Her wedding—indeed, all of the previous day—seemed almost surreal. Waking without Kintail beside her—albeit in his bed—had made everything else seem like an illusion. She missed him, too, for she looked forward to continuing the delightful exercises they had begun.

Realizing that Mauri still waited patiently for a response to her question, Molly said, "I came to see what I can do to help you."

"Ye'll do naught today," Mauri said firmly, drawing her away from the others and speaking in a low tone that would not easily carry. "A proper bride doesna show her face for four days after her wedding."

"Do Highland husbands generally lock up their wives, then?" Molly asked with a wry smile. "Kintail seems to have forgotten to do so."

"He ha' forgotten more than that," Mauri said flatly. "He should be here wi' his bride, but he and our Patrick think Donald be up to more mischief than just inflicting his heathenish presence on your wedding, especially since he had his own men waiting yonder for him today."

"I thought there were watchers," Molly said. "How did Donald's men get here without warning?"

"Ye canna stop them coming to meet their laird when their laird be here," Mauri said reasonably. "Some o' our lads rode wi' them, o' course, and when Donald and his lot left, Ian Dubh and Malcolm followed, saying Donald may ha' more men hidden hereabouts. He'll likely head north to meet his fleet, they said."

"Did Kintail and Sir Patrick follow them, too?"

"Nay, the pair o' them and Thomas MacMorran took Lady MacRae and Bab back across the loch in one o' the boats," Mauri said. "Likely, they'll return soon."

"Someone's coming now," Doreen said, turning as hasty steps approached the kitchen. "Thomas!" she exclaimed happily when the tall young man-at-arms entered. "My mistress be looking for the master. Where did ye leave him?"

Looking apologetic, Thomas said to Molly, "He didna return with us, mistress. He said he were in a mood to walk round the loch instead. He's no alone, though. Sir Patrick sent two MacRae men with him. They be well armed, all three."

Molly felt no concern for Kintail's safety. He seemed somehow invincible, but his choice of activities for the day after his wedding disturbed her.

"Did he offer any reason for this walk of his?" she asked.

Thomas seemed suddenly reluctant to meet her gaze.

"What is it, Thomas?" Doreen asked. "What's amiss?"

"Naught," he replied, glancing at her. Then, drawing a deep breath and looking directly at Molly, he said, "The laird be in a fashious mood, is all. He said he were unfit for company and that a stretch o' his legs would do him good. But he isna a fool, no wi' Donald likely up to mischief, as he is, so, he did agree to take the two other lads along."

Realizing that Doreen and Mauri were also evading her gaze now, Molly knew that they, and Thomas, too, all thought that somehow she had angered Kintail. She nearly told them that she had done nothing of the sort but thought better of it. If she had learned anything about her new husband, she had learned that he would not like hearing that she had discussed his private business with others.

It also occurred to her that she might have done something unwittingly. Since her memories of the previous night seemed untrustworthy, such a possibility did exist. There being therefore nothing she could say that would ease their concern, she was grateful when Thomas took advantage of the silence to say diffidently that he wondered if Doreen had time to take a wee walk with him.

"Since Donald will likely make trouble soon, we must snatch what time we have, lass," he said, smiling at her. "We've things to discuss, ye ken, but I've scarce had two minutes o' your time since we came here."

When Doreen began to list things she ought to do instead, Mauri laughed and told her to get along. "I've plenty of women to help me," she said. "They'll all be off by end of day, but for now, ye go wi' your Thomas. And, mistress, ye should go along back upstairs. I warrant the laird will expect to find ye where he left ye."

Molly obeyed, not because she believed that Kintail would expect her to stay in his bedchamber but because she wanted to think. Her thoughts provided little guidance, though, and the hours passed slowly. When he had not returned by late afternoon, she went downstairs again.

"It seems odd that he would stay away so long," she told Mauri.

Mauri laughed. "No so odd, m'lady. If Wild Fin's in a temper, nae man will hurry him."

Mauri said nothing about Molly's going back upstairs after that, and Molly realized that the older woman feared now that she worried about Kintail's safety. However, she worried only that she might unwittingly have been the one to put him in a temper. She had not the least idea how she could have, though, and her own temper was beginning to stir.

Clearly wanting to distract her thoughts, Mauri gave her

a box of recipes collected over time by various mistresses of the castle, and suggested that she select a few dishes from them that might please her. Molly was still poring over these in a small chamber near the kitchen when at last she heard Kintail's voice.

Closing the box of recipes, she jumped to her feet, but he was already in the doorway, filling it. He wore chain mail, sword, and dirk, but he had taken off his helmet—and his gloves if he'd worn them. His dark hair looked damp and curly.

She reached out to him, then pulled her hand back, feeling strangely shy.

"What the devil are you doing, hiding away down here?" he demanded, looming over her, his look and tone revealing that his mood had not improved much since Thomas had left him.

"I was choosing recipes," she said. "You were gone all day."

"I know," he said, shoving a hand through his hair and looking rueful. "I've been busy, lass, but I've returned now, and what do I find but that my wife has hidden herself away to read recipes." His gaze swept over her from head to foot, and she saw that his eyes were gleaming as hungrily as they had the previous night.

Her body responded instantly to that look. Holding his gaze, she smiled and said, "I could tell you that I was looking for ones that would please you."

"You could," he said, reaching out to tweak a curl that had escaped from her coif. "But I have learned to doubt such words from your lips, lassie. Have I told you that you have beautiful lips?" he asked, bending to kiss them, while still holding the curl coiled round his finger.

The kiss began gently but soon deepened, becoming more possessive, more demanding, and her lips parted when his tongue pressed against them. An arm slid around her, pulling her closer, and when her breasts met the hardness of his shirt of mail, their nipples came alive, pushing against her bodice. His fingers slipped free of the curl twined around them, and moved to stroke her left breast.

"Just touching you makes my hands tingle," he murmured before kissing her again. His touch and his kisses were doing more than that to her.

He was very large and very near, making her conscious of how small the chamber was. She heard faint noises from the nearby kitchen, but they did not trouble her. She cared only about him and the feelings he stirred in her.

Breaking off the kiss, he said abruptly, "Can you swim?"

She blinked, struggled to regain her wits, and then nodded warily.

"I thought as much," he said with satisfaction. "Knowing how capable you are on a horse and with a longbow, and how determinedly you seek to do whatever you want to do, I dared to hope that you could."

"Why?"

"Because I am going to take you to a secret place I enjoyed as a child and to which I return when I want to be alone."

"Do you want to be alone tonight, then?"

"I want to be private with my wife. Will you come with me?"

"Aye, sir, of course I will, if you wish it."

He gave her a look that told her he had thought she might say something else, or perhaps that he had hoped she would, but he said only, "Good."

"Do we go at once or should I change to some other dress?"

"I don't care a jot what you wear, but you'll want a mantle for afterward, and a warm one, at that. The afternoon has been fine, but the night may turn cold."

"Do you really mean to swim, sir?"

"I do."

"Is it not too late in the day? It will be suppertime soon."

"And it may well be dark before we swim, lass. Wait and see. Now, go and fetch that warm mantle and a pair of stout shoes. I'll see to the rest."

When she rejoined him, he also carried a mantle. She learned that Mauri had packed a supper for them and that he intended to carry the bundle himself.

"Do we not take horses?" she asked, remembering the day he had taken her around to meet so many of his tenants.

"Nay, we'll walk." The narrow-eyed look he shot her reminded her that he had forbidden her to ride, but he did not mention that, and she was grateful.

The tide was in, but one of his men waited in a rowboat, evidently expecting to row them across to the mainland, but Kintail dismissed him and, keeping sword and dirk near at hand, took up the oars himself. Away to the west, the sun was dipping below the tops of the hills, and the last glittering pink and orange paths along the water's surface were already fading to silver.

On the other side, after tying the boat, they walked through the village and beyond. When they reached the shore again, Kintail said, "We're on Loch Long now. My childhood spot is about a half hour's walk from here."

It proved to be a sheltered, curving inlet, surrounded by woodland. The dusky light turned the calm water into a flat, gray, oblong mirror. At the east end of it, the rocky bed of a burn marked the head of the inlet. Molly guessed that at snowmelt, the burn tumbled noisily into the loch, but now it trickled. Between the woods and the edge of the loch, a narrow, curving, sandy beach girded the slender inlet. Birds still twittered in nearby trees, oblivious to the visitors.

Kintail spread his mantle on the sand and set Mauri's bundle on it. Then he turned toward Molly, the hungry look back in his eyes.

Suddenly nervous and unsure of herself, and feeling vulnerable, she said, "Why did we come here, sir? Shall we eat our supper now? Is it safe? What happened last night? I own, I do not remember everything that happened, but what I do remember was very pleasant. Did I do something to displease you?" She knew she was babbling, but she could not seem to help it.

"We are safe here, lass, and what happened last night had naught to do with you," he said. "I just want to be alone with you in a place where I can be more certain that no one will interrupt us."

"But what happened to make you so angry today?"

"A man gets angry when his body behaves strangely and he cannot control it. Mine did that last night, and I cannot explain why. I heard voices, but no one was there, and that put me off. I remember holding you close to me, still hearing them, and then I seem to have fallen asleep. All I know now is that I do not want anything to distract me when I make love to my wife tonight."

"I fell asleep, too," she said. "It seems odd for us both to have done that."

"We were overtired, I expect, but Mauri told me that you had a good sleep."

"And you had a long walk today," she reminded him. "I'll wager that you must be tired again."

"Aye, perhaps," he said. "But if we swim, I'll wake up, I promise you."

"But it is still light enough for someone to see us!"

"Not for long, and what if they do?" he added with a teasing grin. "Did you worry about that when you swam on Skye?"

"No, but I never saw anyone else when I did."

"You must have had a teacher."

"I was a child then and swam in my shift."

He frowned. "It is exactly as I have said, then, and Mackinnon granted you far too much freedom for safety. Don't try that with me, lass. I'd be angry if aught happened to you through your defiance or even through careless disobedience."

A little shiver shot up her spine at his tone. "What would you do?"

"We needn't discuss that now," he said. "As to watchers, I have never seen anyone else when I've come here, and it will be dark soon. Moreover, I doubt that anyone would disturb us even if they did chance to see us. Come here."

She hesitated, but when he quirked an eyebrow at her, as if he were mocking her hesitation, she stepped forward to stand before him.

His eyes looked black, and his voice sounded deeper than usual when he said, "You may help me remove this shirt of mail."

She had never done such a thing before, but he showed her how to work the fastenings, and when they were undone, he pulled off the heavy garment by himself. It clinked like coins when he dropped it near one edge of the spread mantle.

He continued to instruct her until he stood clad in only his long shirt and netherstocks. Then, reaching for her lacing, he said softly, "Now, it is my turn."

As his hand brushed bare skin at her throat, her body tensed in wary anticipation of what was to come.

Although his fingers moved lightly over her, they seemed to leave trails of fire wherever they touched her even before he removed her bodice and undid her skirt and petticoat. When the latter two garments fell to the sand, she stood in her thin shift. She could still hear a bird or two in the woods, so she could be confident that no watchers lurked nearby unless someone had come earlier and lay hidden and still. Nevertheless, she felt exposed, as if there were eyes in every tree.

Unnaturally nervous and suddenly wanting to delay things, if only for a moment, she said, "What did those voices you heard last night sound like?"

Kintail smiled.

He was still too near and she wanted to step back, to give herself room to breathe, but she did not think he would let her. At the same time, in response to his crackling vitality, heat sizzled through her, urging her to draw him closer. She had to struggle to look interested in his reply to her question.

"I don't know what they sounded like," he murmured, untying her coif and casting it aside. "Like people, I suppose, but as if they were floating near us. I've never heard their like before."

"Do you believe in spirits, sir?"

"You can call me Fin when we're alone, lass. I'm your husband now."

"Aye, well, do you believe in them?"

"I think you know the answer to that. Were you not present when Ranald MacVinish tried to persuade me that he'd killed a cow at fairies' urging?"

She nodded. "It was the wicked Host, he said. Folks do say that Highland spirits—fairies and the like—are mischievous, even wicked."

He reached to stroke her cheek, his touch setting nerves dancing in parts of her body far from her face. "And what do folks say about your Border spirits?"

Trying to think but finding it hard now to concentrate on

anything beyond the sensations surging through her body, she said, "That . . . that they are different, more practical and . . . and more helpful. Perhaps if you would listen to those voices you hear, you might learn more about them," she added in a rush. "Perhaps you need only let yourself see and hear what stands before you."

"I don't want to talk about fantastical nonsense, lass. Let's swim." He bent to remove his netherstocks.

Instantly diverted, she said, "Are . . . are you going to take off *everything*?"

He grinned over his shoulder at her, then cast his shirt aside. "I already have," he said, standing proudly bare on the sand. "So will you if you are wise. You won't relish walking home in a wet shift."

Without waiting for her to make up her mind, he bent and caught the hem of her shift in both hands, and stripped it off over her head. When she hastily covered her breasts with an arm and the private place at the fork of her legs with the other hand, he reached for the plaited coil of hair at the nape of her neck and freed it, using his hands as combs until her hair spilled down her back in a thick, loose curtain.

"By heaven, you're beautiful," he said, gently moving her arm aside and stroking her breast. "I like the way just touching you makes me feel."

She wanted to say something similar to him, but she could think of nothing suitable, other than to say that his touch made her feel good, too. She could not think at all. Her body felt like a mass of flames, but he took her hand and drew her into the water. Its icy chill banished the other feelings in a trice.

"Ohh, but it's cold!"

"Just a wee bit cooler than the air," he said. "Wait till you're in. You'll see."

She knew he was right, and realizing that in the water she

would not feel so exposed to those eyes hanging from every tree limb, she pulled away from him and splashed forward, grateful to discover that the sand continued under the water for some distance. At her swimming place on Skye, one had to creep over sharp rocks, and if one were not careful, some were sharp enough to cut a foot.

Hearing him splash behind her, she sprang forward in a shallow dive. Using her hands to pull herself deeper, where she hoped he could not see her in the fast failing light, she swam away from the shore with wide, sweeping arm strokes.

She was congratulating herself on a deft maneuver when a large hand clamped around her right ankle and pulled, startling her so that she breathed in a mouthful of water. Fighting upward, she broke the surface, gasping and coughing.

Kintail surfaced right beside her. "Still cold?" There was laughter in his voice, but one large hand moved to cup her elbow, holding her steady so that she could concentrate on catching her breath again.

She was certainly no longer cold. Indeed, the flames had returned, but the water felt warmer now and caressed her body sensuously. Drawing a deep breath, she let it out again and said, "You can let go of me. You need not hold me now."

"I want to hold you," he murmured. "Lean back against me."

It was as if no other people inhabited the world but the two of them, floating, and as if nothing else existed in the world but the sensations flowing through her, the water lapping gently against her, and Kintail floating with her, barely moving.

Even the birds' twittering had ceased, leaving them in silence to savor the sensual caress of the water.

Moving slowly but with a deftness at odds with Molly's

languorous mood, Kintail grasped her around the waist with both hands and turned her to face him.

Accusingly, she exclaimed, "You can touch the bottom!"

"Aye," he said. "Put your hands on my shoulders."

His shoulders—the greater part of them, at least—were out of the water, and he held her so that now the two of them looked eye-to-eye, her breasts touching his chest. He drew her closer until his lips met hers and kissed her lightly, then more firmly. His lips were warm.

"Wrap your legs around my waist," he said, and the command sent a bolt of lightning through her body.

Without a word, she obeyed him, savoring each new sensation, amazed that she had never imagined such intense feelings could exist.

"Now, kiss me."

Again, she obeyed, touching his lips with hers, but when she would have drawn back, his arms slipped around her, crushing her to him. His lips felt hot against hers, and demanding. She could feel the tip of his tongue then, as if he tasted her. Then it slipped between her lips and into her mouth, finding her tongue and teasing it.

She squirmed against him, and her arms slid around his neck. Every nerve reacted now as if her body had plans of its own. His hands, freed of the need to hold her, moved upward to cup her breasts. His thumbs brushed her nipples, making her gasp and squirm even more. Then one hand moved to her waist and around to her bottom, shifting her a little. She heard him groan, deep in his throat.

His other hand moved gently between her legs, touching her where no one had touched her since her infancy, and then it seemed as if his hands were everywhere, moving with more urgency. His whole body seemed to be moving. Disoriented, realizing that she had shut her eyes, she opened them and saw that they were much nearer shore than she had thought. The shadows had blackened. It was dark. She no longer cared if eyes dotted the trees, not even when she realized that he was carrying her out of the water.

He strode to the mantle he had spread on the sand and, kneeling, laid her gently upon it. Then he straightened and reached for her mantle but did not attempt to dry her or himself with it. He just pulled it over them. It was enough.

Her moved slowly, taking his time. His kisses warmed her, for he kissed her everywhere and stroked her with his hands, moving one between her legs again, caressing her there, and using his fingers to stimulate and prepare her, until she ached and moaned for him to claim her. When he moved over her at last, she gasped again but this time in anticipation, and as he slowly entered her, she felt an ache, then more pain, but she nearly cried aloud when he stopped.

He grew still, his senses clearly on alert, and she remembered the eyes in the trees—and what had happened the previous night.

Speaking low, she said, "Not voices again!"

"Not voices, lass, a ship—a galley or birlinn." He eased himself out of her.

Turning her head, she saw the dense shadow on the water. It was perhaps as large as the boats Mackinnon had transported her baggage in. A thrill of fear shot through her, but she said with forced calm, "Did you ask someone to fetch us?"

"I did not." His voice was grim, and she felt him reach for his sword and drag his mail shirt toward them. "Now, hush and be still," he said. "I do not think they can see us. The sand is light, but with the mantle covering us, we should look like just another shadow. It is too dark for them to see what color anything is."

In the stillness, she could hear water lapping gently on the sand and, distantly, the creak of oars in their rowlocks.

Then another sound came across the water—a low-pitched, warbling whistle.

She felt Kintail relax and let out a breath. "It's Patrick with the birlinn," he murmured. Then, in a low but carrying voice, he called, "Here, on the sand."

To Molly, he said, "Move quickly, lass. He cannot have come merely to speak to me. Something's amiss. Can you dress yourself if I do up your laces?"

"Aye," she said, taking the shift he handed her and slipping it quickly over her head. Realizing then that, besides Sir Patrick, there had to be other men in the boat, she added anxiously, "Where are the rest of my clothes?"

"Here." He shoved her things toward her.

Scrambling into her skirt, she said, "How did he know where to find us?"

"He knows my ways as well as I know his, lass, but he would not disturb us without good cause."

He spent more time helping her than dressing himself, with the result that the boat beached nearby before he had donned more than his shirt and netherstocks. She was still trying to twist her wet hair into a braid when Sir Patrick's tall, broad-shouldered figure leaped from the boat and strode toward them.

"I hope you can forgive this interruption, my lady," he said as soon as he was close enough to speak in hushed tones. "Fin, there's trouble to the east. Some of our lads found three bodies half buried near the wee glen this side of the head of Loch Duich. If you'd turned a few yards off the track today, you'd have stumbled onto them yourself. We think Donald must be responsible. Ian Dubh, Malcolm, and the others lost sight of him, and we've had no trouble brewing hereabouts but his." He paused, and then added, "One of the dead men carried a letter from Jamie to you."

"Did you bring it?"

"Aye, but there is no light for reading, and I'd as lief not burn torches when we don't know who might be slithering through the shrubbery. The message will keep until we return to the castle. There's worse, though," he added. "One of the Murchisons from Glen Shiel came to tell us that someone killed Dougal Maclennan and his entire family. The folks there fear more attacks will come."

Shocked, Molly said, "Dougal Maclennan? Our priest?"

"Aye," Patrick said. "And his murderers must be the same men who killed Jamie's messenger. They evaded our watchers, Fin."

"Our men were not watching Glen Shiel," Fin reminded him. "Nor could they watch all the MacLeod land south of Kintail to Kylerhea."

"We know Sleat was on Skye before the wedding," Patrick said.

"Aye," Kintail agreed. " 'Tis likely that, knowing most folks hereabouts would be at the wedding, he hoped his own presence there would lull suspicion that he was up to mischief."

Molly said unhappily, "But he was up to mischief all along."

"It seems likely," Patrick admitted.

"It *is* likely," Kintail said. He put his arm around her and gave her a firm hug as he said to Patrick, "We'll leave at sunrise to see that Dougal Maclennan and his family are properly tended, and then we'll track the villains to their leader before they can harm anyone else. I have had enough of Sleat's antics. I want him and his men out of Kintail for good."

Chapter 17

Back at Eilean Donan, Fin kissed Molly and sent her to bed, knowing he would be up most of the night with Patrick and the others, organizing supplies and men to hunt down the priest's murderers and rid the area of Sleat. He hated to send her away, though, and he could tell she hated to go. Their time on the inlet had been magical. It seemed that he had only to touch her to make his whole body vibrate with longing. The feeling was indescribable, unlike anything he had felt before.

She paused at the doorway to the stairs and looked over her shoulder. She looked wistful and utterly desirable. "You will take care, won't you?"

"Aye, lass," he said. "You and I have unfinished business. I'm not likely to let anyone kill me before we've seen to it."

She blushed, looking more beautiful than ever despite her still damp, salt-stiffened hair and mussed clothing. When she turned slowly away without another word, a new concern occurred to him, and he said, "One moment, madam."

She turned back. "Aye?"

"You are not to go outside these walls," he said, hardening his tone, wanting to be sure she understood that he meant it. "Not for any reason. I'll leave Ian Dubh and Thomas MacMorran here with a few men; so, as long as you do not venture outside, you will be safe. As I told you before, it takes only a handful of people to defend this castle. Just keep the portcullis down and stay inside till we return." He paused, then added firmly, "I want your word that you will obey me."

She gazed at him for a long moment without speaking, and he let the silence lengthen until he heard some of his men shifting their feet and knew that they wondered at her daring. He said nothing even then, but he felt the muscles in his jaw tense. Surely, she would not choose this moment to defy him again.

At last, quietly, she said, "How long will you be gone?"

"I don't know," he said. "That will depend on how much damage Sleat has done and how long it takes us to track him down. I'm sending Patrick to Skye with a pair of galleys to see if Mackinnon has had news of Sleat's movements. It may be that the villain intends to land more men near Kyle to launch an attack through my western lands. If so, Patrick and I may well trap them between us. Others will soon learn of the trouble here and come to help, but in the meantime, we don't know how many men Sleat has, where they are, or how long trapping them will take."

She nodded. "Very well, sir, I will do as you bid. However, you must know that I will use my own judgment if you are away overlong."

"If you do that, lass," he said grimly, "you had better hope when I do return that I agree that your judgment was sound."

She gave him look for look, then turned and left the hall.

"It's a good thing you are leaving Ian Dubh in command here," Patrick said. "He'll see to it that her ladyship does nothing foolhardy."

"Aye, and Mauri will look after her, too," Fin said. "Now, where is this letter of Jamie's? Have you read it?"

"I have not. 'Tis a royal message, I'll remind you, sealed and addressed to you, so I did not dare. Indeed, 'tis a wonder the assassins didn't find it. Our lads said it was tucked just inside the man's jerkin." He extracted a folded, red-sealed sheet of parchment from beneath his mantle and handed it to Fin.

Breaking the royal wax seal, Fin smoothed the parchment. "It is indeed from Jamie and apparently in his own hand," he told Patrick when he had read the first few words. Frowning as he read on, he added, "He writes that he is clarifying the message Lady Percy will have given me. Who the devil is Lady Percy?"

"Percy is an English name," Patrick said thoughtfully.

"Aye. I don't like any of this," Fin said. "Jamie writes that Sleat, having threatened to raise all the Highland west against him, his grace requires the aid of his loyal clans, particularly the Mackenzies and MacRaes. He writes that Sleat's army numbers fifteen thousand and his navy boasts a hundred galleys. He will soon march south, and his fleet will accompany him down the coast, Jamie says."

"Fifteen thousand men and a hundred galleys?" Patrick's eyebrows shot upward. "I don't believe it, Fin. Sleat cannot have that many."

"'Tis not unusual for exaggerated accounts to reach Stirling," Fin said, "but our own information suggests, does it not, that he *has* begun to move."

"Aye," Patrick agreed grimly. "What else does Jamie write?"

"That he suspects the fine hand of England's Henry in all of this," Fin said.

"Jamie always suspects the fine hand of Henry—in everything."

"Aye, but this time he warns me not to trust Lady Percy, despite the purported motive for her visit, but at all cost to keep her at Eilean Donan until she is ready to return to Stirling. I do wish he had thought to tell me who the devil she is, but I begin to suspect that she is either dead or has fallen into Sleat's clutches."

"Well, at least we need not fear England's Henry, as far north as we are."

"Don't count on that," Fin said. "Evidently, Jamie suspects that Henry is supporting Sleat financially, that he intends to invade Scotland and will time that invasion to accord with Sleat's move south in order to trap the Scottish forces between them. What with Henry's persecution of those who do not like his new church, we know that many refugees have crossed into Scotland, fleeing his wrath. Not only does their departure anger him more but few doubt that he wants to control Scotland as punishment for our refusal to reform our own Kirk."

"Does Jamie say what he and his other nobles will do to stop Henry?"

"Aye, he says the Border lords are raising the Borderers to block Henry's invasion, whilst his grace gathers ships to challenge Sleat's fleet."

"He will find it hard to raise even fifty galleys along this coast," Patrick said.

"He knows that," Fin said, swiftly scanning the rest of the missive. "He also knows that Sleat has no cannon. So, Jamie is arming as many large ships as he can to sail up the coast and challenge Sleat's fleet, hoping that if they blast Sleat with cannon-fire, they will halt his advance south. That will take time, so we are to keep Sleat busy here as long as we can."

Patrick crooked an eyebrow. "What do you say then? Does this news alter our plans for the morrow?"

"It does not," Fin said. "We leave at dawn, but we'll leave fewer men here, I think. Sleat has no cannon, and against anything less, Eilean Donan is impregnable. If we can find Sleat and render him unable to lead his army and fleet, we will eliminate the problem that faces us and solve Jamie's problem for him, as well."

From one of the bartizan towers extending from the walkway atop the northwest side of the keep, Molly glumly watched the men depart the next morning, disappointed that Fin had not sought her bed during the night but understanding that he had much to do.

Doreen had been waiting for her when she retired to her bedchamber and had helped her wash the salt from her hair, scolding her but laughing, too, at her tale of the nude swim. Molly had considered going to Fin's room when she was ready for bed but decided against it. If he wanted her, he knew where to find her.

He had wakened her at dawn to bid her farewell, kissing her deeply and lingering long enough to remind her of why she would miss him. If he had slept, she knew it had been only a few hours.

Despite Doreen's ministrations, her hair was still damp when he woke her, but she had gotten up after he left, brushed it briskly before the fire, and now, nearly dry, it was braided and twisted tidily into a coil beneath her coif.

By the time she had reached the battlements, Fin had already crossed the narrow channel to join the main portion of his army. That body consisted of a number of men-at-arms in mail shirts and an even larger number of ragged-looking, bare-legged, bare-chested ones. Fin wore his chain mail over a shirt and dark leggings, with his green-and-indigo mantle over all. Each bare-legged man wore a short kilt with the long end thrown over his shoulder, and each carried a naked broadsword slanted across his back from that shoulder to his waist on a broad leather strap. In the other hand, each carried a gleaming, wicked-looking dirk. Some carried axes or lances, and others carried longbows and quivers full of arrows.

Most were afoot, but some, like Fin, rode. They all traveled swiftly, following the track along the northeast side of Loch Duich toward Glen Shiel, looking exactly like the barbarians that Molly had once imagined them. She knew that even the men running barefoot would have no trouble keeping up with the horses, for it was their normal custom, and so famous had Highland running gillies become that Archbishop Beaton, the Lord Privy Seal, had once taken a group of them to Rome to show them off to the Pope.

Sir Patrick had already departed and was headed in the opposite direction. He commanded two galleys with forty men each, rowing westward toward Kyleakin. When the last boat and rider had passed from view, Molly turned away and found Mauri standing behind her.

"I think ye should come within, mistress," the older woman said. "The laird did order the postern door shut and sealed afore he left, and the portcullis be safely down, but ye shouldna remain here in plain sight like this."

"Any fighting will take place far from Eilean Donan," Molly reminded her. "Do you fear that Kintail might fail to find Donald's raiders and stop them?"

"I dinna ken what I fear, mistress, but our Patrick and the laird did both wonder at Donald's actions. I wish the old master were still here," she added wistfully. "He and Gilchrist MacRae knew that wicked Donald better than most."

"Eilean Donan is safe, come what may," Molly said, feeling a need to defend Fin but repressing a shudder at the thought of a possible attack on Eilean Donan with so few people left to defend it. The only ones left inside were Mauri, Doreen, Thomas MacMorran, Ian Dubh, and herself, unless one counted wee Morag. Tam Matheson and Malcolm MacRae had ridden with Fin.

"We'd best go down to Doreen," Mauri said with a sigh. "She's wi' my wee lassie in the hall, and they'll both likely be on the fret. The men be looking round, even now, to be certain the castle be secure, and when they've done wi' the searching, Ian Dubh says they'll keep watch from the bartizan walkway."

"There are only the two entrances to the castle, are there not?"

"Aye, the main-gate portcullis and the postern door at the foot o' the northwest tower. That door be thick and heavily barred, and the portcullis be solid oak five foot thick. Its wood were soaked in salt water to pack the grain, and it be bound wi' iron rods as well. Likely, it'll not even burn, they say, so we'll be snug enough." Mauri stood at the entrance to the stairway. "Do ye come in now, mistress."

"From which direction would an attack most likely come if ever there were one?" Molly asked as she moved to follow her.

"Yonder to the west if ye're thinking o' Donald and his lot," Mauri said, pointing. "We'd ha' warning afore they could reach us from the land, so they'd come from the sea, and there be room for only a few boats to beach, any road."

"Then mayhap I should stay here and keep watch until Thomas and Ian Dubh come upstairs," Molly said, hesitating at the top of the stairs.

From below, Mauri said, "Nay, mistress, come ye down

to Doreen. Whilst Patrick and his men be watching the Kyle, there be naught to worry us here."

Reluctantly Molly followed her down to the great hall, where they found Doreen rocking wee Morag in her cradle. The hall was silent except for the rhythmic rocking of the cradle and intermittent sucking sounds the dozing baby made. She had tucked the middle fingers of her right hand into her mouth, and from time to time, she sucked rapidly then stopped again.

Looking at wee Morag sent a shiver of unexpected apprehension up Molly's spine. If an attack did come, how could three women and two men protect the child? Donald the Grim doubtless would like nothing better than to wipe the Mackenzies and MacRaes from the earth, so he could include their land in his reclaimed lordship. His men would show no compassion for a baby who was kin to the MacRaes. Had Fin been mad to leave the castle without stronger defenses?

Although Mauri drew a stool near the cradle and sat down to converse with Doreen, Molly could not settle down and wait patiently for Thomas and Ian Dubh. She paced the floor, wishing that she could think of something useful to do.

"Do you think Thomas and Ian Dubh have manned the towers yet?" she asked a few moments later. "Where are they? Should they not report to us?"

Doreen gave her a gentle smile. "I wish ye'd sit down, mistress. 'Tis most unlikely that aught will occur whilst the laird be from home. Will not Sir Patrick see anyone who approaches from the sea? And will not the laird hunt down the Glen Shiel raiders and their wicked leader?"

"But the raiders did reach Glen Shiel!" Molly said, putting into words at last the nagging worry that had been dancing voiceless in her mind since the previous night.

"Think, Doreen—Mauri! Kintail mentioned a track to the south, from Kylerhea."

Frowning, Mauri said, "If the raiders be Donald's, they could ha' avoided Mackenzie and MacRae lands altogether, mistress. The track from Kylerhea crosses MacLeod land. If MacLeod agreed to it, they might ha' come that way."

"Donald was supposed to be heading north to meet up with his fleet," Molly said, remembering. "He came to the wedding from Skye, though, so at least some of his ships may still be there, and if they—" Before she could finish voicing the thought, a shout echoed down the stairwell at the end of the hall.

"Galleys west!"

Mauri's face blanched. "How could ships ha' slipped past our Patrick and his lot?" she demanded. "Donald's fleet lies north o' the Kyle!"

"Perhaps not," Molly said. "If those galleys are Donald's, he sailed around Skye to approach us from the south, through the Sound of Sleat, or he left a few boats at Dunsgaith. It does not matter which it is if he's here," she added. "Take wee Morag to the kitchen, Mauri."

"But they canna get into the castle," Mauri protested.

"If they *do* manage to break in, you must tell them that you are a newcomer, that one of the wicked Mackenzie men abducted you and your bairn but a sennight ago," Molly said. "They might believe you, and if they do—"

"But I canna do that! What about my Malcolm?"

"Malcolm would tell you to do it for the child's sake," Molly said, seeing nothing to gain by pointing out that, if the raiders succeeded in breaching Eilean Donan's wall, what Malcolm might say would be the least of their worries.

"Get ye below, Mauri," Doreen said quietly as she stood and thrust the baby into Mauri's arms. "What of us, mistress?" she added when Mauri had turned away. "If we are not to go with her, what do we do?"

"I'll go above to the bartizan, because Thomas and Ian Dubh going to need help," Molly said. "First, I am going to fetch my weapons, though. Would you know how to deal with anyone who approaches the portcullis entrance?"

"Aye, I ken that fine, mistress," Doreen's eyes gleamed. "Thomas showed me the wee chamber that contains rocks and other nuisances ready to rain down upon them, and he said the cauldrons and levers be so lightly counterbalanced that a bairn could tip them if need be."

"Do what you can then," Molly ordered. "Will Thomas and Ian Dubh have sufficient arms above?"

"Aye, they have their bows, mistress, and whilst neither is as fine a shot as Sir Patrick or the laird, they'll no disgrace us."

Nodding, Molly sent her on her way and hurried toward the bedchamber she shared with Fin. His ridiculous command that she not take her bow in hand again until he gave her leave meant nothing now. Doreen would be safe enough in the small chamber above the portcullis and was well able to manipulate the weapons there, but Ian Dubh, Thomas, Doreen, and Molly herself were all that stood between safety and disaster. And no matter what anyone had said to the contrary, the notion that two men and three women could defend the castle by themselves seemed absurd. Formidable though Eilean Donan's walls might be, given sufficient time, a determined enemy would surely breach them.

Reaching the bedchamber, she snatched her longbow from its place on the wall with one hand, and the quiver of arrows from their coffer with the other. Since she had not recovered all of her arrows before Fin caught her the one and only day she had taken her bow out, her store was sadly depleted. She knew that she had too few left to give much of an accounting and wondered if there might be more else-where in the castle. Perhaps Ian Dubh would know.

But when she reached the top of the northwest tower stairs, she forgot her question, for the sight that met her eyes appalled her. The wind blew from the west, where threatening black clouds gathered, and on Loch Alsh, four galleys with sails raised approached the castle at speed, sending up clouds of spray. Each boat looked larger than their own galleys, with banks of long oars on each side lashing the sea in disciplined frenzy. On boats of such size, she knew that each oar often had two men to pull it, which meant forty men or more in each boat.

"Mercy on us all," Molly muttered.

"Aye," Thomas said, glancing at her. He held his long-bow at rest, but an arrow lay across it, already nocked. He said, "Ian Dubh stands yonder, mistress, in the southwest bartizan. I ken fine that the laird would say ye should go below, but I welcome your bow. I warrant ye could shoot the last needle off a pine bough."

"I don't think I could do that," Molly said, "but I have been blessed with unusual skill."

"That ye can even pull that bowstring shows ye ha' skill beyond any other lass I've met. Sakes, but I've known grown *men* wi' less strength than that."

She had never thought much about the strength required to shoot a longbow. She had wanted to shoot one from the first instant of seeing a man do so, and Mackinnon had humored her, as he had been wont to do in most such cases, by providing her with a miniature longbow of her own. As she had grown, he had replaced that bow with longer, stouter ones. Had she chanced to wonder about the strength required for such sport, she would have assumed simply that constant practice had made it possible for her to shoot the heavier bows.

"We'll no shoot till they've landed," Thomas said. "We've few enough arrows as it is."

Reminded, she said, "Are there any more arrows in the castle?"

"We collected all we could find," he said. "The laird's men and Sir Patrick's took nearly all that were here. Thinking they'd be after Donald himself and would control the landscape from Kyle to Glen Shiel, they didna expect an attack on the castle whilst they were away."

"It was another trap, though, was it not? Doubtless, Donald still wants me."

"Aye, and the laird never suspected, because o' the killings and because the call for aid came from a Murchison, and one living inland, at that. His lordship thought—and Sir Patrick did, too—that they'd be protecting us against any such trickery by having Sir Patrick and Mackinnon keep a lookout for trouble approaching from the north and west. But although everyone assured us that Donald's fleet lies to the north, he must ha' kept these few ships and men ready to attack from Loch Alsh. That be his banner on the lead galley, sure enough."

Molly nodded, keeping her eyes fixed on the approaching longboats. They were less than fifty yards from the islet now, approaching in a line, their square sails billowing, their oarsmen maintaining a strong beat.

"Did not Sir Patrick say he knew the messenger from Glen Shiel, Thomas?"

"He knew the family," Thomas said. "Mayhap we should ha' asked the lad more questions, though. Easy, mistress," he added as Molly nocked her first arrow. "Let them come to us. Then make each shot count if ye can."

"I will," she said grimly.

He gave her a sharp look. "That banner—ye ken 'tis

likely Donald himself who leads them. Wicked or no, the man were your lawful guardian."

"Aye, he was," she said, giving him look for look. "Do you fear that I might take his side, Thomas?"

His gaze locked with hers for a long moment. Then, with a slight smile, he said steadily, "Ye've shown nae great liking for Kintail, m'lady."

"I have much less liking for Donald the Grim, and Eilean Donan is my home now," Molly said, suppressing the urge to defend her relationship with Fin, to tell Thomas Mac-Morran that he was mistaken, that they got along much better than she had ever expected them to. Realizing then that the first galley had reached the west shore and was beaching, she said sharply, "Heed them, Thomas!"

He turned and let fly his arrow, all in one smooth and easy movement, and the sound of a man's scream came in return.

"One dead," Thomas said calmly as he nocked his second arrow.

Molly swallowed hard. Until that moment, she had thought only of defending Eilean Donan, not of what that meant in terms of human lives. The knowledge of what she would have to do struck hard, and Thomas had let fly his second arrow before she lifted her bow to take aim.

Men spilled from the first galley as its sail fell, and a second one beached beside it. Arrows flying from the southwest bartizan told her that Ian Dubh had entered the fray and without another thought, she aimed for a man's right shoulder, hoping to wound him so that he could not fight, without killing him.

Her aim was true, and the man grabbed his shoulder, clamping his hand to the arrow and struggling to yank it free. The injured arm hung limply useless at his side.

From the relative safety of the bartizan, as she nocked another arrow and let fly, she saw men slipping around the north side of the castle, heading for the portcullis. Below her, others attacked the postern door. But her arrows and Thomas's were taking a toll. Dead and injured men littered the grassy slope.

"There," Thomas said abruptly, pointing with his free hand. "D'ye see, lass? Donald himself stands below us. Curse him, he stands too close to the wall. I canna get a shot." He moved onto the battlement walkway, careful to keep his head low until he reached the centermost crenel. Carefully, he put his head through the opening to peer down, then pulled back with a grimace. "Had I a few big stones, I could brain the villain," he said, "but from this angle my arrows be useless."

"Never mind him, then," Molly said. "Shoot where you can."

"I've only a few arrows left," he said, turning toward her as he nocked one of them. "We'd best think of—"

Whatever else he might have said she would not know, for an arrow from below cut off his words, striking the side of his head. He fell senseless to the walkway. She saw that he was bleeding heavily, but although she hurried to his side and tried to stanch the flow with a wadded-up handful of her petticoat, he did not respond when she shouted his name, and she had no time to do more.

She rose, nocked an arrow, and with bowstring taut, moved to examine the view from the crenel. She could see more clearly than from the bartizan loops, and before long, she had used up her arrows and all but one that still lay near Thomas. Hoping that Ian Dubh might have more, she hurried to the southwest bartizan, keeping her head low, only to find his lifeless body slumped against the battlement wall beyond it. Bile rose in her throat, but she ruthlessly suppressed her fear. His quiver was empty, and there were no longer arrows flying up from below.

Looking through the nearest crenel, she saw that men on the ground were heading toward the two galleys beached on the shore, and briefly indulged a hope that the attackers were leaving to avoid the approaching storm. But she soon saw that they were doing no such thing. Instead, they began to remove the masts from the beached galleys.

Baffled, having no idea what they could be up to, she returned to where Thomas lay and picked up his last arrow, noting that it had a wickedly barbed head. Looking over the crenel again, she realized with shock that Donald's men intended to use the two masts as battering rams.

Muttering, "Please, let it fly true," she nocked the arrow carefully, knowing there would be little more she could do once she had sped it on its way. Her bowstring taut between her fingers, she waited patiently, surveying the scene and wondering at her own calm. For the moment, no one was shooting at her. Every man in sight was helping with the masts.

She could no longer see the third galley, but the fourth drifted near the southwest corner of the keep, apparently having given up finding a suitable place to land. Its oarsmen had rested their sweeps and had taken up their bows, clearly intending to rain more arrows upon the castle. Searching the Dornie shore in the hope that she would spy help on the way, she saw no one. Looking back at the men preparing to ram, she looked directly into the fierce eyes of her erstwhile guardian.

She still owed him duty of sorts, she supposed. Mackinnon had told her often that she owed much to Donald the Grim, but she had never felt any particular obligation to him. Donald had not abducted her, but he had done nothing to put matters right. She had been as much his hostage as she had been the King's, or Fin's, but Eilean Donan was now her home.

Donald shot her a look that was half sardonic smile, half grimace, and signed to his men to lower the first battering ram into position.

Without a second thought, Molly raised her bow and let the arrow fly. Like the others, it flew straight, striking Donald high in his left thigh.

The look he flashed her then was one of pure rage, and even as men leaped to help him, Donald of Sleat angrily ripped the offending arrow from his leg.

To Molly's horror—and doubtless to Donald's as well— a pulsing fountain of bright red blood spurted forth; and, although his men did what they could to stanch the flow, it persisted until he collapsed, unconscious. One of the men standing at a distance from him shouted, "Ha' they killed the chief?"

"Nay, he's but sorely wounded," shouted another, bending to help Donald. "Carry him to the galley, lads. We'll away from here and tend him properly!"

As quick as thought, the raiders carrying Donald ran for their galleys, and others speedily replaced the masts. A horn blew, pipes skirled, and in moments, the sails were up and all four galleys were away.

Watching them, stunned by what she had done, Molly saw with a sinking heart that the men tending their fallen chief in the lead boat soon moved away from him and took up oars. One man slumped in the stern, head bowed.

"I've killed him," she murmured. "I've killed Donald the Grim. Faith, what will become of me? I've killed a man who stood as guardian to me. I'll go to Hell, as sure as I stand here." Kneeling swiftly beside Thomas, and seeing that his head still bled, albeit sluggishly, she said urgently, "Thomas, don't you dare die, for I need you! We all need you. For mercy's sake, stop bleeding and wake up!"

To her astonishment, the bleeding stopped, but although she shook him and called his name, Thomas did not stir. She ran along the walkway to Ian Dubh, remembered with a start that he was beyond help or helping, and ran downstairs to find Mauri and Doreen.

Chapter 18

The threatening black clouds in the west had moved much nearer by the time the three women managed to drag Thomas MacMorran and the body of Ian Dubh each into the shelter of the nearest bartizan.

"We must get Thomas downstairs where it's warm," Doreen said anxiously.

"Aye," Molly agreed, "but if you know how we can carry him down those stairs, I do not. Fetch blankets. We can at least keep him warm until the others return."

"I'll fetch the blankets," Mauri said. "And I'll find something to cover Ian Dubh, too. It dinna be proper, leaving him lying there all alone as he is."

Repressing an impulse to point out that Ian Dubh was beyond loneliness or caring about proprieties, Molly fixed her attention on Thomas, knowing that Mauri had volunteered to do the fetching so that Doreen could stay with him, and willing that young man to open his eyes. In moments, they heard Mauri's quick steps, returning up the stairs.

Molly glanced toward the doorway, and just as she did, she heard Doreen gasp. Looking back, she saw with relief that Thomas had regained consciousness.

"I'm no dead yet, lass," he said to Doreen with a weak smile.

"Near enough," she snapped. "D'ye no ha' sense enough to duck when arrows fly at ye, ye feckless bairn?"

His smile widened. "Evidently not," he said meekly. "I need a proper wife to teach me such lessons."

"Oh, Thomas, hush! This be scarcely the time to be talkin' o' wives. Those horrid raiders ha' killed Ian Dubh!"

"Nay, not Ian!"

"Aye," Doreen said. "Art cold, Thomas? We must get ye warm. There be a storm coming. We can see it yonder, all puffed up black and ready to blow."

"Ye're blathering, lass. 'Tis shock, most like, and gey natural. More to the purpose, though, can ye see them villains? What be they up to now?"

Doreen grimaced and glanced at Molly.

Molly said, "They are on their way back to Sleat, I hope. I . . . I shot your last arrow at Donald the Grim and it struck him in the thigh."

"Good lass!" Thomas exclaimed. Remembering his manners, he added hastily, "Well done, mistress. It be a pity ye didna kill the wicked rogue."

"I am afraid that is exactly what I did," Molly said ruefully. "He yanked the arrow out, you see, and its head was sharply barbed. He must have severed a major vessel, because a fountain of bright red blood gushed forth and he collapsed. His men carried him to his galley and they all sailed away, but the ones tending him stopped doing so whilst they were still within sight, so I'm sure he's dead. They must be taking his body back to Sleat. We've seen no sign of them since."

"We will," Thomas said. "They'll be for vengeance, certain sure. Help me up, lass," he added to Doreen. "If there be a storm brewin', I'd as lief be inside by the hall fire. Where lies Ian Dubh's body?"

"We dragged it into the southeast bartizan," Doreen said. "He's under cover, Thomas, so dinna be thinking ye must carry him. I doubt ye can carry yourself."

"Nay, lass, I ken better than to try to shift him. If he has shelter, we'll leave him for the others to tend when they return." He reached for her hand.

Molly and Mauri moved to help, too, but he waved them aside.

"I'll do. Dinna coddle me."

On his feet, he stood still for a minute. Then, insisting that he was as steady as a rock, he managed to totter his way down the stairs with little help from the women, although Doreen stayed near enough to try to catch him if he fell. Considering their relative sizes, Molly was glad that he did not.

As she watched Doreen and Mauri whisking about in the hall to make Thomas comfortable, it occurred to her that a number of men, either dead or wounded, still lay outside. Fin would not have to worry about her leaving the safety of the castle before his return, but she wondered if any of the wounded might pose a threat to him—when and if he came home. The thought chilled her.

Waiting only until Thomas was settled and Mauri had brought Morag upstairs in her cradle, Molly drew her aside. "What about the wounded outside," she said. "Might they not try to ambush Kintail and the others when they return?"

"Nay, mistress, for the folk at Dornie village will warn our lads to take care. The villagers could do naught to help us during the attack, for all their fighting men be wi' the laird or our Patrick, but they'll no let any o' our lads cross to Eilean Donan without first they warn them to look for villains."

"I am going to watch from above to make sure," Molly said.

Mauri nodded, and Thomas warned her to keep her head down. "Just in case one o' that wicked lot still has strength to draw a bow," he added grimly. "Give a shout when the laird comes. We'll ha' to raise the portcullis."

Promising to be careful, Molly hurried back up to the battlements, and although she still fretted at the possibility of danger below, she saw little sign of activity and settled herself to wait as patiently as she knew how.

It was impossible to control her thoughts, and the fear that Fin had been ambushed like his father, and might lay dying or dead somewhere in the windy, starless night, made her wish that she could fling herself on a horse and ride out in search of him. Despite her fear, knowing what he would do if she did find him, not dead but alive and angry, still had the power to send a shivery thrill up her spine.

"Claud, what is it?" Catriona demanded, grabbing him by both shoulders and shaking hard. "What's wrong with you?"

"Dinna speak, Catriona," he groaned. "Your voice beats against me ears like the thunder does beat in yonder storm clouds."

"But why?" Bending nearer, she peered into his eyes and gave his shoulders another shake. "What is amiss with you?"

"I used me powers," he muttered. "Mam did warn me that I'd feel summat whenever I use them now, but she didna say I'd feel such a pain. I canna move a muscle, lass. Aye, and I'm no tae be wi' ye, either," he exclaimed, remembering. "Ye mun get from me! Where am I?"

"In the laird's peek overlooking the great hall. I found you here."

"This be as far as I got, I expect, afore the darkness overtook me," he said.

"But what did you do? Was it something horrid?"

"Nay, lass, only what me bounden duty demanded. Now, go, I beg o' ye. Every moment I'm wi' ye, me powers'll grow gey weaker, Mam said."

"First, tell me what you did!"

"Nay," he said, his voice fading to a thready murmur. "I canna. Ye'll be wroth wi' me, for it willna serve your laird, but only my Maid."

"Tell me! I'll not leave until you do."

He scarcely heard her, but he did not care. The world around him swirled again into blackness.

The storm struck with fury before the men returned. Nevertheless, Molly huddled in the bartizan, keeping watch. When she saw them at last, hours later, she saw as well that Mauri had been right, for despite the lashing winds and rain, they approached with care and encountered no trouble. They were but shadow figures, some wading across the channel through knee-deep water, others rowing boats.

When lightning flashed again, she thought she saw Fin. Hugging herself, she watched carefully, but she did not see him again, only dark, moving shapes, and several of them were hurrying toward the entrance. Heart pounding, she ran downstairs, certain that the others would need her help to raise the portcullis before they could learn who had lived and who had died. Thomas MacMorran was still weak, but she and Doreen could raise it together, she was sure.

Thomas laughed at her suggestion, insisting that he was perfectly fit. When he would not be talked out of it, Doreen went with him, declaring that if he so much as strained a muscle in the attempt, she would throttle him. He draped a muscular arm around her shoulders and said she could help him stay upright while they climbed to the room containing the mechanism that worked the heavy gate.

Molly stood staring at the hall entrance, wanting to run out into the storm to find Fin but knowing instinctively that he would not like it if she revealed any doubt of his abilities. Would they all be safe? Would Fin be glad that they had protected the castle or furious to learn that she had not only taken up her bow and arrows again but had accidentally killed Donald the Grim? Anticipation warred with her fears, but fortunately, her wait was brief. He strode into the hall with Tam Matheson moments later, before Thomas and Doreen had returned.

Fin's gaze swept the chamber, and casting aside her false dignity, Molly ran to him, flinging herself into his arms.

"Did anyone outside give you any trouble?" she demanded.

"Not a whit," he said, wrapping his arms tightly around her. "Did you doubt me, lass?"

"Never," she said, snuggling into his embrace. Despite his wet clothing, she pressed hard against him, hugging him back.

He murmured to the top of her head, "The men Sleat left behind will not trouble anyone again." Then, holding her at arm's length, he added as if he had just realized the fact, "Your clothing is damp!"

"I've been up on the battlement walk, watching for you. Yours is wet, too."

"I'm sorry about this, lass," he said, giving her upper

arms a squeeze. "I should have known better than to think he had so easily given up getting you back."

His simple remorse banished any lingering worries. Ignoring the feelings that his touch stirred in her body, and ignoring, too, the voice in her head suggesting that she invite him to retire at once to his bedchamber, she said, "I do not see how this could be just about me. I'm married to you now. What could he hope to achieve?"

Still looking rueful, Fin said, "It may be that he thinks he has only to declare our marriage null before he can marry you where and to whom he chooses."

"It no longer matters what he thinks," she said, "but does his attack here mean there *were* no raiders in Glen Shiel? Was it just a ruse to draw you away?"

"Oh, there was a raid," he said grimly. "Dougal Maclennan and his family are dead. The raiders were Donald's men, too, but I believe his sole intent was to draw me away from Eilean Donan so he could attack here unopposed."

A shout from above drew his attention. "Patrick must be back," he said. "He'll be wroth that Donald's galleys managed to slip past him."

"I do not think they did," Molly said quietly. "We believe they came from the south, from Sleat, just as the Glen Shiel raiders probably crossed at Kylerhea."

"You've thought it out right carefully, sweetheart," he said, putting an arm around her again. The endearment warmed her heart, but his next words made her chuckle. "Has anyone thought about supper?" he asked. "It looks as if this deluge means to continue till morning, so we should be safe as mice in a mill tonight."

Guiltily, Molly looked at Mauri, but the older woman nodded reassuringly. "If ye've two lads willing to help serve, laird, I ha' food enough," she said, turning toward the kitchen. "There be soup keeping warm on the hob."

"Fetch it to table at once," Fin said heartily. "I swear I could eat enough for ten tonight. Were you badly frightened, lass?" he asked Molly.

"I had no time to consider my feelings," she said. "From the moment we first saw them, we had so much to do, and then Thomas was hit, and . . . and Ian—"

"Thomas MacMorran? Is he hurt? Where the devil is he? And where—?"

"Here, laird," Thomas said, entering with Doreen at his side, and looking much steadier on his feet. "I am well, barring an unpleasant ache in my head, but I count my headache good fortune compared to Ian Dubh's fate."

"Ian Dubh? What of him? Where is he?"

"He was killed, sir," Thomas said, glancing at Molly.

Fin was silent, clearly shocked. Then he, too, looked at her. "Why did you not tell me this at once, lass?"

"I had no chance before now," she protested. "You've been asking questions, but you haven't asked till now about what happened here. There is something more you should know, too." She described the final moments of the battle, adding that she had not meant to kill Donald. "I aimed for his thigh, and the arrow struck true, but he yanked it free without taking even ordinary care."

"A lesson in patience, perhaps, but that is all," Fin said with a shrug. "Do not let it trouble you. We'll none of us miss Donald, and you've doubtless saved hundreds of lives. I'll send word to Jamie. He'll certainly not grieve."

Sir Patrick came in then, and while Fin and Thomas reported the news to him, Molly went to help Mauri and Doreen in the kitchen.

Supper was a relaxing meal despite the excitement of the day, and when Doreen rose to help Mauri afterward, Molly asked her to have someone fill the tub in Kintail's bedchamber for her and build up the fire there, as well.

"I want a hot bath," she said. "All I washed last night was my hair, and after everything that's happened today, I feel grimy. The men will talk here for hours yet, so I should have plenty of time for a proper bath."

"Aye," Doreen agreed. "I'll see to it straightaway."

As Molly left the hall, she saw that Fin was still deep in conversation with Patrick and the others. He waved but otherwise seemed to pay her no heed.

Upstairs, she went to her own bedchamber first and searched her chests until she found a nightdress she liked that she had not yet worn at Eilean Donan. Made of cream-colored cambric, it was fashioned simply, like a shift, but embroidered with a blue Celtic motif and edged with delicate lace. It felt like the right night to wear it.

Several lads with buckets of hot water soon filled her bath, and one carried in another of cold water that he placed near the tub to cool the bathwater if necessary.

Doreen arrived shortly after the water bearers had gone.

"Ha' ye got your French soap, mistress?"

"Aye," Molly said, already stripping off clothing. "Help me with my laces."

Moments later, she stepped into the tub and, with a deep sigh, sat down and leaned back. It was the largest tub she had ever bathed in, and lined with smoothly beaten silver as it was, it was also the most comfortable. She decided that Fin's size was an advantage in that respect if in few others.

The thought made her smile. Truth be told, his size was an advantage in myriad ways, and she admired it—at least, she did as long as he was not angry with her. At such times as that, his size gave him an unfair advantage.

"Fetch a net for my hair, please," she said to Doreen. She had twisted the braids into a topknot, but curls had escaped, and she did not want to take wet hair to bed with her a second night.

Doreen handed her the soap and drew up a short, three-legged joint-stool to set the little soap dish on. Then she went to Molly's bedchamber to fetch the hair net, and Molly began to soap all the bits of herself that she could reach, using a small towel to scrub her face.

Sliding down into the water to rinse herself, she rested her shoulders against the sloped back, pressed the hot towel against her cheeks, and shut her eyes, relaxing. When the door opened, she said drowsily, "Just slip the net on over my hair, Doreen. I may never move again."

"Oh, I hope you will move a little, sweetheart." Fin's voice, teasing and sensual, startled her into opening her eyes.

"You," she said accusingly, "are not Doreen."

"And you," he retorted with a grin, "are very perceptive."

"I like your tub," she said, folding her arms across her breasts and watching him warily. As usual, her body was responding to his presence, making it hard to sit still. He had taken off his weapons, helmet, plate, and mail, and stood now in only his shirt, braies, and boots. The lacing of his shirt was open.

"I'm envious," he said, still grinning. "Can you really stretch out your legs?"

"Aye, easily. My toes touch the end, but it's the biggest tub I've ever seen."

"I think I should have a larger one made," he said. "Big enough for two."

"You can use this water when I've finished," she said, wishing she could relax and hoping Doreen would not walk in.

To be naked in a bath, attended by the personal servant who had tended one from childhood, was one thing. To be naked in a bath with one's husband in the room was something else. But to be naked and aroused in a bath with both of them there, watching her, was not an experience she wanted to face.

Fin watched her appreciatively. Although she did not realize it, the situation was as new to him as it was to her, because he had never watched a woman bathe before, and she was lovely to watch. She had looked at first as if his entrance had not disturbed her in the least, although she had crossed her arms protectively over those luscious breasts of hers. But when she offered him the use of her bathwater—a common enough suggestion in any household—she had blushed, and now she seemed to have fixed her attention on scrubbing the very skin off her face.

With her red-gold curls piled in loose plaits atop her head, her face looked pixielike, her lovely eyes enormous. They revealed a greenish cast that he had not seen before, and their dark lashes sparkled with tiny drops of water, like diamonds. Her skin was smooth, rosy from the hot water, and enticingly touchable. He wanted to lather every inch of her with the bar of soap in the dish on the stool beside her.

"Will you hand me that towel, please?" she asked a moment later, gesturing toward the washstand with one hand while still covering her breasts with the other.

"Where is Doreen?" he asked, realizing that she had expected him to be the maidservant, and that Doreen must have meant to be there to hand her the towel.

"She went to fetch a net to keep my hair up. I think she realized that you had come in, though, or she would have come back by now."

He liked the way the curly tendrils that had escaped the coil atop her head wisped around her ears and cheeks. One trailed down the back of her neck and he wanted to touch it, to let it wrap itself around his finger. Doreen would not return, and the soap glistened temptingly in the dish on the stool.

"The towel?" Molly said.

"I don't think you're quite clean enough yet," he said, bolting the door.

Picking up the wet soap, he moved the little dish to the floor and sat down on the stool. The thought of touching her, of sliding the soap around on her smooth skin, was almost more than his body could stand. A particular part of it was fairly shouting at him to snatch the lass from the water and take her to bed. But anticipation would only increase his pleasure, and hers. He was going to take his time and enjoy himself.

She watched him silently, her beautiful eyes wide and wary.

With the soap in his right hand, he reached with his left and gently moved the protective arm hugging her breasts. Feasting his eyes on their plump splendor, he dipped the soap in the warm water, and then used it to lather them. When they were silky and gleaming, he let the soap slide into the water with her and stroked the lather with both hands.

"That is French soap," she murmured, eyes locked with his. "It will melt."

"I'll buy you more," he said, watching her eyes widen as he stroked the mark on her left breast with a soapy finger, then slid it lower to caress the nipple.

Her voice was a ragged whisper when she said, "French soap is expensive."

"I'll tell Jamie he owes my lovely wife a bar of French soap. In the meantime, you talk too much." Leaning forward, one hand still resting on her silken breast, he kissed her. He had intended the kiss to be light, provocative, but when his lips touched hers, the jolt that struck him nearly unmanned him. Heat flamed through him, setting every nerve afire.

He moved his other hand to cup the back of her head, holding her while his lips pressed harder against hers and savored their response. He moaned deep in his throat, and his tongue demanded entrance to her warm, inviting mouth.

His right hand continued to stroke her body, gently at first, then more hungrily, sliding over her breasts to her smooth belly and lower. Just as his fingertips touched the soft curls at the juncture of her thighs, he shifted direction, holding her silent with his kisses while he searched in the tub for the bar of soap.

She wriggled, but her little tongue stayed busy, playing with his, teasing him.

Finding the soap, he lost it again when it slipped from his fingers and slid under her knees. Reaching between her legs, he captured it again and began to soap the insides of her thighs, moving nearer his goal with each stroke. When she moaned and wriggled more, he touched her nether lips with the bar of soap, delighting in her gasp of pleasure. He let the bar slide free of his fingers again and touched her where the soap had touched her. Her body was warm and welcoming, and it took only a few gentle caresses after that to bring her to her peak.

He held her until the spasms eased.

She had shut her eyes. When she opened them again, he said, "I'll fetch that towel for you now."

When he released her, she grabbed the sides of the tub with both hands, as if she feared she would slide under the water if she did not hold on.

Grinning, filled with anticipation of what was to come, Fin jerked a towel from the washstand rod and turned back.

The damned voices could chatter all they wanted to tonight. As things were now, they wouldn't faze him.

Draping the towel over a shoulder, he turned to get hot water from the hob and pour it into the cold pail.

She continued to watch him, her eyes luminous with sensual pleasure.

"Stand up, sweetheart. I cannot rinse the soap off you whilst you huddle in the water. Moreover, that water must be growing chilly by now."

Slowly, using one hand on the tub sides to balance herself, she stood up, but then she gazed at him steadily and lowered both arms to her sides. Her breasts glistened, firm and shapely, their only flaw the mark that the hot key had made on the soft upper swell of the left one. Her arms were softly rounded, as were her hips and bottom, and her legs were long and slender. Her grace stunned him, and despite the fiery, impatient demands of his body, he stared like a moonstruck lad.

To think that Donald had dared try to take her from him . . .

Her eyebrows lifted slightly, as if she wondered at his hesitation. Her expression grew wary again, as if suddenly she were uncertain of herself.

"You are so beautiful," he said quietly as he poured the rinse water over her, taking care not to get her hair wet.

"I'm weak, sir, and I'll soon get cold if you do not give me that towel!"

"I'll dry you myself," he said, holding out a hand to her. "Step out of the tub and move closer to the fire so you don't become chilled."

She obeyed, stepping onto a rug near the hearth, still watching him.

"Shall I do your back or your front first?"

Her body trembled. "You choose," she said, her eyelids lowering slightly, lashes aflutter.

He smiled. "Art trying to seduce me now, lass, or unman me?"

Suddenly shy, she looked at her toes. "I thought you would want . . ." She swallowed and then added in a rush, "I have never felt anything like that before—what you just did to me—but we have not truly bedded yet. I thought you . . ." She faltered, looking at him as if she hoped to read the answer to her thought in his eyes.

"We are not done yet, sweetheart," he said hoarsely. Gently wrapping the towel around her, he turned her face to him, rubbing her through the towel and hoping the fire warmed her. "I just want you," he said quietly. "You are unlike any woman I have ever known, and you stir a fire in my loins that makes me want to take you to bed and keep you there forever."

Without saying more, he scooped her into his arms, towel and all, and moved to lay her gently on the bed.

"I'm still wet," she protested, "and no one has warmed the bed."

"You are as dry as you're going to be for a time," he muttered hoarsely, "and we'll warm the bed ourselves."

She chuckled then, saying, "You are too hasty, sir. What of your bath?"

"I swam last night and bathed the day before," he reminded her. " 'Tis more bathing than most men attempt in a month."

"Still, you must take off the rest of your clothes," she said, pulling the towel out from under her and doing her best to dry herself while in record time he stripped off his shirt, netherstocks, and boots.

Naked, he remembered the fire and went to put more logs on it, but he left all the candles to gutter in their sconces as and when they would. Tonight, he would continue to watch her every expression while he claimed her properly as his wife.

She had slipped under the coverlet and pulled it up to her chin, but he drew it back again, holding it there to look at her and knowing that he would not soon grow tired of doing so.

As he climbed into bed beside her, Molly felt even more conscious of the size of his body than she had before, but she was glad that he seemed to hear no strange voices tonight. His hands were warm, and they stirred more heat in her as they caressed her. Her body had been responding to him from the moment she had heard his voice in the room instead of Doreen's, and in the tub, he had played its tunes as deftly as a piper played his pipes.

He held her in the curve of one arm, lying on his side while his free hand teased the tip of her breast. His hair tickled her cheek. It smelled lightly of the woods and of the leather lining of his helmet. When his lips took the place of his fingers, she gasped as they warmly enclosed her nipple and began to suck. Her body responded as fully as if he had touched her between the legs again. His hand moved lower, teasing her senses elsewhere the way his lips and teeth teased her breast.

Gasping, she murmured to the top of his head, "Tell me what to do."

His lips released her nipple and he looked at her. "Let me feast," he said.

She tugged his hair. "Kiss me first."

Chuckling, he moved up and claimed her lips, his kisses gentle at first, then more demanding. She squirmed against him, hot and ready, and at last, one of his hands eased between her legs, caressing her lightly until, without thought, she moved against his fingers, urging them to do what they had done before.

Instead, they continued to tease until she wanted to scream but could not without stopping his kisses. She was moaning, writhing feverishly, when at last she felt his body ease over hers, and then breath and movement stopped when she felt him easing himself into her.

When he penetrated her, she inhaled with a sharp little cry. It was not the same as in the tub. He moved slowly, and she could tell that he was trying to be as gentle as he knew how to be, but his every movement brought an unfamiliar ache.

Pausing and gently stroking her breasts and belly, he murmured, "It will not always hurt, sweetheart. Your body will soon adjust to mine. You'll see."

"Good. How long will that take?"

He chuckled. "Not long, but it won't happen in a few minutes either."

She did not want him to stop, ache or no ache, but when he moved inside her again, she gasped, and he went still.

"Is it too much pain?" he asked.

"Not really," she said, surprised that he would ask. What little she had heard about husbands had not led her to expect him to show such consideration for her discomfort. "It's just that there are so many new feelings all mixed up together," she said. "Many are delightful, others not." When he did not reply, she closed her eyes and inhaled deeply, letting the breath out slowly, willing the ache to disappear.

His lips touched hers, and she forgot the ache, kissing him hungrily, her tongue dancing with his as she savored the exciting sensations his kisses and caresses stirred in her.

When he began to move inside her again, first carefully

but then with greater urgency, the aching returned at once and she opened her mouth to ask him to slow down, just for a moment. Before she could, his body moved sharply, then more quickly, pounding against hers, and then it was over.

He lay heavily atop her. She could feel his heart pounding and knew that her own was pounding just as hard, but the ache had already begun to ease.

He shifted his position to lie beside her again. Still holding her in the curve of his arm, he drew the coverlet up higher, saying, "You mustn't get cold."

They lay like that for a few minutes, until she felt herself begin to relax.

"Will it truly be easier next time, this part of it?"

"Aye. Does it still hurt?"

"A little," she admitted.

"I'll get the cloth," he said. "You're likely bleeding, but it will stop soon."

He slid out of the bed and walked to the tub to get the damp cloth she had used to wash herself before.

"I can do it," she said, feeling shy.

"Let me." He was deft, gentle, and quick, and when he was done, he tossed the used cloth into the tub and climbed back into bed beside her. Putting his arm around her, he held her close, and a comfortable silence wrapped itself around them.

Moments passed.

"You're no longer a maid, lass," he said.

"Nay," she said, wondering if she was no longer Maid of Dunsithe.

He turned on his side to face her, and his free hand moved idly to stroke her breasts again. To her astonishment, her body tingled and stirred, inviting more caresses. She snuggled closer, smiling up at him, willing him to kiss her. When he did, she felt a sense of power. She had beckoned, and he had obeyed.

He kissed the tip of her nose, her chin, and then reclaimed her lips, lightly, teasingly. His hand was busy, too, stroking her breasts and belly. When a fingertip touched the mark on her breast, stroking it gently, she thought he meant to begin again, and despite lingering soreness, she had no wish to stop him.

He said casually, "Are you certain that no one ever told you how to find Dunsithe's treasure?"

Abruptly sensual lassitude vanished and her spirits fell. "I know only that it is supposed to exist," she said quietly. "Why do you ask about it now?"

"I just thought it seemed logical that, during your childhood, someone must have given you some clue as to where it lies hidden or how to claim it."

As calmly as she could, fighting her disappointment, she said, "Is that why you have been so attentive, so passionate tonight? Hoping I'd tell you all I know about my fortune so you can find it and protect your castle against future attacks?"

"I ask because it occurred to me to ask when I touched that mark, and because I have the right," he said. "I am your husband, lass. What is yours is mine. It has naught to do with what passed between us tonight."

"Well, I don't know any more about it than you do," she said bluntly. "I'm tired. Can we go to sleep now?"

"Aye," he said in much the same tone, "but tomorrow you can ready yourself to leave Eilean Donan."

"Leave?" Shock surged through her as her worst fear was confirmed. Eilean Donan was no more her real home than any of the others had been. "You mean to send me away just because I cannot tell you where to find Dunsithe's treasure?"

"Nay, lass," he said more gently, slipping his arms around her and drawing her close again. "I am sending you away because Patrick, Thomas, Malcolm, and I are all convinced that Donald's men won't rest until they have avenged his death. I want you where I know you will be safe."

"But where?"

"I'll send you to Jamie. He will not deny you royal protection, and I cannot think of anywhere you could be safer than at Stirling under his care."

"But I don't want to go to Stirling. I can be more useful here."

"I did not ask what you wanted to do. I don't deny that you did well today. Thomas told me that your skill amazes him."

"But this is my home now. I belong here!"

"You will go to the King," he said implacably. "I do not want my wife on the battlements fighting alongside my men, risking her life and possibly—now—the life of my heir as well."

"Very well, then, I'll go," Molly said stiffly. "Good night, sir." And with that, she turned over, determined to ignore him. It was a wasted decision, though, for he held her close, his powerful body warm against hers, but he said no more and she decided he had fallen asleep.

She realized as she dozed off that she had wasted the time she had spent searching for her lacy nightdress.

Fin lay quietly awake, holding her, wanting to tell her he did not want to send her away. He dared not, though. Given even a little encouragement, she would fight to stay, and he could not allow that. Not only would she put herself in danger but also he had to think of Eilean Donan and Kintail. If he died, and she was already carrying his child, she carried their future in her womb. It was long before he slept.

Chapter 19 _____

Claud struggled to waken, vaguely aware that something was happening, but his body refused to cooperate. Shrieking struck his ears from every side, growing louder, refusing to let him rest.

The Host! Terror stirred his consciousness as nothing else could have. He opened his eyes.

Although the sight that greeted him was terrifying enough, it was not the Host. His mother stood before Catriona, but Maggie had not done the shrieking, for Catriona was still at it. Claud had never seen her so animated.

"Stay away from me, you cursed old besom," she snapped, arms akimbo. "You may say what you want to your son, but you wield no power over me."

Claud struggled to speak, to warn her, but even had he managed to do more than open his mouth and gasp, it was too late.

Maggie raised her hands, and Catriona flew backward and up through the air, still shrieking. When she landed, she was hanging by the back of her gauzy green gown from one of the hall banner poles, arms and legs waving wildly.

"You are mad, old woman," she screamed. "How dare you do this to me!"

Claud held his breath.

Folding her arms across her chest, Maggie glowered up at Catriona. "Dare, is it? 'Tis no I wha' dares, ye wicked, boiled-brained callat. Didna my Claud warn ye that he stood tae be broken by the Circle for the things ye plagued him tae do? I'll wager he did, but ye paid his warnings nae heed and continued tae sway him tae your own selfish aims so ye wouldna ha' tae stir yourself tae serve your ain laird."

"I did not! And even if I did, it is no concern of yours. Now, let me down!"

"I dinna want tae hear another word from ye, ye triple-turned slut," Maggie snapped. "Haud your whisst!"

"How dare—!"

Without unfolding her arms, Maggie flicked a finger, and although Catriona's lips continued to move, no sound issued from them.

Maggie said in a quiet but carrying tone, "Now that a body can hear herself talk, it occurs tae me, my wee wicked baggage, that ye ha' twice used the word 'dare' in speakin' tae me. Can it be possible that Claud failed tae tell ye that I am myself a member o' the Circle?"

Catriona ceased her flailing, and her eyes rounded in disbelief that soon altered to trepidation.

"Ah, ye begin tae see your peril, do ye? I warrant we'll soon hear ye tryin' tae apologize. Before ye do, however, tell me this. Did Claud no tell ye he'd suffer punishment that would grow fiercer, the more time he spent in your company?"

Catriona hesitated only for a moment before nodding.

"How wise ye are no tae lie tae me," Maggie said gently. "Ye'll find a way off that pole in time, but ye'll find, too, that your powers ha' diminished. Since ye'd rather persuade someone else tae do your work for ye, ye can ha' little use for them, but I'd urge ye to take special care lest ye lose them altogether."

Catriona's mouth was agape. She had not looked at Claud, and he doubted that she knew he was watching. She had not taken her eyes from Maggie.

"Ye o' the Highland lot tend tae forget that the Circle has the power tae call ye tae account for yourself," Maggie said. "Ye'd best think, before we do that, how ye can atone for your wickedness. We'll want tae hear that ye've learned a lesson. Until then, the sound o' your voice will burden nae one. Come along, Claud."

He had believed that she was as unaware of him as Catriona was, but clearly, even though she had not looked at him, Maggie knew he was awake and alert. He wanted to tell her that he could not move a muscle, but he had sense enough to try first and found, to his astonishment, that his pain and weakness had disappeared. If he stumbled getting to his feet, it was no more than usual.

He said nothing until they were well away from Catriona, but at last, curiosity overcame his determination to remain silent.

"I didna go tae her, Mam," he said. "She found me there."

"Nae matter," Maggie said. "I wouldna ha' lifted my spell from ye so soon, Claud, for ye deserve still tae bear it. But circumstance be altered now, and ye must go wi' the Maid."

"Go! Whither?"

"She goes tae Stirling Castle tae seek the King's protection," Maggie said. "I would ha' gone wi' her myself, but now I must look after the Laird o' Kintail in that silly strumpet's place. I just hope ye've learned *your* lesson, my laddie."

"I have and all," Claud said firmly. "Still, ye should stay

wi' the Maid, should ye not? What if I make another mistake, and all goes amiss?"

"She'll be safe wi' the King," Maggie said. "Moreover, having stripped Catriona of her powers, I be responsible now for her laird as well as for our Maid, and he faces invasion if the Macdonalds seek vengeance for their chief's death."

"Did their chief die?" Claud asked, astonished.

"Ye were there, dolthead, when she shot him wi' the arrow. Ye saw him."

"That man were their chief?"

"Aye, did ye no ken that?"

"Nay," Claud said thoughtfully. "I had had all I could do tae guide her arrows, what wi' the pain ye gave me when I used me powers."

He could tell her more about that incident, but he was uncertain how she would receive the news, so he decided to wait until he could prove to her that he could protect the Maid. She would see. Indeed, the whole Circle would see that their Claud was a cannier lad than they knew.

"Wake up, Molly. The storm has blown over, and it is time to go."

She opened her eyes to find Kintail leaning over her. It was still dark, but he had lighted one of the candles on the wall, and its flickering orange-gold glow behind him gave him an eerie, ghostly look.

"What time is it?" she asked groggily.

"Not yet four," he said. "I want to get you away as soon as possible, before Sleat's people have had time to gather themselves. We don't know who will take command, but we do know there is bound to be turmoil at first, because the only obvious successor is his son, and the lad is too young to command Sleat's men. They'd not heed him if he tried."

She tried to blink sleep from her eyes, to collect her thoughts. Once again, someone was uprooting her and it seemed that she had no say in the matter.

"I do not want to leave," she said, sitting up. Though she had said it before, she tried again. "I am your wife, sir, and this is my home. My place is here."

"Your place as my wife is wherever I say it must be," he said. Then, more gently, he added, "We'll not fratch over this, sweetheart. I want you safe. I am sending you by sea to Dunbarton, and from there to Stirling, to Jamie."

"So you will not even take me there yourself," she said, allowing some of the bitterness she felt to color her tone. "You will send me there like a parcel." She knew she sounded childish, but she did not care. She was tired of being a pawn in this game of power that men insisted on playing only with each other.

"Sweetheart," Fin said, coaxingly now, "I'm sending you to Jamie because it is my duty, both as your guardian and your husband, to see to your safety. And I send you rather than escort you for two reasons. First, my place is here with my people. With Ian Dubh gone, I must sort out some things, and I need Patrick with me, because I mean to make him my new constable here. I'll be sending Tam Matheson and Thomas MacMorran with you and Doreen, to look after you."

"Only those two?"

"Nay, lass. You'll have sixteen oarsmen besides, all stout men-at-arms, but 'tis Tam and Thomas who will see to your safety, and they who will hire riders in my stead to protect you on the road from Dunbarton to Stirling. And, too, they will remain with you at Stirling to see to your needs until I can fetch you home again."

"You said two," she reminded him. "Two reasons that you do not go."

"Aye," he said with a straight look. "The second is that my presence would make your journey more dangerous, because Sleat's men would likely recognize me if they should intercept the birlinn. Moreover, I dare not leave Eilean Donan undefended again, because now that they have made one attempt, they are bound to try again, if only to prove that they *can* take the castle."

"I should not be amazed, I suppose, to learn that you care more about your castle than you do your wife," she said.

Yanking back the covers, he pulled her from the bed, holding her with her feet off the floor as he had that day at Dunakin and giving her a shake.

"Don't talk nonsense," he snapped.

A shiver shot up her spine but she told herself that he did not frighten her. It was merely that she was still naked.

"Put me down, Fin," she said, striving to sound calmer than she felt.

He held her there for a moment, and then did as she asked, but he shifted both hands to her shoulders, gripping them tightly so she could not turn away.

Her feet were bare, and the floor was cold. *She* was cold. She wriggled her toes and crossed her arms over her chest, seeking warmth.

Looking directly into her eyes, he said, "You are my wife, Molly. I cannot send the castle away, nor can I send my tenants, but I can send you. Moreover, I believe that if Thomas and Tam can get you beyond Kylerhea and the east coast of Sleat before daylight, you can be safe before Sleat's lads are awake and alert."

Alarmed, she forgot her cold toes and her fears. She said, "Is there no way to avoid Sleat's coast?"

"Not without sailing all the way around the north end of

Skye and passing Dunvegan," he said. "Not only would that route nearly double the length of your journey, but we cannot count on MacLeod's friendship. All hangs on the choice of Sleat's successor. The likelihood is that his death put an end to the Macdonald claim to the Lordship of the Isles, but his people will seek vengeance. I want you away before they can find their feet—and their new leader. As it is, you'll not pass beyond the Point of Sleat before daybreak, but we usually enjoy a morning mist these days, so you should be safe enough. I'll miss you, lass."

Unexpected tears stung her eyes. "Will you be safe?" she asked, her voice little more than a whisper.

"Aye, sweetheart, you've only to ask Patrick and to remember that I've the MacRaes as my shirt of mail and the luck of the Mackenzies to protect me."

"The luck of the Mackenzies did your father no good," she said as a tear spilled over and down one cheek. She made no move to brush it away, wanting only to gaze at him while she still could.

He reached out and wiped the tearstain away with the back of a finger, then bent and kissed her cheek. Then the finger tilted her chin up so that he could kiss her lips. "I am not my father, Molly. Do you remember what they call me?"

"Aye," she said, her voice choked with tears. "Wild Fin Mackenzie."

"Remember that," he said as he used his shirtsleeve to dry her tears. "Mauri would tell you no to fash yourself over the laird, for he's a wicked one and there be none tae best him."

A watery chuckle escaped her, for aside from his voice being much deeper than Mauri's, he sounded just like her.

"That's better," he said. The door opened, and he added, "Here is Doreen now. She has already packed such clothing as you can take with you, but I'll give you a letter for Jamie before you leave. He'll see that you have means to acquire any new clothing you need at court."

Doreen looked surprised to find her mistress standing nude beside the fully dressed laird, but she snatched up a robe and, with a smile, draped it over Molly, saying cheerfully, "We be going to see the King, mistress."

"Aye," Molly replied unenthusiastically.

Fin shot her a quizzical look, but he said only, "I'll leave you to dress now, lass, but do not tarry. The boat is ready to leave."

She did not want to go, but he was leaving her no choice, for although her tears had moved him, it was not enough to make him let her stay. To rail at him or Doreen would avail her nothing, nor could she spoil Doreen's excitement. Therefore, she would put a good face on it and do what she must. Visiting the King's court began to seem more intriguing then, for it occurred to her that she might meet someone there who had known one or both of her parents. To learn more about either one of them would make the journey worthwhile.

"Farewell, lass," Fin said as he helped Molly into the sixteen-oared birlinn and guided her toward the bow. Then, bending near so no one else would hear him, he added as she took her seat beside Doreen, "You're to obey Thomas and Tam as you would me."

Molly looked at him through a new batch of tears that she had been fighting ever since they had stepped outside together to walk down to the boat. She wished she could see him more clearly, but the man holding the only torch Fin had allowed was standing on the shore some distance away.

Fin's order surprised her, for Tam and Thomas were but common soldiers.

As if he had read her mind, he said, "They serve you, but if you meet with a crisis, I have told them you will not question their commands. Is that clear?"

"Aye," she said, drying her tears with a handful of her cloak, grateful that the others had not seen them. "I'm not a fool, sir, but do not leave me long at Stirling."

"I'll come for you myself, sweetheart, as quickly as I can," he said. "Once we see what Sleat's men mean to do, I'll need only time enough to set things in train here and see that everyone understands that Patrick is my new constable."

She nodded, and he put a finger under her chin, making her look at him.

"Will you trust me to see things right, Molly?"

"Aye," she said, narrowing her eyes. "Will you trust me?"

"You carry my name, my reputation, and quite possibly my heir in your care," he said with a teasing smile as he kissed her lightly. "I must trust you."

He returned to the shore then, and she watched as he moved to stand with the other men. He dominated them all with his size alone, but there was more to his presence than mere size. He dwarfed the other men in personality, too.

He was still watching her, and when she raised a hand in farewell, he responded. It was too dark to see if he smiled. Her heart ached to stay with him, but she would not cry again.

The air grew chillier as the birlinn moved away from the castle into open water. She and Doreen huddled together in their heavy cloaks, and she watched until dark mist swallowed the castle.

The oarsmen did not speak, and rags muffled the sounds of the oars in the rowlocks. At the tiller, Tam murmured from time to time, giving commands, until they approached the opening of the narrow strait between Skye and the southern part of Kintail. After that, he made barely discernible hand signals when he wanted the oarsmen to pull harder on one side or the other.

The eastern sky grew steadily lighter as they made their way through the strait. Thomas put up the sail for a time, because the wind blew from the northwest and was strong enough to aid the rowers. Beyond the mouth of Loch Hourn, the sail came down again. They had entered the Sound of Sleat, and ahead to the west lay the Sleat coast. The birlinn hugged the opposite shore. No one spoke a word.

The sky was growing lighter, for at that time of year dawn came earlier each day. Without the sail, it would take longer to cover the nearly ten miles they must travel before they would be safely beyond view of Sleat, and Molly knew that although Dunsgaith, Donald's castle, sat on the far side of that peninsula, his men patrolled the shoreline along the Sound of Sleat.

Their birlinn flew no banner, which might in itself be enough to draw notice, but perhaps with all the unrest Donald had caused, wary travelers often failed to identify their boats. One could hope so, at least.

The wind picked up, and since it still blew from the northwest, they had little worry now that any of Sleat's people could hear them. The oarsmen removed the rags from their rowlocks to make the rowing easier, but Thomas and Tam agreed that the sail should stay down a while longer.

The sun was peeking over the eastern horizon when they neared the opening of Loch Nevis and approached Mallaig Head. The Sound of Sleat was nearly five miles across at this point, and Thomas moved at last to put up the sail.

Doreen sighed. "I vow, I have been holding my breath

since we left Loch Duich in fear that someone would hear or see us."

"Don't stop holding it yet," Molly advised. "Look yonder to the west."

On the far horizon, two low white clouds seemed to roll across the water toward them. Presently, just as Molly feared, it became apparent that they were clouds of spray. Rising out of each was a single square sail.

Even as he rapidly hauled up their own sail, Thomas shouted at the oarsmen to pick up their pace. "Put your backs into it, lads. They be nae friends o' ours!"

Despite their efforts, the other galleys drew inexorably nearer. Until the pair had closed half the distance, Molly glimpsed their hulls only occasionally amidst the spume set up by the banks of long oars on each side. With their sails' aid, they drove the slender, low-set galleys at a scarcely be-lievable speed.

"Thomas, they'll soon be upon us!" she cried, pointing.

He had already recognized the danger. "We canna outrun them, lads," he said. "They'll be Sleat's boats. We must yield and hope they dinna ken who we be. If they ask, we be loyal followers o' Mackinnon."

"An we each take two o' the bastards, mayhap we can win free, Tam," one of the oarsmen shouted.

"Ye'd ha' to take more each than two," Tam shouted back. "Do as you're bid lads. If they ram us, we're for a swim, so pull nearer to shore. Mayhap someone can win free if need be."

Molly saw Thomas lean closer to Tam, saw the other man shake his head, then seem to argue some point or other. Thomas patted Tam's shoulder, then hunched low and began to ease his way between the oarsmen toward the bow. Crouching some distance away, he slipped off his tartan mantle and tossed it to Molly.

"They be Mackinnon colors, mistress. If ye wear it over yours, mayhap it will lend credence to our tale."

"What is Tam doing?" she asked, noting that the younger man was standing now. He had cast aside his cloak and was pulling off the precious boots that Sir Patrick had given him.

"I've told him he must go over the side as we turn," Thomas said. "He doesna swim as well as I do, but he still runs like a running gilly, and whatever comes o' this, we'll want a man free to report back, if need be, to the master."

"Without his boots?"

"Sakes, mistress," Tam said, "I never had boots afore these. Me feet be tough as whitleather."

She smiled, but to Thomas she said, "They mean to harm us, do they not?"

"We dinna ken that yet." He smiled reassuringly at her as he signed to two of the nearest oarsmen to make space for Tam Matheson.

The younger man stripped to his short kilt but retained his dirk. When he moved up beside Thomas, Molly heard him say, "I dinna think I dare take my sword, man. I'm no so good a swimmer as it is."

"Leave it, then," Thomas said. "Ye'll make the shore easily, because you can swim with the current here, and we'll use the birlinn to shield you from Sleat's galleys. Slip overboard now, and quickly."

Without another word, Tam eased over the side, and they watched him make for shore. They were close, within twenty-five yards of the headland, and Molly watched tensely, looking from the swimmer to the oncoming boats and back again.

"Heel to port now, and turn sharp about, lads," Thomas shouted. "We'll make them keep their eyes on us, and pray that they dinna see our Tam."

"Yield to them when we draw near, Thomas," Molly said, striving to sound calm and still watching Tam. "It would be useless to defy them, especially since I'll wager they want nothing more than to learn who we are."

"Aye, mistress, likely ye're right, but face toward the front now," Thomas said. "Ye men, look to your oars and heed my commands. I dinna want to see a single man glancing toward shore."

The oncoming ships came fast, so fast that it was easy to see why men called such galleys the greyhounds of the sea. They had a certain grace, even beauty, but just then, Molly thought of them as anything but beautiful. She could see Sleat's banner flying from each one.

In minutes, the two galleys had closed on the birlinn. Thomas MacMorran stood, his sword in its sheath, his arms raised high, commanding his men to hold.

"I be Thomas MacMorran o' Dunakin," he shouted, fighting to keep his balance as his oarsmen's blades dug hard into the water and slowed the birlinn. "We travel in peace," he cried to the lead boat. "What do ye want wi' us?"

In reply, the newcomers swept up in fine style, scarcely slackening speed until they were right in front of them. Then, pulling up dramatically with back-watering sweeps of their oars, they brought the great sails crashing down at the exact moment that the lead craft's helmsman, bearing on his tiller, swung his ship across the birlinn's bow.

Thomas shouted for his oarsmen to yaw to starboard, but despite their quick response, the two boats met in a crunching thud that jarred every tooth and bone in Molly's body and jolted her from her seat. If there was damage, it was solely to the smaller boat, for the sides of the galley rose half again as high as the Mackenzie birlinn. From her perspective, she could barely see any oarsmen in the larger boat.

"At them, lads," a voice above her head commanded gruffly.

To her horror, men-at-arms leaped from the galley into the Mackenzie boat, swords at the ready. Her oarsmen, taken by surprise, were no match for the assault, and it was over in moments, wholesale slaughter.

Still standing, sword high, Thomas stepped between the women and the invaders, only to be driven back by men stepping right onto the bodies of dead and dying oarsmen. He leaped onto an oarsman's bench, his sword slashing, but his attacker's sword dove under it, and Thomas tumbled backward into the water.

With a scream of terror, Doreen leaped up to scramble to his aid, but Molly grabbed her skirt and hauled her back onto their seat. Both women leaned over the side to watch for him to surface, but he did not.

"Thomas! Oh, Thomas," Doreen screamed.

Molly pulled the sobbing maidservant into her arms. Tears streamed down her own cheeks, and nausea roiled her stomach as she gazed upon the carnage.

"I bid you good day, Mistress Gordon. I had hoped that we'd meet again."

Senses whirling, she looked up into the eyes of Donald the Grim.

"But you died," she exclaimed. "I saw you die!"

"Your eyes deceived you," he said mockingly. "I was grievously wounded, but God in His mercy saw fit to stop the bleeding, and I am, as you see, wholly recovered. We are going to sink your boat, lass," he added matter-of-factly, "so perhaps you should climb into mine. We have a long journey yet before us."

Chapter 20

"Beg pardon, laird, but ye've a visitor asking to see ye."

Looking up from the list he had been making of needed supplies, Fin said impatiently, "Who is it?"

"She says her name be Lady Percy, sir."

Fin glanced at Patrick, beside him at the high table in the hall, and raised his eyebrows. "Show her ladyship in."

The gilly hurried away to do his bidding, whereupon Patrick said, "At least now we'll learn who she is." Noise at the entrance drew his attention, and he whistled low and appreciatively.

Fin nearly did so, as well.

Lady Percy was a beautiful, elegant woman, and that despite looking as if she had traveled some distance to see him. Recalling that Jamie had warned him to keep her close at Eilean Donan, he eyed her searchingly. She looked harmless enough, he thought, but was that not ever the way with the fair sex?

"Good day, Lady Percy," he said politely. "Welcome to Eilean Donan. I am Kintail, and this is Sir Patrick MacRae, my constable here."

"My lord." She made a graceful curtsy, allowing her dark

blue surcoat to fall open and reveal an amazing expanse of plump creamy bosom barely contained in a low-cut, lace-edged, yellow silk bodice. Fin heard Patrick's appreciative murmur but controlled his own expression without difficulty.

He said evenly, "Although Kintail is a barony, madam, I have not yet been elevated to the peerage. In Scotland, unlike England, I must take my seat in Parliament before anyone need address me as 'my lord.' How may I serve you?"

She straightened, and again her beauty struck him hard.

Her black-fringed gray eyes were nearly as beautiful as Molly's. Her dress was fashionable, expensive, and became her well. A lacy, pearl-embroidered caul confined her golden blond hair without hiding its splendor, and the leather shoes peeping from under the edge of her skirt boasted gold rosettes. Slender and sensually curvaceous, she carried herself in a way showing her awareness of the effect her appearance had on men. Her skirt was wide and her bodice tight, but as she moved, one could see that her underpinnings were simple, lacking the stiffness of boning and tight corsets, and revealing the lines of her body exquisitely.

Despite this blatantly sensuous behavior, her demeanor remained respectful and serious as she replied, "I have come to see my daughter, sir."

Fin raised his eyebrows, surprised. "Your daughter, madam? Enlighten me, if you please. Where do you expect to find her?"

"Why, here, sir. I am told that she recently became your wife."

He stared at her, stunned, but he could not doubt the truth of her words. No wonder her eyes reminded him of Molly's. They were identical.

She said softly, "You did not know? Percy was my second husband. My first was Lord Gordon of Dunsithe.

Please, sir, where is Molly? She is the only daughter left to me, and as you must know, I've not seen her for years."

"Your brother is the Earl of Angus," Fin said, understanding why Jamie wanted him to keep an eye on her. For reasons understandable to anyone who knew his history, the King suspected the motives of anyone connected to Angus.

The smile that touched her lips was sad. She said, "I pray you will not be so cruel as to prevent me from seeing Molly, sir. I . . . I have come a long way."

"Indeed, madam, so long a way that although you were within a few miles of Eilean Donan days ago, you traveled on without stopping to see your daughter. Perhaps you would like to explain that omission to me."

Her cheeks reddened, but her steady gaze did not waver. She said, "Brigands attacked my party. Surely, if you know I was in the vicinity, you learned that, too."

"Aye, for we found the men they murdered. Who attacked you?"

Her hesitation was so brief that had he not been watching carefully he might have missed it. Recovering, she gave him that direct, guileless look again and said, "I did not know them, sir. They were typical Highland barbarians, I believe, but thankfully, they did me no harm and let me go again this morning. Thus, I have come to you now. I want to see my daughter, and also bring you a message from James, the King."

Reaching inside her surcoat, she slid a leather pouch she wore on her narrow belt from side to front and opened it, extracting a small, scrolled missive that bore a miniature of James's privy seal.

When she handed it to Fin, he paused to examine the seal.

"This appears to have suffered some damage," he said, giving her a look as direct as any she had given him.

She did not flinch, and this time, she did not blush. "It has come a distance, sire, and as you see, I have kept it on my person. If the wax grew warm . . ." She shrugged as if to say that he could fill in the rest for himself.

Wondering who else had read it, Fin broke the seal and scanned the message quickly. It was much shorter than the one sent with the man who had been killed, merely introducing Lady Percy to Kintail's notice, begging him to render her such aid as she requested, and adding that his grace hoped the Mackenzies, who had remained consistently loyal to the Crown, would continue to serve his royal interests against Donald the Grim. It was just as well, Fin thought, that he had already sent a pair of running gillies to Stirling with word of Sleat's death. Jamie would be delighted to receive the news.

Quietly, his guest said, "Pray, sir, may I see Molly?"

"You come too late for that, I'm afraid," he said, setting the letter aside with other documents on the table. "She departed this morning for Stirling."

Her expression froze. Exerting visible control over herself, she said, "She is riding, of course. If I leave at once, I can catch up with her party before day's end."

"She is not riding," Fin said. "I sent her by sea."

"No!" She clutched a hand to her bosom, and the color faded from her cheeks. "Oh, pray, sir, tell me that you did no such thing."

Feeling cold, Fin stood up and stepped around the table toward her.

Lady Percy took a hasty step backward, her face as white now as alabaster.

"What the devil is this?" he demanded. "Why should I not send her by sea?"

"Because . . . Oh, mercy!" She took a deep breath, let it out, and said, "Surely you sent her with escorts, sir—a fleet of swift, well-armed galleys."

"It was one boat, a birlinn," he snapped. "Now, tell me what is amiss, or by heaven, I will—"

Without another word, Lady Percy crumpled to the floor.

"You've frightened her to death," Patrick said, moving swiftly to her side and dropping to one knee to shake her. "Madam, my lady, wake up!" Looking up at Fin, he said, "I'll fetch Mauri. She'll know what to do."

Fin nodded and then took Patrick's place when that gentleman hastened from the chamber. As he knelt beside Lady Percy, he caught a wisp of motion from the corner of his eye.

Quickly turning his head and seeing only swirling dust motes in a beam of evening sunlight, he turned back to his fallen guest. Shaking her again, harder than Patrick had, he had the satisfaction of hearing her groan.

"Collect yourself, madam," he ordered harshly. "I must know what has upset you. I know that your so-called attacker the other day was Donald the Grim, but I suspect you were either in collusion with him or that you somehow managed to escape his men. What I do not know is how cozy you were with him before his death, I think you had better tell me everything, and at once."

Moaning again, she sat up and allowed him to help her to her feet. "I . . . I apologize for allowing myself to be overcome, sir," she said faintly. "I . . ." Words failed her, and tears welled in her eyes.

"You are overset," he said. Drawing her toward the nearest bench, he waited only until she sat down, before he said firmly, "You must tell me what you know, madam. Is Molly in danger?"

"Aye," she said flatly. "Donald must have her."

"Donald? Do you mean Sleat's whelp, Donald Gorm?" He shook his head. "He cannot have taken charge of his father's men. He is too young. By heaven, madam, if you are making game of me, I will make you wish—"

"Donald the Grim is not dead, as you think, but danger-ously alive, sir," she said steadily. "He told me he nearly died. They thought he severed the major blood vessel in his leg when he yanked out the arrow that struck him, but the bleeding stopped, and he is quite well now, I promise you."

"Then may the devil take him!" Fin exclaimed. "He has captured Molly?"

"All I can tell you for certain is that he intended to take me south to Dunbarton, for he hoped—" Breaking off, she licked her lips, then added hastily, "That plan is of no con-sequence now except, until early this morning, he . . . he threatened to take me with him. Then someone brought him word of a birlinn in the Sound of Sleat. He said it was 'them, trying to sneak by.' "

"Them?"

"Aye, sir, 'them.' I paid little heed to his discussion, be-cause I believed the information he received did not concern me. I learned long ago that powerful men react badly if one reveals too much interest in their affairs, and I was careful not to anger Donald. His temper is . . . is perilously volatile."

"That's true enough," Fin agreed grimly, wondering if she knew that men had said as much of his own temper. "What then?"

"Donald and his men set out at once, and although he did take me with him, he put me and my woman ashore at Kylerhea, where he arranged for horses and a few men to es-cort us. I had told him from the outset that I came to the Highlands in search of my daughter. He knew that I wanted to visit her before I continued to Stirling, and he said he had no objection. Before, whenever I pressed him to let me do so, he mocked me."

Fin suspected that there was more to her tale than she was admitting, but she had told him enough to get on with.

"If Sleat captured Molly, will he not take her back to Dunsgaith?"

"I do not believe so," she said. Her color had returned, but her voice retained a note of urgency as she said, "He was prepared for a sea journey, sir. He had two large galleys with those very long oars that take two men to manage each one. Such galleys are very fast."

"Faster, certainly, than the birlinn I sent Molly in," Fin muttered as much to himself as to his guest.

Lady Percy said quietly, "You should know, too, that Donald spent much of the time I was with him questioning me about Dunsithe and the Maid's portion."

"What did you tell him?"

"What *could* I tell him? I know no more about it than anyone else. Think you, sir, that had it been otherwise my brother would have allowed me to keep such a secret to myself? You know naught of Angus if you believe that. He may keep secrets of his own," she added bitterly, "but he does not allow his sisters to do so, particularly sisters born on the wrong side of the blanket. He thinks we were born merely to serve him and his political interests."

Fin believed her. He had heard nothing about Angus that would lead him to suspect the man of being soft toward the women in his life. If she had known the whereabouts of Molly's fortune, she would have admitted as much to Angus the first time he questioned her. "You think he will take Molly to Dunsithe," he said.

"Aye," she said. "I think he means to see if she can find the treasure for him." She nibbled her lower lip as if she might say more, but Patrick and Mauri entered just then with Lady Percy's attendant.

Fin turned his attention to Patrick, saying, "Have the lads provision the galleys. Sleat has captured Molly and is taking her to Dunsithe in hopes of laying hands on her fortune. I mean to leave at once."

"The devil fly away with Sleat!" Patrick exclaimed angrily.

"I'll take both galleys," Fin said, "and I'll want the strongest oarsmen you can find. Sleat will want to avoid the Sounds of Mull and Jura, knowing Jamie's friends will be watching for him, so if I take that route, I can make up time. Still, I've none to waste. The journey will take three days, at least."

Quietly but firmly, Lady Percy said, "I am going with you."

Fin ignored her, fixing his attention on Patrick and what he wanted done. "Take Malcolm," he said. "He can help organize the men. I want you to think also of who we know in the Borders who may prove friendly to me."

"You must take me with you," Lady Percy insisted.

"Madam, you and your woman are welcome to stay here until I return. I will bring your daughter back to you as swiftly as I can, but you are not going with me. Believe me, you would only be in the way. Now, please—"

"One hesitates to contradict a man of your size and temperament, sir, but I can do more to help you acquire Border friends than Sir Patrick can. I am still a Douglas, sir, and in these circumstances, I believe that the Border Gordons will also aid me. I have friends in both camps, you see, and you will save a great deal of time if you make landfall short of Solway and ride the rest of the way. Have you access to horses? Indeed, sir, have you ever sailed those waters before? I have, often."

Fin was silent, but he looked at Patrick.

That incorrigible young man smiled ruefully. "She has you there, laird. We've no one here who kens that part of Scotland. Nor can I think of anyone to whom we might turn for aid without first applying to James for references. If we consider men we knew at St. Andrews, we may think of someone, though."

"We've no time for that," Fin said. "And I know of no one."

"If that is not reason enough to take me along, I'll offer another," Lady Percy said. "The plain fact is that if I show up at Dunsithe, Donald is bound to let me in."

Fin's eyes narrowed. Harshly, he said, "Just what *is* your relationship with Sleat, madam?"

With a wry little smile, she said, "Not what you are thinking, but you may find the truth much worse. Just as I carried a message to you from Jamie, I carried another to Donald. It was not from Jamie, however."

"From Angus?"

"Aye, one was from him," she said, watching him warily now. "I also carried one from Henry of England, and—"

"So Jamie was right," Patrick breathed.

Paling, she looked at him, then back at Fin. "Jamie knows?"

"He suspects," Fin told her. "He also suspects that Henry is financing Sleat's rising. What about that, madam? And do not think to cozen me into taking you to Dunsithe," he added, seeing a calculating look leap to her eyes. "You will remain here, but first you will tell me all you know about Sleat's dealings with England."

"You will need me at Dunsithe!"

"We cannot even be certain he is making for the Borders," Fin said.

Patrick, looking past him toward the entrance, said, "Perhaps we can."

Turning, Fin saw Tam Matheson being helped through the doorway. The lad was wheezing heavily, nearly winded.

"Tam!"

"Aye, laird," he gasped. "Some villain be flying that devil Sleat's banner. He's taken the mistress, sailing south!"

"Sleat's alive," Fin told him. "Whereabouts did he overtake you?"

"Loch Nevis, they call it. I've run all the way."

"The others?"

"All dead," Tam said with a groan. "Thomas sent me into the water afore they caught us. Be ye sure it's Sleat himself, laird?"

"I'm sure." Fin turned to Lady Percy and said grimly, "Very well, madam, you may come with me, but do not think you have won much. We're going to have a long talk about Henry and your part in this. Moreover, you'll go without your woman, and at the first complaint, I'm likely to throw you overboard."

Patrick said, "I'll give the men your orders, Fin, and then I'll need a few moments to change clothes and gather my things together."

"You're staying here," Fin said. "I need you in command here, because Sleat may have left men and boats behind, hoping I'd leave the castle undefended."

For a moment, it looked as if Patrick would argue, but wisely, he just nodded and left the hall.

"Now, madam," Fin said, "you may begin, and do not leave anything out."

She seemed willing to talk, but her tale was tangled and filled with bitterness. That she blamed her brother for her unhappy past was plain. That she enjoyed the freedom of her recent life as a widow was also plain. What was not plain was her true position with regard to the daughter whom by way of farewell she had branded with a red-hot key.

Twice during their conversation, Fin experienced again the strange sense that something moved just at the edge of his vision, but each time, when he turned his head, he saw only more dust motes in the fading sunlight.

Propelled by a brisk wind from the northwest, Fin's galleys followed the same route that the birlinn had taken, through Kylerhea into the Sound of Sleat, past Loch Hourn, and along the coast toward Loch Nevis and Mallaig Head. Increasing darkness gave them cover, but Fin kept a close watch on the opposite coast, in case Sleat had left more galleys lying in wait. None challenged him.

Tam Matheson, recovered already from his long run, rested in the stern of the lead galley, tending the tiller. Lady Percy, swaddled in a heavy, hooded cloak, sat beside Fin in the bow. She had scarcely spoken since leaving Eilean Donan and was presently watching the dark coastline on their right.

Tam shouted, "Will we catch them, d'ye think, laird?"

"Aye," Fin replied. "If this wind holds, we should make it in the same time as Sleat, even if his boats are faster. We have extra men aboard, so some can rest whilst others row, and our route is shorter than Sleat's. We'll take horses from a place called—" He looked at Lady Percy. "What was that name again, madam?"

"Ballantrae," she said, glancing at him, then looking back toward the coast.

"How far is this Ballantrae?" Tam asked.

She was not paying heed. "Kintail," she said, pointing, "is that not someone waving to us yonder?"

Shifting his gaze to follow her gesture, Fin discerned movement in the dark shadows on shore. Then a spark flared, a torch burst into flame, and he saw a broad-shouldered male figure waving it back and forth.

"Likely, it be a trap o' some sort," Tam said, peering into the darkness.

"Are you certain that Sleat's men killed all of ours?" Fin demanded.

"I did think so," Tam said. "His lot spilled into the birlinn and slashed everything in sight."

"Not the women, though."

"Nay, laird. They helped the two women into Sleat's galley afterward, and then they sank the birlinn. I saw nae man leave the sinking boat, so I took off running like Thomas MacMorran said I should, to tell ye what happened."

"You did well," Fin said, "but I think we must see who that is on the shore."

Commanding the oarsmen on the left to back water and those on the right to stroke hard, he swung the galley toward shore. The second boat followed.

Before they reached the shallows near the wooded shoreline, Fin was able to make out the familiar features of Thomas MacMorran.

Tam and the others recognized him at the same time, and it was all Fin could do to mute their cheers. He saw Thomas douse the torch and fling himself into the water near the shore, taking great strides as far as he could walk, then swimming the rest of the way. Willing hands hauled him aboard the lead galley.

Grinning widely, Fin clapped him hard on both shoulders and gave him a shake by way of welcome. " 'Tis glad I am to see you safe, Thomas MacMorran."

"Nae more glad than I be, laird," Thomas said with a responding grin.

"But how did ye do it, man?" Tam demanded.

"I fell overboard," Thomas said. "Then I dived under the

birlinn and swam underwater to the other side o' Donald's galley. Nae one looked for a body there, ye ken. When I'd caught my breath, I swam underwater till I reached the last galley and stayed alongside it until they passed by the sinking birlinn. It didna sink in a trice, ye ken, but took a goodly time, so I stayed alongside it. By the time it sank, Donald and his lot were too far away to tell if I were a swimmer or just a wee bit o' flotsam, so I swam here and waited for ye."

"I ran all the way back to Eilean Donan," Tam said in indignation.

"And a good lad ye were to do that," Thomas said, grinning. "I could see nae reason to wear myself out when I knew ye would fetch him and he wouldna waste time. Sakes, man, I were near frozen to death!"

"A good run would ha' warmed ye."

"Me fire did that."

"Enough, you two," Fin said, chuckling. "Don't waste your energy on each other. Save it for Sleat."

"Aye, well," Tam said, clapping Thomas on the back, "we'll take care o' Sleat, never fear."

"Sleat is mine," Fin said curtly.

Chapter 21

Molly awakened to find sunlight streaming into the barren bedchamber through an unshuttered window. The air felt chilly, no fire burned in the fireplace, and the bed hangings smelled musty. She and Doreen had shaken them, but she suspected they still harbored spiders and other such creatures.

Sitting up in a bed likely to have been one her parents had allotted to guests they considered insignificant, she saw that Doreen still slept on the pallet near the cold hearth.

Taking care not to disturb her, Molly whispered, "Maggie? Are you here?"

No answer.

A little louder, she murmured, "Maggie, please, come. I need you!"

Doreen stirred and opened her eyes, still red from weeping over Thomas MacMorran's loss. "Did ye call me, mistress? Shall I get up and bang on that door? Likely, it'll still be locked, ye ken."

Molly sighed. "Don't bother. There is a bedpan, which I've already used, and I don't care if I starve. I'd as lief never see that villain again."

She would have to, though, for she had no choice, and having seen what Donald was capable of, the prospect chilled her. Even if she could take care of herself, which was doubtful, she had Doreen to protect, as well.

They had arrived at the castle the previous night after a tedious sea journey and a long overland trek. After making landfall, they had waited near the beach while some of Donald's men had gone away and returned after an hour or so with ponies for their leader and the women. Molly had feared they would camp again, as they had done the two previous nights, and that she and Doreen would spend yet another night fearing for their virtue, but Donald had ordered everyone to move on.

Darkness fell before they reached the castle, but there was a moon, and Donald knew the way.

They had entered through the main gates, and men-at-arms were there to welcome them. That they were Donald's men rapidly became apparent, as did the fact that they were guarding Dunsithe despite James having ordered the change of wardship, and despite Molly's marriage to Kintail.

Donald took the women into the great hall, a chamber Molly struggled to recognize from her childhood memories. Dim though those memories were, the Dunsithe she remembered was colorful. Bright banners had hung from numerous staffs jutting high from tapestry-covered walls, and silver and gilt plate had decked the high table. All that remained from that time was the Gordon coat of arms over the fireplace, but its paint was dim, its colors badly faded.

"Welcome home, Mistress Gordon," Donald said sardonically.

She had given up reminding him of her marriage and new title. He had ignored her when she'd mentioned those details before. It was as if her marriage had never taken place, despite his having been there to witness the ceremony.

Taking her cue from him, she kept silent, wishing the place did not look so cheerless. The remaining furniture included only rough trestles and benches. Even the high table looked the worse for wear, its elaborate carvings broken or badly scratched, its polish faded. The walls and floor were bare, lacking any sign of the colorful arras and carpets that had decked them in the past.

She was still gazing about curiously when Donald slapped her.

Gasping, she raised a hand to her stinging cheek and glowered at him, struggling to repress her fear.

He said evenly, "When I speak, mistress, you will reply."

Pressing her hands against her sides to still their trembling, she said, "I have nothing to say to you."

"Oh, but you do," he said, thrusting his face close to hers. "Moreover, if you do not find your tongue and your memory swiftly, I've a deal more where that slap came from. You will quickly learn that defiance is unwise."

Raising her chin, she said, "I do not know what you expect me to say. I have told you before that I know nothing about my fortune, let alone where it is hidden, so I cannot imagine what you expect me to tell you now."

"I have thought long and hard about your denials, lass," he said harshly. "For you to know nothing makes no sense."

"Nevertheless, it is the truth."

"You must know enough to claim what is yours," he insisted. "I do not doubt that you expected Kintail to bring you here, or that he meant to do so as soon after the wedding as possible, but I made sure to leave him no time for that."

"Is that why you attacked Eilean Donan?"

" 'Tis one reason. I had hoped to take you with me after the attack, but you thwarted me. And before you defy me again, lass, I'd remind you that I still owe you for what you did to me that day. If you think I'll have any qualm about doing what I must to force you to reveal what you know, remember that."

Although the knowledge of what he was capable of doing terrified her, she managed to look stonily back at him.

"It is late," he said then. "I'll give you what's left of the night to consider your choices, but by morning, you'd better come to your senses." Nodding to one of his men, he ordered him to take the women up to a suitable chamber.

So relieved had Molly been that Donald had not separated her from Doreen that she had gone quietly. But now, considering what lay ahead, she was only grateful that she had managed to sleep. She had feared she would be wakeful, especially since the hard bed boasted only a thin blanket and no pillow, but the moment her head had touched the mattress, she slept.

Clearly, Doreen had slept soundly, too, but her face was wan and her despair plain, as it had been for the past three days, since they had watched Thomas topple into the sea and disappear. She looked at Molly now, visibly bewildered, and said, "I canna believe I slept so hard."

"I, too," Molly told her. " 'Tis as well that we did, though."

"Aye. We'll manage the better for it, but what will happen now? Will Donald leave us be if ye tell him what he wants to ken?"

"We'll never know that," Molly said with a sigh. "I know nothing. I thought you understood that."

Doreen shrugged. "I dinna ken much about me betters, m'lady. Ye were nobbut a wee lassock when Donald o' Sleat brought ye to Dunakin, but still it does seem odd that ye'd ken naught o' your own fortune."

"Nevertheless, it is the sad truth."

The rattle of a key in the lock was the only warning they had before a man-at-arms entered and said, "The master wants ye to join him below, Mistress Gordon. Ye're to stay here," he added when Doreen got up and moved to stand by Molly.

"My mistress requires hot water before she will be presentable," Doreen said stoutly. "Surely, ye canna take her to your master straight from her bed."

"Hush your gob, lass, unless ye want to feel the back o' me hand."

"Never mind, Doreen," Molly said hastily. "We have no choice. I'll go with him. Please, do not hurt her," she begged the soldier.

He shrugged. "I've nae quarrel wi' the lass," he said.

Passing him, Molly followed the twisting stairway down to the hall, where she found Donald finishing what appeared to be a large breakfast. The smell of roasted meat assailed her nostrils, and her mouth watered. She was hungry.

A number of his men lounged about the dreary great chamber, polishing weapons or armor, eating, or talking.

Donald said, "Well, lass?"

She hesitated near the doorway, her fear of him flooding back. "I can tell you no more than I did last night," she said. "It won't matter what you do to me. I cannot reveal what I do not know."

"We'll see," he said. Turning his attention to her escort, he said, "What would you recommend, Colson, to make a lass tell you all she knows?"

Gritting her teeth, Molly forced herself to keep her eyes on Donald.

The man beside her chuckled. "I dinna ha' trouble wi' my lasses, master, but if I did, I'd put her across me knee and teach her better manners."

"Aye, we could start with a good hiding," Donald said thoughtfully. "Or I could strip you naked, Mistress Gordon, and beat you senseless in front of my men. Which would you prefer?"

The thought that he might do either turned her blood cold, but she did not believe he really expected her to answer such a question.

"Bring her here," he ordered grimly.

Clamping a large hand around her upper arm, the man-at-arms jerked her forward until she stood right in front of Donald, and in her determination to keep silent she bit her lower lip. Tasting blood, she met his gaze.

His slap this time was so hard that only the bruising grip on her arm held her upright. "I warned you," he said.

Tears sprang to her eyes, and she felt blood trickling from her lip to her chin, but a vision of Fin brought confidence, and she said, "Kintail will kill you for this." She was amazed at how calm she sounded.

"Mayhap he will," Donald retorted. "But as you have learned, lass, it is not so easy to kill me, and he is not here, is he? No one is here who can help you. Remember that before you speak impertinently to me again."

She could not deny her fear of him, but neither could she imagine anything she could do to alter the situation. Whatever Donald the Grim chose to do to her, she could not prevent, but she would not let him steal her dignity—not easily. He would have to work much harder to accomplish that.

"Stir up the fire, Colson," he commanded his man-at-arms. "We must not let the lass grow too chilly."

When Colson released her and turned away, Donald reached out, grabbed her, and jerked her toward him. Gripping the front of her bodice in both hands, he ripped it open, revealing her thin shift.

Her teeth began to chatter.

"Beg pardon, master," a man's voice said behind her.

"There be a Lady Percy at the gate wantin' tae speak wi' ye straightaway."

"The devil there is! Are you sure that is her name?"

"Aye, master. Lady Percy, she said."

"Did she say why she would speak with me?" Donald asked curtly.

"Nay, only that ye'd be glad tae see her and well recompensed forbye."

Donald frowned, and Molly held her breath. Surely, he would neither beat her nor do anything else so horrid in front of a female visitor. But when she tried to draw the parts of her bodice together, he slapped her hands away.

"Leave that. We'll see what her ladyship thinks of your predicament. But the rest of you lads, clear out. I don't need an army to protect me from women."

Molly kept silent, hoping to find an ally in the visitor, believing that no woman would stand silently and watch another brutalized.

Colson went out, taking the other men with him.

The woman he returned with a few minutes later was not what Molly had expected to see. Not, she realized, that she had had reason to expect anything in particular. But this woman was younger than she had supposed and beautiful. Lady Percy wore a fashionable riding dress and carried a whip, and if she looked tired and as if she had traveled some distance, her greeting revealed only satisfaction at finding her host willing to receive her.

"How fortunate that you traveled south, sir," she exclaimed as she hurried in. Briskly drawing off her gloves, she moved toward the fire, chattering on with only a brief glance at Molly. "And how wonderful that you have prepared such a warm fire. It is uncomfortably chilly outside today."

"What brings you to Dunsithe, madam?" Donald's voice

was harsh, but it contained suspicion as well. "You have traveled with amazing speed."

The visitor shrugged. "She was gone when I got there, so I rode straight on to Stirling and thence to the Borders."

"In three days?" His skepticism was plain.

She raised her eyebrows. "Border women can ride for much longer periods if necessary, sir. Art furious with me for coming? I trust you will not remain so when I tell you *why* I've come. I've seen Angus! And, what's more, I've brought what you've been waiting for, from . . . from another." Casting a sly look at Molly, she added, "I must say no more, though, in front of your friend."

"My friend?" It was Donald's turn to raise his brows. "Do you not recognize the lass, madam?"

Lady Percy laughed, a tinkling, light laugh. "Mercy, sir, *should* I know her? I vow, I never saw this one at Dunsgaith. From the state of her clothing, I'd guess you brought her along for your own purpose, which would explain why you put *me* off your boat so abruptly. Did you go right back then and collect her? You said you would go to Dunbarton and then Stirling, so you can imagine how startled I was to find that you had never reached Stirling at all. To learn only this morning that you were here at Dunsithe seemed providential, for being only a few miles away—"

"How came you to be only a few miles away?" he interjected.

"Faith, sir, did I not tell you I have been with Angus and that I bring you a particular item from England's Henry that you have long waited to receive? Shall I be more direct?" she asked with a coquettish look.

"Why should you not?" he retorted. "We need keep no secrets from Molly."

Bewildered, Molly stared from one to the other, surreptitiously trying to hold her bodice front together without Donald noticing.

He was paying no heed to her, however, for he watched his visitor narrowly.

Lady Percy gazed back at him in dawning astonishment. "Molly? Truly?" She clasped her hands to her bosom, glanced at Molly, then back at him. "Pray, tell me that you would never jest about such a thing, sir, I implore you!"

He shook his head, still watching her closely.

She turned back to Molly then, and tears welled into her eyes. With a watery smile, she held her arms wide and said, "Molly? My darling girl, you cannot know how I've longed to hold my beautiful daughter again."

Shocked, still not understanding, Molly stared at her.

"Precious one, do not deny me the moment I've waited so long for. Oh, darling girl, embrace me, do! Know you not your own mother?"

Molly's knees threatened to fail her. She did not move.

Not far away, Fin lay stretched on his stomach on a hillside with Tam beside him. Thanks to favorable winds, they had made excellent time, and they had learned soon after making landfall that Sleat had beaten them to the west march by only hours. Lady Percy had done as she promised, too, procuring horses and a guide for them from a solemn Douglas kinsman who had asked no questions.

Fin had fifty men with him, but he knew that Sleat had more, and by the solid look of the castle, it was shut tight and guarded well. He had told Lady Percy that he meant to attack as soon as she could bring him information about Sleat's defenses, but he could see no way that an attack would do him much good. The castle, although supposedly abandoned for years, looked formidable. It occupied the crest of a low hill, and although his present hilltop was nearby and he lay concealed, anyone on Dunsithe's battlements commanded every approach and would see him and his men if they moved any nearer.

Like Eilean Donan, Dunsithe's well sat safely inside the curtain wall, and he knew that if Sleat had left men to guard the place, they would be well provisioned. Therefore, a siege was unlikely to succeed, because Fin had few friends in the west march even if Lady Percy's kinsmen should continue to be helpful. It was more likely that the Kintail men would stand alone, and if Sleat simply kept Lady Percy inside, Fin would not benefit by anything she might learn.

Movement stirred at the edge of his vision, but as usual, when he turned his head sharply he saw no one. At least . . . He narrowed his eyes. There was still some sort of movement, hazy, uncertain, as if a breeze swirled dust about. The wind had died, though. Not so much as a hint of a breeze stirred.

His men waited silently behind him, below the crest, confident that he would find a way to free their mistress and defeat Sleat. Little did they suspect his uncertainty. He wished Patrick were there. Patrick always had ideas, and although most of them seemed daft, they often worked. Fin started to smile, but the image of Patrick's grinning face faded, replaced in his mind by Molly's serious one.

Where was she? What was she thinking? She would not be as confident as his men were that he would rescue her, and even though the lass had heart, she was likely frightened. He had to get to her. The thought that Sleat might harm her terrified him, and why else would the villain have seized her and brought her to Dunsithe but in the hope that she could lead him to her fortune? Even if she could, how could Sleat keep it unless he stole it and murdered her to cover his theft?

Again, movement stirred just beyond sight. Again, he turned and saw . . .

"Tam, look yonder," he muttered, pointing. "Do you see anyone near that thicket of trees? A figure, mayhap a countrywoman?"

Tam glanced obediently toward the trees but shook his head, saying quietly, "Nay, laird. We came that route ourselves, and we ken fine that nae one were there then. I've been keeping a sharp eye out since."

"Good man," Fin said, frustrated. He could still see movement. Indeed, he could make out a figure in the shadows beneath the trees, childlike in size but looking more like a woman old enough to be his long-deceased mother. Was she gesturing to him? He squinted, trying to see her more clearly.

Beside him, Tam muttered, "Be aught amiss, laird?"

"Are you certain you see no one yonder?"

"Dead sure. What d'ye see?"

"We've got to get to the mistress," Fin said harshly, still watching the thicket. It *was* a woman. He could see her more clearly and wondered why Tam did not, for she appeared to be jumping up and down now and waving her arms madly. Surely, she was some odd hallucination.

He had scarcely slept since learning that Sleat had taken Molly. Doubtless his mind was playing tricks. She was clearer than ever now, still waving and dancing. Her mouth was open. Was she shouting at him? Why could he not hear her? He had heard voices when he did not want to. Why could he not . . .

What was it that Molly had said to him that night at the inlet when she had asked him if he believed in spirits? Something about just listening, just allowing himself to see and hear what was before him. He was willing enough, but how?

"Wait here," he said to Tam.

"Where be ye going?"

"Yonder, to the woods. If someone wants to help us, I must learn what she can tell us."

"But there be no one there," Tam protested.

"Be silent and wait," Fin snapped.

Keeping low, he moved swiftly toward the thicket of trees and shrubbery that crowned that part of the hilltop. The rest of his men waited beyond it. No one could have sneaked past them, so how could any woman possibly . . .

Molly needed him.

He should be studying Dunsithe, learning all that he could learn abut it, perhaps moving to the far side, using what vantage he could from nearby hilltops, although he could not count on all of them to be as empty as this one. Had Dunsithe been his to defend, he would have kept watchers on every nearby hilltop.

Had Sleat kept watchers here? Was it possible that they had fled when they saw him and his men coming? Did Sleat know they were here? Was he just waiting for Fin to make his move?

Realizing that he had lost sight of the little woman, Fin hesitated. He had reached the trees, and they provided sufficient cover for him to stand upright, so he did. Doubtless, she had been only a figment of a wishful imagination.

He needed help. "Where are you?" he muttered desperately.

"Over here."

He nearly didn't hear her, and hearing her, he nearly didn't see her. When he did, he had an urge to shut his eyes. She looked furious.

"Who are you?" he asked.

Without answering—or answering so softly that he did not hear—she turned and walked away. She was much smaller than she had seemed before, like a small child, and he was afraid he would lose sight of her if he did not hurry, although that seemed ridiculous, because one stride of his equaled six of hers. Still, she moved swiftly, not having to duck and bend as often as he did.

"Wait," he said urgently, keeping his voice down and hoping she would hear. "Where are we going?"

She stopped and turned, hands on generous hips, scowling at him.

"Ye're a one for chatter, and nae mistake, but we've nae time for it. Ye ha' work tae be done. Can ye whistle up your lads, or d'ye need tae fetch them?"

"Aye, of course, I can whistle them up, but why should I?"

She glowered at him. Could she be leading him into a trap?

Hands still on her hips, brows knitted, she said, "I were going tae take ye by yourself, but I ha' thought better. Ye'll need more swords than your own, and that be plain fact."

"But where—?"

"Whisst now, will ye whisst! I never saw such a one for talking when he should listen. Our Maid be in dire straits, so if ye want tae help her, ye'll do as I bid ye and nae more backchat."

"But who are you?"

"I be Maggie Malloch, nobbut that's tellin' ye anything. Now then, will ye call your men, or will ye no?"

"Not until you tell me where you are taking me," Fin said.

"Into Dunsithe," she said. "Will that suit ye, d'ye think?"

Putting two fingers to his lips, he gave a low, trilling whistle. He could see Tam from where he stood, but he could not see the others. Gesturing to Tam to follow him, he followed the tiny woman. The name Malloch meant nothing to him. He had never heard it before, so he could not judge her allegiances, but she seemed to know Molly. For the moment, that was enough.

"What d'ye want o' me, laird?" Tam said, coming up with him.

"We're following her," Fin said, pointing to his guide.

"Who?"

Realizing that Tam still could not see her, Fin hesitated. When he did, the small, plump figure ahead seemed to fade. That was enough to persuade him.

"Just follow me," he ordered, "and be sure that the others do, too."

"But where are we going?"

"Into the castle. I've found a secret way in. Don't ask questions," he added harshly. "Just do as I command."

Eyes widening, Tam nodded, and soon fifty men were hurrying along behind the little woman. Fin had not realized that the thicket extended so far. It seemed to follow the curve of the hill, but instead of moving up toward the top again, to head toward the castle, they traveled steadily downward.

He wanted to ask more questions, but as the thought crossed his mind, her figure dimmed. Hastily, he decided just to go where she took him. Her figure sharpened then, letting him follow easily. If he had to duck under branches, he was unaware of it. So, too, was he unaware of the men behind him. He had eyes only for the hurrying figure ahead.

They crossed a bubbling burn, and just beyond it, the little woman disappeared into the hillside.

Breaking into a run, Fin followed, and he nearly ran right into a rock slab before he realized there was an opening behind it. The opening looked too narrow for him, but hearing her voice beyond, urging him on, he walked into it, and to his surprise, it seemed to widen to accommodate him. He walked into a tunnel.

He heard the men muttering behind him now and turned to tell Tam to quiet them. They had to be a considerable distance from the castle, but without knowing what lay ahead, he wanted them quiet. It would not do for Sleat or any guards he had set at the other end to hear them.

It occurred to him then that he could see more clearly than one ought to see in a tunnel. He could still see the tiny woman ahead of him, but more than that, he could see the walls, ceiling, and floor. Something glowed in the dirt, some sort of low, ethereal light. That someone had used the tunnel often at some time was clear. Passing an alcove with a pair of rusty trunks of a type that generally contained weapons, he realized that the Gordons probably had built it as a precaution against siege. The question was whether Donald the Grim knew of it. Lady Percy probably knew, Fin realized. And if she knew, it was possible that Sleat did, too.

Hesitating, wondering again if they were running into ambush, he glanced back to see his worry mirrored on Tam's face. Looking forward again, he discovered that he had lost sight of his guide.

He stopped. What now? It was possible that she had just disappeared around a bend in the tunnel or perhaps into another alcove like the one containing the weapons chests, but it was also possible that danger lurked ahead, and his men's lives depended on his making the right decision.

As that thought crossed his mind, an image of Molly banished it. What Sleat might be doing to her did not bear thinking about, and with no way into the castle but this one, it would be folly to leave the men behind. They would go forward. He would put his trust in the tiny woman, but he would keep his wits about him.

Fin drew his sword.

Chapter 22

Molly had allowed the tearful Lady Percy to embrace her, but she felt no sense of familiarity. She had no recollection of her mother hugging her during her childhood. The memories she did retain of Eleanor Gordon were of a bright creature, flitting hither and yon, never lighting anywhere, and certainly never sitting still long enough to hold her or her tiny sister, Bess.

Donald said dryly, "Your daughter does not appear to be overjoyed by this reunion, madam."

Releasing Molly, Lady Percy stepped back and said ruefully, "She has little cause to greet me with joy, I fear. I did not know what good fortune I enjoyed until Angus took it all from me. He stole my life," she added bitterly.

"That would imply that you have been dead for some dozen years, madam, yet here you stand alive before us," Donald retorted.

"Faith, sir, I lost my husband and both of my children in a matter of days. What more is there to a woman's life?"

"You scarcely can blame Angus for Gordon's death. Your husband died at the hands of one of his own tenants! As for the rest, it appears to me that Angus paid you well for your loss by marrying you to the powerful Percy family."

"An English family, I would remind you, and certainly that stale marriage was not enough to make up for wee Bessie's death, which, I would also remind you, occurred whilst she was in Angus's custody, mayhap to assure that Molly became Dunsithe's sole heiress. Nor could anything have made up for losing Molly," she added with a wistful, damp-eyed look that stirred Molly's quick sympathy.

Donald said sharply, "You said at the outset of this conversation that you had brought something for me. What is it, and where is it?"

"Aye," Lady Percy said. "That is to say, I bring word of—"

"So you have brought nothing but more words. Seize her, Colson."

"No! Henry is sending the money you requested. Angus promised that I shall have it tomorrow!"

"Aye, and we all know how much we trust Angus," he said sarcastically.

Lady Percy flushed. "Please, sir. Upon my honor, I will see that—"

"Your honor is worth no more than his," he said. "Did you not tell me you suspect him of having stolen your daughter's inheritance?"

"I *do* believe that," she said forcefully. "What else could have happened to it? You did not see Dunsithe in those days, but the night Angus came to take away my daughters, this hall was resplendent with silver and gold, fine furnishings, and colorful banners. Every room boasted such things. And there was money, chests full of it. I never asked for anything that Gordon did not provide—dresses and jewels. Oh, the jewels, sir! One would have to see them to believe their magnificence."

Her eyes shone at the memory.

Glancing at Donald, Molly saw him frown. "Enough," he said curtly. "When Angus left with your daughters, you were still here. Do you expect me to believe he took so much without your knowing?"

Lady Percy nodded. "He locked me in my bedchamber, because I grew hysterical when I realized he was taking both of my daughters, and when I won free again, everything had disappeared, including the servants, although he had left his men to watch the place. They must have stolen it all that night. Angus came for me two days later and carried me off to Tantallon, his castle by the sea. I stayed there, within arm's reach of my daughter but never allowed to see her, until he had his final falling out with the King and we escaped to England. I never saw Dunsithe again until today."

"A pretty tale," Donald snarled, "but a false one, I'll wager. One frequently hears that Angus is but a pensioner at Henry's table, forced to do Henry's bidding. How can that be if he possesses as much wealth as you say he stole from here?"

"I do not know," she replied. "It is true that one hears such things, but perhaps Henry took all Angus had and gave him just enough to let him keep up appearances. That would be ironic, would it not?"

Donald looked long at her. "Madam," he said at last, "I do not believe that Dunsithe's treasure ever left Dunsithe, for as long as Angus controlled the Maid, he controlled her fortune. After all, he could not have known that his royal regency would end only a few months later, forcing him to flee Scotland."

"But—"

"Silence," Donald snapped. "It is clear that Gordon or some of his minions managed somehow to hide her inheritance, but he must have intended her to claim it. Therefore, she must know how to do so."

Lady Percy looked speculatively at Molly. "I do not see how she could know more than I do," she said thoughtfully. "She was not yet six, after all, when Angus took her. And her father died suddenly. It is not as if he had known he would die and took opportunity to whisper some secret in her ear, or that she would remember it now, even if he had. Do you recall any such thing, Molly?"

"I have already told him that I do not," Molly said, still trying to digest the notion that the beautiful Lady Percy was her mother. "I barely remember Dunsithe. I have lived the greater part of my life on Skye, after all."

"There, you see?"

"Nevertheless, madam," Donald said, "she is the key to Dunsithe's fortune, and if she does not know more than she has told me, it will go badly for her, because one way or another I mean to learn all she knows. I'm told she bears a mark on her breast in the shape of a key and that you put that mark on her yourself."

"Aye, I did, to my shame," Lady Percy said with a look of deep remorse. Avoiding Molly's gaze, she added, "Her nurse and I discussed the likelihood that her appearance would change over the years, and I feared someone might try to put a false Maid in her place. The mark was meant to keep that from happening."

"What key did you use? What did it open?"

"Faith, I do not know! 'Twas years ago, and the key was just one her nurse found when I asked her to fetch one."

"I do not believe you," Donald said. "It is too great a co-incidence that we search for a hiding place whilst the lass bears the mark of a key." He glanced from one to the other. "Believe me, one of you will tell me what I want to know."

"You are mistaken," Lady Percy said urgently. "We know nothing!"

With a sneer, he said, "We'll begin with the lass. You will not like hearing your daughter scream, madam. I shall begin by giving her just a little pain, but I'll wager that if she tolerates that without talking, she will not hold out long against more of the same pain you gave her when you bade her farewell."

"No!" Lady Percy rushed at him, catching Colson off guard. The man-at-arms leaped to grab her, but he was not quick enough to do so before she flew at Donald, raking his cheek with her fingernails, drawing blood.

Donald caught her arms, twisting them hard as he flung her away. When she landed in a heap near the hearth, Molly turned to run to her, but Donald caught her, his hand gripping her arm so tightly that she knew he would leave bruises.

"Colson, pick Lady Percy up and see that she watches closely whilst I question the lass. I believe her ladyship will quickly remember which key she branded her with and where she hid it afterward. I'll acquit you of knowing what that key will open, my lady, but only because I believe Angus would long since have forced you to tell him anything you knew. Since it is patently obvious that he did not, perhaps he never learned about that mark."

"I tell you, I know nothing that can help you," Lady Percy cried.

"One of you knows something," he retorted harshly, "and the quickest way to learn which of you it is, is to question the lass. I don't doubt she could watch you suffer pain without blinking an eye, since she scarcely knows you, and her last memory of you is painful, but you are still her mother, are you not?"

"Oh, please, sir, do not!"

He was still holding Molly tightly, but she was frantically looking around the hall in search of a weapon to aid her. Surely, there must be something. Even as the thought crossed her mind, a glint of light sparkled on the handle of the dirk Donald wore in the sheath on his belt. She eyed it obliquely. Did she dare take it?

Donald was watching the other two. Lady Percy continued to argue with him as she struggled in Colson's grip, and Colson had all he could do to hold her.

No one was looking at Molly.

Slowly, carefully, she inched a hand toward Donald's dirk. Only the two men remained in the hall, but she had no illusions. Even if she and Lady Percy managed to incapacitate them, many more of Donald's men were outside; however, she decided to worry about that only if the need arose. Fixing her attention on the dirk, edging her hand toward it, she shifted her body slightly to conceal what she was doing from Colson.

Her hand touched the hilt of the dagger.

They were still arguing. She paid no heed to what they said, even when she heard Lady Percy cry out as if Colson had hurt her. She dared not listen or look. She had to keep her attention on the dirk. Giving a slight tug, she found that it moved easily, more easily than she had dared hope.

A sudden silence filled the chamber.

Quick as thought, Molly snatched the dirk from its sheath and turned its point toward Donald's side.

"Release me," she snapped, "and step away!"

He did not obey, merely raising his brows as he said lightly, "You do not look like much of a killer to me, lass."

"I nearly killed you once before," she reminded him.

"Aye, from a distance and with an arrow. But had it not been for my own foolishness in yanking it free, you'd have done me no great harm. As it was, the bleeding stopped more quickly than I had any right to expect. I doubt that you have the nerve to plunge that blade into living flesh."

"Don't tempt me," she said, hoping she sounded more sure of herself than she felt. "I am perfectly capable—"

She cried out when he grabbed the hand holding the dagger. She heard Lady Percy shriek again but she was too busy struggling with Donald to see what the others were doing. Her very determination to prevent him from taking the dagger seemed to give her strength she had never known before. Suddenly, she had both hands on the hilt, although how she had freed the one from his grip she did not know. Slowly, ever so slowly, she forced the point inward again, toward him.

Strong hands grabbed her from behind, and shrieks and shouting echoed all around her as Lady Percy and Colson joined the struggle. Colson's enormous hand smacked down atop hers on the hilt of the dagger. Then Molly was free, spinning away from Donald.

She landed hard on her backside on the floor.

The two men leaped apart, still facing each other, and as they did, Lady Percy crumpled to the floor between them. Bright red blood oozed through her clothing from a wound in her side.

Molly stared at her in shock, willing herself to move, finding that she could not. Her legs and feet felt as if they had turned to wood.

"No," she moaned as tears poured down her cheeks, and whatever held her let go. Flinging herself down beside her mother, she clutched at her and pressed her hand against the wound. "Don't die," she cried. "Not now, not here!"

Donald caught her and wrenched her upright. "So you do care, do you?" he said, giving her a shake. "Not that it matters. The way she's bleeding, she'll not live long, and I'll soon send you to join her if you don't tell me what I want to know."

"You murderer! I wouldn't tell you anything even if I did know!"

"We'll begin by having these rags off you, I think," he growled, jerking her around to face him and grabbing the front of her shift with both hands through the torn bodice. "I want to see the imprint of that key."

"If you do, it will be the last thing you see in this world before you enter the next," Kintail snapped from the rear of the hall.

Astonishment, delight, and relief surged through Molly as she whirled to reassure herself that Fin was really there.

He stood in the doorway, sword unsheathed and at the ready, his rage making him look larger and more dangerous than ever. Two men flanked him, and such was her delight at seeing him that she nearly failed to recognize them. One was Tam Matheson. The second, to her amazement, was Thomas MacMorran.

Colson whipped his sword from its sheath, held it up, and stood balanced on the balls of his feet, waiting for a command from his master.

In that brief silence, Molly heard Lady Percy give a shuddering gasp. The sound chilled her and tied knots in her stomach. Was it possible that she had found her mother only to lose her forever?

Terrified, she wanted to pull away, to run to her, but she dared do nothing to distract the men lest one of them act in haste or folly. Only when Donald released her and stepped away to draw his sword did she rush back to Lady Percy, and even then, she did not take her eyes from Donald, fearing he might turn his sword on them, might even be so dastardly as to use them as his shield.

He was paying them no heed, though. His gaze was fixed

on Fin. "Have you defeated all my men, then?" he demanded.

"We have," Fin said. "They await you in yonder courtyard."

"They can continue to wait till I have dealt with you, sir," Donald said. "Or are you such a coward that you will not fight me?"

Molly, kneeling now beside Lady Percy, glanced at Fin to see that he was watching her, apparently unconcerned that Donald had spoken to him.

"Art safe, sweetheart?" he said gently.

"Aye, sir," she said, swallowing hard. "He did not hurt me."

"Who tore your gown?" His tone was edged now, ominous.

She dampened dry lips, not wanting to tell him, knowing that she would feel responsible for Donald's death if she named him for such a deed.

"I tore it," Donald snapped. "If you don't like it, do your worst!"

"Tell your man there to surrender," Fin said. "Mine are two to his one, and they will show him no mercy if he challenges them."

"And if I win?"

"If you win, you and your men can go free, for I will be dead."

"And the lass will be mine again, as will her fortune?"

"Which is why you will not win."

"Why should I trust you?" Donald demanded. "What is to keep your men from killing me after I've killed you?"

"My word is good," Fin replied curtly. "You should know that, Sleat, although the fact that you doubt it makes me wonder if you have any sense of honor at all. Not that it matters now," he added. "You won't suffer the lack much longer. Now, tell your man to stand down."

"Put away your sword, Colson," Sleat said.

When Colson had sheathed his weapon, Fin said, "Tam, take him out to join the others. The lad tending the injured woman can stay."

Bewildered, Molly looked at Fin, then at the equally baffled Tam, wondering what "lad" Fin was talking about. Donald and Thomas looked confused, too.

But Fin was unaware, for he went right on speaking to Tam. "When you've seen to that chap, come back so that Sleat does not attempt to strike down Thomas if he does succeed in besting me. If he wins fairly, your only task is to see that our men leave this place safely and with my honor intact. Is that clear?"

"Aye, master," Tam said, glancing uncertainly again at Molly.

She returned her attention to Lady Percy. "Please do not die, madam," she murmured, stroking her cheek. "All will yet be well. The bleeding is slowing, so mayhap the wound is not as deep as I'd feared, or it missed vital organs."

The stertorous gasping continued.

The sudden clash of steel on steel startled her even though she had expected it. She turned to watch, fearfully.

Both men were strong and quick, wielding the cumbersome weapons as if they weighed half what they did. Each time the swords crashed together, Molly held her breath, but she was certain from the first what the outcome would be. Fate would not be so cruel as to take Fin Mackenzie from her just when she had come to appreciate him, to admire him—nay, to love him with all her heart.

That thought startled her as much as the first clash of swords had.

Fin slipped on a slick flagstone, and she tensed as Don

ald leaped in for the kill, but even as Fin was going down, he managed to parry the stroke and recover his footing. After that, the end came swiftly with no quarter asked or granted. A final, slashing stroke from the shoulder, ending in an upward cut to the neck, and the thing was done.

Molly turned from the awful sight as Donald crumpled to the floor, his head nearly severed from his body.

Fin flung his sword aside and rushed to her, and she was on her feet before he reached her, throwing herself into his arms.

"Oh, thank the Fates that you are safe, but how did you get in?" she cried.

"I found a secret tunnel," he said. "Are you certain he did not hurt you?"

"I'm sure. He threatened to make me tell where my fortune lies hidden, and that frightened me, because I could not tell him what I do not know. But then you came, and he—" She broke off, burying her face against his chest, not minding in the least that her cheek pressed against the hard chain mail under his baldric.

His arms tightened around her, and they stayed like that for a long, satisfying moment. Then his hand clasped her chin and gently tilted it up, and his warm lips claimed hers.

She responded at once with a sigh, but the kiss was all too brief, for she remembered her injured mother and stirred to pull away.

At the same moment, he released her, saying, "We must tend to Lady Percy."

Thomas MacMorran was already kneeling beside her, and when Fin spoke, he looked up at them and said, "She's been stabbed, laird."

"Aye," Molly said, "and it was all my fault. I took Donald's dirk whilst he argued with her, and when he grabbed it and tried to twist it from my hand, she leaped in to help me and he stabbed her. Is she going to live, Thomas?"

"I canna say, my lady. She's bled a great deal, but the bleeding ha' stopped now. Time will tell the rest."

"Where is the lad who was tending her earlier?" Fin asked.

Thomas looked at him and shook his head. "I saw nae lad, laird."

"Nor I," Molly said.

"Well, I saw him," Fin said firmly. "A small man, quite small, in fact."

A prickling sensation stirred along the back of Molly's neck. "How did you find the tunnel, sir? I did not know that Dunsithe boasted such a thing."

"There was a plump little woman," he said. "She beckoned to me, and I followed. Then, somewhere in the tunnel, she disappeared. I feared we might be walking into an ambush, but we came to a door that opened into a corridor, and from there, we were able to steal up on Sleat's men from behind. After that, it was quick work, but I never saw that woman again. I don't know where she went."

"I think you must have seen Maggie Malloch," she said quietly. "She has told me that because you have the gift of second sight, you can see her people but only if you allow yourself to do so."

"Maggie Malloch is the name she gave me, lass, but who is she?"

"She is the same Maggie who told me the mark on my breast will fade away in time," Molly said. "She calls herself a household spirit, a sort of benevolent fairy. She and her son, Claud, have followed me since I left Dunsithe. The 'lad' you saw earlier, tending my mother, may have been Claud. They seem to have some special healing power, so perhaps she will live, as you did when you fell from your horse, and as Thomas did after the arrow struck him, and Donald after I shot him." She frowned and then added thoughtfully, "If you can see Maggie and Claud, perhaps they can help us find my fortune."

"I am not sure that, even now, I'm ready to believe in fairies," Fin said, smiling. "As to your fortune, though, perhaps I do know something about that."

"But how could you?"

"Coming through the tunnel, we passed two large chests. I'll wager we'll find that they contain what everyone has sought here for so long. Would you like to see them? Thomas can watch over your mother. He can help her as much as anyone can, and Tam will return any moment."

"I'm here, laird," Tam said from the doorway.

"Help Thomas carry Lady Percy to the settle and see if you can find some blankets to cover her," Fin ordered. "My lass and I are going to see if this fortune of hers is mythical or real."

Molly said, "Find her a pillow or some cushions, Tam, and see if you can find someone who knows about healing. In truth, sir," she added to Kintail, "I'll not feel right leaving her just to look for that blighted treasure. I know you want to find it, but—"

"Nay, lass, it can wait. I suggested it only—"

"The treasure? Molly's fortune?" To their amazement, Lady Percy sat up on the settle as soon as Tam and Thomas set her down on it.

"Mercy," Molly exclaimed, running to clasp her hand and peer anxiously into her face. "Have you recovered so quickly, madam?"

Smiling lovingly at her, Lady Percy said, "I remember flinging myself at Donald to keep him from harming you, and then feeling a sharp pain." She looked down at herself and fingered the bloody rent in her gown where the dirk had pierced it. "His blade cannot have done much damage, though, for I feel no pain now, I promise you. What's this you were saying about the treasure?"

Fin said, "My men and I entered this castle through a tunnel. Do you know aught of such, madam?"

"A tunnel? Nay, sir, I do not, but they say that Dunsithe conceals many secrets. Do you think you can find this tunnel again?"

"Oh, aye," he assured her. "If you have truly recovered, we'll look now."

"Indeed, sir, I must see this, and pray, call me Nell, for we are all family now." To their surprise, she got to her feet, shook out her skirts, and seemed to be completely healthy again.

Her swift recovery delighted Molly and told her that whatever Fin might think to the contrary, Maggie and her minions had taken a hand in the game.

Fin led the way out of the great hall and down a corridor that appeared to end in a wall of solid stone. To her astonishment, he walked up to the wall and reached around the side of the largest stone. Gripping it, he pulled, and like a door, the whole stone wall swung silently toward them, revealing a gloomy tunnel, like an extension of the corridor. It led into eerie darkness.

"Will we not need torches?" Molly asked.

"We'll send for some later if we do need them," Fin said. "First, though, I want you to see it the way we did, if you can. The walls seemed to glow, but everything here has been so odd that I do not know if they will do so now or not."

Pulling the great stone door shut behind them, he said, "Wait until your eyes adjust. If it is as it was before, we'll see our way easily."

"I never even heard rumors that this tunnel existed," Nell

said. "In sooth, I do not remember that stone corridor approaching its entrance."

"It has been over a decade since you were here," Fin reminded her.

"True, and the whole castle looks different now that it is no more than stone walls and floors and a few rough benches and tables." She sighed.

Molly had been staring into the distance ahead, scarcely heeding their conversation. "Look," she said. "The walls and floor *do* glow."

"Follow me," Fin said, taking the lead. "The chests lie not far from here."

In minutes, they reached the two large, dusty, ironbound chests. Molly bent swiftly to the first one.

"It is locked," she said. "Since we do not have a key, we'll have to break it open, and it is too heavy for us to carry back into the hall. I cannot even shift it."

"Likely, the key is one of that bunch on the wall above it," Fin said.

"Where?" Molly and Nell said as one.

"Here," Fin said, reaching past them to touch a place on the wall.

Molly saw nothing but the rough-hewn stone of the passage wall. "There's nothing there," she said as he pulled his hand away, looking bewildered.

"But I can see them," he protested. "It is a large bunch of keys like a chatelaine that one's wife or housekeeper would carry at her kirtle. I see them, but when I try to touch them, I touch only wall."

"Perhaps Maggie Malloch or someone like her has cast a spell over them," Molly said matter-of-factly.

Fin shot her a look, then cast another, more speaking one at Nell, but he did not dispute Molly's conclusion.

"Who is Maggie Malloch?" Nell said.

Although Fin gestured to Molly to keep silent, she ignored him and said, "Did you ever hear of fairies or other wee folk at Dunsithe, madam?"

Instead of scoffing, as Fin clearly expected, Nell chuckled. "Dunsithe means 'hill of the fairies,'" she said. "As a result, the whole area abounds with tales of the wee folk, and I certainly heard many of them when I lived here. I cannot say I believed them, but many folks hereabouts swear they are true. Can you really see a bunch of keys on that wall, sir?"

"I can, madam, and since I can, perhaps I am meant to reach for a particular key. Can you describe the one you used to burn—?"

Nell raised a hand in protest. "Pray, sir, do not remind me again of that horrible moment! I thought I was doing right, protecting her, but I have heard her shrieks in my dreams ever since. Truly, I do not recall which key I used."

"Try, madam. Try to remember."

Her grimace was visible even in that dim light, but she said, "Try as I will, I see only a key that seemed small till I pressed it to Molly's flesh and she screamed."

"The ones on the wall all look larger than what you describe," he said, frustration clear in his tone.

"I wish I could see them," Molly said.

He looked at her speculatively. Then, as if he were speaking his thoughts aloud, he said, "It is your fortune, lass. I can claim it only through you. Mayhap that fact is the true key to the treasure. When I touch you, touch your . . ."

He hesitated, looking at Nell. Then he seemed to give himself a shake, as if to clear his head.

Turning back to Molly, he said, "When I touch your breast, I feel an odd tingling sensation. It is not merely sensual, although I've told myself that's all it is. Indeed, I believed it was a simple reaction to my intense physical feelings for you, feelings I have experienced since the night we first met. However, that particular sensation remains significantly different from any other I've felt, ever. Perhaps, just as any claim I have to your fortune comes to me through you, my ability to touch what I see also lies in you."

He said no more, letting his gaze lock with hers as if he willed her to come to a similar conclusion but was content to let her do so without further urging.

"You think that if you touch the mark on my breast," she said, following his reasoning easily, "you may also be able to touch what you see on the wall."

"Perhaps," he said. "Art willing to try it, sweetheart?"

"Do you want me to leave?" Nell asked. "I own, I am dying to know what will happen, but if you would prefer to be alone whilst—"

"No, madam," Molly said, smiling at her. "You must stay." She turned back to Fin and, gazing into his eyes, opened her bodice and loosened her shift for him.

"Touch the mark of the key," she said. "See if it will help you choose the right one."

His expression softened, and she felt a jolt of longing. She wanted to be alone with him, to send the rest of the world away. Except insofar as Dunsithe's treasure meant a great deal to him and to the people of Kintail, it meant little just then to her.

Gently, he reached out and touched the mark on her breast with two fingers. She looked down at them, long and slender. The fingertips felt chilly for that first instant but warmed at once. Her gaze met his again, and he smiled, then turned to face the wall where he had seen the keys.

She closed her eyes, waiting, savoring the touch of his fingers on her breast, a feeling she had feared she would never experience again.

When she felt him reach for the keys that only he could

see, Molly opened her eyes to see his hand leaving the wall, empty. The keys had not moved.

Fin sighed in disappointment, and let his hand fall away from her breast.

"Wait," she cried, realizing in that instant what she had seen. "I could see them! Oh, touch the key mark again!"

He did so at once, and the keys reappeared, just as he had described them to her, a large ring such as many women wore clinking at their kirtles. One key glinted like silver, brighter than all the others.

Without a thought, she reached for the ring and found herself holding the silver key. How it had leaped from the ring to her hand, she did not know.

"Faith," Nell exclaimed. "How did you do that?"

"Try it in the lock of the chest," Molly said, offering the key to Fin.

"Nay, lass, it is your fortune and your key." With a smile, he stepped back, gesturing toward the two chests.

Molly moved to the first one, knelt beside it, and inserted the key in the rusty lock. It went in easily, but it would not turn. Disappointed, she moved to the second chest and repeated the attempt. Again, it went in, but this time the key turned easily. She lifted the lid, and although the light in the tunnel was dim, they could see all they needed to see.

The chest was empty.

Chapter 23 _____

Fin knelt quickly beside Molly when she sat back on her heels, unable to hide her disappointment. Putting an arm around her to comfort her, he reached into the chest with his free hand, sweeping it to touch every side and the bottom, in case the contents might be proving elusive in some fashion, as the keys had earlier.

"Can *you* see anything there?" Molly asked. "Am I just unable to do so?"

"Nay," he said. "The chest looks and feels empty to me, too. Although . . ." As the new thought struck him, he reached for her arm and turned her to face him. "Let me touch the key mark again," he said, slipping his hand beneath her shift to touch her warm breast. "Mayhap . . ."

But when he touched the mark, he felt no tingling sensation, so he was not surprised when she shook her head. The chest was simply empty.

"I don't understand," Nell said. "There ought to have been something in it, certainly, but what did you expect to find, sir? It might have contained money, I suppose, if my husband had hidden some here before his death, but both of these chests together are much too small to contain all that was lost."

"They are not too small to have held gold coins, jewelry, or other small items of great value, however," Fin said. "You told me yourself that a vast quantity of jewelry disappeared. In any event, it is unwise for us to linger. My men passed through this tunnel, you will recall, and I'd as lief none but the three of us know about this. Lock up the chest, sweetheart. It can keep its secret for now. We'll decide what to do about it after I figure out how to deal with Donald and his lot. I certainly can't carry these chests home in a boat full of Macdonald prisoners."

Molly had already moved to close and relock the open chest, and he saw now that she was having difficulty with the key.

"What's amiss?" he asked.

"It won't turn."

He took it from her and tried it himself, only to find that she was right. It would go into the lock, but no matter how hard he twisted it, it would not turn.

"Let me try the other chest again," Molly said. "Perhaps one has to open them in a certain order."

Fin stepped aside to give her room, and Nell moved closer to watch.

"It's useless," Molly said. "It goes into the lock, but it still will not turn."

"It seems to me that your wee folk are the wicked sort," Nell said, shaking her head. "They gave you the secret but have stolen the treasure."

Molly shook her head. "I do not believe Maggie Malloch would do such a thing. We simply have not yet solved the whole puzzle."

"Can you not summon this Maggie Malloch?" Nell asked.

"She has never come at my behest," Molly said. "Moreover, if Kintail saw her earlier, I'd expect him to see her now if she were present. I think we must solve this puzzle ourselves."

"But what else can we do?"

Fin said, "If that key won't open the other chest, it won't, but we may think of some other way after we've given it more thought. In any event, I mean to take both chests back to Eilean Donan until we can solve this mystery."

He reached for the empty one and found that it was light enough for one man or certainly two men to carry. Glancing at Molly, he said, "I thought you said this chest was too heavy to move."

"I thought it was," she said. "Try the other one."

The second refused to budge an inch.

"I'll have some of my men collect them both," he said.

"And what if my key disappears again?"

"It won't," he said confidently. "Now that it is in your possession, I think you will find that even if someone else manages to take it, he will be unable to use it for anything. At all events, we'll do some thinking and confer with Thomas and Tam. I do wish Patrick were here, though."

He led the way back to the castle, and the women followed, emerging from the tunnel into the stone corridor. But the corridor was no longer bleak or bare. Rich arras draped its walls, candles burned in silver sconces along the way, and a long, magnificently colorful carpet covered the floor.

The three of them exclaimed aloud, and then stood and gaped for a long moment, but when they forced themselves to move on, it was to find that the great hall, too, was transformed. Splendid arras cloths draped all but one wall, and on both long walls, colorful banners on gilded poles lined the chamber's length.

The high table was no longer battered and plain but

highly polished and decked with silver and gold plate. Carved and cushioned chairs surrounded it, and carpets more magnificent than the one in the corridor were scattered over the flagstone floor. Weapons and shields hung from the undraped wall, all polished and gleaming, many bejeweled or boasting gilded hilts and decorated sheaths. Plush velvet cushions graced exquisitely carved benches along the walls.

"It is as it was the night Angus came," Nell said, clearly still in shock.

"I remember it now," Molly said. "But why has no one else noticed this miraculous change? It is far too quiet. Where is everyone? And what, pray, did they do with Donald's body?"

"I expect Thomas and Tam carried it outside," Fin said. "Recall, sweetheart, that most of my men were with our prisoners in the courtyard."

Again, he led the way, and when they passed through the anteroom, they saw that it, too, had changed. Arras draped the walls, and a long, carved and cushioned bench stood along one wall that earlier had been bare.

Outside, they discovered the greatest change yet.

"Where the devil are my prisoners?" Fin demanded as he opened the door.

As Molly peeped around him to see only the fifty men from Eilean Donan, lounging at their ease in the courtyard, a familiar voice spoke from the anteroom.

"Ye ha' nae prisoners the noo, Kintail."

Fin and Molly whirled around as one.

Nell started at their sudden movement but otherwise seemed only bewildered to see so few men where she had expected to see many.

"She canna hear or see us," Maggie said. She perched on a cushion atop the carved bench, arms folded across her chest, her pipe cupped in one hand.

"Us?" Molly exclaimed. "You mean she cannot see Kintail or me either?"

"Dinna be daft," Maggie retorted.

Fin said gently, "She means that Lady Percy cannot see the man sitting beside her. He's the same man that I saw before, tending her when she was hurt."

"But I cannot see him!"

"Nay," Maggie said. "Claud hasna the power tae render himself visible tae most folks o' your world. Ye can see me, because I do ha' the power. I thought I explained that tae ye long since, but we didna discuss Claud much. The laird can see us both, because he has the sight, but ye canna see my foolish Claud."

"Who are you talking to?" Nell demanded. "I do not see anyone!"

Maggie gestured slightly with her pipe. "Now she canna hear ye when ye speak tae me, either," she said, "and she'll ask ye nae questions after, for when she speaks again, it will seem tae her that nae time has passed."

"What happened to my prisoners?" Fin demanded.

"Since the spell be broken, they never were here," Maggie said. "Ye'll note that your lady's gown be nae longer ripped, and your shirt o' mail be gone."

Fin clapped a hand to his chest, and Molly looked down at her bodice. Not only did it no longer show damage where Donald had ripped it, but it looked clean and fresh. So did Fin's clothing. She noticed something else, too.

"My mother's dress is not torn or bloody where Donald's dirk stabbed her."

"Aye, sure," Maggie said. "All is as it would ha' been had my Claud no interfered on the day Donald the Grim attacked Eilean Donan. Donald should ha' died then, ye see. Now, as far as anyone will recall who were concerned in the attack, or in any o' the events that followed, Donald *did* die on that day, and Dunsithe appears as they remember it when ye arrived. The laird's men-at-arms believe they escorted ye both tae Dunsithe from Kintail merely so the laird could inspect his fine new property."

"But others know that her fortune has been missing for years," Fin protested. "Many have seen the bare walls, and many have searched under every stick and stone. What do we tell them?"

"Tell them naught," Maggie said with a twinkle in her eyes. "It be your own business, be it not, and none o' theirs."

Fin looked at her for a long moment and then grinned. "Aye," he said. "That might work."

"You have only to fly into a temper, sir," Molly said sweetly. "No one dares to question Wild Fin Mackenzie."

He raised his eyebrows. "No one?"

"Well, almost no one," she answered, smiling at him.

"Cheeky lass," he retorted. Then, turning back to Maggie, he said, "You say that your Claud interfered the day Sleat attacked Eilean Donan?"

"Aye, 'twere Claud stopped Donald's bleeding, thinking our Maid wanted the vile creature tae survive when fate had deemed otherwise. Nae one can say now if he acted out o' poor judgment or stupidity, nae more than they can say one way or another about him causing the pair o' ye tae meet on Skye, or causing James tae transfer her writ o' wardship and marriage tae ye from Donald the Grim."

"Claud did all that?"

"Aye. He meant well all along, o' course, but it seemed tae him and tae others, too, that each thing he did proved a mischief and did nae good. He faced dire trouble within our clan for his actions."

Molly said hastily, "But if he did all that, Claud is responsible for our coming here and finding my fortune, is he not?"

"Aye," Maggie said with a grimace. "Truth be told, a body canna ken what energies be set loose when she casts a magic spell. It be clear now that poor Claud and others, too, may ha' acted under the spell that protected your portion. Only ye could remove it, ye see, for only when ye came back tae Dunsithe and took the key from the wall wi' your own hand could ye open the two chests."

"I could open only one of them," Molly told her. "Is there another key somewhere, or should the one I have open both of them?"

Maggie frowned. "Ye could open only the one?"

Molly nodded.

"Then ye ha' nae right tae the other," Maggie said, still frowning thoughtfully. "The spell allows only the rightful heir tae open it."

"But if I am not the rightful heir, who is?"

"Your father had but one other child," Maggie said.

"Bessie?"

"Aye."

"But Bessie's dead! She's been dead since soon after they took us away! Angus said so. Everyone said so!" A chill shot up Molly's spine. "Do you mean to tell me that's not true—that Bessie is alive?"

"I dinna *mean* tae tell ye anything," Maggie said. "I believed the bairn had died and that ye'd inherited her portion. But if ye canna open yon chest, I'm thinking there be wickedness afoot, and the rightful heir tae the other chest lives."

"Mercy, then, where is she?"

"That I canna tell ye, for I dinna ken," Maggie said. "Truth be told, even if I did, our rules wouldna let me tell ye, any more than they permitted me tae tell ye how tae claim your portion. Although I set the spell, I canna undo even a part of it. That be its greatest protection, since I canna tell anyone else how tae meddle with it, either. A secret shared be nae secret at all, ye ken."

"I must speak with my mother," Molly said. "She must know something that will help us find Bessie."

"Aye, I'll release her," Maggie said, "but ye should ken first that just as other folks' memories ha' altered with the breaking o' the spell, so too will her ladyship's memory o' what transpired these past days fade and change. Only ye and the laird will remember, and if ye try tae explain what happened tae anyone else, ye'll find your memories o' this day dimming, too."

Alarmed, Molly said, "We won't forget that Bessie is still alive, will we?"

"Nay, I'll leave ye that," Maggie said. "And I'll allow her ladyship's memory tae fade more slowly than the others', so that if she kens aught o' this wicked business, she can tell ye. Farewell now. Ye've work tae do."

When Maggie faded from sight, Molly said, "Did Claud say anything?"

"Not a word," Fin said, "but he looked quite pleased with himself."

"I'm glad that he helped my mother," Molly said, adding as Nell stirred, "Can you hear us now, madam?"

"Of course, I can," Nell said. "Why should I not hear you when you are standing right here beside me? You have no answered my question, either. To whom are you speaking?"

"We have been talking to Maggie Malloch," Molly said "When you asked your question, she did something so tha you could not hear any more, and she said that when you di hear us again it would be as if no time had passed. And so is."

"Mercy, do you mean that you said more than just that b I heard?"

"Aye, she told us everything is as it would have been ha

Donald died the day he and his men attacked Eilean Donan," Molly explained. "Also, all the men believe that they came to Dunsithe only as our escort, that Kintail is merely inspecting the property he gained by marrying me."

"But what of me? I remember perfectly well that Donald abducted me and held me prisoner at Dunsgaith and then that he and I were here with you."

"You, too, will forget in time," Molly said quietly. "As we will. But there is one thing that you will not forget, madam, and it is the most important thing of all. You will recall that my key did not open the second chest."

"Aye," Nell said. "Did you learn its secret from your Maggie?"

"We did, but it is not what we expected. Apparently, I am not heiress to the contents of that chest."

"But if not you, then who?"

"Bessie."

Nell stared at her, her face draining of color. Her chin trembled, and when she tried to speak, at first there was no sound. Then, at last, she spoke, her voice no more than a whisper. "Bessie is dead," she said. "Angus told me so."

"Angus lied," Fin said.

"I know how you must feel," Molly told her quietly, touching her arm. "It was a great shock for me, too."

"You cannot know how I feel," Nell said, hugging herself as tears spilled down her cheeks. Then, eyes widening, she reached for Molly's hand and clutched it tightly, drawing her close and hugging her. "I sound like a shrew, I know, but you are not yet a mother, nor have you ever lost a child. Faith, even I do not know how I feel!" Her hands shook, and her chin quivered. "H-how can this be? Are you sure?"

Molly nodded, and Fin said gently, "If Bessie were dead, Molly would be her heir, and her key would unlock the chest."

Nell inhaled deeply, struggling visibly to control her emotions. "Too much has happened," she said. "I cannot think, but I can well believe that Angus lied. He does so frequently, although he does not tolerate liars, himself."

"Can you recall nothing that he might have said over the years to reveal what really happened to her?" Molly asked.

"No," Nell said. "Nothing. We must find her, though."

"Excuse me, my lady," Doreen said from the doorway, "but Cook desired me to tell you that your dinner is ready to serve."

"Doreen! I thought you were locked . . . that is . . ." Molly floundered, looking to Fin for help.

"She thought you were still attending to things in her bedchamber," he said with a smile.

Doreen shook her head. "Nay, master, I finished there long ago, and I ha' been helping in the kitchen just as I do at home. Be Lady Percy ill, sir?"

"No, no," Molly said, surprised that Doreen knew Nell's name. "She is just a little tired, I expect."

"I'm famished," Fin said heartily. "We will come at once. What of my lads?"

"They are to eat in the lower hall, sir, as they did yesterday."

"Ah, of course," he said. "Come along, ladies. There is naught to be gained by keeping good food waiting."

Feeling dazed, Molly let him take her hand, and Nell followed silently behind him. Doreen helped serve the meal and seemed to remember nothing other than that they had arrived the day before after a tedious sea journey and that the only people they found in the castle had been looking after things until its new owner arrived. If she knew about the mystery regarding its contents, she said nothing to indicate as much.

Nell was quiet, but she revived a little as the meal progressed, touching one item after another as the magnificent serving dishes appeared, saying that she had believed she would never see them again and perhaps she would soon find Bessie.

Molly glanced at Fin more than once, wondering what he was thinking.

If Maggie's words meant that the three of them would eventually forget everything that had happened, just as Fin's men had already forgotten, what else might they forget?

His gaze met hers, and the warmth she saw in his eyes seemed to flow into her. When he tore a piece of roast chicken from its bone with his teeth and chewed it, still watching her, an unexpected bolt of yearning shot through her.

"Madam," he said a moment later, turning to Nell, "I warrant you would like some time alone with your thoughts and to become reacquainted with Dunsithe, so if you have no objection, Molly and I will bid you good night now. We have much to talk about, and I confess, I have sorely missed my wife."

"I believe you, sir," Nell said with a wan smile, idly shredding a roll. "I will sit here for a time, I think. I am finding it hard to come to terms with all that has happened in these past few days."

"You must do as you like," he said gently. "Doreen can help you choose a bedchamber and help you prepare for bed. Molly will not need her tonight."

Nell managed a smile for Molly. "I hope you want me to stay, love. Having waited so long to find you again, I shall be reluctant to curtail our reunion."

"I want to know you better, too, madam," Molly said, moving to hug her again. "I just wish you could remember something to help us learn where Bessie is. I want to find her."

Fresh tears filled Nell's eyes. "I can think of nothing," she said, "but I will soon have to face Angus, and I dread it, for I know not what I will say to him. He frightens me witless when he is angry, and since I was supposed to carry messages back to him and to England's Henry from Donald, Angus will be angry that I have failed. Still, I'm angry, too, and perhaps I can make him tell me what really happened to our Bessie."

"Do not endanger yourself," Molly said. "I do not want to lose you again."

"You won't, my love, but go now and be with your husband. I shall be quite all right here on my own."

Needing no further urging, they bade her good night.

Conscious of Fin beside her, Molly suddenly felt much as she had on her wedding night. Her skin prickled, and her body felt warm and moist. Remembering the huge bathtub in his bedchamber at Eilean Donan, she smiled.

He put his arm around her and drew her close. "Art sleepy, lassie?"

"Nay, sir. I feel warm and . . . and . . ."

". . . and lusty for your husband, I hope," he said with a chuckle. "I spoke the truth, sweetheart. We've business to sort out, and although I warrant we may need assistance with the part that involves Dunsithe, the rest of it is our alone to determine. What say you to the notion of naming Patrick constable here?"

"We cannot live at Dunsithe, can we." She made it a statement, not a question, as she moved ahead of him to the spiral stairway leading to the upper floors.

"I must stay with my people, Molly. We can visit here as often as you like, but when we are away, we should have someone in residence whom we can trust to look after the place properly, to tend its lands and its people."

"I like Sir Patrick."

"I, too, and I will miss him, but I know no one in the Borders whom I would trust as I trust him, and Malcolm and Mauri can look after Eilean Donan whenever we come to Dunsithe to visit."

"Will Patrick agree?"

"You know that he will agree to anything I ask of him. Moreover, he will make friends here far more quickly than I would." They reached the landing at the next floor, and he opened the door to the first chamber they came to. "This will do," he said, peering into the elegantly appointed room. Someone had lighted the fire, and its golden light played on the wall hangings and embroidered bed curtains.

"It is my parents' room," Molly said. "I remember it now that I see it again. What if my mother expects to sleep here?"

"She will not. It is the master's chamber, and she is well aware of the proprieties of such. Moreover, I intend to lock the door. We want no interruptions tonight." Suiting action to words, he shut the door and shot the bolt.

Then, turning, he drew Molly into his arms and kissed her. "I feared that I might have lost you," he murmured.

"I, too," she said. "That I had lost you, I mean."

"Would that have distressed you, lass?"

"More than I could have guessed when I arrived at Eilean Donan," she said.

His fingers touched her bodice where the rip had been. "Others may believe that Donald never was here, but I will never forget what he did, sweetheart, or what he threatened to do. It is not pleasant to be the means of another man's death, but I confess that I feel a certain satisfaction in knowing I avenged both my father's death and your abduction."

"My second abduction," she murmured, not caring much what he said, so long as he kept holding her.

He did not reply. His fingers toyed with her lacing, and she could feel the warmth of his hands through the material.

"It is my turn to undress you," she reminded him.

"So it is."

There were no difficult fastenings, since his shirt of mail had vanished, but she took her time, enjoying the chance to tease him for once. Unlacing his shirt, she slipped both hands inside it, stroking his chest lightly, then pulled the shirt free of his breeks. She would have played with it longer, but he caught hold of it by the hem and yanked it off over his head. When he would have thrust off his boots and breeks next, she stopped him.

"Be patient, sir," she said, grinning.

"I am not a patient man," he growled.

"Then you must practice to be more so."

"Cheeky lass."

He caught her shoulders and pulled her close, cupping her chin and raising it to kiss her. His lips were hot against hers, and for a moment, she forgot her appointed task and enjoyed the sensations his kisses stirred through her body. His hands moved to her breasts, and she realized that she was in danger of losing herself in the passions he was arousing.

Gently breaking off the kiss, she said, "Do you want to wear your boots and breeks to bed, impatient one, or will you let me help you take them off?"

His response was half groan, half chuckle, but he said, "If you think you can pull my boots off, go ahead."

Knowing better than to give him a chance to begin kissing her again just then, she knelt swiftly to obey, and once his boots were off, she moved to unlace his breeks, taking her time, using her fingers, lips, and hands to good purpose until she heard him gasp with pleasure.

Looking up into his eyes, she smiled and said, "I believe I am learning how to serve you well, am I not?"

"You are," he said, his voice catching on the words as if it were hard for him to breathe properly.

When he was naked, she began exploring his body with tiny, light kisses, moving slowly from his knees upward.

Expecting certain, inevitable distractions, Fin had intended to let her lead the way, to enjoy himself and the feelings she stirred in him. He kept reminding himself of that intention while her lips and hands busied themselves, but he had not counted on his body's profound reaction to her slightest touch.

He wanted to see her naked, to watch the firelight play on her smooth skin. He wanted to touch her everywhere, and bend her to his will.

She was playing with him, teasing him, taunting his lust for her. Her lips were hot against his skin, her fingers stirred lust wherever they touched him. Those busy lips and fingers reached only his thighs, therefore, before he suddenly leaned over, scooped her up, and carried her to the high, curtained bed. His breathing was more ragged than ever, and his hands were urgent as they dealt with her clothing.

Molly stifled a bubble of laughter when Fin snatched her up and carried her to the bed, but soon, she was as naked as he, and he moved over her to claim her again as his wife. Her body leaped to his in response, and she was astonished by how easy it was to pace her actions with his and to stir him to even greater passion. Every move was instinctive, and every new sensation stirred pulsing fire through her, increasing her ardor until the final surge threatened to overwhelm them both.

Afterward, as she lay with her head on his shoulder, he stroked her gently, idly, for some moments before he murmured, "I noticed something else that is different, sweetheart."

"What?"

"The mark of the key has nearly disappeared from your breast."

She looked down and saw that he was right. Maggie had promised that the mark would fade, but it looked almost as if her breast had never been burned.

"All that has happened here seems strange," she said, "but things are certainly better now than before. It will be wonderful if we can find Bessie."

"We'll find her," he murmured. "I love you, Molly."

A rapping at the door startled them, and at the same time, they heard Nell's voice. "I'm sorry to disturb you," she called, "but I thought you should know that I've found a box of Gordon's documents concerning Dunsithe."

"Excellent," Fin shouted back. "I'll study them carefully—tomorrow!"

"I've thought of something else, though," she said, her voice low-pitched and tense. "I think I may know where we can find Bessie."

Molly sat up, ready to let her in, but Fin held her and said, "Are you sure?"

"No, and I could be wrong. Indeed, I cannot even recall the name of the woman who may help us. I'm not sure Jamie will remember her either, but I met her at Stirling. She's a horrid woman, so I do not know whether to hope or to pray."

"Then that, too, can wait until morning," Fin said. "Good night, madam."

After a pause, Nell said, "Good night, my dear ones."

They heard her quick footsteps fading into the distance as he said gently, "Did you want to discuss it all with her now?"

"She may forget everything by morning."

"She won't forget that," he said. "Maggie Malloch said we'd remember that your sister is alive, and any memories Nell may have of her whereabouts have nothing to do with what happened today. Whatever she remembered tonight will linger and may even be clearer tomorrow, but we will do as you choose." His hand stroked her belly lightly.

"We'll wait," she said. "We're going to find Bessie, and despite what Maggie said earlier, I believe she will help us. She seemed angry to learn that someone had hidden the truth from her. She won't let them get away with it."

"Excellent; so where would you like me to touch you next?" he asked, his sensuous tone stirring the embers inside her.

"Here," she said, showing him and stirring in languorous delight when he complied. Nevertheless, before long, an errant thought struck her.

"Did I hear you say that you love me?"

"I did. You are mine, Molly, my lass, and will remain so for all of our days."

"I love you, too," she said, "but just remember one thing, Fin Mackenzie."

"What's that?" he asked lazily, toying with the tip of her breast.

"You no longer have license to accost innocent maidens walking home on dark nights."

"I'm still master here and at Eilean Donan," he said.

"You'll have to keep me happy if you want to prevent such events in future."

"Recall my skill with a bow and arrow, sir. I can render you unequal to—"

"You win, sweetheart," he interjected swiftly, wincing. "I promise, on my oath, to remain true to you forever. Now, go to sleep."

Chuckling, she snuggled against him. When she heard his breathing slow and deepen, she sighed and snuggled closer, taking comfort from the warmth of his body, knowing she belonged with him and that she had found her true home at last.

Sleepily, she murmured, "Thank you, Maggie Malloch, wherever you are."

I hope you enjoyed *Abducted Heiress*. When it was suggested that I include fairies and their ilk in Fin and Molly's book, I studied many fairy and spirit legends from the Highlands and Borders of Scotland. Much of the information I've used comes from two sources: *The Clans of Darkness*, edited by Peter Henning, and *The Fairy Faith in Celtic Countries* by Walter Y. Evans-Wentz. I am also indebted to the latter for certain details of the crofters' *ceilidh* at the beginning of the story.

After studying fairies, I looked for Scottish historical events that might plausibly have relied on "fairy intervention." When I came upon the story of the 1539 attack on Eilean Donan, I knew I'd found what I wanted.

The versions differ drastically (especially those offered by the Macdonalds, Mackenzies, and MacRaes), but to take the widest extremes of each, imagine as many as fifty galleys full of Macdonalds (each galley holding approximately forty to fifty armed men) attacking a castle that contained only three men, who defended it successfully. Surely, fairies must have had something to do with it, especially when one takes into account the small size of Loch Duich and the area around the castle.

After discussing this attack with the present Laird of Kintail, I decided to use his version primarily and adjust it to suit my story. Citing an 1886 Edinburgh reprint of *History of the MacRaes* by Alexander MacRae of Kintail (1587–1634), he suggested a more probable number of three to four galleys. He also provided me with the names and ages of the five people in the castle during the attack: Mauri and Malcolm MacRae, their infant daughter Morag, Ian Dubh Matheson, and Duncan MacRae, who shot the famous arrow that killed Macdonald of Sleat. Sir Patrick MacRae is patterned on Duncan, who became constable of Eilean Donan in 1539 after the death of Ian Dubh Matheson Fernaig, who was killed during the attack.

For those of you who are purists when it comes to British titles, let me assure you that Fin Mackenzie is not Lord Mackenzie. In sixteenth-century Scotland, a barony, with all its rights and privileges, including the power of the pit and the gallows, did not necessarily mean the baron could call himself a lord. According to Sir Ian Moncrieffe of that Ilk (*The Highland Clans*, Barrie & Jenkins, Ltd., 1977) Kintail was erected into a barony in 1508. However, there was no "Lord Mackenzie of Kintail" until 1609, when the position was raised to the peerage, giving the holder of the title the right to sit in the Scottish Parliament and call himself a lord. To call Fin "Mackenzie of Kintail" is accurate and is the manner for equivalent titles of the period (various Douglases, Scotts, Macdonalds, etc.).

The Mackenzies did hold Eilean Donan in 1539, but both Fin and Molly are fictional characters, and MacRaes now own the castle.

I would like to extend a heartfelt thank you to Donald R.

MacRae, the present Laird of Kintail, for his help in understanding Eilean Donan's history (and for his extraordinary patience in answering my many questions). I would also like to thank him for permitting me to "rewrite" his family history, even to the extent of letting a female shoot that MacRae arrow. When I asked if he would mind my doing that, he did suggest that for a female to use a longbow would be implausible, but when I pointed out that she had fairies on her side, he agreed that it would be possible and told me about the wee people who inhabit the woods of Kintail. It is his description that I used for the glade in the first scene with Catriona and Claud, and he is also my "authority" for the sensation of peripheral movement that one experiences when one first begins to realize that wee people are nearby.

I would also like to thank Pam Hessey, in particular, and other members of the California Hawking Club, in general, for helping me get the hunting scene right. And I must thank Nancy and Charles Williams for their unfailing support and their help in tracking down research books. Many thanks also to Suzanne and Jim Arnold of Serenery for providing so many great pictures of Eilean Donan to refresh my memories of the castle and its splendid setting, and to all the dedicated folks who man the clan tents at the numerous Scottish and Highland Festivals in California, Washington, Oregon, and Arizona who have enthusiastically assisted me in my research. Last but hardly least, special thanks go to Maggie Crawford, Beth de Guzman, and Karen Kosztolnyik, my editors at Warner, for their generous advice and encouragement when it came to blending the fairies' world with Fin and Molly's. It's been great fun.

If you've enjoyed *Abducted Heiress*, I hope you will

look forward to reading the adventures of Molly's little sister, Bess, when she meets Sir Patrick MacRae. *Hidden Heiress* will arrive at your favorite bookstore in summer 2002. In the meantime, happy reading!

Sincerely,

Amanda Scott

Return to the misty isle of Scotland, where
Bess Gordon's story unfolds in a magical world
of romance, fairies, and intrigue. . . .

HIDDEN HEIRESS

by Amanda Scott

Available from Warner Books
in Summer 2002

For a sneak preview of *Hidden Heiress,*
please turn the page.

Hidden Heiress

The Scottish Borders, March 1541

"Elspeth!" The feminine shriek rang through the sun-dappled woods.

Silence followed. Not even a bird twittered.

"Elspeth, where are you? Her ladyship wants you, and if I have to search for you, be sure that you will regret it. Come home at once!"

More silence. No breeze stirred, no leaf twitched. It was as if every living thing in the woods held its breath, so quiet that one could hear the rushing of a burn some distance away.

Minutes passed without a sound, but no more shrieks shattered the silence; and at last a small cottontail rabbit hopped out from beneath a bush, paused, and looked about. Apparently satisfied that the offensive intruder had departed, it turned its attention to a nearby patch of new grass.

When the *chip-chip-chwee* of a chaffinch sounded

from a treetop, echoed immediately by the chattering of a squirrel, a certain thick clump of shrubbery slowly parted in front of what looked like a rock slab, and a face appeared.

It was a lovely face, oval with high cheekbones, black-fringed gray-green eyes, a tip-tilted, freckled little nose, and full, rosy lips. The slim, arched eyebrows were considerably lighter than the lashes but many shades darker than the flaxen hair that fell in a long silken sheet, framing the pretty face. The eyes were wide and watchful. The head turned cautiously, looking to the right and to the left.

The bunny continued to graze, the birds to sing.

One small, rawhide-shod foot stepped forth from the shrubbery, followed by the other, whereupon the slender figure of a young woman, seventeen or eighteen years of age, was revealed. She wore a simple faded blue gown with a plain white apron, and if she had earlier worn the customary white coif and ruffled cap that most females wore in daytime she had mislaid both elsewhere.

Free of the shrubbery, she paused and listened and one could see that her fine, straight hair reached all the way to her hips. Apparently realizing that required some sort of confinement, she reached back over one shoulder with both hands and gathered i flipping it forward to plait it with quick, experienced fingers.

The birds continued to sing, and although the li

tle rabbit had stopped grazing and seemed alert to possible danger, it did not dart away.

The plait finished, albeit loosely and showing little indication that it would remain so for long, Elspeth Douglas drew a deep breath and exhaled. She would have to go home now, and on the way, she would have to think of an acceptable excuse for her tardiness. Not that any excuse would help if Lady Farnsworth was already angry with her, but at least Drusilla had gone away. She could be sure of that, because the young woman was wholly incapable of keeping silent, let alone of moving silently enough to fool the birds and other creatures of the woods.

That she had to return was a pity, because the day was a particularly fine one for April, and she enjoyed the solitude of the woods. Moreover, she could not be sure that Drusilla had shrieked the truth at her. The elder of the two Farnsworth daughters might easily have come looking for her without a command to do so, because Drusilla was not kind and often exerted herself to make Elspeth's life difficult, and others' lives as well. Less than a week before, her complaints that Sir Hector's falconer had dared to flirt with her had cost the man his position.

As these thoughts flitted through Elspeth's mind, a new sound intruded on the woodland peace. Although distant, it was nonetheless easily identifiable as the baying of sleuthhounds, and it sounded as though they were heading toward her.

To hear such sounds in daytime was unusual, for the hounds generally were used for chasing reivers, and reivers generally did their reiving by moonlight. Doubtless, someone was either training his dogs or—although the season was young yet—using them to hunt rabbits or deer. In either event, she knew she would be wise to leave the woods before the hounds surged into view. No animal had ever harmed her, but a sensible person left unknown dogs to themselves.

Elspeth turned reluctantly homeward, but she had taken only a few steps when, just as she sensed a presence looming behind her, a large, warm hand clamped over her mouth and a muscular arm wrapped tightly around her torso, lifting her off the ground and holding her securely against a hard, masculine body.

Kicking backward, her heel connected solidly with a shin, and she had the satisfaction of hearing a muffled grunt of pain, but her captor did not release her. Instead, his grip across her chest tightened, making it hard for her to breathe.

She kicked a second time but missed, whereupon a low voice growled in her ear, "Easy, lass, I mean ye nae harm, and if ye cripple me, I'm sped."

Elspeth stopped struggling, realizing that further such efforts would be useless. He was too large, too strong. She would hurt only herself.

"Good lass," he said. "What lies yonder behind that shrubbery?"

His hand was still clamped across her mouth. When she tried to twist away from it, he said, "I ken fine that ye canna speak, lassie, but I'll ha' your word first that ye willna shriek."

She hesitated, then nodded.

He moved his hand enough so that she could talk but kept it near enough to let her know that he would clap it across her mouth again if she tried to scream.

When she did not speak at once, he said more urgently, "Be there a cave there, where ye were hiding?"

"Aye," she said, "but 'tis only a shallow one."

"Big enough for the pair of us?"

"Since I cannot see you, I do not know how large you are," she said.

"Large enough," he said, and to her surprise she detected laughter in his voice. "I'll put ye down, lassie, but if ye shriek, I swear I'll throttle ye."

He set her gently on her feet, and she turned to face him.

She had known from the way he held her and the ease with which he had lifted her that he was a large man, but the reality was greater than she had imagined. He was a full head and shoulders taller than she was, which made him at least two or three inches above six feet, a height unusual among Borderers, who tended to be small and wiry. His shoulders were very, very broad.

He had thick, dark hair, but where a shaft of sunlight touched it, it gleamed with auburn highlights. His eyes were stone gray, set deeply, with lashes long enough and curly enough to be the envy of many a woman, and laugh lines at the outer corners. His eyebrows were thick and straight, like hasty slashes in a drawing. His other features were well chiseled, as if a skilled sculptor had modeled them. His complexion was tanned and ruddy. His beard was short and well trimmed, emphasizing the strong, straight lines of his jaw. He was the handsomest man she had ever seen, and his intense, penetrating gaze stirred feelings in her body the likes of which she had never known before.

He wore the tawny breeks and brown doublet of a hunter but carried himself with an arrogance that showed he thought he was superior to most other men. Doubtless, his size gave him that confidence, she decided, his size and the sword and dagger he wore at his side. Certainly, he looked capable of wielding both weapons expertly.

His voice was deep and pleasant, but his accent puzzled her. He spoke broad Scot, of course, but the cadence was neither that of a Scottish Borderer nor yet quite that of an English Borderer. Still, to her finely tuned ear, it sounded nearer the latter than the former, and England was only a few miles away.

Bluntly, she said, "Are you English?"

"Nay, lass, I be as much a Scot as ye be yourself, but we'll no fash ourselves over me antecedents just now if ye please. Will I fit into yon cave o' yours, or no?"

"Aye," she said, measuring him again with her eyes, "but barely."

"Then we'll ha' tae cuddle up a bit, I expect."

"You cannot keep me with you," she exclaimed as nerves stirred in places she had not known she had nerves. The thought of cuddling with him was not at all distasteful. Still, she said firmly, "I must go home straightaway. Surely, you heard Drusilla calling me!"

"I didna recognize that infernal shrieking as 'calling,'" he said. "What a heathenish voice that lass has got! Still and all, I collect that Drusilla must be your sister and 'tis rude o' me tae condemn any kinswoman o' yours."

She opened her mouth to correct him but, instead, said weakly, "I must go."

"Nay, lassie, I canna afford tae trust ye that far, I fear. Ye'll bide wi' me in yonder wee cave till the danger be past."

With a sigh, she nodded and turned to lead the way, pausing when she reached the thick bushes in front of the opening. Clearly, the dogs had his scent, and she wondered when it would occur to him that simply hiding in the cave would not be enough to shield him from them.

The cave was larger than she had led him to believe, but it was not deep enough to protect them both from discovery or attack, and she could hear the dogs more clearly now. They were rapidly drawing nearer.

"Who is chasing you?"

"My erstwhile host," he muttered.

"I beg your pardon, sir. I do not understand what you mean."

"Them be English soldiers, lass, and no pleasant folks at all. Now, get ye inside," he added, this time his words a clear command. He held the bushes apart and nodded at her to go first, following her at once.

Inside, enough light penetrated the shrubbery to reveal the walls of the cave, and he grunted at the sight. She could stand upright, but he could not, and although they could sit, they would be more vulnerable to attack on the ground.

He drew his sword. "This doesna seem tae be the best place for concealment after all, lass. We've no retreat here, and they'll easily track me tae this place. Mayhap ye'd better leave me, after all. I'll no want ye tae suffer for helping me."

She had been trying to think of a way to persuade him to let her go, but at these words, perversely, she changed her mind. "One moment," she said, turning away. "I have something that might help."

He made no move to stop her when she bent to retrieve the jug that some weeks before she had placed on the floor of the cave near the wall.

"What be that stuff?"

"Aniseed," she said. "Sir Hector's huntsman told me that it is one of the few things that will put sleuthhounds off their scent. One of the local reiver bands uses it frequently, he says."

"Ye begin tae intrigue me, lass," he said. Taking the jug and removing the stopper, he sniffed and grimaced. "Ha' ye tried it on your own hounds?"

"Not yet," she admitted. "I did think, however, that it might prove useful if Drusilla ever sent our dogs to find my hiding place."

"Do I just shake it out on the ground yonder?"

"Aye, but perhaps you would be wiser to let me do the shaking. If someone should see me, he would think nothing of a young woman walking in the woods."

"I'll let ye, but only if ye promise to do it quickly and come back here," he said firmly. "I'd no trust the men wi' them dogs tae act honorably wi' any female."

She did not argue with him, nor did he repeat his insistence that she return. She had a feeling that it did not occur to him now that she might disobey him. What man, she wondered, had that sort of confidence in his ability to command others? Surely, he could not be only a common huntsman.

He held the shrubbery aside for her, and she hurried out, going the way he must have come, toward the barking dogs. They were only a few minutes away now.

When she had gone as far as she dared, she shook aniseed from the jug. Realizing at once that such a method was less than efficient, she poured some into her hand and then flung it, as if she were scattering grain for chickens.

The dogs were closer yet, not more than a half mile away.

Backing toward the cave, she scattered more aniseed as she went, taking care to scatter it heavily over the route they had taken after he captured her.

As she neared the cave, still scattering the pungent herb, she wondered if she had taken leave of her senses. She had only his word that the men hunting him were English. They might as easily be Scots, chasing a thief or murderer, but she could not shake the notion that returning to him represented safety while remaining where she was represented danger. She had no time left to make for Farnsworth Tower. The dogs would be upon her before she could cover half the distance.

They were too close even now for comfort. What if they could catch her scent in the air? Deerhounds and many sleuthhounds possessed that ability.

Running now, still flinging aniseed across her path, she saw that he was still holding the bushes apart for her. Diving toward them, she stumbled, but he caught her arm, steadying her and drawing her into the sanctuary of the cave.

"Take some deep breaths, lass," he recommended calmly. "Ye must steady your breathing, or the hounds will hear ye. Their sense o' hearing be nigh as acute as their sense o' smell."

The sound of the dogs changed. They had been baying in a rhythmic way, all of them making a similar sound, but many were yelping now, in some disorder.

"They've come upon the aniseed," he murmured. "Be still now. Not a movement, not a word."

"I am not a fool, sir," she said.

Nevertheless, she was grateful to feel his large body close to hers. Big, warm, and solid, it made her feel safer despite the increasing danger outside. Her fears continued to ease only to return threefold when she heard the sound of hoofbeats and knew they announced riders following the hounds. Chills shot through her body. She had not let her thoughts dwell on the men with the dogs.

Swallowing, she did what she had done since childhood whenever she felt herself in danger. She thought about something else, pretending that she was far away, in a very safe place. The warmth of the large body next to hers made it easier than usual to return to memories of her early childhood, of a large, muscular man—her father, surely—holding her close. She basked in that warmth, telling herself that she was on the shore of a pond with her father, surrounded by woods that were a haven of safety, the only sounds those of birds and squirrels, and the occasional splash of a fish leaping to the fly that twitched at the end of her father's rod.

When her companion's hard, muscular arm draped itself across her shoulders, she leaned into it, forgetting that it belonged to a stranger, accepting its comfort without question or comment.

Through the shrubbery blocking the entrance, she could see the dogs now, at least a half score of them, and she saw at once that the aniseed had put them off their scent. Three bunched near a tree, and feeling the body beside her stiffen, she wondered if that was where he had stood, watching her emerge from the cave.

Riders appeared, guiding their ponies through the trees toward the dogs.

"Damnation," one of the men exclaimed. "They've lost him!"

"Look up in the trees," another voice shouted. "Mayhap he's climbed one of them and is hiding in its branches."

They were English voices, so at least he had told her the truth about that.

"As I recall, there'll be a brook or a river to the

east," another shouted. "Mayhap he walked into it to cover his trail. Send the dogs along its banks on both sides, and I'll wager we'll find him again in short order."

"How far away is that burn?" her companion murmured when the area nearby had fallen silent again.

"Five minutes' walk from here," she murmured back.

"And where does it lead?"

"Its source lies in the hills north of us. It flows southwest into Annan Water and thence into Solway Firth."

"And if they follow it on north?"

"They'll pass Farnsworth Tower," she said. "The burn provides our water."

"Farnsworth Tower is your home?"

"Aye."

"Surely those English will not remain long on the Scottish side of the line," he muttered as if he were talking to himself.

Elspeth said gently, "If they have declared a hot trod, they can remain in the west march for six days."

"How so?"

"Well, if I am remembering Border law correctly, either side can declare a hot trod up to six days after a crime and anyone chasing a criminal may cross the line as long as they are in hot pursuit of him."

"And how is it that a lass like yourself kens aught o' Border law?"

"Sir Hector frequently serves as clerk when opposing march wardens meet for Truce Days, and he often explains such laws to us at home."

"I see. Six days, eh? But it means only that they can cross the line for six days after they discover the crime, and only if they know who they are chasing?"

"Aye, but Sir Hector says that many interpret the law to mean that if they follow at once, they can search for the full six days. Did they follow you at once?"

"You mean directly after I committed my crime?"

Again, she detected laughter in his voice, but this time it annoyed her. "I do not think that felonious activity should be a matter for humor, sir," she said primly.

He chuckled. "Doubtless you are right, lass. I confess, I've been up to my ears in felonious activity for so long now that I've forgotten how most folks tend to view such behavior. At present, however, I care only about saving my skin."

"Your accent has changed," she said.

"Has it, then? I ha' a knack for picking up cadences from whomever I'm speaking with unless I take care no tae let m'self. Doubtless I ha' just picked up a bit o' your pretty speech, for ye dinna talk like a common Border wench."

"I speak as Drusilla and Jelyan speak," Elspeth said. "Sir Hector taught us all to speak properly."

"Ye ha' two sisters, then. What be your name?"

"They call me Elspeth," she said, believing it unnecessary to explain to him that Drusilla and Jelyan were not her sisters. "What of you?"

"Ye should call me Patrick," he said. "That'll be sufficient."

"The men who seek you, what will they call you?"

Again, he chuckled. "Ye be too wise for your own good, sweetheart. It doesna matter what they will call me."

"It will matter if they seek you at Farnsworth Tower," she pointed out, ruthlessly ignoring the way the casual endearment stirred her senses. "I am in trouble already for being away so long. If they learn that a villain is running loose hereabouts, they will likely ask me all manner of questions. Did I not see or hear the dogs? Did I perchance see the man?" She grimaced. "I am not a good liar, sir."

"Then you must practice," he said with a wry grin. "Believe me, practice makes nearly anything possible. I know that much for a fact."

"Lying is not a skill that one should aim to perfect," she said curtly.

He did not respond. Indeed, she thought he looked regretful, and the look stirred her sympathy. She wanted to smooth his furrowed brow, to make him smile again. She swallowed hard, mentally scolding herself as harshly as ever Lady Farnsworth or Drusilla had scolded her. Clearly, she had lost every ounce of good sense she possessed the moment she laid eyes on the villainous fugitive.

She could not hear the dogs any longer, but the shrubbery rustled. A breeze had come up, and if it was blowing from the west, as most breezes did in that area, it might well blow sounds of baying and barking away to the east.

"What will you do now?" she asked when the silence began to hover uncomfortably between them.

"I must think about that," he said. "If ye be right, and them villains mean tae stay this side o' the line for six whole days, I must go tae ground somewhere I doubt I can get by wi' posing as a traveler, wending me way north tae Stirling."

"Nay, you are too large to pass as a common Borderer. Moreover, everyone hereabouts knows every one else. Must you go to Stirling?"

"Aye, in time, I must."

"A fortnight after the Queen's new bairn is born which will be any day now, we of Farnsworth Towe and others from these parts, will travel to Stirling. she said. "The King is to hold a grand celebration i honor of the child's birth, all the grander if it shoul prove to be a son. Travel will be easier for you the perhaps."

"Aye, if I had a safe place tae stay, so I could affor tae wait that long."

Another idea stirred in her mind, but she rejected it. She had already been foolish enough for one day. Indeed, most sensible people would call her foolhardy to linger thus, chatting with a felon and confiding her family's plans to him.

"How far is it from here to Farnsworth Tower?" he asked.

"No more than a twenty-minute walk," she said.

"Will you tell them about me?"

She hesitated, knowing it was her duty to warn everyone about a scoundrel in the area. If Drusilla, or even Jelyan, found out that she had kept such information to herself, she would face dire punishment. But try as she might, she could sense no danger in the man, and over the years, she had learned to trust her instincts.

"I'll tell no one," she said. "But I must go home."

"It should be safe now," he said. "Listen for the dogs, though, and if ye hear them, make for an open space, preferably one wi' a good many folks about."

She nodded, and when he parted the bushes for her, she stepped past him, feeling the energy from his body as she did. Glancing up at him, she opened her mouth to bid him farewell, and then shut it again, uncertain what to say.

He smiled, revealing strong white teeth, and his eyes twinkled. " 'Ware strangers, lass," he warned.

The absurdity of such a caution coming from him made her smile back. "I'll be careful," she said.

"See that you are," he said more sternly. "And, lassie, bind a ribbon round that plait when ye get home, lest ye be punished for untidiness."

"Yes, sir," she said, automatically responding to what was a common command to her.

"And, lass . . ."

Annoyance stirred, but she paused again, forcing patience. "Aye?"

"Thank you," he said gently. "I am greatly in your debt."

"Good-bye, sir," she said, turning away without telling him he was welcome to her help, although it doubtless amounted to aiding and abetting a felon. But even with her back to the man, she could sense his strong vitality, and she did not want to leave him, not—or so she told herself—with danger possibly still at hand. Swiftly, she turned back, and without giving herself a chance to think more about what she was doing, she said, "Do you ken aught o falcons or hawks?"

A flashing grin lit his face. "Aye, I ken everything about them," he said. "Why d'ye ask?"

"Because Sir Hector's falconer left a sennight age and presently Sir Hector has only one careless lad t look after his birds. You would need to know only much as the lad knows, although it would not hu to know a bit more."

"I see that ye're either hard o' hearing, lass, or th ye ha' the good sense no tae believe a man wh claims tae ken all there be tae ken, but I spake the truth. I warrant there be few men wha' ken as much as I do about birds o' prey. I were raised wi' such. Do ye mean tae hide me in a falconer's cot?"

"Ours had no cottage," she said. "He dwelt in a small chamber near the kitchen. The mews contain no residence, only room for the birds."

"How many birds?"

She shrugged. "I do not know exactly—only three or four, I think. The lad warned Sir Hector that he might have to put one of them down. He said the bird started and before he could control it, it broke two of its primaries. I am not entirely certain what that means, but Sir Hector told him to wait a day or two."

"Faith, he cannot mean to put down a gallant fellow or lass only because of a couple of broken feathers. I can see that ye need me as much as I need your sanctuary, lass. By heaven, I'll do it."

"Mercy, can you repair broken feathers?"

"I can, and if ye be a good lass, I'll show ye how tae do it yourself. But how will we introduce me fine skills tae Sir Hector? I canna walk home wi' ye. 'Twould be tae shred your reputation an I did such a thing. In any event, I dinna ken what Sir Hector can be thinking, letting ye wander about at will like this."

"If you are going to scold, we will part at once and

you can seek your own fortune," she said tartly. "You are hardly in a position to preach good behavior."

"So ye've a temper, have ye? Well, sheathe it, lass, because ye willna win any fratching contest wi' me. Consider that I've only tae pick ye up and carry ye home bottom upward over me shoulder—"

"You wouldn't!"

"Would I not?" His feet were set apart, and now he hooked his thumbs over his sword belt and gazed at her sternly. A prickling awareness engulfed her, not that he would harm her but that he would carry out any threat that he made.

Choosing her words carefully, she said, "It would be wiser, I think, if you were to present yourself to Sir Hector later today. If you tell him that you heard at a tavern or some such place that his falconer had left unexpectedly and that, therefore, you decided to apply to replace him . . ."

"Aye, that might suffice," he said when she paused expectantly. "Be there any other odd detail that I should ken about the position?"

She frowned. "I do not know much more about it myself."

"D'ye no ken why the last chap left, then?"

Smiling sweetly, she said, "He was impertinent to Sir Hector's daughter."

"Aye, sure, and bein' that I'm an impertinent lad m'self, 'tis a good thing ye **had the foresight tae warn** me." He frowned, adding gently, "Now, tell me tha it was yourself to whom the man dared be impertinent, and I'll have yet more business to attend to before I can leave for Stirling."

His accent had altered again, but she did not think it wise to point that out to him just then. Instead, she said, "I doubt that the poor man was impertinent to anyone. Drusilla complained that he looked at her oddly and insisted that he be turned off."

"Farnsworth Tower sounds like it harbors some verra pleasant folks," he said. "Almost do I look forward tae spending some few days in their company."

"Understand me, sir," she said. "I can be of no assistance to you in gaining employment there. You must speak to Sir Hector, and you must not mention me."

"I ken that fine, lass. Dinna fash yourself, for I'll no betray ye. I'll hope tae see ye again, though, so I can show ye how tae mend a feather properly."

She smiled but wondered if she had lost her senses. Doubtless, she had accomplished nothing more than the potential introduction of a murderer into the Farnsworth household. The thought widened her smile. Whatever he was, she was certain the man was no murderer. Nor was he what he claimed to be, however. She wondered if she would learn who he really was before he had to leave.

Sir Patrick MacRae watched the lass hurrying northward. Then, swiftly and silently, he followed her, wanting to make sure that she reached her destination safely and hoping that he had judged her motives accurately.

The thought that she could be laying a trap for him was not one he could afford to set aside in favor of a pair of beautiful gray-green eyes and an innocent face. For all he knew, she suspected him of even more dastardly deeds than those of which he was guilty and would betray him the moment she got home.

He had heard of Sir Hector Farnsworth but knew little about him. If the man served as a clerk for Truce Day meetings, one could suppose that he believed in the rule of law, but Patrick had heard Sir Hector's name in another context, as well. If the man proved false, Patrick would be sped, as would the so-important mission that had taken him to England and now brought him to the Borders.

Elspeth was a bonny lass, though, and he certainly did not regret meeting her. Not only did he have a keen eye for beauty but she had also stirred a protective vein in him that had laid dormant since the day eight months before when he had left his laird and lady at Stirling Castle, where the laird was a hostage of the King of Scots and would remain so until Patrick completed his mission.

He watched now unseen from the shelter of the woods as Elspeth hurried toward a distant tower and its surrounding stockade. When she was safely inside, he walked back to the cave, keeping an eye out for the searchers but thinking hard.

What information he had gleaned in England would do little more than reinforce the belief of his principal that Henry the Eighth sought to bring all Scotland under his greedy thumb. Before he left the Borders, he needed to confirm certain other details that he had come to suspect, or prove them wrong. And in the meantime, he had to move with extreme caution, because the landscape teemed with potential enemies.

Whether bonny Elspeth was one of them remained to be seen.

About the Author

AMANDA SCOTT, best-selling author and winner of the Romance Writers of America's RITA/Golden Medallion and the *Romantic Times'* awards for Best Regency Author and Best Sensual Regency, began writing on a dare from her husband. She has sold every manuscript she has written. She sold her first novel, *The Fugitive Heiress*—written on a battered Smith-Corona—in 1980. Since then, she has sold many more, but since the second one, she has used a word processor. More than twenty-five of her books are set in the English Regency period (1810–20), others are set in fifteenth-century England and sixteenth- and eighteenth-century Scotland. Three are contemporary romances.

Amanda is a fourth-generation Californian who was born and raised in Salinas and graduated with a bachelor's degree in history from Mills College in Oakland. She did graduate work at the University of North Carolina at Chapel Hill, specializing in

British history, before obtaining her master's in history from California State University at San Jose. After graduate school, she taught for the Salinas City School District for three years before marrying her husband, who was then a captain in the Air Force. They lived in Honolulu for a year, then in Nebraska for seven years, where their son was born. Amanda now lives with her husband in northern California.

VISIT US ONLINE @ WWW.TWBOOKMARK.COM

AT THE TIME WARNER BOOKMARK WEB SITE YOU'LL FIND:

- CHAPTER EXCERPTS FROM SELECTED NEW RELEASES

- ORIGINAL AUTHOR AND EDITOR ARTICLES

- AUDIO EXCERPTS

- BESTSELLER NEWS

- ELECTRONIC NEWSLETTERS

- AUTHOR TOUR INFORMATION

- CONTESTS, QUIZZES, AND POLLS

- FUN, QUIRKY RECOMMENDATION CENTER

- PLUS MUCH MORE!

Bookmark Time Warner Trade
Publishing @ www.twbookmark.com